"With all due [illegible] novelist James F. David's *Footprints of Thunder* is worlds better on entertainment, intellectual, and readability levels. Terrific suspense, living, breathing characters that you care about (both two-legged and four-legged), and skilled writing by an author with fortissimo imagination. Do not miss *Footprints of Thunder*. It's one of the greats that will knock your socks off."

—Naomi M. Stokes, bestselling author of *The Tree People*

"An interesting novel, with the kind of situation I like: contemporary human beings encountering dinosaurs. It's exciting, and sometimes brutal, with an intriguing rationale."

—Piers Anthony, author of *Isle of Woman*

"For those who can't get their fill of dinosaurs and a lot of action, try this splendid story of man's deed coming back to haunt a modern world. . . . Magnificently executed."

—*Star-Banner* (Ocala, Florida)

"James F. David's *Footprints of Thunder* is an outstanding work of imaginative fiction. I devoured *Footprints of Thunder* in one sitting."

—Douglas Preston, bestselling coauthor of *The Relic*

"Believable characters and riveting, nonstop action ultimately sustain this fanciful dinosaur tale." —*Booklist*

"In *Footprints of Thunder*, *Jurassic Park* goes head to head with *The Stand* in an apocalyptic epic that will send you reeling."

—Robert Gleason, author of *Wrath Of God*

FOOTPRINTS OF THUNDER

James F. David

TOR®
A TOM DOHERTY ASSOCIATES BOOK
NEW YORK

NOTE: If you purchased this book without a cover you should be aware that this book is stolen property. It was reported as "unsold and destroyed" to the publisher, and neither the author nor the publisher has received any payment for this "stripped book."

This is a work of fiction. All the characters and events portrayed in this book are either products of the author's imagination or are used fictitiously.

FOOTPRINTS OF THUNDER

Cover art by Paul Stinson

A Tor Book
Published by Tom Doherty Associates, Inc.
175 Fifth Avenue
New York, NY 10010

Tor Books on the World Wide Web:
http://www.tor.com

ISBN: 0-812-52402-0
Library of Congress Card Catalog Number: 95-21887

First edition: October 1995
First mass market edition: July 1997

Printed in the United States of America

0 9 8 7 6 5 4 3 2 1

Acknowledgments

I would like to thank everyone who encouraged or tolerated me during this project. Thanks to Mark, who gave me the initial push to get started, Carol McCleary for seeing the potential, Bob Gleason and Greg Cox for many good suggestions and for pushing me to a new level, and to my wife, Gale, for hours of reading and rereading.

Abby, Katie, and Bethany—this is why Dad sat at the computer all those hours.

Dramatis Personae

Oregon

Kenny Randall—Student at Oregon Institute of Technology, and a member of the group.
Dr. George Coombs—Former professor of anthropology, now a chiropractor.
Dr. Chester Piltcher—Professor of system science at Oregon Institute of Technology, and the leader of the group.
Phat Nyang—A student at Oregon Institute of Technology, computer programmer, and a member of the group.
Mrs. Wayne—Member of the group and New Age believer who communicates with a spirit guide by the name of Shontel.
Petra Zalewski—Student at Oregon Institute of Technology, and a member of the group.
Colter Swenson—Student at Southern Oregon State College, and a member of the group.
Ernie Powell—Friend of Mrs. Wayne, and a member of the group.
Robin Kyle—Deputy sheriff, Jackson County Sheriff's Department.
Jill Randall—Kenny Randall's sister, and tour guide at the Oregon Caves.
Robert Jenkins—FBI Special Agent.
Shirley, Jay, and Kimberly—Rangers at the Oregon Caves National Monument.
Bill Conrad—Colonel in the U.S. Air Force.
Angie Conrad—Wife of Bill.
Dr. Terry Roberts—Psychologist.
Ellen Roberts—Wife of Terry.
John Roberts—Son of Terry and Ellen.
Ripman and Cubby—Friends of John.
Carl, Bobby, Kishton, Butler, and Miller—Motorcyclists from Carlton, Oregon.
Vince Peters—Chief of Police, Carlton, Oregon.

Stanley "Coop" Cooper—Reserve officer, Carlton, Oregon.
Rita Watkins—Stranded motorist.
Chrissy Watkins—Rita's daughter.
Matt Watkins—Rita's son.

FLORIDA

Ron Tubman—Owner and captain of the deep-water sailboat *Entrepreneur*.
Carmen Perez-Tubman—Wife of Ron Tubman.
Rosa Perez—Carmen's daughter.
Chris Tubman—Ron's son.

NEW YORK

Mariel Weatherby—Resident of apartment bordering the New York time quilt.
Luis Ibarra—Resident of apartment bordering the New York time quilt.
Melinda Ibarra—Wife of Luis.
Gene Diamond—Host of radio show *Night Talk*.

HAWAII

Emmett Puglisi—Assistant professor of astrophysics, University of Hawaii.
Carrollee Chen-Slater—Assistant professor of botany, University of Hawaii.

WASHINGTON, D.C.

Elizabeth Hawthorne—White House chief of staff.
Scott McIntyre—President of the United States.
Dr. Nick Paulson—Science advisor to the President.
Dr. Arnold Gogh—Former science advisor to the President.
Samuel Cannon—Director of the CIA.
Phil Yamamoto—Sergeant, U.S. Air Force.
Natalie Matsuda—Secretary of Defense.

Prologue: Corn Fall

The pickup sped through the forest past the marker indicating the border of the Indian Reservation. Unnoticed by the passengers, the forest changed. Hardy pines replaced the water-loving firs, the mountains melted into hills, and the highway convolutions became mere curves. The truck was moving down the eastern slope of the Cascades into the rain shadow that was the high desert of eastern Oregon.

It was opening day of deer season, at least it would be at daybreak, and the pickup was loaded with essentials. In the back were a tent, three sleeping bags, fishing rods and tackle, two cast-iron frying pans, a propane lantern, three 30.06 rifles, and two cases of beer. In the cab three eager college students kept themselves awake by talking sports and sex. Few cars were on the road, and only an occasional sign advertising the reservation resort, Kah-Nee-Tah.

It was nearly 2:00 A.M. when the pickup pulled itself free from the forest and into the expanse of the plains. The passengers fell silent, their eyes no longer confined by the evergreen walls. They were forest dwellers who found thick stands of evergreens, mountains, and waterfalls commonplace, so the browns, grays, and muted greens of the arid plains were seductive. There were no clouds in the sky, and when the passengers tired of wide open plains, they savored the wide open sky. To enhance its splendor, they turned off the lights of the pickup, and the vehicle moved across the plain with only the moon to light its way. At a wide spot in the road, it stopped, and two of the passengers got out, stretching their legs, arching their backs, and staring at the sky. The driver lay down on the seat of the cab, stretching his legs out the driver's door and his arms out the other.

After a catlike stretch, he moved to the doorway of the cab and leaned across the top of the pickup, looking across the desert. The cool autumn air sent goose bumps up his arms, invigorating him and clearing his brain. Then something bounced off the top of the cab in front of his face. It was a dried piece of corn.

"All right, who's the wise guy?"

The other two were staring at him blankly when another piece of corn landed on the ground between them. Then another, and another, joined the first. They looked up to see where it came from, but there was nothing to see but stars. More corn fell, sprinkling the ground and people, stinging them where it hit. When the corn began to fall harder, they climbed into the safety of the pickup. Still the corn fell in torrents, sounding like hail as it pounded the vehicle.

The passengers stared out the windshield as the ground quickly covered itself with the brownish yellow kernels. Then, just as suddenly as it had started, the corn fall stopped.

The young men opened the door tentatively and slowly climbed out. There was still nothing in the sky but stars, but the evidence of the strange shower was all around them. The driver kicked at the corn on the ground and then cleaned it off his pickup to look for damage.

"That's the strangest damn thing I've ever seen," the driver said. "Where do you think it came from, Jack?"

"How should I know?" Jack replied. "I don't think they even grow corn around here. Hey, where did Kenny go?" They both looked around, and then called out Kenny's name.

"I'm back here." They found Kenny Randall kneeling down behind the pickup. He was dumping a jar of Tang onto the ground.

"What are you doing, man? That's *my* Tang!"

Kenny ignored the driver, finished dumping out the powder, and then filled the jar with corn from the ground. He didn't say much after that, and he wasn't much fun. Even in camp, he just sat and stared at the jar of corn.

Jack got a three-point buck on Saturday and he and Robbie skinned it. Robbie caught half a dozen trout Sunday morning, but Kenny didn't have much of an appetite. When they broke camp Sunday afternoon Kenny, still absorbed by the corn, said very little all the way back.

PreQuilt

I. Residence Hall

. . . and there shall come a time when the present shall be joined together with the past . . .
—Zorastrus, Prophet of Babylon

Oregon Institute of Technology, Klamath Falls, Oregon
PreQuilt: Saturday, 2:00 a.m. PST

Kenny Randall looked doubtfully at the pile of belongings on his bed. They would never fit into his pack. Pulling out his essentials, he finished stuffing his yellow backpack. The gun was last; he wanted it accessible. But its outline showed clearly through the thin yellow nylon. When he wedged the gun on the inside it rubbed against his spine through the pack. Finally he wrapped the weapon loosely in a towel to help hide the deadly shape.

Kenny checked his watch and then sat down at his computer and ran the simulation again. He tried feeding in more of the Zorastrus data, but the outcome was the same. After a dozen runs he gave up. Kenny envied the long dead prophet. He had only predicted what Kenny would have to live through.

He took one last look around his littered dorm room. Textbooks, mostly dealing with industrial management, papers, notebooks, pens and pencils, were in apparent disarray, but Kenny had his own system of organization. One pile was for his computer programming class, the one next to it was for his systems management class, and the pile sticking out from under the bed contained last year's work. There was another year's worth of work deeper under the bed. More books and papers were piled on the closet floor, with a seldom-used typewriter.

The computer on Kenny's desk was surrounded by its own peculiar debris—boxes of discs, disc holders, a mouse and mouse pad, a printer, and stacks of computer paper. Next to the computer was a pile of newspaper clippings. On the shelf above the computer was a rack of books with titles like *Stranger Than Fiction*, *Strange Facts*, and *The Unexplainable*. At the end of the shelf was a jar of dried corn.

There wasn't anything Kenny particularly valued in the room, but he felt a sense of loss anyway, knowing he would not see any of it again. He checked his pack one more time, to make sure the gun didn't show, and then he closed and locked the door.

The dorm hall was quiet, and all the doors were shut. The last of the late-nighters had drifted off to bed about half an hour ago. On this Saturday morning no one was likely to stir until nine or ten. It was better this way, Kenny knew. He was weary of talking to people who were deaf to what he had to say, though it was unlikely anyone would talk to him now anyway. He had become genuinely unpopular in the last few months. Ever since his discovery he had tried to tell them, to show them, but they treated him as a joke. For their sake he hoped they were right, but for his sake he was going to do something about it.

An empty elevator was waiting for him, and he left the building without looking back—even though the dorm had been his home for the last three years he had always disliked it. Even the name of the dorm was ridiculous: Residence Hall. One night after a few too many beers, he, Jack, and Robbie had printed out official-looking signs on Kenny's computer and posted them around the building. RESIDENCE HALL FLOOR, one said, RESIDENCE HALL HALL, another said. Even RESIDENCE HALL WALL, and RESIDENCE HALL TOILET. It was the kind of thing that was funny when you're drunk but seemed dumb the next morning. Still, none of the other residents tore the signs down for months.

He found his dark blue Toyota in the parking lot. The odometer had twenty-eight thousand miles on it, but it had rolled over two years ago. The upholstery was shot, and the passenger window was stuck closed, but the car would not quit. He was briefly apprehensive—in all his careful planning he had never considered the possibility that his ten-year-old Toyota might be the weak link, trapping him with the unbelievers. Now he pumped it twice, relieved when as usual it started the second time.

As he was pulling out of the parking slot, he noticed a yellow bumper sticker on the Escort parked next to him. Written in calligraphy, it read simply *Shit Happens*. Kenny forced a nervous laugh. "You got that right," he said out loud. "You sure got that right." Then Kenny left the parking lot for the last time.

When he reached Dr. Piltcher's house, Phat, Colter, and Petra were already there, packing the RV and the van for their trip. Kenny found Dr. Piltcher and Dr. Coombs staring at a computer screen. Kenny could see the simulation he and Phat had developed running on the screen. A well-worn copy of an ancient manuscript lay open next to the computer. It made an odd sight, the ancient and the modern sitting side by side. The two scientists looked up when Kenny came into the study. There were dark bags under their eyes.

"Have you been running the simulation all night?" he asked.

"Yes," Dr. Piltcher said. "Dr. Coombs and I fed in more of the Zorastrus data. It didn't make any difference. It's going to happen."

"I know," Kenny said.

There was nothing more to say, so Kenny left the scientists to help the others. While they were packing, Mrs. Wayne arrived with Ernie Powell in Ernie's pickup truck, its bed loaded with more supplies. Dr. Piltcher had advised them all to prepare for the worst.

When everything was packed it came time for good-byes. Dr. Coombs shook Kenny's hand without a word, but Kenny knew Dr. Piltcher would have something to say.

"Won't you change your mind, Kenny?" Dr. Piltcher asked. "Come with us. We should be together when it happens. I think you need to be with the group."

Kenny knew Dr. Piltcher's concern was genuine. Kenny had become introspective as the summer wore on. By the season's end he rarely participated in the group discussions, and even Phat couldn't draw him out. Kenny had tried to stay engaged but wasn't like the others. He couldn't compartmentalize his life, set aside his fears and live normally. In fact, now his fears were his life. He needed family, not friends. He didn't understand why, so he said simply, "I need to be with my family."

"So you're going to go through with it?" Dr. Piltcher asked, not expecting an answer. "Take this with you. I copied some of the Apocrypha of Zorastrus for you. It might help."

Kenny took the sheaf of papers from his friend and mentor and placed them next to his backpack.

"Be careful, Kenny. We'll look for you after it happens . . . if we can."

"Thanks. The group meant a lot to me." Kenny's voice cracked, so he immediately lowered his head, holding back the rest of what he had planned to say. Instead he and Dr. Piltcher stared at their shoes for a full minute and then Kenny managed to steady his voice long enough to tell them, "I'm going now."

Dr. Piltcher nodded and then shook Kenny's hand, as did everyone in the group except Mrs. Wayne, who knocked his hand away and wrapped her arms around him. When she finally released him he saw tears in her eyes. Turning away quickly to hide the moisture in his own, he climbed into his battered Toyota. He backed slowly down the driveway, knowing he probably wouldn't see any of them again. They were all still waving good-bye when he turned onto the main road and drove out of sight.

---

2. THE ENTREPRENEUR

Until meteorites fell in 1803, scientists were certain that reports of stones falling from the sky were legends. It makes one wonder what other mysteries should be revisited.

—E. Suzuki, *Belief and Behavior*

Naples, Florida
PREQUILT: SATURDAY, 9:03 A.M. EST

The *Entrepreneur* was a thirty-five-foot fiberglass deep-water sailboat, rigged for the open sea. The original production hull had been modified with a three-foot cabin extension, bowsprit and pulpit, and webbing of double lifelines. The mast was forty-five feet of extruded aluminum supported by one-quarter-inch stainless steel shrouds. A gleaming white, slim hulled beauty with a fin keel, the *Entrepreneur* was everything Ron Tubman always wanted in a yacht, and more, and it was finally his.

Carmen and her daughter were aboard, stowing gear for the voyage. Ron still thought of Rosa as Carmen's daughter, though they had been a blended family, or at least mixed, for eighteen months now. Everyone was consciously trying to blend, and Chris had surprised him, warming up to Carmen as quickly as Ron had. He remembered joking with Carmen about her close relationship with her new son, suggesting a reconsideration of Freud's theory about Oedipal conflicts.

Rosa was a different story, however, with no sign of an Electra complex toward Ron. She was cordial with her new brother Chris, even affectionate at times. Brother and sister roles were new to both of them, and they had quickly formed a bond. Even before the marriage, Rosa had gone out of her way to do things with Chris—just as she went out of her way to avoid Ron. Maybe, Ron thought, it was the age difference between Rosa and Chris that made it easy for them to be friends. Rosa was six years older than Chris, and they had different interests and roles in the family. The spliced siblings had never competed for affection from their parents. But Rosa remained deliberately distant, cool and aloof to Ron. She visited her father every other weekend and made it clear she didn't need another. Ron didn't know if Rosa had harbored fantasies about her parents reuniting after their divorce, but Carmen's remarriage would have abruptly ended such a dream.

Still, Rosa had shown faint glimmerings of interest in the sailboat, and that tiny spark was more than Ron had seen in eighteen months. Now he was hoping that the time at sea, away from the distractions of school, television, and boys, would help him form a bond with Rosa. If not, at least he'd have the pleasures of sailing.

Ron shouted down the dock at Chris, who was leaning over the bow swishing a piece of line in the water.

"Hey, Chris! Permission to come aboard?"

Chris looked confused for a minute and then stood erect, brought his hand to his forehead in a salute, and said, "Permission granted." Ron returned his salute and then climbed over the double railing. For perhaps the hundredth time, Ron saw that Chris was a miniature version of himself, with sandy blond hair, blue eyes, and fair—now sunburned—skin. It looked like Chris would someday reach at least his father's five foot ten inches. Both were dressed in nautical white T-shirts, shorts, and deck shoes, and Ron admitted to himself that father-and-son outfits made him feel a little silly.

"Ready to sail, First Mate?"

"I've been ready for an hour. . . . I mean, everything's shipshape, sir."

"I'm going to check on the stores."

Chris ran back to whatever he was doing on the bow while Ron stepped down into the cabin. With only eighty-five square feet of living space, it was tightly packed with necessities and comforts. A propane stove, a refrigerator, and a sink with foot-pump faucets, one for freshwater, and one for saltwater, made up the *Entrepreneur*'s galley. The table in the center of the cabin was actually the cover for the two-cylinder diesel engine. The berths doubled as storage space, and the head was forward in the bow. A small chart table folded down from the wall, and the *Entrepreneur*'s speedometer, chronometer, dinometer, and compass were mounted on the wall above the folding chart table. The radio direction finder, depth finder, and the short-wave radio were mounted below it.

Carmen and Rosa were sitting on the opposing bunks talking when Ron stepped down into the cabin, but stopped as soon as he came in. Rosa and Carmen were nearly as similar as Ron and Chris, sharing short brown hair, brown eyes, and thin arms and legs. But while Carmen was filled out, teenage Rosa still looked gangly.

"Are you ladies ready to go?"

Rosa looked down, folding her hands into her lap, and Carmen gave Ron a "don't make a big deal out of this" look.

"Rosa doesn't want to go."

"But it's all set, and it's only overnight."

"No, I mean she doesn't want to make the sail to Bermuda. A month on the ocean is a long time to be away from your friends."

"It's not just my friends," Rosa said. She raised her head and stared defiantly at Ron. "It's my dad, my real dad. I don't want to be away from him that long. I mean, Mom, you have Ron, and even Chris, but Dad's got no one but me. If I'm gone he'll have no one."

Out of the corner of his eye, Ron saw Carmen bite her lip. Given the history of Rosa's father, Ron doubted the man would be lonely. Ron knew Carmen's marriage had broken up because of her husband's repeated affairs. He also knew Carmen had hidden that from Rosa.

"You'll be together," Rosa continued, "but he'll be alone for a month. I just can't do that to him."

Ron wanted to protest that it wasn't a month at sea, only a week. Well, he reflected, a week each way, with a two-week layover—but he heeded Carmen's warning look.

This trip was meant to be a trial run for the Bermuda voyage. They were to sail out from Naples, Florida, spend the night, and then sail back. The kids could get their sea legs, and Ron could prove to the kids, and Carmen, that he could navigate. He even planned to do it without the RDF system. This was supposed to be a warm-up for the big event, and he wasn't ready to give up the voyage to Bermuda yet.

"Well, I think we can talk about this," Carmen said. "Can't we, Ron?"

Ron nodded, but hoped that after a couple of days at sea Rosa would fall in love with deep-water sailing, just as he had.

"Let's talk about it at sea," he suggested. "I think so much more clearly when there is nothing to see but blue sky above and blue sea below. Rosa, loose the stern lines. Carmen, help Chris with the bow lines. We sail!"

"Don't you give me orders, Captain Bligh," Carmen warned playfully.

"Please?"

Carmen smiled, wrapped her arms around Ron in a brief hug, and then climbed up on deck. His good feelings restored, Ron thought of gliding across the sea using the stars to guide his way in the calming emptiness of the ocean. Then he thought of Rosa. "Please love sailing, Rosa," Ron whispered to himself, "please." Then he climbed to the deck and started the engine.

3. GUN IN THE DARK

At that time a great wonder occurred. The forests were ignited and a multitude of abominable vermin appeared.

—The Shu King, the Canon of Yao

Oregon Caves
PREQUILT: SATURDAY, 10:25 A.M. PST

Dr. Terry Roberts was watching his wife feed Wheat Thins to the chipmunks. Ellen was making a trail using little pieces of the crackers, trying to entice the chipmunks closer and closer. The chipmunks were resisting, though, as if they thought she might lead them to their doom. Terry stifled a laugh at the absurdity of the idea. Ellen was the last person who would harm chipmunks. Terry had even seen her digging carefully in the garden to avoid hurting worms.

Her head down, Ellen was laying a trail for another chipmunk. Her curly brown hair was just long enough to hide her profile as she bent over. In her oval face, the brown eyes, nose, and mouth were distributed and proportioned nicely. The chin was narrow, even pointy. Still, most everyone who met her would call her pretty, although no one but Terry would call her beautiful. At five feet ten she was nearly the same height as her husband. After walking together for twenty-five years they had developed the same gait, and from a distance it was hard to distinguish one from the other.

Though Terry's brown hair wasn't as curly as Ellen's it was almost her shade. Otherwise he was about as average physically as a person can get in height, weight, speed, and strength. Only Terry's intellect was exceptional, but even there he didn't quite qualify as truly brilliant. A guidance counselor had once referred to him as "marginally gifted."

A short, stocky young woman dressed in a park ranger's uniform walked through the people milling around the entrance to the caves. With a serious look on her face she announced in a businesslike manner that all those holding tickets for the ten-thirty tour should gather together. As Terry and Ellen joined the group, the guide gave directions.

"Please enter the caves single file and wait for me inside the entrance. Have your tickets ready."

Ellen went first and Terry handed theirs to the guide. She tore it neatly in half and then handed it back. Terry and Ellen joined the group inside the mouth of the cave and waited for the guide to start her spiel. Terry was surprised to find himself excited about the tour, and whispered in Ellen's ear, "Ready for an adventure?" Ellen didn't answer, she just shrugged her shoulders.

Kenny hung back from the group gathering for the tour. He didn't want his sister to see him or she might call security. With his ticket in hand he went over what he would say to her. He had tried to convince her before, but he had been clumsy and unsure of himself. Now he had proof. He had Dr. Piltcher's pages from the Apocrypha of Zorastrus, and Kenny could tell her about the computer simulation, and how it was all leading to something big, and something soon. That should convince her, he assured himself; he didn't want to use his other plan.

Kenny unzipped the top of his pack and pushed the towel aside, exposing the gun. He fingered the weapon and wondered if he could actually use it. He decided he could. He couldn't save himself and leave his sister to go through it alone. She might hate him now, but soon she would understand.

Kenny put on his pack and joined the group. His sister didn't notice him until she took his ticket.

"Get away from me, Kenny."

"I've got proof, let me show you," Kenny began.

"I don't want to hear it."

"There was this prophet Zorastrus, and everyone thought he was crazy but it turns out he was right—"

"I've got a tour to lead, Kenny. Go tell it to a priest."

"Please, Jill—"

"No, Kenny," she said, and then turned to go.

"I've got a ticket, Jill."

"You don't want a tour, you just want to harass me."

"I won't say a word. I just want to be with you."

"I can't stop you, but if you start preaching that end-of-the-world nonsense, I'll have you arrested."

Kenny nodded agreement and then joined the tourists.

Terry stood behind Ellen with his hands on her shoulders. Their group was mostly couples. One couple had to be newlyweds; young, and pretty, they never let go of each other's hands. Another young couple had two boys, about eight and ten, who whispered and giggled to each other. There was a prosperous-looking older couple that seemed to be retired and enjoying it. Terry suspected that a Silver Stream trailer was waiting for them in the parking lot.

Another man came through the cave opening carrying in a backpack a baby wearing a hat with Mickey and Minnie Mouse designs. Her mother followed, trying to wipe the baby's face while the baby kept turning her head, gurgling. The wife was wearing a Mickey Mouse T-shirt and the husband's shirt advertised KNOTT'S BERRY FARM. Terry imagined their car's bumper stickers said TREES OF MYSTERY and VISIT DRIVE THRU TREE.

Finally a middle-aged interracial couple entered. The woman was white and carefully groomed and coordinated from the scarf that tied up her blond hair to her color-matched L.A. Gear shoes. In ten years she would be "fat," but today she still qualified for "voluptuous." The man—the only black man in the group—was also the tallest, at least six feet tall. He would be doing some ducking on this tour. While Terry hated stereotypes the man's short, neatly trimmed hair and good posture made Terry suspect the man was in the military.

The last member of the group, a college-age kid with a yellow backpack, stood out because only he was unaccompanied. Terry wondered vaguely about the bulging pack, deciding he had taken the DON'T LEAVE VALUABLES IN YOUR CAR signs seriously.

"My name is Jill and I will be your guide for a sixty-minute tour of the Oregon Caves. The temperature inside the caves is a constant fifty-six degrees, and although that sounds cool, the high humidity will keep you quite comfortable. Electric lights were installed in the cave in 1956, in order to protect both visitors to the caves and the caves themselves, so flashlights and lanterns are not necessary."

Terry noticed that nearly everyone carried a portable light.

"Smoking is not allowed in the caves, and we ask that you do not leave litter or gum in the caves."

Ellen dutifully pulled a piece of tissue out of her pocket, wrapped up the piece of gum she had been chewing, and dropped the wad back in her pocket.

After some instructions to "not straggle" and "stay on the trails" she led them into the caves. The air was cool but comfortable, and as they hiked along, those with jackets took them off and tied them around their waists. The electric lights along the trail made flashlights unnecessary, and they slowly disappeared into pockets. Periodically, when the group stopped, the guide explained some feature of the cave.

"If you look through this opening, which was made in 1967, you can see the natural color of the cave walls. The original explorers of these caves used torches to light their way, and, as you can see, the soot from the torches discolored the walls and ceiling. Originally the caves were snowy white as you can see through this opening . . ."

It had been Ellen's idea to stop at the caves on the way back from a convention—really a vacation—in Los Angeles where Terry had presented a paper on dysfunctional families but skipped most of the other sessions. Cruising up I-5, Ellen had studied the literature she picked up at a visitors' information rack at a rest stop. Ellen was in a tourist mood, and it had been years since they'd visited the Oregon Caves, so they cut off the interstate at Medford and headed west to the caves. After a morning tour they'd still make it back to Portland that night.

Vaguely remembering his last tour through the caves, Terry was anticipating one particular part: When the guide turns out the lights, it's the first and only time most people experience total darkness. Terry recalled feeling the darkness around his face as his eyes vainly struggled to detect something. In retrospect, it seemed unpleasant, but, strangely, Terry was looking forward to it again.

As the tour progressed members developed an informal understanding. The couple with the baby hung back, since the baby's noises distracted the guide. Front positions were reserved for the older couple since they listened more attentively than the rest. The little boys went wherever they wanted, and the parents didn't care. The young man with the yellow backpack was always in the rear, staring at their guide, a sad determined look on his face.

The group came to a large cave with several branching passages, its well-packed trail testimony to the previous thousands of tourists. The guide, directing them into a side passage that dead-ended into a small cave, stood by the entrance and let the group pass.

"You will now experience something that few of you have had the chance to experience. Total darkness."

Immediately the lights went out. Several people gasped as their eyes became useless. Then the lights were back. There were murmurs of relief and cheerful kidding among the members of the group, until a masculine voice ordered: "Stay where you are and don't move."

"Kenny, what are you doing? Are you crazy?"

Terry turned with the group toward the voices. The kid with the backpack was standing by the entrance with a gun in his hand, the guide at his side, her mouth and eyes open in disbelief. More murmurs from the group but no longer cheerful. The little boy whispered he was scared. The baby gurgled cheerfully while she yanked on her dad's hair. Terry noticed the black man start to move from the back of the group toward the kid.

"I said don't move." As he spoke the kid turned the gun toward the man, who froze in midstep, his face determined—while Terry felt near panic.

"I want everyone to sit down right where they are. Sit down. You too, Jill. Now!"

Everyone but the guide sat down. Terry noticed the military man sat down last, his eyes never leaving the gun in the kid's hand.

"Kenny," the guide pleaded softly. "Please put the gun down. You're scaring everyone. There are kids here. You're scaring the kids."

"It's your fault, Jill. I tried to get you to listen. It's going to happen . . . happen soon. I want my family with me when it does. At least you, Jill. Now, sit down!"

At the last words, the kid shoved the gun in the guide's face, and the shock sent her stumbling back a few steps until she melted into the group, which sat in stunned silence.

Terry thought about the guide's reaction. The kid called her family, yet the guide seemed genuinely frightened, and that was a red flag. The kid had strong feelings for the guide, and yet she was afraid he would use the gun on her. Terry didn't need his professional training to diagnose Kenny as unstable and potentially dangerous.

The group sat in silence, the only sound the collective deep breathing. Finally, the old lady spoke.

"Son," she said, attracting his attention. "I've never heard of anyone hijacking a cave tour before. What is it that you want?"

"You won't believe me! No one will believe me! My own sister won't believe me."

"I promise to listen to you and keep my mind open. Ask Hank, here," the old woman said, indicating her husband. "He'll tell you I'm a good listener. Have to be when you live with Hank for forty years."

Hank smiled at his wife, but the kid with the gun didn't.

"You won't believe me, but if you want to know . . . I'm going to save you. At least I think I am."

Nervous conversation spread through the crowd. The old woman ignored it and asked, "What is it that you think you're saving us from?"

"He's crazy," the guide responded. "He's hooked up with a bunch of flakes that think the sky is falling."

Anxiety washed across the kid's face, and he reddened. He looked away from the old woman to his sister, pain in his eyes. Then, with what could have been embarrassment, he said, "I'm saving you from the end of the world!"

4. Offshore

We were three days into the desert when the flood occurred. Great waves washed over our caravan. Three men and two camels of great value were lost. When the waters receded we were surrounded by a great number of fishes. The water was of no use because it tasted of salt.

—Abu al Assad, 1413

Off Naples, Florida
PreQuilt: Saturday, 1:35 p.m. EST

Ron was so obvious about trying to please Rosa that even Chris noticed it. "Geez, Dad," he said finally, "why don't you just kiss her?" Ron took the kidding but didn't give up trying to get Rosa interested in sailing. He showed her how to mind the helm, hoist and lower the sails, told her what the different sails were called, and explained the compass and what a heading was.

He let her take the helm and talked endlessly about his experiences at sea and the time he had sailed with his uncle in the greatest of the offshore races, the Fastnet. With forty-one other entries they had set sail from Cowes on the Isle of Wight, raced to Fastnet Rock off the coast of Ireland, and then back to Plymouth, England. Thirty-two competitors finished that year, and Ron's uncle's boat finished seventeenth. But that seventeenth place was as good as a victory in Ron's memory. They had raced through fog banks, fought whirligig currents, and finished in the middle of the pack. But they had finished. Ron talked about it with more passion than Rosa had ever seen in him, and as a result she listened respectfully. Even Chris, who had heard the story for years, listened attentively this time. Telling the story at sea gave it a feeling no living room could.

In the afternoon Ron brought out the sextant and tried explaining navigation to Rosa and Chris. Carmen sat at the helm, a bemused look on her face.

"The key to figuring out our position is what we call the navigational triangle. We start by identifying three points on the earth's surface. We know where the earth's pole is, so that is one point."

"Which pole?" Chris cut in. "There's two, you know."

"Yes, I know. The closest pole, in this case the North Pole. We also know the geographical position of stars and planets . . . that means where the star or planet is over the earth's surface."

"But the earth is turning," Rosa pointed out.

"Yeah," Chris echoed, "the earth is turning fast. Maybe a million miles an hour."

"Yes," Ron said with exaggerated patience, "the earth is turning, but not millions of miles an hour, more like a thousand. That's why we need a clock, a very accurate clock."

"The one in the cabin, right?" Chris said.

"Right, Chris. We leave that one in the cabin because it's set to Greenwich mean time and must be exactly right. Then, I set my watch by that clock."

"I thought you used the radio to set your watch," Rosa pointed out.

"I use the radio to see how far off our clock is from Greenwich mean time. They broadcast Greenwich mean time signals so people at sea can check their clocks."

"And if their clocks are off they can't navigate?" Rosa asked.

"Yeah, they get lost forever, and become ghost ships," Chris said.

"No, they just need to correct their calculations based on how many seconds off their clock is. You were right about the earth moving, but we know where a star will be above its surface at a given time. We use the *Nautical Almanac* to find that out." Ron held up the book. Chris reached for it, but Ron pulled it out of his reach. "I'm not finished yet. Okay, so we know where the pole is, and we know the point on the earth's surface where a star or planet will be directly above at a certain time of the day. Then we use our position to complete the triangle."

"But if you know where we are why do you have to do all this?" Rosa asked.

"Yeah," Chris echoed his new sister. "If we know where we are why do we have to do this?"

"We don't know exactly where we are, we estimate it based on course and speed from our last position. But an approximate position isn't good enough. We have to know exactly where we are. This is where the sextant comes in." Ron lifted it out of its box. Chris made a grab again, but Ron held it up high. "I use the sextant. Maybe I'll show Rosa how to use it if she wants."

"What about me?" Chris whined.

"Well, maybe," Ron said doubtfully. He looked to Carmen for help, but the look on her face said she was enjoying his predicament.

"We know the three points of our triangle, and based on that we know, at a certain time, how high the star should be above the horizon. We use the sextant to read the exact height of the star above the horizon, and mark the time of the reading. Then, since we know for sure two points of the triangle, we can adjust the position of the third point based on the difference between our estimated altitude of the star and the actual altitude."

Ron looked around at his miniaudience. Carmen was still grinning, Chris was staring blankly, and Rosa glared angrily at him. Ron couldn't imagine why his navigation lesson would make her mad. Then Rosa blurted it out.

"This is geometry, isn't it? This is some sort of trick to get me to do homework, isn't it?"

"No, it's not a trick. It is geometry, but I thought you would be interested. . . . I mean, you have to do this to sail offshore."

"Just what I want to do, float around the ocean doing geometry. Just how often do you have to do these calculations?"

"Seven or eight times a day. You do the first before sunrise, a couple of sun sights in the morning, a noon sight . . ."

Ron stopped talking. He knew he was making Rosa's hostility worse.

"Eight times a day? You have to do the calculations eight times a day? And you get to get up early to do them? What a sweet deal."

"Well, it's not that bad. Most of the calculations are done

for you, you just use the tables, or the electronic navigator in the cabin."

"I know if I tried to pay someone to do my geometry homework you would ground me forever. And now I'm supposed to do yours? Well, if I have to do geometry to sail, it's another good reason to stay on land. There all you have to do is read the signs, or a map."

"But the stars are the map out here."

"Yeah," Chris cut in, "the stars are a map. Kind of a connect the dots."

Ron scowled at Chris while Rosa got up and stomped down the deck to the bow. Carmen gave Ron a look that said "You should have known better." Ron thought about Rosa and then he thought of Bermuda, and then he got depressed. Chris was still sitting there with him, looking at the sextant. Maybe, Ron thought, if I get Chris interested Rosa will come back.

"You want to see how the sextant works, Chris?"

Chris lit up like a kid on Christmas morning.

"Yeah, sure. Can I hold it too?"

Ron spent a few minutes with Chris, showing him how to sight the sun and the horizon and make the readings. It was clear Chris mostly wanted to look through the sextant's telescopic sight, so Ron gave up and let him. Rosa never came back. Instead she was sunbathing on the bow. Finally, Ron set Chris up with a fishing pole and then settled in next to Carmen at the helm.

The *Entrepreneur* sailed southwest into the afternoon. When Ron dropped the sea anchor they ate. Carmen had cooked crab in the icebox, and they cracked and ate it with salad, and soft bread sticks. The lunch warmed Rosa's heart enough to get her talking to Ron again. After lunch Chris talked them into playing spoons, his favorite card game. Carmen had never played, and Chris expertly explained how the cards are passed in a circle until a player gets four of a kind, and then picks up one of the three spoons on the table. Then, in a race, the other players try to grab the remaining spoons. Chris cautioned her not to get faked into grabbing one too soon but in the first round feigned a grab and tricked her. Laughing as they played, they shared a good feeling. Finally, Carmen announced it was time for swimming.

They spent the next hour jumping off the stern into the warm blue waters. Finally, exhausted, the kids stretched out on the bow to warm themselves while Ron and Carmen settled in the stern.

"You're being too obvious, you know?" Carmen said. "About Rosa, I mean. You can't force her to want to go to Bermuda."

"I know. I gave up after the navigation debacle."

"That was pretty funny. Trying to get a teenager to like sailing by teaching her geometry. Did you notice things went better after you stopped trying?"

"Well, we did have a good time after lunch. But we can play cards at home. That has nothing to do with sailing."

"But we don't play cards at home. The kids have their friends and TV. You and I have our jobs, and we tend to bring them home with us. When was the last time we played cards? I mean all of us, as a family?"

Carmen was right, Ron admitted. The isolation of offshore sailing had brought them together. Perhaps Rosa would never love sailing, but the experience might help meld the family. That was more important than a sail to Bermuda, Ron told himself. He tried telling himself that again, but still a part of him wanted Bermuda, and it wasn't looking good. Ron leaned back, looking up into the clear blue sky, and silently hoped nothing else would go wrong.

5. Hostages

I was awakened this morning by the sound of pounding on my roof. I went to the window to see a most surprising sight. Dried fish were pouring from the sky onto the houses and into the street. When the shower ended the natives collected the fish into baskets. My aide estimated that 3000 to 4000 fish had fallen.

—Colonel Witherspoon, India, 1836

Ashland, Oregon
PreQuilt: Saturday, 3:40 p.m. PST

Deputy Sheriff Robin Kyle was parked with his feet stretched out on the front seat of his patrol car. He wasn't asleep but was only about one level of consciousness away, his eyes partially open, semialert for criminal activity. Of course much criminal activity—or even traffic—would be rare on this particular dirt road. That was why Kyle had picked this patrol. He had no intention of ruining a beautiful fall day by actually catching a criminal. He wasn't lazy, exactly, it was just that relaxation came naturally to him, and since there was very little real crime in Jackson county, he believed he was making best use of his time.

Occasional calls and assignments could be heard over his radio speaker, but he had turned the radio down low enough so it didn't distract him. A horse clip-clopped past his cruiser, ridden by a teenage girl. Kyle alternated between watching the rider's and horse's rears wiggle rhythmically. He picked up his radar gun and aimed it at the retreating behinds. Too bad, he thought, they're within the legal limit. He was still watching the behinds when he heard his unit number. He ignored it the first time but reluctantly answered it after the second call.

"Sorry to bother you while you're so busy, Kyle," Karon, the dispatcher said, as if she knew what he was doing. "But we got a call that only you can answer. Seems they've got a hostage situation in the Oregon Caves."

Kyle pounded the side of his head like something was stuck in his ear.

"You said in the Oregon Caves? What kind of hostage situation, Karon?"

"The usual kind, Kyle! Someone with a gun is holding a dozen people hostage down in the caves. Says he won't kill them as long as no one interferes."

Kyle was trying to understand why someone had selected a cave to take hostages in. Certainly it would be a difficult place to assault, and guns would be almost useless. Any wayward shot would ricochet wildly, killing indiscriminately. Still it wasn't like hijacking a jet. A jet could take you somewhere. Even a bus could do that, but not a cave. And this particular cave was in the middle of nowhere.

"That's mighty peculiar, Karon," Kyle cut in. "Someone selecting a cave to hold hostages in! I got a dollar says he wants free transportation to a worker's paradise somewhere. Have there been any demands?"

"Negative, Kyle. You ready for the strange part? The guy with the gun says he's saving the people in the cave. Says he doesn't want to be alone after it happens."

"After what happens?"

"After the world ends."

"What do they want me for?"

"They're looking for officers with cave experience. They heard about your rescue training."

Kyle winced at the mention of that. He had taken the special training as an excuse to take two weeks off, drink beer with some friends of his, and get a little extra in the paycheck each month. In the two years since the training he had helped recover one dead body from a plane wreck, and helped pull a hiker with a broken leg up a twenty-five-foot slope. Kyle wanted to tell Karon that his training was for rescuing people who want to be rescued, not for going in after some self-destructive nut. Kyle didn't seem to have a choice, however.

"Okay, Karon, tell them I'll pick up some gear and head on over, but it'll take a couple of hours." Kyle was hoping the situation would be resolved long before he could get involved.

"They know that, Kyle, they said there was no hurry. The guy in the cave isn't going anywhere."

6. Kid with a Gun

Not one will get away, none will escape. Though they dig down to the depths of the grave from there my hand will take them.

—Amos, 9:12

Oregon Caves
PreQuilt: Saturday, 3:42 p.m. PST

Ellen and Terry were sitting down, using each other as backrests. Most of the others in the cave were either lying down or leaning against the cave walls. The initial panic the group experienced had died down. Nothing had happened since the kid had scared off the next tour group, pointing his gun at the members entering the cave as he told them to "get out and stay out." The kid made no demands or political statements, but it was clear he wasn't going to let anyone go either. Occasionally his sister would plead or try to reason with him, but each time she was rebuffed. Finally she gave up and sat in silence with the rest of the hostages.

Terry was mentally reviewing what he knew about hostage situations. If they remained captive long enough, and if the conditions were harsh, some would come to sympathize with the hostage-takers. Persistent anxiety, with no control over the situation, causes one to identify with the source of the anxiety, in this case the kid with the gun. Terry remembered one case where hostages were held in a bank vault for three days. The police turned off the air-conditioning, poisoned the food, and provided minimal water while the gang holding the hostages sexually abused the women. Yet, when finally released, many of the hostages expressed concern about what would happen to their captors.

The two boys were throwing rocks in the back of the cave.

Terry turned to look at them and noticed something peculiar. The military man was no longer toward the back of the group, but in the middle. The kid was sitting with his knees up to his chest, and staring straight ahead. The gun was still in his hand, although it was pointed toward the ground. Terry pulled his own head to his knees, put his arms on top, and then lay his head down sideways so he could watch the military man.

It took a long time, but Terry could see what was happening. Every once in a while the military man would stretch a leg, or an arm, or arch his back and yawn. And every time his leg came back down, or he finished stretching, he would be an inch or two closer to the front. Terry watched him move an arm and rock sideways. A few minutes later he stretched the other arm and rocked back the other way. He was now two inches closer. It was like watching a clock. It took patience, but if you stared long enough you could see the minute hand move.

The military man's moves rekindled Terry's sharp fears; waves of panic swept him. What if the kid noticed? What if the military man did something? What if he did something that made the kid punish the group? On the other hand, Terry didn't know enough about the kid's condition to be certain that he wasn't a danger.

Terry had once worked with a paranoid schizophrenic named Larry who was high functioning. He lived in his own apartment, held down a laborer's job, and took good care of a white Persian cat named Katrina. If it hadn't been for his persistent claims that a group of telepathic Masons were trying to kill him, Terry would not have been treating Larry. Then one day a salesman wearing a Mason's pin came to Larry's door. Larry shot the salesman in the chest, later claiming self-defense. Larry ended up in the state mental hospital and Katrina in the animal shelter. Could this kid be another Larry? Did Terry want the military man betting all of their lives that he wouldn't be another Larry?

Terry gently pushed Ellen into a sitting position, and then cleared his throat.

"What is your name?" he said weakly. Then, in a stronger voice, he repeated himself. "It's Kenny, isn't it?"

The kid raised his head, his eyes glassy. Slowly his head

turned in Terry's direction. Terry noticed the gun followed his stare. Even when Kenny was finally facing Terry, he wasn't sure the kid was seeing him.

"I said no talking."

The kid said it without conviction. Terry assumed he was as bored as the rest of them, and probably more scared.

"It's Kenny," his sister answered for him. "Kenny Randall, the nut case."

Kenny glared at his sister, but the gun remained pointed at Terry.

"I'm Terry, Kenny, and this is my wife, Ellen." Terry thought about telling Kenny he was a psychologist. Sometimes troubled people found that reassuring. On the other hand, many people who have had institutional experiences harbor hostility toward psychologists. Terry decided it was too soon to mention his profession.

"Kenny, Ellen and I are scared, and I bet you are too. Are you scared, Kenny?"

Kenny's eyes were still unfocused, but he seemed to be taking the whole group in. Terry wondered if he was monitoring the progress of the military man.

"I don't want to talk about it."

"What don't you want to talk about, Kenny?"

"About what is going to happen."

"Kenny, I want to understand this. What is going to happen?"

Kenny's eyes finally focused on Terry. His direct stare, gun in his hand, twisted Terry's stomach into a knot.

"I already told you. The world is going to end."

"How, Kenny? How will the world end?"

"You don't believe me. No one believes me. I tried to tell people but no one would listen. No one would believe me when I told them. I even tried to show them, but they wouldn't see it." Then with bitterness in his voice, and a nod toward his sister, he added, "Even my own family wouldn't believe me."

Terry had worked with a number of paranoid patients before and Kenny seemed to have the symptoms. Kenny believed he had secret knowledge, something he had discovered and something only he could understand. If Kenny was paranoid then he was potentially dangerous.

"Kenny, you haven't told me about it yet. I promise you I will try to understand."

"I told you, he thinks the sky is falling," Kenny's sister said.

Kenny's eyes flamed and his face reddened.

"You never really listened to me, did you, Jill? I never said the sky was falling. I said things were falling from the sky. There's a difference, a big difference. I have the proof too, but you wouldn't look at it, would you?"

Terry saw Kenny's anger was welling up and worried it might drive Kenny to lash out—maybe with the gun. Terry decided to try again to deflect Kenny's attention from his sister. He could see Kenny loved her, but her comments were provoking Kenny's anger.

"Kenny, I really would like to hear your story—theory."

Kenny sat silently, breathing deeply and staring at Terry. Terry, afraid that murder was going through the kid's mind, was relieved when Kenny finally spoke.

"All right, smart man. Can you understand why corn falls from a clear blue sky? Can you understand why people suddenly burst into flame? Can you understand how whole civilizations simply disappear? At first we couldn't either. But then we found someone else who had seen it, someone a long time ago. Everyone thought he was crazy too. He understood it, and so did we finally. We proved it just as scientists should. We had the data, the theory, and the evidence, and still no one believed us."

Kenny looked lost in thought for a minute, a pained expression on his face. Then Kenny's expression changed to profound sadness, and he spoke again.

"I wish to God that corn had rained on someone else. Maybe I was meant to know. Maybe I stumbled into it accidentally. It doesn't matter now, it will be over soon."

From a professional viewpoint, Terry saw much to explore in what Kenny had blurted out. He was emoting freely, and if this had been a therapy session Terry would have followed each lead deep into Kenny's subconscious. Things falling from the sky, people burning, the mention of God. Were people being burned for their sins? Who were the "we" Kenny referred to and who was the person from long ago? But Kenny wasn't a patient and certainly wouldn't cooperate. Terry knew he had to focus on their immediate situation. Even the briefest therapy was no good here.

"Will we burst into flame, Kenny? Is that what's going to happen?" Terry worried that Kenny might have a can of gasoline in that yellow backpack, and when the world didn't end he might try to simulate it.

"No, we're not going to burn, at least I don't think so. Not down this far. I hope not, but I don't . . ." Kenny's sentence trailed off and his face showed confusion and then anger. "How am I supposed to know? Jeez, I'm not some sort of Einstein. I only know it's going to happen." Kenny glanced at his watch. "And it's going to happen soon."

"Are you expecting a nuclear attack, Kenny? Is that why some people will burn?"

"No, nothing like that . . . well . . ." Kenny's lips pulled up briefly into a smile. "In a way it is a nuclear attack. But it is more than that, it's natural too."

"A natural nuclear attack. Can you explain that, Kenny?"

Kenny quickly lost his smile.

"No, I can't. I won't. If I'm wrong you'll all be free soon. If I'm right you'll be thanking me. I won't talk anymore."

Kenny dug into his backpack and brought out a handful of granola bars and tossed them into the group.

"Here, eat something."

Slowly the group passed them around. Only the children ate.

7. Chicken Little Summer

Seven solar ages are referred to in Mayan manuscripts, in Buddhist sacred books, in the books of the Sibyl. . . . The "suns" are explained (by the sources themselves) as consecutive epochs, each of which went down in a great, general destruction.

—Immanuel Velikovsky, *Worlds in Collision*

Oregon Caves
PreQuilt: Saturday, 4:15 p.m. PST

Kenny sat with his back to the cave entrance and his eyes fixed forward. He couldn't bring himself to look any of them in the eye. It was too painful. He could see what they were thinking. It didn't matter what the old lady said, or the other man. They all thought he was crazy. But I'm not crazy, he told himself over and over again. I'm not crazy! He wished the others from Dr. Piltcher's group were here so they could back him up, testify to what they all sincerely believed. They had figured it out, but more importantly they had proved it.

Their first real success came just after the Fourth of July. Kenny and Phat had worked every night in June on the program, trying to refine the geographical and temporal predictions, but felt trapped in a vicious cycle. If they could successfully predict even a single fall, they could refine their model, but until they predicted a fall, the imperfect model couldn't define the location of an event. So night after night the other students and volunteers sat at picnic tables in the campgrounds, and by propane light combed through newspapers searching for the impossible. Dr. Piltcher and Dr. Coombs sat at another table, poring over the Zorastrus manuscript and other ancient texts, trying to find historical data to help shape the model. Phat and Kenny sat in Dr. Piltcher's RV, writing and rewriting the program. Around eleven the group would drift off to bed. Mrs.

Wayne usually retired just before eleven, when her spirit guide Shontel made herself available. Sometimes Ernie Powell sat with Mrs. Wayne and listened to her messages from "Shontel," but most nights he spent a few minutes in the minivan picking up the baseball scores before retiring to his tent. On some nights Petra Zalewski and Colter Swenson took a sleeping bag and went for a walk. Petra was a student at Oregon Institute of Technology, but Colter was enrolled at Southern Oregon State College, which he'd chosen from a list of best "party schools" he found in *Playboy*. They had been strangers before joining the group. Dr. Piltcher and Dr. Coombs often debated late into the evening, long after Kenny and Phat exhausted their creative reservoirs.

The pattern continued, day after day, week after week. Every few days Dr. Piltcher and Dr. Coombs came to Kenny and Phat and asked for a location and a date. Kenny and Phat ran the program and made the prediction. Then the group would be on the move again. They had started in South Dakota and were working roughly west while zigzagging north and south. Kenny knew if the predictions brought them to the Pacific Coast without success it would be over.

The break came one night in a Montana campground near Glacier National Park. They spent the early part of the evening shooting off fireworks to celebrate the Fourth of July, and then settled down to comb through local newspapers for any strange events that would fit the model. It was nearly eleven that night when Petra found a story in a local weekly paper about a boy swept off a three-wheeled motorbike by a flash flood. The boy suffered a broken arm. Two peculiarities made the story stand out. First, although flash floods were common, there had been no rain to account for the flood, at least none anyone reported. The article quoted a weatherman describing it as a freak local shower. The second peculiarity was that the nearly drowned boy said the water tasted salty. After hearing the story, Dr. Piltcher finger-combed his thin white hair ten strokes before responding. Ten strokes meant he was convinced.

"That's one," he said, turning to look at Dr. Coombs. "It's coming, Doctor."

Dr. Coombs nodded solemnly.

"Mr. Randall, Mr. Nyang," Dr. Piltcher continued. "Add this to your model."

Kenny and Phat had taken the data and tried to fit it to the model. Failing that, they worked late into the night adjusting the model to the data. The next morning Dr. Piltcher and Dr. Coombs arrived with the expected request for the location and the time.

"Thirteen days, plus or minus forty-eight hours," Phat said.

"And the location?" Dr. Piltcher asked.

"I've always wanted to see Yellowstone National Park," Kenny answered.

They stayed three more days in the campground, making side trips to libraries, retirement homes, and newspaper offices in local towns, looking for more reports of unusual events. Petra and Mrs. Wayne were assigned to find and talk to the boy or his family about the incident. They found the boy and visited the site, but found no evidence that would help confirm the incident. No pockets of water, no fish, no aquatic vegetation. Dr. Piltcher remained certain though. "This," he said after finger-combing his hair six times, "was an event."

They camped outside of Yellowstone for a few days, making side trips to libraries, newspaper offices, and museums, and then moved in early one morning to make sure they could get enough campsites together. Yellowstone was the worst possible location to experience an event. It was forested and mountainous, and while there were numerous meadows and fire-thinned sections of forest, visual identification of an event would be near impossible. Dr. Piltcher was particularly frustrated, because he felt so close to success and saw it slipping away. As the first possible date approached, Dr. Piltcher and Dr. Coombs worried over how to distribute observers. Finally they decided on high viewpoints, open meadows, and the flat open spaces that housed the tourist facilities.

The first day of the event window Kenny was assigned to a spot near Old Faithful to watch the open areas around the lodge. Petra was assigned a trail head leading to a high meadow where she camped and watched. Mrs. Wayne drew a viewpoint overlooking the Grand Canyon of the Yellowstone. Phat Nyang was dropped at road's end on Mount Washburn, with a backpack full of camping gear and enough food for a few days.

He was the most experienced backpacker in the group and the best equipped to climb the trail toward the peak of Mount Washburn. Colter Swenson went to Roosevelt Lodge to watch the open meadows there. Ernie Powell stayed at Lake Village by Lake Yellowstone, although Dr. Piltcher admitted if it happened somewhere over the huge lake, it would be hard to spot. Dr. Coombs and Dr. Piltcher were kept in reserve to begin a rotation in the watch they might have to keep up for eight days.

Everyone rotated from site to site, taking turns off watch to sleep and eat. Dr. Piltcher even admonished them not to go to the bathroom unless they were relieved from watch. "But don't just watch," he told them over and over, his hands relentlessly combing his hair. "Listen. Listen to what the tourists are saying around you. This park is full of tourists, all of them with their eyes wide open, and their camcorders running. We might not see it, but somebody must." It was painful to see Dr. Piltcher. He finger-combed his hair incessantly and was always flushed and sweaty. He was short, overweight, and two years past retirement age, and Kenny sometimes worried that he might have a heart attack.

Kenny had gone to Dr. Piltcher the previous November, after his experience with the corn fall. Dr. Piltcher was the only one who had listened to him. Kenny had tried to interest his friends and family in what had happened, but to no avail. His father had just laughed at him. His sister was skeptical. Still, Kenny's obsession with the corn fall grew.

Kenny spent most evenings and weekends in bookstores looking for books on the kind of events he had experienced. He found those books, and more. He found old newspaper records of things falling from the sky, and of people disappearing. He found records of people and things bursting into flames. He found mystery after mystery; but he found no theory to link these events, let alone to explain them. Then he found the story in the newspaper about the mother and daughter in a park buried in flowers that poured from the sky. That's when he got his idea.

He began working on his computer, logging the events, looking for patterns, looking through the eyes of his theory for a way to explain away the mystery. Kenny wanted corn, ice, water, and fish falling from the sky to become natural and predictable. But he had little success until he met Dr. Piltcher. On a flyer tacked to a bulletin board in the Student Union building, he read that Dr. Piltcher would be giving a talk the next night on "Cataclysm and Its Role in Cultural Development."

Kenny had heard of Dr. Piltcher. Among the students, the professor had a kind of disreputation as a brilliant man who collected degrees like others collected coins. He wandered from university to university teaching different subjects and earning new degrees. He started at Yale as a geologist, then taught at the University of Michigan as a zoologist, and then briefly at BYU and Oregon State University as a lecturer in paleontology. Somewhere along the way he picked up degrees in computer information science and management. His interest in systems approaches to civilizations and organizations, and the climate of southern Oregon, lead him to OIT. Kenny overheard one faculty member describing Dr. Piltcher's academic career as working down the ladder of success.

His last eight years had been spent teaching in the systems science program at OIT. Until his retirement he had been a lackluster teacher in his field but dynamic when chasing rabbits through his lectures. All a student had to do was make a reference to some obscure subject and Dr. Piltcher would be off on the new topic, only to discover twenty or thirty minutes later he had been sidetracked. His passion for the obscure shone through as he held bored management students spellbound when he rhapsodized about the books of the Sibyl, or the annals of the kings of Tezcuco as recorded by the Native American scholar Ixtlilxochitl. Where Dr. Piltcher was dry as dust when talking about Theory Y management and the Hawthorne effect, he would speak with passion about the Buddhist sacred book *Visuddhi-Magga.*

The flyer's reference to "cataclysm" brought Kenny to the lecture hall the next night. Thirty people sat scattered in a room built to hold one hundred. Most were community residents who lived on the fringe, drifting from one New Age philosophy or religion to another. Some of the others were elderly, drawn to anything that was free and maybe interesting. There were a few students there besides Kenny. Although Kenny didn't know Petra's name then, he picked her pretty face, long brown hair, and slender shape out of the stragglers who entered as the lecture began. Mrs. Wayne was there too, the opposite of Petra, plump and busty, with rounded features and bottle blond hair.

Dr. Piltcher was introduced by Dr. Coombs, whom Kenny didn't know. Dr. Coombs wasn't on the faculty at OIT. A tall man, well muscled and tan, Kenny would later discover that Dr. Coombs was a local chiropractor who had taught anthropology for years at the University of Oregon but then opted out of the publish-or-perish environment of academia.

Dr. Coombs listed Dr. Piltcher's numerous degrees and papers, and then introduced the night's topic by describing Dr. Piltcher's research into ancient history and geology. The introduction ended to light applause. Kenny noticed Mrs. Wayne applauded loudest of all. At the podium, Dr. Piltcher placed a sheaf of yellow paper on it, pulled a pair of glasses out of his pocket, perched them on his nose, and began.

The lecture described how fossil remains of hippos were found in West Yorkshire, England, 1450 feet above sea level. Dr. Piltcher pointed out the absurdity of hippopotami in the northern latitudes of England, climbing the hills to their resting place so far from the sea. Dr. Piltcher argued the only reasonable explanation was geologic catastrophe. In the past when the climate of the earth was uniform from pole to equator to pole, the poles were thirty degrees warmer than they are today. Under those conditions the planet would support near-tropical growth from the equator to near the poles. In that era, Dr. Piltcher theorized, there was no tilt to the earth's axis. But the passage of a large comet or planet changed all that. The resulting tilt cooled the poles, warmed the equator, and created the distinct seasons we experience.

Kenny found himself absorbed. Soon he realized he was beginning to feel the same way about the hippopotami as he had when the corn fell out of the sky.

The lecture was followed by a debate between Dr. Coombs and Dr. Piltcher. Dr. Coombs argued that the presence of hippopotami remains could be explained by a migration of hippos leaving North Africa, perhaps by the Nile. Dr. Coombs argued the animals could have swum ever northward, pausing in their migrations in the winter, swimming north only during the warm summer months. Eventually they would have reached England and worked their way to the places in England where they were found.

But Dr. Piltcher immediately and vehemently disagreed. "What would motivate the hippopotami to move from warm equatorial waters to the frigid waters of the North Atlantic?" he thundered. "How could a hippo survive in such a radically different climate?"

"They did not survive," responded Dr. Coombs. "Isn't that the point? The hippos could not survive in the climate they had migrated to."

"But what motivation? What instinct would drive them north? And when they reached the north, what would drive them inland and up the hills and mountains to die?"

"Why do whales beach themselves?" Dr. Coombs challenged him. "Perhaps if they had legs they would not only beach themselves but crawl up the nearest mountain."

"So why do we not see hippopotami migrating today?" came Dr. Piltcher's reply.

The debate went back and forth for twenty minutes. As Kenny listened he realized it held no acrimony. Rather, it seemed like a well-orchestrated performance, with Dr. Piltcher given the more dramatic role. Dr. Coombs responded reasonably but without Dr. Piltcher's passion and volume.

Afterward a few people went up to talk with Dr. Piltcher and Dr. Coombs, but Kenny held back, embarrassed to speak of his experience in front of strangers. Most of the people had gone except Mrs. Wayne, Petra, and Dr. Coombs, who seemed to be preparing to leave with Dr. Piltcher. Kenny swallowed his embarrassment and called out Dr. Piltcher's name when he passed.

"What is it?" Dr. Piltcher replied.

"Something happened that I wanted to tell you about . . . this corn just started falling out of the sky . . . I mean it was strange . . . right out of the blue. I'm not making this up. It really happened! And I have a theory of why it happened . . . only an idea, really. I thought you might be able to help me understand it better."

Kenny paused, wishing he had thought out ahead of time what he was going to say. It sounded so lame to him, so vague. Kenny paused, waiting to get brushed off again, or worse. He expected a blank look or exasperation from Dr. Piltcher and amusement from Dr. Piltcher's followers. To his amazement he found interest in their eyes and welcome from Dr. Piltcher.

"That's a story I'd like to hear, but not here. I need my coffee."

Kenny followed the chiropractor's minivan to the edge of Klamath Falls. Down a long drive, a two-story frame house sat in an unkempt cluttered yard. Inside Dr. Piltcher's home every wall was covered with floor-to-ceiling bookshelves. More books and boxes filled with papers and journals were stacked on the floor, almost concealing a soiled flowered carpet. The others in the group, experienced visitors, picked up stacks of books and papers off the overstuffed furniture and added them to the piles on the floor. Kenny followed their lead and made space in a lumpy armchair. While Mrs. Wayne and Dr. Piltcher disappeared from the room to make coffee, the others discussed the debate over the hippo fossils. Kenny listened, but felt uncomfortable and ignored. When Dr. Piltcher and Mrs. Wayne returned, Dr. Piltcher turned immediately to Kenny.

"Well, Kenny. Tell us about what happened to you," he urged encouragingly.

Feeling more at ease, Kenny started into his story slowly, describing the hunting trip and the strange corn shower, how he was led to research other strange events through books and articles. As he talked they listened with rapt attention, no disbelief on their faces, until he found himself not only describing the event but also his feelings. He shared his awe and fear when the corn fell. He described his estrangement from his father, friends, and finally his sister.

He could tell by their eyes that almost everyone in this cluttered room had shared his experience; they all actively listened. When he was done there was silence. He watched for reactions from the group, but they all turned to Dr. Piltcher, who sat combing his thinning hair with his fingers. Then he spoke.

"Sound familiar to you, George?"

Dr. Coombs was rocking in his chair, with his arms folded behind his head, studying the ceiling. Ten years younger than

Dr. Piltcher, balding and gray-templed, Dr. Coombs stopped rocking long enough to answer. "That it does, Chester."

"Let's start with the easy one, shall we?" Dr. Piltcher suggested. "Burning sulfur falling on Sodom and Gomorrah. Destroyed the whole damned city—pun intended. Your turn, George."

"Frogs falling on Egypt, as recorded in the Bible and Midrash." Dr. Coombs said it without taking his eyes off of the ceiling.

"The biblical plagues are too easy. Locusts and flies also came out of nowhere. Too easy! How about the hail of hot stones as recorded in the Mexican *Annals of Cuauhtitlan*?"

"Could have been meteorites," Dr. Coombs countered.

"Nonsense. Thousands of hot stones falling like hail and bouncing around setting things on fire? Meteorites burn up in the atmosphere more often than not, and even if they reach the ground they most assuredly don't fall in groups like hail. Your turn, George."

"Manna from heaven," Coombs suggested, then leaned forward and spoke to the group. "Manna was described by the Israelites as a yellowish seed that tasted like oily honeycomb. Most likely it was the seed of a plant, but no one has been able to explain why it fell from the sky. Come to think of it there's no reason it couldn't have been corn."

Dr. Coombs turned, his pale eyes gleaming in his well-tanned face, looking straight at Kenny and disconcerting him. "They did grind it and bake bread with it just like corn," Coombs added. "And they certainly wouldn't have seen corn before."

"Not bad," Dr. Piltcher said. "You're still pulling from the Bible and the Talmud, but it's creative. Let me take ambrosia from you. Homer and Hesiod both refer to honey from heaven."

"The hymns of *Rig-Veda* refer to *madhu* falling from clouds."

Dr. Piltcher cleared his throat derisively. "That's just another name for ambrosia."

"Maybe. But if you won't give me credit for it I'll take the red dust that fell on the Mayas."

"Let's stretch this a bit. Kenny said something about fish falling from the sky. What if bigger things fell? What about that, George? Suggest anything to you?" Dr. Piltcher paused and turned to the rest of the group. "Remember back to our debate over the presence of hippos in Europe." Dr. Piltcher looked first at Petra and then Mrs. Wayne. "Is there another way the hippopotami could get to England?"

Mrs. Wayne cleared her throat and then suggested in a high-pitched voice, "They fell from the sky?"

"Possibly. Possibly. If corn can fall, if fish can fall, why not a hippo?"

Kenny was surprised. Dr. Piltcher was now willing to abandon the cosmic cataclysm theory he'd espoused only an hour earlier, a thesis that had cost him much time and effort. Kenny had always agreed that new theories were accepted only when those defending the old theories died off. But Dr. Piltcher showed surprising flexibility for a scientist.

Dr. Coombs rocked forward again, stretching out his feet and knocking over a pile of books. "It might explain some other mysteries. Did you know they found the skeletons of two whales in Michigan? Michigan! Awfully far from the sea, wouldn't you say?" Dr. Coombs said to the group while looking mostly at Kenny. Not to be outdone, Dr. Piltcher added to the whale stories.

"Found a whale skeleton in Quebec too. Six hundred feet above sea level. Oh, now that I think about it, they've found whales, hippopotami, rhinoceroses, and elephants in the most unlikely places. Even in Antarctica. Not to mention the coniferous trees found in both the arctic and antarctic—"

"And, of course, the most famous of all," Dr. Coombs cut in, "the leopard on Mount Kilimanjaro."

"George, what's the name of that Babylonian prophet, the one who was stoned for knowing too much?"

"Zorastrus, I believe."

"Yes, yes. Quite brilliant, he collected events like Kenny has been describing too. No one believed him either, of course."

Dr. Coombs rubbed his chin with his hand and looked concerned for a minute and then said, "This Zorastrus might be worth looking up, I seem to remember he had quite a lot to say about the future."

"Something to pursue later, eh George? But you do see what I'm getting at," Dr. Piltcher mused. "Until tonight, finding animals in unlikely locations was explained either through migration, which is highly unlikely, or cataclysm, like the shifting of the earth on its axis, which is also unlikely. Having them fall from the sky is beautiful in its simplicity. But the sky-fall theory lacks a cause . . . a source for the effect."

Dr. Piltcher paused and turned to Kenny; the others in the group all did too. Now more comfortable he told them about the flower fall, and the mother and the daughter, and his theory. As he spoke he watched their faces light up. They began to add to it. They brainstormed. And the theory began to grow.

Kenny became part of the group that night. He knew other people would call the members of that group kooks, or weirdos, and Kenny would have too a few months ago. But he saw things from the inside now. It was an odd group of people, but receptive and even warm.

After that Kenny spent every Saturday night with the group. He got to know Mrs. Wayne and witnessed her contacts with Shontel, the spirit guide. He became friends with Petra. He met others too. An elderly couple who ran a local convenience store alternated coming on Saturday nights. They only listened, though, and never participated. Others, like Bonnie Smith, came occasionally but were never part of the core. Bonnie showed up one night with another student, Colter Swenson, who listened attentively but kept glancing at Petra. The next Saturday Colter showed up without Bonnie and sat by Petra. Colter became a regular after that. There were others who came occasionally but were never part of the core.

Two weeks later Dr. Coombs arrived at the meeting all excited. He had managed to track down a translation of some of the writings of Zorastrus. He did indeed live in ancient Babylon and was called a prophet right up until they stoned him to death. Dr. Coombs was particularly excited by the discovery of something called the Apocrypha of Zorastrus. Some scholar had separated out Zorastrus's collection of stories of things falling from the sky and other bizarre phenomenon from his "serious" works. Confirming Kenny's corn fall in an ancient document was reassuring to Kenny. They also found Zorastrus had his own theory, a theory disconcertingly similar to Kenny's.

With the discovery of the Apocrypha of Zorastrus the group

began to meet more often. Now the group spent Saturday nights trying to understand the events Kenny had researched and those in the Zorastrus manuscript. They considered other theories besides Kenny's and that of Zorastrus, including those contributed by Shontel, but always returned to Kenny's explanation.

Phat Nyang showed up one night, recruited by Dr. Piltcher to work with Kenny on computer modeling the theory. Kenny and Phat worked out a crude computer model suggesting possible causes. The group critiqued it, and the model was refined, again and again. As summer approached they made plans to utilize the model. Dr. Coombs offered to provide financial support for the summer project.

Kenny now found himself walking around the geyser basin at Old Faithful for the tenth time. It was more than a mile out to Morning Glory Pool, and he could make the circuit and be back before his pickup time. It was the third day of the eight-day watch, and he had walked to the pool four times a day, looking at the skies and meadows surrounding the geysers. A small herd of elk were grazing near Castle Geyser and Kenny paused to watch them before continuing to Morning Glory Pool.

That had been a disappointment to Kenny. It was only pale blue, not the bright blue-green of the pictures on the postcards. His trail guide explained tons of coins thrown by tourists had changed the temperature of the pool, causing the colors to fade. The trail guide referred to the penny-tossing tourists as vandals. Kenny felt disgust and loss.

Kenny started up the boardwalk to the viewpoint. Ahead of him he heard loud laughter and looked to see two well-muscled men about his own age leaning over the steaming water. As he approached one of them spat a big wad of gum into the center of the pool. The other one laughed uproariously and then flipped a coin in after the gum. Kenny's temper flared as the man prepared to flip another. Grabbing the hand with the coins, Kenny slapped it down onto the wooden railing. Money clattered onto the boardwalk and the man yelped from pain.

"Whatcha doing, man?" he yelled.

Now the other one stepped forward, his face contorted in menace.

"You'll ruin the pool doing that," Kenny explained. "I didn't mean to hurt him, but really, that will change the color of the pool. Maybe plug it up."

"That's our business," the big one responded, and punched Kenny in the solar plexus. Kenny's breath exploded from his body and he bent in half. Then he felt his head jerked up by the hair and he found himself staring in the angry face of the man. "You got something to say, you say it to me, not my friend. You understand?"

With that Kenny's head was slammed down into the railing. Kenny put his hands on the rail, protecting his face from the second blow.

"Stay out of our way!" the man yelled and then slapped Kenny's head.

Kenny leaned on the rail, smarting from the slap and gasping for breath, and watched the two men walk down the boardwalk and out of sight. A family with two kids came down the walk and Kenny turned toward the geyser, trying to hide his face. A few seconds later he felt a touch on his arm and turned to see the mother looking concerned.

"You're bleeding. Are you okay?"

"Yeah, fine. I just slipped. Hit my head."

Kenny put his hand to his forehead and a trickle of blood ran down into his eyebrow. He dabbed his forehead with tissues the woman offered and found them soaked with blood. Then he felt something in the wound. Kenny accepted a couple more tissues and then thanked the woman and excused himself. He would need to clean the wound.

As he approached the lodge, an attractive young woman in a ranger uniform watched him closely and then turned and fell in beside him.

"You better let me take a look at that," she said.

"I'm all right, really."

"No, you're not, and if you think you are, you're delirious. You see, I've got you coming and going."

Kenny turned to look at her. She looked determined, so he let her guide him into the lodge, down stairs marked EMPLOYEES ONLY, to a small first aid station. The ranger opened a cabinet and began dabbing Kenny's wound with an alcohol-soaked wad of cotton.

"You've got something in this wound."

"It's probably splinters."

"How did this happen?" As she talked she searched through the cabinets.

"I slipped, tried to catch myself and ended up banging my head on the railing."

"Uh-huh. Here they are."

She turned with a pair of tweezers and went right to work on Kenny's forehead. The first two splinters came out easily with little pain. The next two were a different story.

"This might hurt a little," she warned after Kenny winced.

She was on her third probe when another ranger led a woman of about thirty into the room, followed by two women about the same age. All of them were wearing cycling clothes.

"Good, you're here already, Leslie. I've got another customer for you."

When Leslie turned to look at the newcomers Kenny got a clear look at the injured woman. She was holding a blood-soaked handkerchief to her head, just above the ear.

Leslie acted surprised. "Two head wounds in one day? I'm usually treating scraped knees and bee stings."

"And occasional buffalo gorings," the second ranger added.

"Steve, you didn't need to say that. I'll be finished here in a second."

Leslie dug the last splinter out, dabbed the wound with peroxide, then covered it with a bandage. Before he left, Leslie was talking to the new patient.

"How'd this happen?" she asked as she guided the woman into the chair Kenny had vacated.

"Some sort of freak hailstorm, I guess. We biked over to Black Sand Basin and were walking the trail when these huge hailstones started pounding us."

"Those weren't hailstones," one of her friends corrected. "They were chunks of ice. The chunk that got Gayle was six inches across and it was a small one. I swear some of those that hit the geyser pool were two feet at least."

Kenny remained frozen in the doorway. He realized he had just missed the event they had been waiting for. He listened intently to the narrative, becoming more convinced with every word. Then he sprinted back to the pickup point. They were close this time. Closer than they had ever been.

The others were excited by the news. Kenny, Phat, and Dr. Piltcher immediately returned to the campsite and began modifying the model to make it fit the new data. The others fanned out, looking for other witnesses, who gave descriptions nearly identical to those of the women. Phat and Kenny ran the computer simulation again two days later and they traveled to a spot near Provo, Utah. After seven days there, nothing had happened. Then Mrs. Wayne turned up an article about a house that burned up two days before they arrived when the linen closet suddenly burst into flames. Dr. Piltcher combed his hair a couple of times before agreeing to count it as an event. The model next sent them to Las Cruces, New Mexico. They were still setting up camp when they heard of a backyard swimming pool suddenly overflowing with saltwater and drowning a family dog. They chased the next events to Colorado and then to Idaho, where they arrived the day after the campground had been showered with gravel. That's when Dr. Piltcher called a halt to the chase.

Dr. Piltcher and Dr. Coombs became reclusive for a few days, poring over their notes and manuscripts, and debating vigorously. Finally one evening, they came to Kenny and Phat in the RV.

"There is," Dr. Piltcher said, "a fundamental flaw in our thinking."

Kenny and Phat listened attentively.

"This may not be a static phenomenon. What I mean is we have been just missing the events. They happen either before we arrive, or as soon as we arrive. I think we misled you with our historical data. We relied too much on the Zorastrus manuscript. Zorastrus detected the pattern but he didn't have enough data to refine his model. It lacked temporal specificity. I'm trying to say Zorastrus, and we, believed the events occurred at regular intervals. That's not the case. We now believe the events in the past occurred in waves. Waves that become farther apart as you move into antiquity. The events we are tracking, however, seem to be getting closer together."

From then on they fully understood the implications of the

model and began to fear the future. Each day after that Kenny's anxiety grew slowly and steadily toward the panic that drove him to desperate measures. It was the panic that made him purchase the gun and plot to kidnap his own sister.

He couldn't stand being a pariah much longer. *Whatever is going to happen*, Kenny prayed, *let it happen soon.*

---

8. Cave Crisis

The Lord thundered from heaven, the voice of the Most High resounded amid hailstones and bolts of lightning.

—Psalm 18:13

Oregon Caves
PreQuilt: Saturday, 7:30 p.m. PST

It took Deputy Kyle over four hours to reach the Oregon Caves. It was normally less than a two-hour drive, but he had been extra cautious and slow to get started. First he stopped by the station and picked up his climbing gear. He brought two 165-foot kermantle ropes, an assortment of oval and D carabiners, tapers, camming devices, pitons and a piton hammer. He then realized his climbing shoes and helmet were at home. While he was home he decided to change into his climbing clothes. After all, he reasoned, there might not be a place to change at the caves. As long as he had his clothes off he decided to shower. He made one last stop at McDonald's for a Big Mac, large fries, and super-size Coke. As a concession to the repeated requests for his presence at the cave, Kyle violated his personal rule about never eating while driving. Ten minutes down the road he spilled secret sauce on his climbing shirt.

When he arrived at the cave Kyle was disappointed to find that the hostage situation had not been resolved. A park ranger ushered him through the excited crowd of spectators that had gathered around the park entrance. Off to one side Kyle spotted a small group of people who were probably the hostages' relatives. They looked at Kyle's climbing gear hopefully.

In a small building near the cave entrance, fifteen people were in a strategy meeting. Three wore climbing clothes. Kyle decided they were either rangers or state police. Two other men wore ties. Kyle was introduced around to handshakes and "glad you're heres" from everyone in the shed, comments that made Kyle apprehensive. The two men in ties turned out to be FBI agents, and Jenkins, who had wet armpits, turned out to be in charge.

"Glad you made it, Officer Kyle. We've been waiting for you. I understand you've had some experience at this."

"I'll do whatever I can." Kyle tried to say it like he meant it.

"Good. I understand you finished top of your class in marksmanship too."

Jenkins was referring to Kyle's training in special weapons and tactics. It had been another opportunity to spend a couple of weeks with his buddies, drink beer, and end up with a little extra in his paycheck.

Kyle laughed, and then said, "Oh not me, sir. I wasn't at the top of my class."

"Oh, where did you finish?" Jenkins seemed concerned.

"Second," Kyle said reluctantly.

Jenkins looked relieved, and his partner broke into a smile.

"That should be good enough," he said. "You're much too modest, Officer Kyle."

Kyle grinned weakly, nodded, and promised himself never to take another special training course again.

"Now listen up everyone," Jenkins said. "Now that Officer Kyle has arrived we can get started. We are going to assign a few of you to positions inside the cave. There are only two entrances to the cave where the hostages are being held. Most of you will be assigned to positions around the main entrance. Fortunately, the egress is actually quite narrow and you will have a clear line of fire. Unfortunately, if you do fire you can't miss the target or the ricochet could kill a hostage."

"Won't a hollow point load minimize ricochet?" one of the state policemen asked.

"Minimize, yes, eliminate, no. There will be no firing unless I give the word."

"Excuse me, Agent Jenkins," Kyle interrupted. He didn't like the direction of the meeting. "I seem to remember from my training that the best way to handle hostage situations is to negotiate. The best weapon in these situations is time. Wear the criminal down, maybe send in some tainted food. I'd say, for the hostages sakes, we should give this another day or so before we attempt a rescue."

Jenkins stared at him quizzically.

"Thanks for your advice, but this situation is a little different for a couple of reasons. First, we are getting no demands. Every time we attempt to negotiate he refuses to talk. He doesn't seem to want anything and has no political agenda that we can discern. Second, the man holding the hostages seems to have a deadline in mind. He keeps saying things like 'it will be over soon' and 'I'll let them go when it's over.' It's a vague deadline, apparently meaningful only to him, but he appears to be getting more agitated. If he does go off the deep end . . . well, I'm not waiting for that to happen."

He was staring at Kyle when he paused, so Kyle nodded firmly with a serious look. As expected, Agent Jenkins took that as agreement.

"Officer Kyle," he continued, "we've got a special job for you."

Kyle felt like saying "Yippee."

"These rangers here"—once again Jenkins nodded toward the other climbers—"tell me there is another entrance to that cave. They say that getting there is not an easy climb. That's why we waited for someone with your experience. They'll show you the way. We'll give you four hours to get into position. Then we cut the lights and you position yourself in the cave. Then we'll distract him and you can take him from behind."

As it turned out four hours was barely enough. The other climbers, Jay, Kimberly, and Shirley, were rangers. All were athletic and had the weathered appearance of people who spent more time outdoors than in. None looked older than mid-twenties. Both Shirley and Kimberly were somewhere between plain and pretty. They were both brunettes, with short hair, but Shirley seemed more animated, and her face had a few laugh lines. As the leader, Shirley directed Kyle to leave his kermantle and other gear in his car. This was strictly a free climb.

They set off through the trees following a little-used hiking trail. It climbed gradually, but steadily. Kyle soon found himself breathing hard but tried to disguise it. After about a mile they branched off onto a barely discernible path. Another half mile through the trees, up a rocky slope, and there they faced a door in the side of the hill, a big wooden door painted institutional green, with a hasp and large lock. Shirley unlocked the door and led the way in. Kyle hesitated. Standing there on the side of a mountain, about to enter the door to the underworld, felt magical, unreal, and unsettling.

The trip inside the cave was anything but magical. Shirley and the others were small enough and lithe enough for spelunking, but Kyle was built more for digging tunnels, not crawling through them. Twice he got stuck. Shirley had to pull on one end and rangers Kimberly and Jay pushed on the other. After three hours of crawling on his belly, squeezing through rock-strewn passages, and being pushed and pulled by his guides, Kyle was tired, sore, and had a new appreciation for toothpaste.

They finally reached a chamber large enough to stand in. Shirley, who didn't seem to be winded, put her finger to her lips and pointed up at the ceiling, where Kyle spotted a dark hole. When Kyle shone his helmet light toward it, Shirley slapped her hand over it and jerked him to one side.

"Careful, he might see it," she whispered. "You'll have to go first from here. We'll follow you."

"But I don't know the way. Why don't you lead?"

"You have to go first. You've got the gun. Once we're in the chimney we can't pass each other. If you get stuck, you'll have to get yourself unstuck."

Kyle thought about offering Shirley his pistol. He thought about it seriously.

"All right," he said finally, "is it just straight up?"

"You need to shinny up the chimney about thirty feet. There you'll find a horizontal tube to follow for another hundred feet. Be quiet, because you'll be above the cave with the hostages.

Don't worry about falling through the opening. The light from the cave below should outline it."

"When I drop into the cave which way is the cover?"

"Right is closer," Shirley said. Then she looked him up and down. "But I think we've got too much man and too little rock. You'll have to scrunch down pretty small. If you have time, go left instead. There's some pretty good stalagmites to hide behind if you can make it."

Shirley smiled at him again and then pointed up to the hole in the roof of the cave. It was smooth on the inside, and he had to stand on his tiptoes to feel a rock ledge. He was too stretched out to get any lift out of his legs, so he pulled himself up with his arms and then jammed his elbows over the ledge to hold himself. As he started kicking his legs, he realized he must look silly to Shirley. Then he felt hands on his rear shoving him up into the cave until he had his legs wedged into the opening. Then one of the hands came back and patted his bottom. He hoped the hand had been Shirley's or Kimberly's and not Jay's.

He put his back against the wall and his knees against the edge and began to inch his way up, first pushing his back up and then his knees. The little light from the helmets of the rangers faded as each entered the chimney. It was perfectly dark, Kyle thought, if you can use the word *perfect* to describe a condition where your most valuable sense is useless. The chimney widened and Kyle had to use more leg strength. He wanted to slow his ascent, but every time he did he was bumped by the energetic climber below him.

He nearly fell out of the chimney when he reached the horizontal tube. He inched up with his legs, and when he brought his back up he flopped inside. Kyle managed to roll over and began inching his way along the tube. His eyes, perfectly dark adapted, could see light up ahead. As he approached the opening to the cave below he slowed his pace. He could feel the climber behind bumping into his feet, and he reached the opening with fifteen minutes to spare.

Someone tugged on his pant leg and then whispered into his shoes. It was Shirley.

"Aren't you going to check the cave?"

Kyle waited long enough for Shirley to think he had not

heard her, then he crawled forward and slowly bent into the opening. He lowered his head until his eyes cleared the edge. Everything was upside down. He jerked his head back up and mentally inverted the scene. All the people were where they were supposed to be.

With one minute to go he inched over the opening and arched over the hole with his hands on one side and his legs on the other. All he had to do now was drop his legs into the cave, hang briefly by his hands, and then drop noiselessly into the cave.

The lights went out on schedule and Kyle dropped. As he swung down into the darkness the rock in his hands crumbled. His swinging legs continued upward as he fell, bringing his head and shoulders down. He hit the cave floor with a loud thump. Pieces of crumbled rocks avalanched down on him. A large chunk smacked him in the face, bloodying the bridge of his nose.

The hostages were screaming and crying and the gunman was yelling for everyone to "stay put" and "keep quiet." Kyle rolled to his knees and started to get up and then he realized he'd lost all sense of direction. One way was the back of the cave wall. Two directions led to safety and one to the gunman. Each second he hesitated seemed like an eternity; the flashlights would be on soon. He flinched when a thump sounded next to him and a hand touched his side, moving up until it gripped his arm. He was pulled up and directed forward into the inky blackness.

Suddenly a light filled the room, and he felt himself being tripped and pushed to the ground. Someone landed on top of him. More tiny spotlights filled the cavern. The gunman yelled until quiet was restored, and as he was yelling Kyle lifted his head and looked carefully around. He was on his stomach behind the stalagmites. He twisted his head around and could barely make out Shirley's face inches from his. In disbelief she shook her head and started dabbing off the blood from the bridge of his nose. Kyle felt like an idiot and began wishing he was back on a country road aiming his radar gun at girls on horses. Shirley finished with his nose and then kissed it. Kyle hoped it was too dark for Shirley to see his face turning red.

Time Quilt

9. Mariel Weatherby

One novel feature of spacetime predicted by Einstein's equations is called a wormhole. These holes in spacetime connect one region of space with another distant region, and one time with another distant time. To travel through one would be to travel through time. One wonders in the vast universe, if there might be other spacetime phenomena that would permit such travel.

—Robert Yee, *The Einstein Revolution*

Somewhere over the Atlantic the laws of time and space were suddenly rewritten, and the resulting effect began to spread east and west. Land suddenly appeared in the ocean—not dropped, but layed down gently on a watery foundation that could not support it, and soon, like ancient Atlantis, those lands were lost beneath the waves. In the skies flocks of seagulls in flight disappeared, as did the military and civilian aircraft in the affected regions. Tourist, pilot, exchange student, airman, and junketing congressman were all treated equally and ruthlessly. The air itself was instantly changed, the replacing air either noiselessly filling the void, or, if air pressure differences were too great, violently expanding. Titanic booms were as common as soft whooshing.

As the effect reached the East Coast it continued on land. Streets, cars, homes, office buildings, and fast-food restaurants were replaced with forest, grassland, ice, lakes, and ocean. With the artifacts of mankind went the people who constructed and inhabited them. Men, women, children, rich and poor, teacher and student, Muslim, Christian, Jew, and atheist, all whisked away together.

The effect was systematic, but not thorough. As the effect washed across the planet's surface, it rippled, leaving some regions untouched. People, awakened by thunderous booms, looked to see neighborhoods sundered, their houses intact, the other side of the street impossibly changed. Inhabitants of other large regions slept through the night, untouched, unknowning, only to wake to confusion.

New York City
TIME QUILT: SATURDAY, 8:35 P.M. EST

Mariel rocked by her open window, her hands crocheting while her mind listened to the sounds of the autumn evening. She didn't get to hear the sounds very often anymore. Summer used to be the best time, but now everyone had air conditioners, and if Mariel opened her window she heard only the hum of electric motors. When she first came to live in her apartment all the neighbors would open their windows in the summer, and Mariel would sit and listen to families arguing, or the sound of radios or hi-fis. There were the sounds of people talking too, and sometimes Mariel could make out a sentence or two and follow the arguments. She never joined in, of course—that would be invading her neighbors' privacy, but she couldn't stop herself from forming opinions. Behind it all was the backdrop of the sounds of New York City, traffic, honking horns, and occasional police sirens.

Mariel could hear the Ibarras having an argument two floors above her. Some of the argument was in Spanish, so she couldn't follow it well. But the rhythm was familiar to her, she had listened to so many arguments in her chair by the window. She didn't have to understand the words to know the argument was about one of three things: money, family, or the kids. Those were the topics when she moved in back in 1955, and it had been those three topics ever since.

Mariel could also hear the sound of a stereo from the MacGregor's apartment below her. From the sound of rap, she knew their son was playing it. It also meant his parents weren't home yet, because they always made him wear earphones when he played rap. Mariel also knew he would be on the phone to his girlfriend at the same time. Sometimes he talked and laughed loud enough for Mariel to hear, and it would embarrass her. She was often embarrassed by the way boys talked to girls today. But still she always listened. It was better than the made-up stuff on the afternoon talk shows.

The air was cool, but Mariel didn't want to close the window. So instead she went to the kitchen and put the teakettle on and then got a blanket for her lap. Mariel returned to her chair, picked up her crocheting, and listened to the argument again.

It was winding down now. The Ibarras never stayed mad at each other for long, not like the Venuccis, who used to live next to her. How many years ago? Twenty at least, she decided. Now, the Venuccis knew how to have a fight. They yelled and screamed at each other, sometimes for hours. Sometimes Mrs. Venucci would throw things and Mariel could hear glass shattering or things banging. When they first moved in Mariel had feared they would hurt each other, but when she saw them in the hallway the next day they never had cuts or bruises. One day Mariel stopped Mrs. Venucci and told her she worried about her. Mrs. Venucci smiled and assured Mariel she was not in any danger. "Sure," she had said, "we fight hard, but we make up harder." Mariel knew that was true. The Venuccis raised seven children in that apartment. The Ibarras must be the same way, Mariel believed. They had five kids.

The teakettle called to her from the kitchen. Then with her cup and saucer she returned to the window. The Ibarras had moved on to making up, and there were no voices now. A few minutes later the rap music suddenly died, and Mariel listened to Cathy McGregor scolding her son and telling him to do his homework. Then Mariel was left alone with the sounds of the city.

She looked down into the courtyard below. It used to be filled with little garden plots, some with flowers, some with vegetables. It was mostly paved now, and ugly garbage Dumpsters sat here and there. The only garden left was Mariel's. She only grew flowers now. She used to grow vegetables till people began stealing them. She wouldn't have minded if they ate them, but most of them were smashed against walls or thrown through windows. Still, the flowers were pretty and a stark contrast to the ugliness of the asphalt and Dumpsters. Mariel loved the garden, but it was harder to grow things ever since the high rise went up across the courtyard. It was an office building, all glass and steel. Mariel hated its sealed glass windows.

Once long ago, Mariel had a friend who lived in the building that used to be where the office building now stood. Sometimes when the kids were at school, Mariel would meet Gertie for coffee and talk. In the summers their kids played in the courtyard together, and Mariel and Gertie would visit or garden.

Gertie moved to Florida years ago and was long dead now, and the building she lived in was ten years gone.

Mariel's life in the apartment had started out quietly, just her and Phillip. Then the children had come, filling their lives with activity and stress; stress she missed now. When the three children were growing up Mariel had lots of friends, most of them the parents of their children's friends. Phillip's work gave them friends too. There was business entertaining and dinner parties. If they weren't guests, they were hosts. They were involved in their children's schools too. School plays, music lessons, and a myriad of other activities kept them constantly on the go. Mariel had scarcely a minute to herself in those days and relished the few hours a week she could sit by the window and listen to the sounds. Then the children had grown. Now they all lived in other states and called infrequently. She had Phillip for a few years after the children were gone, and many friends still, mostly connected with Phillip's work. Then Phillip died suddenly, and with him went the parties and many of her friends. Soon all Mariel had were acquaintances, no friends. Now she only went out three times a week, and then only to do shopping. She used to go to church on Sunday, but then the church had closed and moved to a new location in a better neighborhood. Now Mariel watched church on TV, but it was hard to make church friends through a TV. Her life was quiet now, like the end of the arguments she listened to over the years. Mariel longed for the activity again, for someone to argue with.

Mariel looked up at the sky for stars. But the bright moon and city lights meant she couldn't see any. The city wasn't the place to look at stars, Mariel knew. She never had a good view, of course, but when she had something to do, something to occupy her time, she never thought about stars.

Now Mariel thought about the stars and the moon, and other things, a lot. Her oldest son wanted her to move to Ohio with him. She could see the stars there, he assured her. But she didn't want that. She didn't want a piece of his life. She wanted her own life, even if it was mostly memories now. No, she would live in the apartment until she became a memory too.

Mariel turned on the TV and flipped through the channels with the remote control. As usual there was nothing on she wanted to watch. Sometimes she thought of getting cable TV. The television guide told her she could get shows like "Father Knows Best" and "Mr. Ed" on cable. It was expensive, though, and she hated paying for what she should be getting for free. She finally settled the dial on a situation comedy. The laugh track told her the jokes were supposed to be funny, but they weren't. They were bathroom jokes for the most part, and Mariel had never liked that kind of humor and she didn't appreciate the filthy language in her home. She turned the channel to a TV movie. A young couple were kissing open-mouthed. The woman was naked from the waist up, and Mariel could see the side of her left breast pressed up against the man's bare chest. Mariel had been shocked the first time she had seen this on TV, but now it was routine and boring. She supposed the networks would soon have to show all of the actress's breast to keep people interested, and she only hoped she wouldn't live long enough to have that on her TV screen. She clucked her tongue at the half-naked couple, then turned the channel just as the couple fell onto a bed. She tried the rest of the channels but it was more of the same.

Mariel turned off the TV and turned on the radio. There was lots of filth on the radio now too, but you could still find something worth listening to if you searched. They ran old radio shows sometimes, and there was big band music if she wanted that. Tonight, though, she wanted to listen to talk, and there was lots of talk on the New York City airwaves. Mariel tuned in one of her favorites. She wasn't loyal to any of the shows. If they talked of sex or politics, or if they ran down religion, she would tune them out. Mariel had long ago settled her opinions on all those topics.

Tonight people were calling in with movie trivia questions or just to talk about favorite scenes from films. Mariel settled in to listen. For a while they talked about last lines in movies. Mariel knew the last line in *The Wizard of Oz* right away, it was "Oh, Auntie Em, there's no place like home." She also knew the last line from *Gone With the Wind*, but it took three callers to get "tomorrow is another day." Everyone kept guessing "Frankly, my dear, I don't give a damn." Mariel was enjoying the movie memories, trying to remember where and with whom she had seen the movie. Then someone changed the topic to actors who played James Bond. Mariel had seen some of the James Bond movies with Phillip but never liked them. They were too violent, and Mr. Bond was certainly oversexed. Still, she remembered both Sean Connery and Roger Moore had played James Bond. Someone called in to say that David Niven had played James Bond too, in a movie called *Casino Royale*. She'd never seen it but couldn't imagine David Niven as James Bond. David Niven was a gentleman, he wouldn't behave like that secret agent. She would have searched for another station, but she was waiting to hear who the fourth actor was who played James Bond. She was still rocking, crocheting, and listening by her open window when she drifted off to sleep.

Mariel woke when her head hit the floor, but she kept her eyes tightly shut till the pain and shock subsided. Opening her eyes to total darkness, Mariel found herself and her chair tipped over onto the floor, and the only light was moonlight from the window. The power was out again. Mariel still hurt from the fall—and because she was old, she admitted it to herself, she knew there was real danger of breaking bones from even a small fall.

She lay still, waiting for the pain to seep away so she could feel her bones, but now she began to think she was deaf. There were no city sounds as there should be outside her window. Mariel felt her legs and arms. She would be sore for a month but nothing was broken. She felt around on the floor for her glasses, found them in one piece, and put them on. Then she got slowly to her feet.

She needed candles and they were in the hall linen closet. Mariel started forward, confident of her footing even in the dark, but she took only two steps before she kicked something on the floor. She bent down and picked up the blue vase from her end table. Whatever had knocked Mariel over had knocked off her vase. Mariel proceeded cautiously after that and found the floor littered with lamps, pillows, and knickknacks. The contents of her apartment had been tossed around, as if by a hurricane. Slowly she walked down the hall to the closet, carefully testing the floor before she placed each foot.

The candles were where they should be and she found a

holder with them. Unfortunately the matches were in the kitchen.

The candlelight lit up the room like a search light. It was a mess. Dishes and canned goods had fallen from the cupboards, littering the floor and counters. Mariel lit another candle, securing it with dripped wax on a plate. In the living room she set up two more candles and then used the one in the holder to look for her portable radio in her bedroom.

There she found broken glass all over her bedspread and on the floor. The window frame was empty. Mariel shook her head in disbelief. What could have happened? She clucked her tongue at the work it would take to make her apartment neat again and then found her radio along with her flashlight, which she decided to save in case she had to go outside.

Mariel tried the radio. Most of the local stations were off. Those still broadcasting weren't talking about the power loss yet. Back in the kitchen she tried the phone. It was out too. That concerned Mariel a little. Usually the phones still worked when the power went out. But she picked her rocker up and sat down by her window, listening to her portable radio.

When she turned to look outside she got the shock of her life. The office building that had replaced Gertie's apartment building was gone, and so were the buildings behind that. As far as Mariel could see in the moonlight there was nothing but grass.

Mariel stood at her window like thousands of other New Yorkers, trying to understand what she was seeing. She had fallen out of her chair, she was sure of that. She didn't remember hitting her head, but maybe she did. She felt her face and skull but found no lumps or blood. But if she wasn't delirious what had happened to the building? To the city? Mariel was thinking of walking across the hall to ask Mr. Moreno if there was city on his side of the building when there were loud footsteps outside her door followed by a pounding. Mariel took her candle and walked to the door and peered through the peephole. It was too dark to see, so Mariel shouted, asking who was there. Luis Ibarra responded, and Mariel opened the door to see him wearing only a pair of jeans.

"Are you all right, Mrs. Weatherby?"

"Yes, Luis. Thanks for asking. Luis, as long as you're here, would you mind looking out my window? I can't seem to see the city anymore."

"Yes, I know, Mrs. Weatherby. You're not crazy. We can't see it either. I checked out the other side of the building. It's still there. Man, this is some kind of weird. We're thinking of getting the kids out. If we go I'll come for you."

"No thank you, Luis. I'll be fine."

"It's too weird to stay, Mrs. Weatherby."

"I'm staying. By the way, I couldn't help but overhear the argument you and Melinda were having. I do hope you settled it. You're such a good couple. I told my daughter she should be so lucky to be as happy as you and Melinda."

"Oh yeah, it's all forgotten. You've got to come with us, Mrs. Weatherby."

"Get back to your family, Luis. No, wait a minute."

Mrs. Weatherby used her candle to get back to the kitchen and emptied her cookie jar into a paper sack. Then she took them back to Luis.

"Give these to your children. If they're scared it will calm them down."

Luis took the bag without protest. "I'll come back for you if we leave."

"I won't leave my home. Good night, Luis."

Mrs. Weatherby returned to her window and sat looking out into the new meadow. She found she wasn't afraid. Mariel had once heard a talk show guest say people are afraid of only two things: death and the unknown. Mariel disagreed. People her age were not afraid of death, they had seen too much of it and lived with it too long. As for the unknown, Mariel relished it. Her life had been one of unrelenting sameness for nearly a decade.

She could hear the sounds of the city from the other side of the building, but the meadow made no sounds. It looked to be an endless sea of grass. No, not just grass. Mariel cursed her old eyes and the darkness and strained to see better. She removed her glasses and cleaned them but to no avail. Something was sparkling in the grass in the distance. It was water. The meadow ended in a swamp. Mariel wished she hadn't given Phillip's binoculars to Phil Junior. There was much to see in this meadow, and even more just out of her visual reach.

Mariel turned on the radio. None of her favorite stations were on, but she found a station carrying the Gene Diamond show. He was obnoxious and profane, and Mariel seldom listened to his Night Talk show, but they interrupted it often with news and that's what she wanted to hear. Gene was talking to someone named Roland from Salt Lake City, Utah.

"Gene, we're never gonna get the truth about cold fusion, because they'll never let the truth out. They've got too much to lose."

"Who's 'they,' Roland?"

"The power companies, of course. You think the nuclear companies and big oil, not to mention coal, are going to let the working man get access to cheap power? Uh-uh. Won't happen. That's why the government's trying so hard to ruin the reps of the inventors."

"So the government, the power companies, the oil companies, and whoever owns the coal reserves in this country all got together and conspired to discredit the inventors of cold fusion?"

"Right."

"So why is it no one seems to be able to replicate the cold fusion experiments, Roland?"

"The government bought off all the scientists."

"Even the scientists in the former Soviet Union?"

"They need the money worst of all."

"Makes sense. Makes sense if you're a paranoid idiot. Let's get another caller in here."

Most nights, Mariel had heard Gene Diamond make rude comments like that. It was a wonder, she thought, anyone would ever call in to his dreadful show. Still they did. Often the same people who had been rudely treated called in over and over. Now Mariel clucked her tongue in disbelief and then turned down the radio. She only wanted news tonight, not chatter. She wasn't feeling lonely, not with a whole new world to explore.

Mariel sat by the window through the night studying the meadow, straining to hear the night sounds it might make. Only once did she hear something that seemed to come from the meadow. It was a low rumbling sound, something Mariel had never heard before.

The sky brightened as the sun neared the horizon, and more of the meadow was visible. The swamp could be clearly seen now and even more distant was a treeline. Mariel reveled in each new discovery. When the sun appeared over the distant trees, Mariel attached a pair of snap-on dark lenses to her eyeglasses and sat in excited expectation waiting for the unexpected.

The sound of voices came from below her. She leaned out the window to see a group of teenagers walking out into the meadow. She could tell by their jackets they were gang members. She had seen them often enough, standing on the streets, harassing the passersby. Mariel and her neighbors had little use for them, but they were the sons and daughters of the neighborhood and you had to take the good with the bad.

The gang members all looked to be boys, but Mariel wasn't good at guessing sex these days. They walked out into the meadow, looking at the grass and talking and laughing. Mariel was surprised by how tall the grass was. It came nearly to the waist of even the tallest boy. She realized she detested having the boys in her meadow—not the boys, only their presence. They weren't part of this new world, and Mariel didn't want it to turn back into what it had been. First would come the teens, then their parents. More and more people would come to the meadow. Then they would divide it up, put in roads, and put in buildings. Soon Mariel would be looking at an unfriendly glass wall again. No, these boys had to go. Mariel was about to yell at them, to tell them to get out of her meadow, when the boys shouted and pointed into the distance.

Mariel tried to spot what had the boys so excited. There *was* something there, coming closer. The boys below turned and ran from the meadow. Mariel clapped her hands in delight. Hooray for whatever had scared the boys from her meadow! Wishing again for Phillip's binoculars, she watched it coming closer. Finally her eyes managed to focus on it, and Mariel knew then the view from her window would never be boring again.

10. The Group

Who can fathom the minds of the gods? There will come a time when the words past, present, *and* future *will have no meaning.*

—*Zorastrus, Prophet of Babylon*

East Lake, Oregon
Time Quilt: Saturday, 7:35 p.m. PST

"Phat! It's getting late, give it up," Dr. Piltcher yelled.

"Soon, Doctor, soon!"

Phat was high in one of the pine trees surrounding their campsite trying to move the antenna for the shortwave radio higher into the tree. They could pick up Petra and Colter at Summer Lake, but not Mrs. Wayne and Ernie Powell at Warm Springs. To help them with the antenna, Phat had stayed longer than he should have, and family was waiting for him in Eugene.

"Come on down, Phat," Dr. Coombs urged him. "I'll get up there and rig it."

"You too big," came Phat's reply. Phat was too gracious to add he thought Dr. Coombs also too old. "Got it."

Phat climbed down carefully, placing each foot solidly on a limb. He wasn't going to risk a fall that might keep him from his family, not at this crucial time.

"Thank you, Phat. Now go! Give my regards to your family."

"I will, Dr. Piltcher. Dr. Coombs?" Phat said, holding out his hand, then shook hands with both men. "See you afterward."

"Remember what to do?" Dr. Piltcher asked unnecessarily, to reassure himself.

"Yes, Doctor."

After Phat drove away, Dr. Piltcher worried about him. The

group had dispersed to await the arrival of the window, all except Phat, who had stayed to help Dr. Piltcher and Dr. Coombs. The window was three days long, but they had never been able to pinpoint events. If something significant came earlier rather than later in the window, Phat was at risk. Dr. Piltcher hoped Phat made it to his family before anything happened.

Dr. Coombs cranked up the shortwave again. Colter and Petra answered immediately; the atmospheric conditions made for good reception. But it took three tries to get Mrs. Wayne and Ernie Powell, who could barely be heard through static. They agreed to check in every half hour.

The half-hour checks continued into the evening, but nothing happened. It was late when Dr. Coombs cooked up a stew for dinner, and they ate the beef and vegetables in silence, soaking up the gravy with buttermilk biscuits. After dinner they built a fire and sat in lawn chairs outside the RV. It was a clear night, and despite the full moon they could see the Milky Way. In the campground other travelers slowly drifted off to their tents or trailers, taking their family sounds with them and leaving the doctors in silence.

The radio crackled to life at eleven. Petra was calling with nothing to report, except a beautiful evening. Colter shouted something unintelligible from the background, eliciting a frown from Dr. Piltcher. The call from Ernie Powell followed, the static just as bad as ever, but they too had nothing to report. Dr. Coombs found a stick and began poking the fire. After sending several showers of sparks into the air, he spoke to Dr. Piltcher.

"You know, Chester, I've been thinking about that static." Dr. Coombs poked the fire again. "I've been wondering if it could have anything to do with the effect."

Dr. Piltcher's eyebrows raised slightly.

"I've been thinking the same thing, George."

Dr. Coombs knew Dr. Piltcher had been thinking no such thing, but he was unwilling to concede an original thought to anyone. It irritated Dr. Coombs only mildly. Dr. Coombs had long ago given up the endless quest for recognition. He was a true scientist now. He wanted only to understand. Whether he or Dr. Piltcher took credit for good ideas, made no difference.

He poked the fire again. "Of course the static could be the effect itself."

Dr. Piltcher's eyebrows went up sharply again.

"Oh, no. I . . . I can't accept that."

Dr. Coombs understood. They both feared what could happen, but they also had invested in it. They, and the rest of the group, had cut their social and professional ties believing something was going to happen. They needed an event more important than a little electromagnetic interference on the radio.

They talked awhile about the static, speculating on its source. As the fire burned hot and bright they sat exchanging ideas, questioning each other, building up and breaking down theory after theory. These kinds of discussions had characterized their entire friendship. Two lonely men, whom others thought odd, drawn together by a common love of the ancient and the mysterious. Not once in their seven-year friendship had they ever run out of conversation, because the world had never run out of mysteries.

The midnight check-in brought no news. Petra reported she would take the first watch, but they could hear Colter giggling drunkenly in the background. Dr. Piltcher's face reddened, but there was nothing he could do. Colter was useful at times, and Petra seemed to need him, but Colter was undisciplined, and—even worse from Dr. Piltcher's perspective—dumb. Petra's attraction to Colter was one mystery Dr. Piltcher could not even begin to fathom. Here was a serious, brilliant young woman, who lived to learn, while Colter was a young man with a mediocre intellect, dedicated to drinking, partying, and apparently sex. Dr. Piltcher could understand why Colter was attracted to pretty and personable Petra. Dr. Piltcher finally concluded Petra's need for Colter must be hormonal.

Mrs. Wayne checked in a minute later and reported no changes. Dr. Piltcher could hear a radio in the background going over the evening's baseball scores—Ernie's Cincinnati Reds were in the thick of the pennant race. Mrs. Wayne also reported that Shontel assured her their prediction was accurate and it would happen soon. Dr. Piltcher thanked her and asked her to pass his thanks to Shontel.

Dr. Piltcher and Dr. Coombs returned to the discussion of the static problem, and the role of sunspots in such interference. They had just begun discussing spot cycles when Petra's voice sounded behind them. They hurried to the RV to respond.

"Something's happened here. It might be nothing, but there was a strange noise a minute ago, a kind of whumping sound. Now there's a range fire east of here. Pretty big one. It came out of nowhere."

Dr. Piltcher and Dr. Coombs turned to look at each other. Dr. Coombs spoke first.

"I expected something more. I don't think this is it."

"Agreed," Dr. Piltcher said. He directed Petra: "You shouldn't get near it tonight. Keep a safe distance and check it out in the morning. We'll contact Mrs. Wayne and Ernie just to be sure."

Dr. Piltcher signed off and then called for Mrs. Wayne. The static had diminished some but was still annoying.

"Mrs. Wayne, Mrs. Wayne. Are you reading me, Mrs. Wayne?"

After a few minutes he switched to calling for Ernie Powell. Neither ever answered.

---

11. PIG PILE

Fiery winds and fierce clouds lashed the world accompanied by violent hailstorms. When the storm abated the beings who had been hidden beneath the earth multiplied upon the earth.

—New Zealand, Maori Oral History

Oregon Caves
TIME QUILT: SATURDAY, 11:05 P.M. PST

Terry saw that the military man had inched his way forward so that he was sitting near the front of the group now. He'd moved there during the blackout. When the kid finally pulled a light out of his pack and snapped it on, the military man was in the front row. The kid was distracted for the next few minutes, screaming out the entrance that he wanted the lights back on, and Terry was sure the military man would make his move, but the kid did a good job of keeping his gun pointed at the group, and nothing happened.

Now Terry wanted to move forward too, but felt it might jeopardize the rescue. So instead, Terry had inched himself a little sideways until there was a clear path between him and the kid with the gun. Terry did not have the training or nerve to do anything alone, but he hoped he could help the military man if necessary.

The chance came sooner than Terry had expected.

He was partially dozing with his head on his knees when another voice reverberated through the cave, startling everyone awake.

"Hello in the cave."

The kid was startled too and stood turning toward the noise. At that instant the military man jumped to his feet and raced toward the kid, who jerked back around, but it was too late. The military man barreled into the kid, knocking him backward, his hands outstretched and reaching for the gun as the kid fell onto his back.

Terry hesitated, but when he realized no one else was doing anything he jumped to his feet and sprinted toward the struggling men. He could see the gun was still in the kid's hand and the military man was trying to hold the gun arm down. At the same time the kid was kicking and shoving and punching with his other hand. Terry dove onto the struggling pair, reaching for the gun. His landing partially knocked the military man sideways, and he lost his grip on the gun arm, which Terry grabbed—then realized that the kid might be too strong for him to control. There was a manic look in the kid's eyes and his strength seemed out of proportion to his body.

The military man was swinging around to get a better grip when another person hit the pile so hard he knocked Terry over the kid's arm and the military man off of the kid entirely. The new person wore a helmet and climbing clothes, and slid so far forward that he was nearly sitting on the kid's face.

Terry realized that he was now lying in front of the gun and the gun was pointed at his leg. He let go and jumped up as a young woman in climbing clothes held him back and then did a knee drop on the kid's solar plexus, ending the fight.

They were soon surrounded by police officers and rangers, and the kid, now handcuffed, had gone from mania to severe depression in seconds. He was crying and begging them to leave him in the cave. "It may not have happened yet," he said over and over again. "Please, let me stay here. Jill! Jill! Please don't let them take me out. It's too soon. Please, Jill!"

Jill began comforting him, repeating "it will be okay," but Terry doubted the kid could hear his sister. The kid was in a different reality.

Finally, Terry heard someone call over the radio for a stretcher, and the police escorted the hostages from the cave. The kid was still sobbing and begging when the hostages left.

When they reached the surface, the police needed to interview all the hostages and have them fill out reports. It took hours.

It was nearly dawn when Terry and Ellen were finally released. As they walked toward the parking lot Terry saw the military man. When his eyes met Terry's, he and his wife began walking toward them. The couples met with hands extended.

"My name's Conrad, Bill Conrad. Good job in there," he said to Terry.

"I only followed your lead. I'm Terry and this is my wife Ellen."

"This is my wife Angie. Man, wasn't that strange?" Bill said shaking his head from side to side in slow movements. "I wonder what he thought was going to happen?"

In the parking lot they found a knot of excited people clustered around a motor home. Terry could hear voices from a CB radio.

"What's going on?" Angie asked.

A couple broke off from the group, anxious to share the excitement with newcomers.

"You're not going to believe this, but something has happened to the interstate. It's gone!"

"What? An avalanche?" Terry asked.

"Maybe," the woman responded, "but that's not the way it sounds. You drive up I-5 and it just ends. Where there was a four-lane highway, now there's grass, trees, and a mountain. Can you believe that? A mountain."

12. Road Games

. . . the day of the Lord will come like a thief in the night. When people say, "there is peace and security," then sudden destruction will come upon them . . .

—I Thessalonians 5:2

Newberg, Oregon
Time Quilt: Saturday, 11:20 p.m. PST

Ripman was keeping time from the driver's seat of Cubby's van while Cubby stared at the Taco Bell sign. John was spread out on the bench behind them. All three of them had Big Gulps wedged in their crotches. Ripman kept calling out the time and revving the engine.

"Two minutes, big guy. You got two minutes! No way you're gonna win. I can taste that pie already."

"Cram it, Ripman," Cubby growled.

All three of them slurped periodically on their Big Gulps. It was the last turn of the last round, and the loser was buying Hostess pies. Ripman was way ahead, so the contest was between Cubby and John.

They were twenty miles out of Portland in Newberg, one of the too-small towns that had nearly faded into obscurity when the interstate had bypassed it thirty years ago. The motels, drive-ins, and restaurants that had eked out a modest living off the highway traffic were mostly gone now, and the town was at the mercy of the big paper mill. Given another two decades of urban growth, Newberg would be absorbed into the urban sprawl of Portland. For now, however, fifteen miles of forests and farms separated Newberg from the city.

John, Cubby, and Ripman normally played road anagrams on 82nd Avenue or 122nd in Portland, but they'd gotten bored and craved new territory. So they found Newberg. There was a little college there, and they drove around for a while yelling out the van windows at the coeds. When they tired of that they found lots of opportunity for their game along the highway.

They started on the west side of town at the Dairy Queen, one of the old-fashioned kind with no eating space inside. A reader board outside advertised specials on blizzards and banana splits.

BLIZZARDS $1.99
BANANA SPLITS $1.99
SUNDAES $1.49

Ripman studied the sign for a minute, waited until there was a lull in the traffic, then reshuffled the letters so the sign read

LIZZARD LIP SUNDAES $99.99

He left the rest of the letters in a pile on the ground. Cubby loved it, and John had to admit it was a high scorer.

John went next, picking the AM/PM sign. The sign read

PARTY TIME?
WE HAVE BEER AND ICE

when they pulled in. John switched the letters around so the sign read

PARTY?
WE HAVE RICE AND BEET

Ripman called it a "piss poor effort," and Cubby just snorted agreement.

When John challenged Cubby to do better, Cubby picked the D & D video sign:

JOIN OUR VIDEO GOLD CLUB
MEMBER DISCOUNTS

Cubby hopped out and came back a minute later. As they pulled out they read

RODEO MOLD ONE DIME

Ripman cackled his approval, pulled into the 7-Eleven and made John buy Big Gulps.

When Cubby finished this round, one way or another he was going to have to tell them he had to get home. It was nearly eleven-thirty, and under no circumstances could he take the chance of staying out past midnight. His parents would be home from their trip by now, and he didn't want them to think he'd been out past curfew every night.

The worst part would be telling his friends he had to get home. "Jeez," Ripman would say, "they've really got you whipped. What a wuss." Cubby wouldn't say much in words, but his crooked smile and raised eyebrows would say as much as Ripman did in words.

John was always the first to have to get home. His father was a psychologist and occasionally taught parenting classes. His credibility depended on how he raised his own kids, so he was meticulous in that area. "The keys to good parenting," his father always said, "are consistency and discipline." While John had a clear set of rules that were virtually inviolable, Ripman's father didn't care what he did, as long as he did it somewhere else. And Ripman was usually somewhere else.

Cubby's father was the worst though. He was the most popular minister in the state and even had a regional following on cable TV. He "trusted" his son. He "trusted" him enough to buy him the van, and "trusted" him enough not to put restrictions on him, except one. He had to be in church every Sunday morning and every Wednesday evening. Otherwise, until he violated his father's trust, what Cubby did was "between his son and the Holy Spirit." As far as John knew, Cubby had never done anything to violate that trust. At least not anything his father knew about. There was no way to know what the "Holy Spirit" knew.

"All right, Ripman," Cubby said with confidence in his voice, "get me under that sign. This is for Hostess pies, right?"

Ripman put the van in gear and pulled up. Before it stopped

rolling Cubby had his head poked up through the sunroof and was holding the long-handled sign changer, which Ripman had "found" and Cubby kept in his van. Overhead signs always earned more points.

Cubby, at six foot five inches with a heavily packed frame, filled the opening in the roof. The football coaches drooled every time Cubby walked by, but Cubby had never had any interest in their game. The biggest guy in school, he was about the gentlest. If you looked at his face closely enough you could see the babyish look of the pale blue eyes and the rounded facial features, but you had to look quick because Cubby had learned that the best way to avoid having to be tough is to look tough. Cubby had the tough look down cold. He'd stare at you glassy eyed and not blink or flinch no matter what you did, and then he would talk slowly, and simply, with a lot of menace in his voice but no cursing. It was pretty effective. John didn't know anyone else who could act that tough without swearing their brains out.

Cubby popped down from the roof and tossed the gripper toward the back.

"Hit it, Ripman."

After Ripman swung out of the parking lot, he and John looked back at the sign, which had started with:

TODAY'S SPECIAL
BURRITO, TOSTATA
OR TWO TACOS AND LARGE COKE
$1.99

Now it read:

TACOS TASTE LIKE BUTS SMELL

Cubby had to invert the *w* to get the *m* and used the *1* from $1.99 for one of the *l*s but there was no rule against it and it could earn you extra points. It was the best anagram of the night, and Ripman was cracking up.

"Elemental. I love it. El-ahh-men-tahl."

Elemental was Ripman's favorite superlative. He used it for everything that pleased him. When John and Cubby first heard him use it they thought he meant *elementary*, like the word Sherlock Holmes was always using to insult Dr. Watson. Ripman was clear though, it was *elemental*, and it meant the simple and basic things—the things that life was really all about. And to Ripman that meant things that didn't depend on other things. That was Ripman's dream. To live a life that didn't depend on other people, on things, or on society.

Ripman was a self-proclaimed woodsman, but you didn't call him a survivalist to his face. Survivalists weren't elemental enough for Ripman. To Ripman the chink in the survivalists' armor was their dependence on technology: freeze-dried food, water recycling systems; solar-powered stills, and automatic weapons. To Ripman, an elemental person was someone who needed only a knife to survive, not an Uzi.

"Elemental!" Ripman exclaimed again. "Cubby, once again you stumbled uncontrollably into a winner." To John he chortled, "Get your wallet out, it's pie time."

Eager to get back, John was just glad the game was over. At the 7-Eleven they all piled out and went in to select their pies. Cubby picked apple, as always. John picked a berry pie and Ripman the lemon. Cubby was reading the front page of the *National Enquirer* when John and Ripman headed out the front door.

"Jeez, John, why do you buy those things?" Ripman asked.

"What things?"

"Those berry pies. I mean it doesn't even say what kind of berries are in it. For all you know they could be dingleberries."

John was going to tell Ripman to cram it when he noticed a car pulling in next to Cubby's van. It was a jacked-up 1969 Chevy Camaro painted primer gray, and it looked like it would always be a fixer-upper. There were two too-large Pioneer speakers wedged into the back window, blasting out some indistinguishable hard rock sound. Now three guys who were looking for trouble climbed out. The driver, the smallest of the three, was a little shorter than John at five foot eight but had huge shoulders and arms. His head was huge too, and his large lopsided mouth was shaped permanently into a wise-guy grin. He looked like a dwarf that had been inflated to normal size. All three guys wore faded Levi's and jean jackets, and their hair was shaved close on the sides. The biggest one was about six feet tall and hung back a little from the other two. He was uncommonly ugly and wore his hair down so that it covered half his pimply face. When the driver stepped out in front of the others, they assumed tough guy poses behind him.

"What are you assholes doing in our town?"

The creep, John knew, was referring to him and Ripman. John also knew a rhetorical question when he heard one. Unfortunately, Ripman didn't.

"You talking to us?" Ripman said, with a surprising amount of menace in his voice.

John had known Ripman since his freshman year in high school. Their homeroom turned out to be PE class and the ex-marine gym teacher had screamed out their names as he worked through the alphabet assigning locker mates. "Ripman, Roberts, number two thirty-eight."

In all the time he had known him, John had never seen Ripman in a fight. Ripman claimed to be six feet tall but was probably a little short of that and on the thin side. He was big enough to discourage the bullies in school, but this one in Newberg didn't look or act discouraged.

The leader snorted, smacked his gum a few times, looked Ripman up and down, then, with catlike quickness, snatched Ripman's pie. The wise-guy grin got bigger as he held it up. Pimples snorted his approval.

The big dwarf turned back to Ripman.

"You want this back, asshole?"

Ripman didn't answer, he just stared defiantly. The big dwarf smacked his gum and grinned some more. Ripman flinched when the hand came toward his head, but then held his ground when the big dwarf squished the pie into his hair.

"All right!" pimples chortled.

With a slow deliberate motion Ripman brought his hand up to his head and forcefully scraped the pie off, throwing it toward the big dwarf's feet, splattering them with lemon filling. Then the door behind them opened and Cubby came out. He was doing his tough-guy routine.

"There a problem here?" Cubby asked in a voice two octaves below normal.

Cubby pushed past the thugs and opened the van door. The

big dwarf was turning red, his blood boiling—apparently he knew his limits and Cubby was a little beyond them. John climbed onto the bench seat in the back, but Ripman surprised him by climbing into the passenger seat. It surprised Cubby too. He almost never drove his van, preferring to ride in the passenger seat, hollering out the window while Ripman drove fast and semirecklessly.

As Cubby started up the van and backed slowly out of the parking slot, Ripman maintained eye contact with the big dwarf. Suddenly the big dwarf spit his gum at Ripman, sticking it to the middle of the passenger window. When Ripman gave him the finger in return, the big dwarf nodded and glared, in commitment to see Ripman another time when Cubby wouldn't be around.

As Cubby headed them north, Ripman sulked, staring at the glob of gray gum. John knew what was eating at Ripman. Unable to handle the situation with the big dwarf he'd violated his "elemental" principle by requiring Cubby's help. They drove out of town in silence and darkness.

Cubby took them east on 99 toward Portland. As they climbed Breed's hill out of Newberg's valley, John could see the lights of the little town below them.

Then the lights went out. John managed to get a "hey" out of his mouth before a sonic boom rattled the van. All three boys gasped, and before their ears and hearts had recovered, the storm hit. The sudden wind drove the van across the lane onto the narrow shoulder of the road, bordered by large rocks. Cubby hit the brakes and fought to keep the van out of the ditch. Gravel machine-gunned the bottom of the van and the tires screeched as the van slid to a stop. Silently, they all stared out the van windows.

The wind roared around the van. John was horrified to see the fir trees on the other side of the road bending in half. Would they reach the van if they fell? The van rocked with each gust of wind and John honestly wondered whether it might be safer to get out. Then behind him, emerging from behind the hill to the west, he saw a funnel cloud was dancing through farmlands, ripping up crops and trees. John was seventeen years old and had spent all his life in Oregon. In that time he had never heard of a tornado in the state.

The funnel was stirring up so much debris and dust that the road and fields were obscured. If it continued on a straight line, John estimated, it would cut across the highway and then continue into the vineyards on the east side. A farmhouse on that side was a little north of the tornado's path. When John looked back he realized the tornado was curving back into Newberg. John sat there helpless, watching in horrified fascination.

The tornado ripped through the nursery at the edge of town, shredding three greenhouses, then lifted into the sky and seemed to dissipate. Seconds later it was back, dropping to earth again, this time into the Ford dealership, first floating and then lifting Aerostars and Mustangs. Then the funnel ascended again, widened into a swirling, angry cloud, and disappeared.

The three of them sat in silence for a minute and then, all at once, clambered out for a better look as the wind died down to a soft, restful whishing sound.

"Elemental," Ripman said, surveying the damage in the valley below. "Let's go take a look at that Ford dealer."

"Forget it, Ripman," Cubby cut in. "Take a look at the road."

John looked back along the highway to Newberg. It was littered with fallen trees and debris from the greenhouses. They would need a chain saw and a bucket loader to clear a path to the Ford dealer. The road ahead was also covered with debris, but no large trees blocked it. With one last look, and another "elemental" from Ripman, they climbed back into the van and headed home. They were all still on adrenalin highs and peppered their talk with "Did ya see that?"

They finished climbing the hill, went down the grade, and hit the stretch where the road split into two one-way sections divided by dense trees. It felt like driving down a dark green tunnel. Suddenly, Cubby hit the brakes, sliding to a tire-squealing stop. Ripman very nearly hit the windshield, and John and his Big Gulp rolled off the bench seat. He came up cussing, but stopped when he looked out. Cubby was ten feet from where the road ended abruptly. The asphalt was neatly cut from one edge of the road to the other, and where the road should have continued was a forest, but unlike the one that had lined the road to Newberg. The spindly second-growth Douglas firs were gone, and in their place were giants, with girths three to four times larger. John stood, his head protruding from the sunroof, and traced one of the giants from its massive base to its crown, towering above him. Had the road been shifted by the tornado? Had these trees always been there, hidden from the road by the firs?

Cubby and Ripman climbed out of the van, and Ripman walked to the nearest giant and kicked it with his foot.

"It's real enough," he snorted, "but I still don't believe it. Where . . . how did it—?"

Cubby's sudden loud sobbing cut Ripman off. John turned to see Cubby drop to his knees, his hands spread wide and his face turned to heaven. He buried his face in his hands and begged for Jesus to take him. Angrily stomping over, Ripman pulled Cubby's hands from his face. Cubby jerked his hands back and shoved Ripman away, the other boy, overpowered, staggered back a few steps, his face red with anger.

"Get away from me!" Cubby shouted, his voice ragged with tears. "Don't you know what's happened? Can't you see it? It's the second coming. It's the rapture. The righteous have been taken from the world and I have been found wanting."

"Don't give me that, Cubby. This is just some kind of landslide, or maybe that tornado did something weird, but don't give me that supernatural crapola."

As Cubby kept on sobbing, Ripman stepped forward, stopped and kicked dirt at the weeping boy, and then stalked to the edge of the forest, peering into the blackness. John approached Cubby but hesitated, embarrassed and afraid. Ripman was an atheist, but John was an agnostic who could be convinced of God's existence by a miraculous event. What force short of a miracle could have delivered the changes? After a few minutes, Ripman stomped back to yell disgustedly, "Stop blubbering, you big baby. I'll prove to you this isn't the second coming. John, watch him till I get back."

John opened his mouth to protest, but Ripman walked off down the road toward Newberg. John watched him until the dark enveloped him, then he turned back to the forest, a forest that hadn't been there a few hours ago.

"I hope you're right about this, Ripman," John whispered, "I hope to God you're right."

13. Flight Delay

The flight leader radioed they were off course and his compass was haywire. The pilots of the other four torpedo bombers confirmed their instruments were going crazy, and then lost contact. After the planes vanished a twin engine Martin Mariner, with a crew of 13, was dispatched to search the area. The search plane was never heard from again.

—Roger Cochran, *Vanished: Secrets of the Bermuda Triangle*

Honolulu, Hawaii
Time Quilt: Saturday, 10:11 p.m. AHT (Aleutian-Hawaiian Time)

Assistant Professor Emmett Puglisi hurried through the airport looking for the arrival monitor. There were few people, but because he feared being late, everyone was in his way. Spotting a monitor, he quickly scanned for Dr. Wang's flight. Emmett was relieved; he still had a few minutes before her flight arrived.

Emmett noted the gate number but only took three steps before he was stopped by a touch on the arm. Emmett turned to see Professor Carrollee Chen-Slater's beaming face. There was nothing subdued about Carrollee, not her smile, not her personality, and not the way she dressed. Today she was dressed in a brightly colored flowered sundress, which on most people would be gaudy, but Carollee added large flowers to her sandals and one in her hair. Carrollee's taste in clothes ran well past loud, and stopped just a little short of being circus garb.

"Hello, Dr. Puglisi," she said with mock formality.

"Hello, Carrollee," Emmett replied warily. He and Carrollee worked at the university but in different departments, and he knew her well enough to be careful of what he said.

"Dropping off, picking up, or going somewhere?"

Emmett considered lying but wasn't good enough at it to fool Carrollee.

"I'm picking up Professor Wang. She's been at a conference on the mainland."

Carrollee immediately cupped her hand, put her nose inside and twisted it, making the universal sign for brownnosing.

"It's not like that," Emmett said defensively. "She didn't want to leave her car in long-term parking, and she doesn't have any family—"

"Or friends."

"I'm a friend."

"You're an obsequious kiss-up who wants tenure."

Carrollee said it with a smile, but it stung anyway. Emmett changed the subject. "What are you doing here?"

"I dropped my brother off. He's going to the mainland for a couple of weeks. That's him over there," she said.

Emmett followed the point to see a uniformed man a few years older than Carrollee standing in a ticket line.

"I'm only doing it so he'll keep buying me stuff in the PX cheap," she added.

"Nice seeing you, Carrollee, but I've got to get down to the gate."

"I'll walk along."

Emmett left reluctantly, with the unpredictable Dr. Chen-Slater at his side. He didn't want her near when he met Dr. Wang, but didn't know how to get rid of her.

"It might be better if I met her alone, Carrollee."

"Want to do your kissing up in private, eh?"

"I'm just doing her a favor. It's just that if she sees us together she might think we're dating or something."

Carrollee laughed softly and then said, "Are you suggesting I'm not fit to be your girl?"

Emmett was pretty sure she was kidding, but admitted to himself he was mildly attracted to her. Carrollee was four inches over five feet and had a round face topped with a mass of short brown curls. Her figure was unremarkable, except for the way she covered it.

"I'm not saying anything about you," he said defensively. "I just know Dr. Wang doesn't think faculty should have personal relationships."

"You mean sex."

"Relationships. It creates complications—"

Emmett never got to finish the conversation with Carrollee because at that moment a loud boom pealed through the terminal. People in the concourse gasped and babies cried.

"A sonic boom?" Carrollee asked.

"Maybe, but it sounded more like thunder to me."

Carrollee walked to a window. Mindlessly, Emmett followed.

"It's a clear sky," she said, puzzled.

No clouds or aircraft were in sight, and Emmett soon gave up and managed to slip away to find Dr. Wang's gate.

Twenty minutes past arrival time a commotion broke out by the arrival monitor. Emmett joined the crowd to find the arrival times gone, replaced by DELAYED. A half hour later the enormity of the disaster was clear.

---

14. TIDAL WAVE

The ocean will become desert and the fish will die in the sea.

—Nostradamus

Off Naples, Florida
TIME QUILT: SUNDAY, 3:12 A.M. EST

An ear-splitting sound blasted Carmen and Ron awake and to their feet.

"Look over there!" Carmen yelled and pointed.

Ron followed her gesture starboard to an island. In confusion, Ron mentally reviewed his charts. There was no island within hundreds of miles of their position. Even if he had made a navigational error, they hadn't been sailing long enough to reach one of the charted islands. As his mind continued to race he realized that there was something wrong with the island they were looking at. It was getting smaller . . . no, it was sinking, and sinking rapidly. His mind hadn't quite grasped the importance of that fact when the kids came out of the cabin, distracting him.

"What was that?" Rosa asked. "I nearly peed my pants. Hey, an island, neat. Can we go there?"

"Can we go there?" Chris echoed. "Hey, where's it going?"

The island was clearly sinking. Just half its original mass was visible.

"Look at the sky," Carmen said.

Ron saw a boiling angry cloud bank above the island. Otherwise it was a clear night in all directions. Lightning suddenly lit the sky, quickly followed by peals of thunder, and Ron realized the clouds were racing away from the island in their direction. More lightning traced constant jagged patterns and lit up the clouds while overlapping peals of thunder sounded nearly deafening.

"Man, almost as good as a laser show!" Chris yelled above the thunder.

"It's too close," Carmen shouted into Ron's ear. "Can we move away—"

A stiff breeze suddenly hit them, interrupting Carmen. It was then Ron realized the danger.

"Carmen! Get life jackets on Rosa and Chris and one on yourself, and get below! Secure everything. Quickly!"

"What's wrong?"

Ron hesitated. Rosa and Chris were staring at him with frightened eyes, but there was no hiding what was coming.

"I think we're going to be hit by a tidal wave."

Rosa and Chris looked stunned, but Carmen immediately took action, herding the kids into the cabin. The breeze was getting stronger and waves were rolling the *Entrepreneur* to starboard. Ron hit the Start button and listened to it crank, his eyes never leaving the sinking island. After a few seconds of eternity the little engine chugged to life, but it wasn't designed for outrunning a tidal wave and could manage only a few knots. Ron hesitated, anguished. Rationally he knew his best chance was to head into the wave, but every cell in his body was programmed to run from danger, not toward it. But the lives of his son and his new family depended on his decision. Finally, he put the *Entrepreneur* in gear and spun the wheel to starboard, and toward the island.

Carmen reappeared on deck with two life jackets. Chris and Rosa were peeking out of the cabin behind her, worried—but

Ron was reassured that they didn't reflect his own mortal terror. Carmen looked around briefly and then turned to Ron.

"Aren't you going the wrong way?"

"If there is a tidal wave, we need to head into it. If we run, it will catch us and swamp us. If it hits us broadside we'll be capsized."

"Won't it swamp us if we run into it?"

"There's a better chance this way."

Ron wanted to say more, but there was no conviction in his words. If he tried to explain more his voice would quiver.

"Really, this is the best chance."

Carmen took the helm while Ron put on his life jacket, cinching it tight. He stepped below to double-check the kids' jackets and weakly attempted reassurance.

When Ron took the helm again Carmen gripped the railing, her knuckles white, as if she expected the wave at any second. The wind was picking up and the clouds from the island were beginning to block out the stars. The lightning was only intermittent now. Ron found the occasional peals of thunder more disturbing than the constant booming, as he reflexively used the pauses to prepare for the next boom. The starry calm night of a few minutes ago was now a stormy nightmare.

Ron looked for the island just as a wave broke over the bow, showering Carmen and Ron with spray. As the *Entrepreneur* crested still another wave, Ron searched ahead.

"Carmen, do you see the island?"

"There, I think there."

Ron looked but saw nothing but waves and spray. At least Carmen confirmed that they were probably heading in the right direction. More waves broke over the bow and Ron began to think they might drown even before the tidal wave sank the *Entrepreneur*. Then Carmen shouted again. "Oh my god! Ron, look at that!"

Ron could see nothing but gray. Then he realized he was looking too low. He tilted his head to see an edge. The tidal wave was nearly on them.

"This is it, everyone. Hang on to something."

The *Entrepreneur* started down into the trough, sliding into the smoother waters before the wave. The dip made their stomachs lurch, and Ron and Carmen gasped as the towering wave rose even higher with each foot of drop into the trough. Then their craft started up the wave. Once more their stomachs churned as they were carried up by combination of wave and engine. The *Entrepreneur*'s bow tilted higher and higher, until Ron feared they would flip over backward. He fought to keep them headed directly into the wave, but the *Entrepreneur*, buffeted by wave and wind, wouldn't stay nose on. For a minute he thought they might make it to the top but then he saw the curl. It wouldn't even be close.

The curl broke over them, twisting the *Entrepreneur* to port and pushing her under the wave. Ron was torn from his place at the helm and thrust deep into the sea, pitched and tossed, and then he heard the screaming. In his panic it took him seconds to realize it was the scream of metal. *Entrepreneur* was losing her mast.

Ron let the currents buffet him beneath the waves. He knew if he started swimming while still disoriented he could swim himself deeper, so instead he let the buoyancy of his life jacket carry him to the surface. As the buffeting died down, he regained a clear sense of up and down. He kicked his legs and pulled upward. His lungs soon screamed and he blew bubbles trying to fight off the urge to open his mouth and suck in the sea. He kicked harder and harder as lights flashed before his eyes. He had only seconds of consciousness left now, and he dreaded the moment when his breathing reflexes would take over, filling his lungs with water. Suddenly he broke through the surface, shooting out of the sea and breaching like a whale. He gasped for air, breathing in sea spray and oxygen all at the same time, when a wave hit him in the face and he inhaled a mouthful of saltwater. He kicked higher out of the water, coughing and sputtering up the brine, his lungs and nose burning.

Searching for the others, he bobbed in the waves which towered over him, but nothing like the tidal wave. He rode up one side and down the other. He knew his family could be only a short distance away and yet not be seen, but he still felt desperate. To his left he spotted something white in the water. He kicked up the next wave and popped up again for another look. The hull of the *Entrepreneur* was bobbing a few waves away. He stroked toward the hull, kicking up at the top of each wave to make sure of his heading, but he saw only the hull: no Chris, no Carmen, and no Rosa.

Ron finally swam down the last wave, riding it right to the hull—inverted, but it looked to be intact. Still he found no sign of his family—*they had to be somewhere, they had to be!* He'd lost one wife, and he couldn't stand losing another, let alone a child. Ron pulled himself to the stern and used the rudder to clatter up on the hull. Then he heard pounding. The kids were still inside.

Ron slid back down into the water and tried to dive, but his life jacket pulled him back to the surface. He unsnapped the catches and shrugged it off. Now he could feel the weight of his shoes and clothes. He kicked off his shoes and pulled his shirt over his head, and then he dipped below the surface, stroking down to the inverted deck. In the murky green he could see the cabin door was open. He swam to it and used the frame to propel himself through the opening. He could see legs ahead of him and he curved up, searching for the air pocket. He burst through the surface tension to find a foot of warm, foul air, but also light; someone had turned on a floating lantern. Ron turned to find Rosa staring at him, her eyes wide with fear. Even soaking wet he could tell she had been crying.

"Thank God. Oh, Ron, Chris is hurt. I can't wake him up and I don't know what to do. I couldn't get him out of here."

Ron looked past Rosa to Chris. He was unconscious, and Rosa was supporting his head, keeping it out of the water. Ron pushed through the water. There was a nasty gash high on Chris's forehead and water dribbled from his hair through the wound, emerging pinkish on the other side. Ron gripped the boy's wrist but couldn't tell if the pounding he felt was Chris's pulse or his own. Ron shook Chris, talking, urging him to wake up. He knew the longer Chris was unconscious the more serious the damage. To keep him alive they had to get him out of the hull and into the fresh air, even if that air was a storm. Tears in his eyes, Ron fully realized Rosa's dilemma. She could have saved herself by swimming under the water and out to the surface, but she had to leave Chris behind to do that. If she tried to take him with her he would drown on the way.

The air was getting worse. Ron knew they still had oxygen, but he and Rosa were beginning to gasp. The only chance was pulling Chris under and letting him inhale the water. He knew from the baby swim class his wife had taken with Chris that newborns reflexively stop breathing when placed under water. Would that reflex still exist in some form? Would a lower part of Chris's brain take over and protect him for the underwater trip? If only Chris could keep from breathing for even thirty seconds, Ron could have him out by then. Then a solution occurred to him.

"Rosa, feel around in the water there. Find some tape, wide tape. It's in the everything drawer."

The "everything drawer" was the place where they put everything that had no other place. Ron kept two or three kinds of tape in the drawer, most of them useful even if wet. Rosa felt around briefly and then took off her life jacket and ducked under the water. While she swam, Ron pulled Chris to the rear of the cabin, where a rack for drying clothes was attached to the wall. He felt around until he found a clothespin, and then started back to Rosa. Rosa was still ducking under the water, occasionally coming up with something in her hand, holding it to the light, and then tossing it aside. She popped up again, this time with a big roll of silver tape in her hand.

"I got some," she said and held it up for Ron to see. She was smiling, happy to be doing anything that might save Chris.

Ron supported Chris while Rosa unsnapped the catches on his life jacket, then they wrestled it off the limp boy. The inert weight of his son unnerved Ron, who struggled to support Chris's head. When the life jacket was off, Ron peeled up a length of tape, then struggled to tear it. It finally tore but folded up against itself. At least, Ron reflected, it was still sticky when wet. Futilely, Ron tried again. The air was much worse and Ron realized they were running out of oxygen. He was about to tell Rosa to swim out when she ducked under the water. Disappointed, he still knew she made the right decision. Now the oxygen would last a little longer. Ron was struggling with still another length of tape when Rosa's hand suddenly appeared out of the water holding an Exacto knife. Her face followed, smiling broadly.

Ron smiled back, grabbed the knife, and sliced off tape, pressing it down firmly over Chris's mouth. Chris began to breathe deeply through his nose, with an alarming liquid sound to it.

"Okay, Rosa, time to go."

Rosa hesitated, her eyes reflecting her concern. "I can help with Chris," she offered.

"You wait on the other side for him and help pull him up."

Rosa nodded, sucked in a deep breath, and disappeared into the liquid gloom. Ron gave her time to swim out, then moved Chris to the opening. He had to push him under a couple of feet of water, through the cabin door, and then out past the helm to the surface. A short swim, but it would be difficult with a dead weight. Ron determined to do it the first time, took several deep breaths, then clamped the clothespin on Chris's nose. Chris immediately began puffing against the tape and Ron saw it wouldn't hold long. He shoved his son down into the water and tried to follow him, but Chris kept bobbing upward. After a couple of attempts he grabbed a fistful of Chris's shirt with one hand, the edge of the door with the other, and pulled Chris toward the opening, like propelling a slow-motion torpedo. Ron strained, trying to push Chris lower with one arm so he would clear the opening and not bang his injured head on the door frame. Chris moved toward the opening slowly at first, and then more quickly.

Now Ron let go of the frame and pushed Chris down with both hands. As the boy filled the opening Ron realized he had overcompensated. Chris was going to clear the top and right door frame easily, but not the left frame. Ron didn't want to slow Chris's momentum so he tried to change his course. He managed to keep the child's head from hitting the side, but the frame scraped down his forehead and then along his nose. When the clothespin scraped off, the convulsions started.

Chris began twitching and jerking, and clawing frantically. Ron tried to steady the boy, but one flailing leg caught Ron in the solar plexus and the air exploded from his lungs. He tried to stay under, but the breathing reflex drove him to the surface. He broke into the air pocket again, filling his lungs with the oxygen-poor air as the water churned with Chris's struggles. Although he needed more oxygen, he forced his mouth closed and his head back in the water; still, he wouldn't be able to stay down long. To his horror, he saw Chris's body still flailing violently, but slower.

Suddenly Chris shot forward through the opening. Surprised, Ron returned to the air pocket, gasping in the nearly spent air, and then dove, following Chris.

Ron came up gasping, the sea air quickly flushing his system of the excess carbon dioxide, and was surprised and relieved to see Carmen helping Rosa shove Chris up onto the hull of the *Entrepreneur*. Ron pushed the boy from below and then climbed up carefully. The boat was still pitching from the aftermath of the tidal wave, although the breeze had died down. Ron looked at the sky: black, not a star in sight.

On the hull Rosa was pulling Chris along behind her while Carmen pushed. It took Ron a minute to see that Chris was moving his legs, trying to help himself along. Relief spread through Ron; his son was conscious—not the same as okay, but in the right direction. He watched helplessly as Carmen took off her life jacket and helped Chris into it. The thought of diving back under the hull sent shivers through Ron, but they needed supplies if they were going to survive.

Ron relaxed, let gravity pull him into the wet blackness, and then dove under the hull. Once inside he didn't bother trying to breathe the stale air; instead he held his breath and pulled open the bunk exposing the storage chest. Survival food and bottled water tumbled out. He grabbed two water jugs and headed back to the surface. He left one jug just inside the door and pulled the other to the surface. His lungs ached when he reached the surface again.

"Carmen! Reach this. I'm going back for more."

Ron found the second jug easily and passed it up to Carmen.

"Ron, what about the life raft? Can you get that?"

The inflatable life raft was strapped to the bow just in front of the cabin. It was packed with survival gear and a canopy. Ron hesitated. He couldn't be sure it was still strapped to the deck.

The *Entrepreneur* had taken quite a beating. His family was temporarily safe on the hull, and he was retrieving food and water they would need. If he tried to unstrap the raft, he would have to do it upside down, underwater, and it might take several dives. He decided on another trip for the gear in the cabin first and was about to dive again when Carmen called down to him.

"Ron, is there a life jacket for Rosa?"

Suddenly, Ron was mortified. In his worry about Chris, he had forgotten about Carmen's child. Ron dove again, and found a life jacket floating in the cabin and wrestled it down and through the opening. It snagged on something on the way out and he had to get another breath before he could free it. Carmen's smile when he tossed her the life jacket meant he could forgive himself.

Nearly exhausted, Ron decided it was time to get the raft. Ron paddled forward to the bow, took several deep breaths, and then dove. He found the raft almost immediately and felt for the straps that held it to the deck. The strap catches were still holding but one of the straps was loose, its cleat torn away.

The raft had a length of cord with a loop on the end, for looping around the arm or leg. Then, when you tossed the raft overboard, you pulled the inflation ring, and the rope would keep the inflated raft from drifting out of reach.

Confident he could locate all the raft's features, Ron returned to the surface to replenish his air supply. On the swim back, he ran into the railing. Now he was getting tired and making mistakes. He wouldn't be able to do many more trips without resting. As soon as he broke the surface he heard Carmen's warning.

"Ron! There's something coming, another wave!"

Ron used most of his remaining energy to sprint to the stern and climb up the rudder. Chris was sitting with his head down, but Carmen and Rosa were staring into the night. Ron turned to their direction and spotted the wave. It was almost on them. Although much smaller than the first wave, it would be even more dangerous. Even in the dark the wave was a chocolate brown color, and full of debris—even whole trees—from the island. The *Entrepreneur* dipped into the trough before the wave, nearly rocking them off the hull, then started to rise as it climbed the wave. As it climbed it started to roll. Then something hit the *Entrepreneur* hard, shaking the hull and tilting it even farther. Chris slid off first, but Carmen and Rosa went with him, their hands gripping his life jacket. As Ron went over he heard pounding and tearing as the *Entrepreneur*'s hull took the beating of the debris. Some swept over the hull, pounding down mud, leaves, and limbs on Ron and his family. Something huge hit the *Entrepreneur*, and Ron felt himself being pulled under the hull by an undertow and fought to stay on top.

Suddenly the wave smashed a tree trunk into the hull of the *Entrepreneur*, nearly splitting it in two. Splinters from the hull showered the family, and everyone tried to kick away from it as the muddy wave finished halving the boat.

Ron swam toward the piece of the hull that still held the raft, but it was sinking rapidly. The tree trunk that had shattered it was between Ron and the raft, and he dove to go under them. As he swam under he realized it still had many branches attached, and he dove deeper. As the hull sank it rolled and Ron easily reached the bow, but it was sinking quickly and pulling him down with it. He hung on to the loose strap and released the catch of the other strap, and the raft began to drift out. The raft was sinking fast. Deftly, Ron pulled the inflation ring and heard the compressed air flood the cells. Ballooning, the raft squirted out from under the remaining strap. He grabbed for it, but it shot out of his reach. His lungs burning again, he kicked for the surface pulling with his arms.

He was farther down than he realized, much farther. His lungs screamed for oxygen and he was flailing like a drowning man. But he surfaced.

When his panic died he looked around. To his relief he saw Carmen had the children organized and was moving them toward the raft. Exhausted, Ron rolled over to his back to float. The sea was too rough, however, and the debris-laden waves kept washing over his face. He gave up and rolled into a breast stroke, reaching the raft at the same time as the others.

"Rosa's hurt, Ron," Carmen said. "Help her into the raft."

Ron swam around Carmen to Rosa and found her grimacing from pain.

"What's wrong? Where are you hurt?"

"It's my side. Something hit me. I think it was a tree."

The raft was octagonal, with four inflated pillars that held the canopy four feet above. The sides were a double row of inflated cells. Ron tried to help Rosa up gently, while Carmen did the same thing with Chris. Finally, Ron gave up on gentle and shoved hard. With a gasp, she flopped into the raft and lay on the floor shuddering. Ron hung on to the edge of the raft, exhausted, then felt Carmen pulling him up. His weight pushed the raft down and a muddy wave washed in and over Rosa. Then he felt Carmen's hands on his bottom and she pulled him up and over. He ended up on his back in the soup on the bottom with Rosa, his head in Carmen's lap.

The raft was rocking and pitching, but still it seemed restful. Occasional waves broke over the raft, but the family was oblivious to them. They stayed like that for a long time.

---

15. Coop

There were thunders and lightnings, and a thick cloud upon the mount, and the voice of the trumpet exceedingly loud; so that all the people that was in the camp trembled.

—Exodus 19:16

Carlton, Oregon
TIME QUILT: SUNDAY, 12:13 A.M. PST

Police Chief Vincent Peters was eating a Mount Vesuvius in the Copper Skillet restaurant. The omelette filled his plate and was covered with chili and sour cream. He knew eating it this time of night meant he would pay in a couple of hours, but that was then and this was now, and he was going to enjoy every bite. That is, if Coop would let him. Reserve Officer Stanley Cooper was across the table working on a Godfather's Special, his eggs covered with spaghetti sauce, olives, and sausage. "Coop," as he liked to be called, was temporarily distracted by the waitress across the aisle, who bent over arranging forks and knives. Then she finished arranging the table, scooped a small pile of change into her palm, and left, Coop's eyes trailing after her.

"As I was saying, Chief, before I got distracted"—Coop wiggled his eyebrows up and down and then continued—"at the rate we're growing, it won't be long before you're going to have to expand the force. I mean we already got a fair amount of fiscal underachievers for a city our size, and I don't have to tell you what that means. We also got ourselves a problem with transients and non-goal-oriented members of society. Just last weekend we ran six of them out of City Park."

Peters was listening to Coop as well as anyone could, but wishing he wasn't. A city the size of Carlton couldn't afford a large permanent force of officers, so they used part-time reserve officers, like Coop, to fill in. Peters needed the reserves, so he took them to lunch occasionally, had them out to his house for barbecues, and was generally nice to them. It wasn't always easy, especially with Coop. More than any of the other reserve officers, Coop wanted to work full-time, but it would never happen as long as Peters was chief.

Nearly everything Coop did irritated Chief Peters. For example, the way Coop talked. "Fiscal underachievers" were poor people, "non-goal-oriented members of society" were street people, and "transients" referred to anyone who ran into trouble with the law but didn't live in the city. Coop once sent a letter to the editor of the local newspaper complaining of "fiscal advanced downward adjustments" in the police department and "downsizing personnel." Peters wondered how many readers knew he was talking about budget cuts and layoffs. There was even an officer who swore on a Bible he heard Coop refer to a pencil as a "portable hand-held communications inscriber." Peters doubted the story. Still, with Coop you never knew for sure.

"It is imperative, Chief, that we plan for such a contingent upsizing of personnel. We don't want to make last-minute hasty decisions that might be regretted later. We need to do some thinking now, establish a line of ascension, and stick to it when the time comes."

"Any ideas, Coop, on who should be on the hiring list?"

"Chief, you know I got more experience and know-how than any other reserve officer. I've paid my own way through three special training schools, done extra duty, why I even learned how to type. I'm not expecting anything in return for all this, you understand, I'm just pointing out my qualifications."

Coop's résumé was interrupted with an ear-shattering noise that shook the restaurant, knocking the copper skillet on the wall behind the cashier's counter to the floor. The windows rattled, and startled gasps came from the other two customers.

"What the hell?" Coop said, with a half-grin on his face. "I do believe we just experienced an unauthorized sonic excess."

If it was a sonic boom, the jet must have broken the sound barrier right over the town. Chief Peters walked outside to look around, with Coop following. The sky was clear directly overhead and filled with stars. Any jet would have already disappeared, so he didn't expect to see one. He looked up and down the main street to find nothing unusual except house lights blinking on here and there.

"Look at that, Chief."

Peters turned to follow Coop's pointing finger. West of town, there was a boiling mass of clouds shooting thousands of feet up into the air, as if buffeted by strong winds. Peters had never seen anything like it. Something had whipped the sky into a frothing madness. As they watched, lightning flashes added to the show, quickly followed by the boom of thunder. Soon they moved back into the restaurant.

"What do you think caused that, Chief, a little ultimate high-intensity warfare?"

Peters knew "ultimate high-intensity warfare" meant nuclear war to Coop.

"I hope not," Peters said.

Coop was clearly disappointed.

PostQuilt

16. The President

It is the ability to successfully draw on the experience of others, as well as their own, that distinguishes great leaders. However, once faced with something outside human experience, they become ordinary with surprising rapidity.

—Carl Comstock, *Decision Makers*

Washington, D.C.
PostQuilt: Sunday, 4:37 a.m. EST

President Scott McIntyre was shaken to consciousness by a secret service agent and his chief of staff. McIntyre knew instantly that it was serious. As chief of staff, Elizabeth Hawthorne had the authority to decide what needed the president's immediate attention and what could wait. Elizabeth believed a rested President was the best kind to make important decisions, so for her no emergency required waking the President. Even when two terrorist bombs went off in New York City and the terrorists demanded the release of political prisoners, she let the President sleep and wake to a fully briefed staff ready for a crisis meeting. When a Russian bomber and an American chase plane collided off the coast of South Carolina, he again awoke to a meeting of an already summoned Security Council. So, if Elizabeth Hawthorne was waking him, it must be serious. He dressed quickly.

Elizabeth was in the Oval Office with Colonel Winfield, the President's special military advisor. The President was amazed at how both of them looked well rested and well pressed. Colonel Winfield's uniform was stiff and smooth, as if it had never been worn, his graying temples neatly combed, and his dark face shaved clean and smooth. Elizabeth was just as well groomed. How the two of them could wake in the middle of the night and pull themselves together so quickly the President couldn't understand. Elizabeth at least had the advantage of age. She was still in her thirties, but Colonel Winfield was well into his fifties and managed the same trick. To look presidential, McIntyre pulled himself erect as he walked into the room.

All the lights were on, including the green shaded reading light on his desk. Still the room looked dark to the President, perhaps because of the dark windows behind the desk. Why is it, the President thought, that the dark of morning is different than the dark of night?

He sat behind his desk, picked up a paper clip and twisted it into a miniature crank, which he would fiddle with all through the meeting. The paper clip signaled he was ready and Elizabeth began.

"Something has happened . . . something strange."

That was all she said. The President looked at her with surprise. Elizabeth Hawthorne at a loss for words? She and Colonel Winfield exchanged glances, but neither spoke.

"What has happened?" he prompted. "Have the Russians invaded the Baltic states? Did California shake into the sea? Have I been impeached?"

"Parts of the country have . . . are . . . experiencing communication disruptions, blackouts, and there have been some disappearances," Elizabeth said.

"Disappearances? Who has disappeared?"

"It's not a matter of who . . . well, I don't mean to overlook the human dimension but . . . Mr. President, it appears that a large section of New York City has disappeared."

President McIntyre was baffled.

"What do you mean 'disappeared'? I can understand devastated, or vaporized, or flooded, but what the hell does *disappeared* mean?"

"It means, Mr. President, that where there were buildings, streets, cars, and people, there is now nothing."

"Nothing? Nothing means an absence of anything . . . a void."

"What Ms. Hawthorne means, sir," Colonel Winfield cut in, "is where there was a city, there is now countryside."

The President sat back in his desk chair, reclining. He was considering the possibility of a practical joke, but Elizabeth was humorless. President McIntyre had never heard her utter anything more than a polite courtesy chuckle now and then. But if this wasn't a joke, then what? Cities don't disappear, at least they never had.

"I'm still having trouble understanding this . . . a section of New York City is now devoid of buildings and streets . . . and people . . . and is now farmland, or something?"

"Yes, sir," Colonel Winfield said, "and the rest of the city is blacked out. The reports are unofficial, but they do seem to be consistent. Inbound commercial flights to Kennedy International have been rerouted . . . and at least one aircraft has been lost. Kennedy International is gone—we've confirmed it with our own flyover."

The President was lost in thought, thinking about what Colonel Winfield was saying. The paper clip in his hands slowed its twirl to a near stop. From experience Elizabeth and the colonel knew not to interrupt; the President processed slowly but thoroughly. Finally the paper clip picked up speed and the President looked up.

"You said 'parts of the country' and 'disappearances.' You used the plural, didn't you?"

Elizabeth stood and walked over to the President's desk.

"Mr. President, there are similar reports from other regions of the country. Blackouts, tornadoes, sonic booms, and sudden disappearances of roads and even whole towns. We don't know how widespread it is, but it is not an isolated incident."

"Colonel Winfield, I want flyovers of as many areas as possible and satellite reconnaissance if you can get it. I've got to see this for myself. If the military hasn't gone to full alert then it should immediately. I want a full intelligence briefing at the staff meeting."

Colonel Winfield nodded and left. Elizabeth turned to leave, but the President stopped her.

"Elizabeth, I've lost track of Sandy's schedule."

"The first lady is in Atlanta, Mr. President. We have no word about Atlanta."

"Thank you, Elizabeth."

When Elizabeth left, the President was staring out the dark window and twisting the paper clip crank around and around.

17. Science Advisor

The morning I arrived in Singapore the heavens filled the street with fishes. When the fish stopped falling the Chinese and the Malays gathered them up, most returning home with an overflowing basket. A most unusual introduction to a most unusual country.

—François de Castelnau, February 16, 1861

Washington, D.C.
PostQuilt: Sunday, 5:13 a.m. EST

There was a phone beeping in Nick Paulson's ear. Nick's head was paralyzed from fatigue but he managed to roll his eyes ninety degrees toward the clock radio. The numbers waved before his eyes for a few seconds and then coalesced into a fuzzy pattern that resembled 5:13. The two glowing globs in the corner were too blurry to read, but they had to say A.M. The phone beeped again and Nick began to wish for the good old days when phones jangled. A jangle can energize you and take you from stage four sleep all the way to consciousness. But a beep just doesn't have the necessary power to blast you from delta waves to alpha waves.

On the second try, Nick palmed the receiver and heard a voice respond to his groggy hello, but it didn't make any sense. Finally he recognized it as belonging to Elizabeth Hawthorne, the President's chief of staff. Elizabeth Hawthorne was a human jangle.

"Elizabeth . . . Elizabeth . . . start over please. I've only been in bed a couple of hours."

"I said, we're calling an emergency Security Council meeting at seven this morning and you are to be there. It would help if you could come in as soon as possible and review some of the reports we have. The President will want your assessment."

Nick was not sure he understood her. Nick had never sat with the Security Council, and he couldn't imagine the kind of emergency that would require a science advisor. Emergencies usually need only two kinds of people, those who can negotiate and those who can kill. Nick was sure he couldn't do the first, and pretty sure he couldn't do the second.

"Elizabeth, can you tell me the nature of the emergency?"

"Not on this line. Dr. Paulson, be here within the hour."

Elizabeth hung up. Good-byes were superfluous to her.

It was then he noticed his heart was pounding. Only two things made Nick's heart pound: sex and fear. Since Kathy had moved out over two months ago, that left only fear.

Twenty minutes later he was directing his Volvo through the empty streets. The rain had stopped and the streets were shiny and slick. Nick ran an electric razor over his face as he drove, clearing away the stubble. He finished grooming by running his fingers through his thinning blond hair. He decided to check the radio for news, hoping to pick up some clue to what the Security Council was meeting to discuss. There was nothing but music on the FM stations, but on AM he picked up part of a news broadcast.

"Bill, how are the people of New York handling this latest blackout?"

"Well, so far, Maria, we have no reports of looting. As our listeners know from past blackouts, some people take advantage of unfortunate circumstances like these. We can only hope that the governor—"

Nick went back to twisting the dial.

The meeting could have something to do with the New York situation, but blackouts normally don't require a meeting of the Security Council. Now if the blackout was caused by terrorist action you might call such a meeting. But why invite the science advisor? It couldn't be a nuclear attack. Nick wasn't on the nuclear response team. Besides, a nuclear blast would certainly have made the newscasts by now. Nick spun the dial looking for more details and rested briefly on a talk show.

"I'm telling you, Gene, this is what I saw. The road is gone, the trees are gone, the old candle factory is gone, everything is gone. Gone, gone, gone! Can't you hear what I'm telling you?"

"Ken . . . Ken, I can hear fine. But do you hear what you're saying? Do you? You want me . . . and my listeners . . . to believe that you turned your back for a second, just a second, and when you looked back everything was snowed in? Ken, it can't snow that fast."

"I didn't say it snowed—"

"Ken . . . let me finish . . . suddenly, without warning, on a sixty-degree night, it snows thirty or forty feet . . . enough to cover a factory? I'm not buying it, Ken. Time to refill your prescription."

"Well why don't you come out here and I'll take some of that imaginary snow and shove it—"

Nick was sorry the line went dead. Ken was about to tell the talk show host something Nick had always wanted to say to a talk show host.

"Naughty, naughty, Ken. We must please the FCC now, mustn't we . . . you butthead. We've got Coop from Carlton, Oregon, on line three. Go ahead, Coop, you're on *Night Talk*."

"Gene, I got another improbable indecipherable for you. There was a supersonic percussion a couple of hours ago from the direction of Portland. I just got back from taking a little reconnaisance ride. I could only make about ten clicks."

"And what did you see on your reconnoiter?"

"It's what I didn't see. Portland."

"You didn't see Portland? It's a good thing you got lost, Coop. Once you've seen the big city you'd never be happy on your farm again."

"I'm no agricultural entrepreneur, and I didn't get lost. Portland did. It's not there anymore and where it used to be there's a forest."

"Coop, what do they drink out there in Carlton, or should I say how much?"

Nick could not believe what he was hearing. Someone was on the radio reporting a missing city and sounding serious. The idea of a missing city was odd enough, but the caller made it seem even stranger. It was something in the way he spoke about it. For one thing the caller sounded excited, not depressed, not bewildered, not even sad. Certainly if a city full of people had disappeared it would be a disorienting experience. But the caller sounded downright enthused.

"I don't imbibe while on duty, Gene, and I consider myself

on duty until this emergency is over. I'm a reserve police officer and proud of it."

"I have reservations about police officers too."

"That's not all of it, Gene. When I was looking through my optical assistance device I spotted a dinosaur."

"A dinosaur? You mean one of those extinct creatures that hasn't existed on earth for a few million years or so?"

"What else could it be? It was either a dinosaur or the only ten-foot lizard I've ever seen. I'm getting ready now to head back and see if I can apprehend the trespassing lizard."

"You do that, Coop, and be sure to call back and let us know when you catch it. Meanwhile I'll alert my listeners to be on the lookout for a missing city." The line was cut and then Gene added, "Bob, let's start screening these calls. Is there a full moon tonight or what?"

Then Gene punched up line one from Sioux City, Iowa.

"Gene, I should of taken your advice." The caller had clearly been drinking.

"What advice was that, Sioux City?"

"You told me to get rid of my wife. We was having trouble . . . she was cheating on me. You told me to take her stuff, throw it out of the house and her with it."

"I remember, Sioux City. So what happened?"

"She took the farm."

"The farm equipment?"

"No, damn it, she took the whole—*beeeeep*—farm."

"Watch your language, Sioux City."

"We had a big fight and I stomped out and jumped into my pickup to go get a beer. I got about halfway down the driveway when I got knocked off the road by a humpin' big noise. I still can't hear so good. When I looked back the place was gone. I got no house, no barn, no stock, no nothing. But I got plenty of nothing."

"You wouldn't happen to have a relative living in Oregon would you?"

"I ain't got nothing no where."

"Well, that brings us to the news on the hour . . . thank God. I'm gonna turn it over to Jim Jenkins with all the latest on missing cities and farms, and when I come back let's talk about something normal like flying saucers, or abortion, but not dinosaurs. I'm Gene Diamond and you're listening to America's nighttime favorite—*Night Talk*."

Nick kept turning the dial, but all the stations seemed to be getting their news from the same source and reported only on the New York blackout.

The security at the White House told Nick how serious the situation was. The guard at the gate had been replaced by marines in uniform with secret service agents mixed in, and Nick was going through his third ID check when Elizabeth Hawthorne took his arm and expedited the process. Nick couldn't help but notice that no one asked for Elizabeth's ID.

"The reports are on my desk. You can use my office."

"Nice to see you too. What is going on?"

"Read the reports. I'm going to stay here and help the others through security. Nick, I think you should know that Dr. Gogh will be at the meeting."

Nick wasn't sure how to take that news. Arnold Gogh was the President's first choice for Nick's job. In fact he held the post for two years. The President had been friends with Gogh when they were both faculty at the University of Michigan. It was a strange friendship—Gogh the physicist and McIntyre the political scientist—a rapport based on compatible political beliefs. When McIntyre left academia for the state legislature Gogh stayed with the university, but he was never really out of touch or influence.

When the Democrats had splintered, McIntyre had coined the name Neodemocrat for the new party. When he ran for the Senate, Gogh took a leave of absence and managed his campaign. When McIntyre ran for the presidency as the Neodemocratic nominee, Gogh was an integral part of the successful campaign. To everyone's surprise he turned down chief of staff; that position went to Elizabeth Hawthorne. Instead, Gogh sought the position of science advisor and then reshaped it in his own image.

He would still be science advisor if it hadn't been for Gogh's penchant for young girls, recorded on video. Gogh had to plea-bargain himself out of jail, and the position of science advisor fell to Nick.

Nick had a reputation as a popularizer of science. His award-winning public television productions brought the mysteries of the galaxy, the seas, and the animal world to everyday people in a way they could understand. Nick's success made him popular with the public, and with politicians, but his reputation as a scientist had suffered. He was no longer a purist. He no longer published in obscure journals that even the specialists ignored. He'd dropped out of the great grant race.

But now he could pursue his first love—all sciences—and it was a trade he rarely regretted. So he produced the television specials, delivered the talks, and served as a liaison between the President and the sciences.

Nick knew that Gogh's presence did not mean McIntyre's lack of trust in Nick. Gogh was part of the President's emotional support network, and with the first lady out of town, Nick assumed President McIntyre might be using Gogh as a surrogate partner. However, Gogh would diminish Nick's influence.

Nick watched Elizabeth walk back to the door and take up an observation post. She was an unusual woman. Not that she wasn't a fine-looking woman. Her hair was silky. Her skin was flawless. Her rarely used smile dazzled, and her figure was made for snuggling up to. But she never posted signs that she was willing or even interested. Elizabeth was carbon monoxide, odorless and colorless. Nick had no doubt she was just as deadly.

Nick found the files on the desk just where Elizabeth had said they would be. They were easy to find, since the desk was bare except for one folder.

The first report, about the New York situation, gave Nick a sick feeling of déjà vu. It wasn't a report about a blackout. The report clearly stated that part of New York City had disappeared. Nick had trouble reading because he kept thinking about the talk show. Three of the callers had said something about things missing. Portland, Oregon, a farm in Iowa, and what had that first caller said? Something about a candle factory buried in snow? What was going on? Nick flipped through the reports. None of them mentioned Portland or anything in Iowa, but there were reports of blackouts, landslides, and bridge collapses. They were mostly from the East Coast and Midwest.

As he read Nick felt as if he had been jangled by an old-fashioned phone. The pounding in his chest built and his breathing quickened. He recognized the feeling right away this time. It was fear again.

---

18. THE MEADOW

The wonders of this age cannot compare to the wonders of the age of no time. In that age we will surely know from whence we came.

—Zorastrus, Prophet of Babylon

New York City
PostQuilt: Sunday, 7:07 a.m. EST

It was coming across the meadow slowly, pausing frequently to get down on all fours with its head in the grass. Then it stood, rising on its two bigger back legs until it towered above the meadow, looking around defensively. It was eating the grasses at a leisurely pace, more interested in food than speed. Mariel was both afraid and excited when she realized it was eating its way toward her window. She watched the huge beast come closer, and with each giant step, the beast loomed larger. First she thought it was the size of an elephant, but now she could see it was bigger. Much bigger.

Filled with new excitement, Mariel knew it was a dinosaur. She was excited and scared at the same time. Her old eyes could finally see it clearly. Grass hung from both sides of its mouth, and it stared at Mariel's building and the other buildings bordering its meadow. From the curiosity she saw in those eyes, she knew this was an intelligent animal. You could tell intelligence by the eyes. In people, too.

Mariel was watching it stuff its mouth with grass again when someone started pounding on the door. She shouted for whoever it was to go away, but the pounding only sounded louder.

Luis was at the door, and she opened it to find him carrying his little girl, Melinda holding the baby, and the other three kids hanging on to Mom, sleepy and confused.

"Mrs. Weatherby, it's time to go. I'm getting my family out. You come with us!"

"Luis, I told you—"

"Mrs. Weatherby, have you seen what's out your window?"

"Yes, Luis. I know what's out there. That's another good reason to stay."

Melinda stepped forward and pleaded. "Mrs. Weatherby, it's too dangerous to stay. We should've gotten out when the buildings disappeared. I mean, that shouldn't happen. Everyone's getting out. The Kaplans and Greccos are gone. Mr. Moreno left an hour ago."

"The McGregors?"

"I don't know," Melinda replied. "I think so."

Mariel didn't like the idea of being in the building alone. If the gangs knew her building was empty they might see it as an irresistible opportunity. She wavered but then shored up her resolve. She hadn't felt so alive in years and wasn't going to be scared out of that feeling.

But Melinda wasn't ready to give up. "That's a dinosaur, Mrs. Weatherby. It could eat you."

"It's eating grass, dear. Thanks so much for your concern. I'm just fine here in my home."

Luis started to argue with her again but Melinda cut him off.

"Luis, the kids. We've got to get them out of here."

Luis looked down and then nodded his head.

"We're going, Mrs. Weatherby. I've got to for my kids. If I can, I'll be back for you."

"Luis, really, I'll be all right."

"If I can, I'm coming back."

Mariel watched the Ibarra family go down the hall to the stairs and then they were gone. She listened to the building. It sounded empty and unfamiliar.

Mariel talked to herself on the way back to the window to fill the emptiness. "Ask me to leave my home? Well, thank you very much but I'll leave when they carry me out." When Mariel reached the window she immediately forgot her fears, for the dinosaur was much closer now, and it was magnificent.

It was as tall as the McGregors' window below her. It walked on its two massive hind legs and had two powerful forelegs. Its three-toed feet were each tipped with long curving claws. Its forepaws resembled human hands with four massive fingers and a thumb on each hand. The fingers ended in curved claws, but the thumb was tipped by a large spike. The skin looked thick and leathery, mottled green and brown. The dinosaur's shoulders were wide, and its thick neck narrowed toward the head, which was mostly jaw. Its dark, deep-set eyes blinked, and two nostrils were set in the tip of its nose. Ridges ran the length of its spine and down its tail which dragged behind.

What kind of dinosaur was this? Mariel wondered. Then she remembered a book she must still have. Looking out the window again to make sure the dinosaur was content eating grass, she took her flashlight down the hall to the bedroom she used for storage. In the closet were old toys and books from when the kids were little. When the grandkids visited she pulled out the old toys and watched them, recalling her own children, spinning the top, cranking the jack-in-the-box, and building with blocks.

But the grandkids were older now, and seldom visited. Mariel felt a twinge of sadness as she pushed the toys aside and dug into the piles of books. Near the bottom of the corner pile she found *The Children's Book of Dinosaurs*. Mariel took it back to her chair, nearly breathless from the exertion and her fear that the dinosaur might have left.

Outside, the dinosaur was even nearer now, still eating; it seemed to have an endless appetite for meadow salad. Mariel flipped through the pages trying to identify her dinosaur. She found pictures of the three-horned triceratops, the long-necked apatosaurus, and heavily armored stegosaurus. But none of them resembled hers. Mariel paused when she came to the allosaurus. The picture showed it walking on two legs, but its head was much bigger than her dinosaur, and it didn't have the thumb spikes. Mariel also rejected the tyrannosaurus. Its head was too big and its arms too small and shriveled looking. Besides, the allosaurus and the tyrannosaurus both had rows of long pointed teeth. Mariel's dinosaur had none of those.

She continued to flip through the pages, pausing frequently to look out her window. Toward the back of the book she found a picture of an iguanodon and knew instantly this was her dinosaur. When she read the part describing its flat teeth she smiled and said, "I knew it, I knew it. You're a vegetarian."

Mariel sat watching the dinosaur, very pleased with herself. The other tenants had gone, scared of an overgrown cow. But she had stayed and how glad she was! An iguanodon. What a nice name for a dinosaur.

The iguanodon ate its way closer to Mariel's building, clearly curious about the strange structure. She could see even more details now. Its skin was a mass of wrinkles and reminded her of the hide of an alligator, except thicker. When it stood to eat it rose eighteen feet into the air.

Later in the morning Mariel took a break. She didn't each much anymore. When there is no one to eat with, appetite diminishes. Mariel was in the kitchen buttering a muffin and wishing the microwave still worked. The kitchen window was too small for a good view, but Mariel kept glancing out. She was putting the muffin and juice on a tray when the view shocked her. The city was back.

Mariel leaned on the sink to stare out the kitchen window. The city was fuzzy and kind of shimmery, but it was there. Disbelieving, she wiped her glasses with the kitchen towel, but when she put them back on, the city was still there. But why was it so fuzzy? Then Mariel remembered the iguanodon and hurried back to the living room and boldly leaned out. It was there eating grass only a few steps from her building. Mariel looked into the distance. The city was there, but very fuzzy and growing dimmer. In a few minutes, as she watched, it faded away before her eyes.

She sat in her chair, confused. She was still trying to understand it all when she heard something hitting the side of her building. Mariel looked out her window to see the iguanodon right below her. It had crossed the last of the meadow and was now sniffing at the McGregors' window. She smiled with delight. It was so ugly it was beautiful. She kept back from the window, peeking over the edge, not wanting to scare it away.

The dinosaur's head ducked and rooted around and came up with a mouthful of flowers. Mariel laughed at the sight of the colorful meal, and then her face fell. It was eating her flower garden. The flowers were already half gone. Furious, she screamed out the window, "You get out of my garden! I mean it. Get back in the meadow where you belong."

The iguanodon turned up its big head, looking at Mariel. The intelligent eyes showed no fear, only curiosity. Mariel screamed at the dinosaur again, but it dropped its head defiantly and pulled up another third of the flower garden. Mariel pulled back, looking for something to drop on the dinosaur. She couldn't sacrifice anything precious from her past, so she grabbed a throw pillow, and dropped it. The pillow fell straight and bounced off the dinosaur's head, landing next to the garden. The dinosaur didn't flinch or move. It just sniffed the pillow and then turned away.

Now Mariel was even angrier. She had wasted one of her favorite pillows and hadn't even got the animal's attention. She needed something heavier. Mariel walked through her apartment looking for something unimportant. In the kitchen she picked up a cast-iron frying pan, then put it down. She didn't want to hurt the creature, only move it. For that reason, she also rejected the idea of canned goods, or jars. Finally Mariel found a five-pound bag of flour in her pantry and carried it to the window. Then she returned for a five-pound bag of sugar. As she leaned out the window, she saw the iguanodon still below her, ripping out more of her flowers. Mariel picked up the flour in both hands, leaned out the window, aimed carefully, and dropped it. This time the iguanodon reacted, flinching when the bag hit and then cringing when the flour cloud enveloped its head. It stood frozen, watching the flour fall. Mariel held her ground when it turned its flour-covered head up and stared at her, then stretched itself to its full height. When its mouth opened and it hissed at her, Mariel stepped back—it sounded like a giant snake and Mariel hated snakes. She screwed up her courage again and picked up the sugar. The dinosaur's head stretched up at her, its mouth opening to reveal double rows of grinding molars. When another hiss started, Mariel held the sugar out the window and let it go. The full bag fell down into the gaping mouth, hitting the thick tongue and bursting open, the sugar spilling over the tongue and pallet and down the throat. Suddenly, the dinosaur jerked its head back and snapped its mouth closed. Mariel could see surprise in its eyes and congratulated herself. Yes, surprise was another sign of intelligence.

The dinosaur shook its head, then opened and closed its mouth a few times, making a smacking sound. Mariel could see the tongue moving in and out. The dinosaur put its head down and sniffed at the garden and the pillow, and then its head came up and it sniffed at Mariel. As she watched, its mouth came open and it hissed again. The dinosaur seemed to want more sugar. Its hiss was turning into an "aaaahhh" sound. It was almost cute. Mariel went to her pantry and dug out the sugar she had opened yesterday for the sugar cookies the Ibarras were now enjoying. Back at the window, the dinosaur was looking around, but as soon as it saw Mariel its head went up, and its mouth came open, and it emitted a loud "aaaaah." Mariel turned the bag upside down and poured the sugar into the dinosaur's mouth. Swallowing, it snapped its jaws closed and began smacking its lips. It looked around again and then opened its mouth and made its sound.

"Oh my, what have I done?" Mariel asked herself. "I never thought you would have a sweet tooth."

Mariel didn't know what to do. She couldn't keep feeding it sugar, but she didn't want it to go away. She was about to get another bag of sugar when the sound of an air horn split the meadow. The dinosaur spun, its tail slamming into Mariel's building. She felt the vibrations. The horn sounded again, followed by the sounds of gunfire.

Now the iguanodon trotted back across the meadow, watching for the source of the sound as it went. Again the horn sounded. More gunfire popped. Mariel looked left and saw another dinosaur running on four legs in the distance, but it was too far away for her to see clearly. The iguanodon receded into the meadow.

Mariel sat back in her chair, feeling sad and lonely again. Her life had gone from dull routine to exciting and frightening and back to dull in a matter of hours. She rocked in her chair and looked out her window. She craved excitement like the dinosaur craved sugar. Reaching over, she turned on her radio and picked up her crocheting. She smiled to herself. Mr. Iguanodon would remember the sugar, and when its sweet tooth started calling it would come home to her, and she would be there.

---

19. SECURITY COUNCIL

If there is a common denominator among these strange falls from the sky, it is the disruption of electric power. Such failures have not been explained by engineers.

—Constance Jones, *Fortiology and the Modern Age*

Washington, D.C.
POSTQUILT: SUNDAY, 7:50 A.M. EST

The Security Council met in the basement of the White House in the Situation Room, brightly lit with banks of fluorescent bulbs built into the ceiling. Nick had seen operating rooms with less light. A table held doughnuts, coffee, and orange juice. The orange juice was untouched, but the coffee pots had already been refilled once. Nick helped himself to a cup.

Elizabeth's chair was next to the President's but pushed back so that she had to lean forward to whisper in his ear, which she did frequently. Nick did not have a regular seat, but Elizabeth motioned him to a chair near the far end of the rectangular table.

The meeting was about to begin when Dr. Gogh arrived. Under his arm he held a folder identical to the one Nick had received from Elizabeth. Expressions of surprise spread around the table, but Dr. Gogh sat down and immediately began poring over his notes. Nick noticed that Gogh's seat was closer to the President's than Nick's.

Because the situation was treated as a military emergency, the CIA, NSA, and defense intelligence reports were at the top of the agenda. Nick's report would be last.

After making sure the armed forces were on full alert and that all SAC bombers were either in the air or on the flight line, the President began taking more detailed reports. The various intelligence reports all focused on the state of readiness of the U.S. armed forces and threat assessment. The immediate concern was the loss of the ELF system—the network of buried transmission lines that made up the extreme low frequency transmission system, designed to keep the nation's fleet of nuclear submarines in contact with the military authorities. The loss of the system would mean dependence on less reliable and more vulnerable systems requiring the submarines to approach the surface to communicate via satellites. One of the naval aides estimated 30 percent of the ELF system was in terrain that was farmland and forest one minute, and arctic tundra the next. Like the others present, the President ignored the incredible changes in the terrain and focused on the relatively inconsequential loss of the communications system.

From all over the country had come reports of huge tracts of land disappearing and being replaced by other terrain, often radically different in climate. Nick new that part of New York had vanished, apparently replaced by grasslands, but other reports confirmed a huge sheet of ice had appeared in Iowa, a tropical jungle in Georgia, and a desert in Ohio. Massive floods were occurring in East St. Louis and other locales. The flooding gave Nick an idea, and he nursed it, temporarily oblivious to the meeting around him.

"No, Mr. President, we have no estimate of the extent of the loss although we have some reports that part of the system we thought was lost may still be intact but dysfunctional. Although the topography has changed, the ELF lines may remain under the surface. We are organizing teams to check on that now."

After Elizabeth leaned forward and whispered in the President's ear again, he asked, "Colonel, do you have an estimate of when the results of that assessment will be available? When you do, would you see that my chief of staff has that? Thank you."

President McIntyre had been twirling a twisted paper clip in his fingers but put it down to run his finger down the agenda. Before he could find his place Elizabeth leaned forward and pointed. The President seemed unconcerned about Elizabeth's blatant intrusion.

The head of the CIA gave the next report. Samuel Cannon was another of the President's old friends. He'd had a rough ride through the confirmation hearings. The Congress was leery of making a former auto executive head of the CIA, but the President had his man in the CIA, qualified or not.

"As I understand your reports, Sam, the events are random and not targeted at military installations. Both civilian and military targets have been hit?"

"That's right, sir," the CIA director confirmed. "Whatever the weapon is, it missed our strategic capabilities. Although we have lost communication with some facilities."

Lost communication or lost facilities? Nick wondered.

"Could the strategy be to take out civilian targets?" the President asked.

"If the targets were civilian then the weapon was just as inaccurate. We have unconfirmed reports of even nearly uninhabited areas being affected. Whatever it was, was powerful but not accurate."

Cannon said it with satisfaction, as if a weapon that could make a third of New York City disappear, never mind three million people, was no threat if it could not be aimed accurately.

Elizabeth leaned forward again and whispered in the President's ear.

"I know you don't believe the Russians are technologically capable of such an attack," McIntyre said, "but it seems even less likely that any other country would have the technology to do this. Is it possible something has escaped our scrutiny? What about the project they have going at the old Chernobyl site in the Ukraine?"

The CIA director and Elizabeth flinched at the mention of Chernobyl. It was clear the President had committed a breach of security just by saying the name.

"Sir," Cannon began cautiously, "I don't think this is the place to discuss the . . . ah . . . other matter."

"I'm not asking you to discuss it, I'm asking you to assess the possibility that it has something to do with what has happened to our country."

The CIA director looked at his assistant behind him, who leaned forward and whispered à la Elizabeth Hawthorne. While they whispered Nick noticed that Gogh was still engrossed in the reports.

"Our best information suggests there is no connection between this latest event and the other matter."

"Is it possible that one of our own projects could have inadvertently produced this effect? Possibly the fusion project, or maybe that muon particle projector . . . or what about the antimatter space drive? I always had doubts about that project," McIntyre said dryly.

"Mr. President! If you wish to discuss these projects we should dismiss all those with inadequate security clearance."

Nick found this discussion particularly interesting. Whatever these black bag projects were, spilling the beans had the CIA director white-faced with rage.

"Calm down, Sam, I'm more concerned with finding out about what has happened than I am about leaking information on pie-in-the-sky secret weapons. I only want to know whether these projects could in some way have produced the . . . the . . . whatever it is that happened today."

The President was visibly angry at the CIA director's resistance to his questions. Elizabeth whispered in the chief executive's ear again.

"Sam, we have dozens of highly classified projects going on right this minute. I mentioned only three. I am ordering that all of these projects be shut down immediately. You understand me? No testing, no operation, no experimentation. Until we know what has happened we're not going to risk having it happen again."

"But Mr. President—"

"No buts, Sam, shut everything down."

Samuel Cannon opened his mouth to speak but then closed it again. It was clear he was not through arguing, but he knew better then to pursue it in this setting. Then the President stunned the CIA director again.

"Have you considered any other sources for this effect?"

"Yes, sir, but the most technologically sophisticated countries are all friendly. We're less certain about the Russian Federation. We know the Baltic Union wouldn't have the sophistication, but the Federation retained most of the U.S.S.R.'s technological capabilities."

"I'm not talking about other countries. I'm talking about other species."

"Animals . . . like whales or something?"

"Sam, I'm talking about the possibility that this is the result of an act by an alien intelligence. Have you considered this? Why not?"

Gogh had stopped reading and was listening intently to the exchange between the President and the CIA director. From his face Nick couldn't tell where Gogh stood on the idea.

"Sir, there is no evidence to support such a theory." The CIA director looked embarrassed for the President.

"There is no evidence to reject such a theory either, isn't that right?"

Sam was nonplussed and began whispering back and forth with his aide.

"We will explore this possibility, sir, perhaps through the SETI people, or Bluebook."

Nick's eyes again went wide. He hadn't heard project Bluebook mentioned for more than a decade. Was it possible that the air force was still exploring UFO sightings? Nick began wishing he always had access to Security Council meetings, they were so full of juicy bits of information.

"Please do, Sam. I know this sounds crazy but I'm serious. I've always believed that somewhere in the universe there has to be another form of intelligent life. This may be the prelude to an invasion, or it could be some kind of friendly gesture. I know what you're thinking, Sam, but check it out anyway. All right, let's continue," the President said, running his finger back down the agenda. This time he found his place without Elizabeth's help.

The next report focused on the civilian situation and contained more reports of terrain changes. The biggest confirmed loss was part of New York City, but there were other losses in Florida, Texas, Maryland, and South Carolina. Most of these were known because of military base losses in the same area. Nick mentally added what he heard on the radio to the list. Civilian losses hadn't been estimated, but Nick guessed they were already in the tens of millions.

The last part of the civilian assessment dealt with communication problems. The country still had a communication network but now it resembled a piece of swiss cheese. Radio and television facilities had disappeared in some regions, while still others had been affected by an electromagnetic pulse. The EMP was weaker than that which accompanies a nuclear blast but was strong enough to damage some remaining facilities. Other holes in the communication network were caused by loss of satellites. What the country was left with was a shattered network where some cities still had local TV, radio, and phone service, while others had long-distance service, but no local.

Nick tried to picture morning in America. Some would be getting up to find their favorite network morning program absent from the airwaves but local news filling in. Others would be waking in the dark, using a portable radio trying to find someone still broadcasting. Everywhere people would be jamming the remaining phone systems to reach loved ones or to request emergency services—services that would be slow in coming.

The report ended with a promise to keep Elizabeth updated. This time when Elizabeth pointed to the President's agenda he looked up at Nick.

"Dr. Paulson, you seem to be next. Would you please give us your report." The President glanced at Gogh briefly before he turned to Nick, who felt like a second-string quarterback thrown into the big game.

"Thank you, Mr. President. First, this is not an attack on the United States." Then he added, as an afterthought, "Not an attack from another country anyway, I will have to consider the possibility of an extraterrestrial source." The President looked pleased that Nick had not thought of his theory, but the corners of Gogh's mouth turned up slightly.

"Nick," the President asked, "how do you know this isn't an attack?"

"This phenomenon has crossed borders," Nick said simply, "and I have seen reports that it may be a worldwide phenomenon. It seems illogical that someone with hostile intent would release a weapon that seems to act indiscriminantly."

The President turned and gave the CIA director an icy stare.

"That right, Sam? I didn't hear anything about this happening in other countries in your report."

"I dealt with only confirmed reports. We have only unconfirmed reports from overseas . . . there was some speculation that the overseas phenomena might have been a smoke screen—"

"That's enough," McIntyre said sternly, cutting the CIA director off. The President's jaw was set and his eyes were cold. "Go on, Dr. Paulson."

"Second, there is no technological or theoretical basis for producing such phenomena."

"Dr. Paulson . . . Nick . . . saying that what has happened couldn't happen isn't particularly useful."

"That's not what I am saying, sir. I am suggesting that this may be a natural phenomenon."

The President was about to speak again when Gogh interrupted. "Natural? There is nothing natural about disappearing cities, and topographical disruption. There is no record of any similar events ever recorded."

"I know it hasn't happened in the modern era, but there are ancient records that suggest something similar. Floods, lost continents, missing peoples, a number of events that are not dissimilar."

Gogh was giving Nick a hard stare, but the President seemed genuinely interested in Nick's theory, so Nick switched into his "explain it to the public" mode. "We've been on this planet for only a tiny slice of geological time. If you think of the life of this planet in terms of a twenty-four-hour clock, then the dinosaurs appeared about an hour ago and people have been here for only the last few seconds. There is over twenty-three hours of clock we are still trying to understand. This could have happened many times before, but we would be unaware of it."

"There would be geologic, or fossil records, of such an event," Gogh insisted.

"There might be such evidence, but without a disciplinary matrix that includes time displacement as part of the theoretical basis such evidence would be explained in terms of existing theory, or dismissed as a theoretical anomaly. One example that comes to mind is the finding of human footprints in the same rock that carries dinosaur footprints. We have assumed that the footprints could not be human because humans and dinosaurs did not exist in the same era. Instead of trying to understand how humans and dinosaurs might have ended up together, we hypothesize an unknown dinosaur that makes a human-looking footprint."

"There was such a dinosaur," Gogh interrupted.

"There was a dinosaur that made a footprint that did resemble a human's, yes. But to explain the human-looking footprint found in the riverbed rock, you have to add erosion. Enough erosion to remove the foreclaws."

"It is a reasonable hypothesis," Gogh persisted.

"Reasonable, yes, but Occam's razor tells us to take the simplest explanation, and that is that those are human footprints."

"It's not simpler at all. Putting humans and dinosaurs together violates a century of research supporting the theory of evolution."

"Not if time displacement had occurred. Some dinosaurs could have been displaced and for a short time coexisted with humans."

While Nick was talking, Elizabeth whispered in the President's ear. This time he waved his hand at her in dismissal.

"Dr. Paulson, you mentioned time displacement," the President said. "What is it you are talking about?"

Nick was surprised by the question. It was clear to him what had happened because he had a theory that allowed him to organize the bits and pieces of evidence. But the meeting's various reports dealt with the impact, not the event.

"Yes, sir. I believe that the best way to describe the situation is time displacement. Sections of our present have been replaced by sections of the past. Think about the reports: sections of land suddenly snow covered, deserts, lava flows, tundra, jungle—all could be from our past."

"But snow is certainly common enough even in this age, and lava, and desert. I see nothing that requires us to assume any kind of time disruption. Why not topographical displacement?"

"There are also reports of dinosaurs."

Everyone at the table straightened up and began murmuring. Nick looked around the table. All the officials were talking to their aides, or one another about the dinosaurs.

The President spoke first. "I've seen no reports of dinosaurs.

Where are there reports of dinosaurs, Elizabeth? Sam? What's this about dinosaurs?"

"I don't know where Dr. Paulson got that, Mr. President," Cannon said. Then he resumed whispering with his aide.

Everyone turned to Nick. Nick decided not to mention the radio talk show.

"It is an unconfirmed report, sir, but it would be consistent with time displacement. I would like to pursue it further."

"Dinosaurs," the President mused, "imagine that. Dinosaurs." Elizabeth whispered in his ear again and he roused himself from his reverie.

"Dr. Paulson, please pursue your theory, and somebody find out about those dinosaurs! Sam, I want to see even the unconfirmed reports. Elizabeth will arrange the next meeting. In the meantime I would like all of you to continue to gather as much information as possible and begin to formulate a plan to deal with what has happened."

"Deal with it, sir?" Nick asked in surprise.

"Yes. I want a plan to reverse what has happened."

The President tossed his twisted paper clip onto the table and it skittered toward Nick, who collapsed back into his seat, expelling his breath. The President had seen too many bad science-fiction movies. This wasn't some invasion from outer space where some generic "scientist" would create a deus ex machina to make everything right again. This was the real world, even with time, space, and the entire universe altered.

Nick sat at the table long after the others had left, thinking about his own theory. If he was right, it was a new world now. Would the old rules of civilization apply in a crazy quilt world of the ancient and the modern? The dinosaurs had ruled their world as surely as humans did theirs. What would happen when they met? What was happening?

20. Into the Forest

I found my sister, Wilhemina, burned to death in her bed in our home in Whitley Bay. The bedclothes were unscorched and there were no signs of fire anywhere else in the house. The police suspect me, but only the devil himself could burn a person to charcoal and not set the bed on fire.

—Margaret Dewar, March 22, 1908

The Newtonian, Einsteinian, and quantum views each approached the universe in a unique way, but all agree that human needs, and wants, are not considered as the laws of physics are played out. So it was that as the effect wrought havoc across the planet, it did so remorselessly. Some children staying with grandparents or friends were whisked away, leaving parents with no clue where to look, and with no hope. Fathers and mothers away on business trips never returned, or had nothing to return to. Parents separated because of strife, could never reconcile—too much time and space between them. People out late found no home to return to, and those at home waited in vain for loved ones to return.

But as ruthless as the effect was with human feelings, it was almost gentle in its dealings with the physical. No person or animal was halved or quartered by the effect, nor was a single finger or limb lost. Time, space, and matter, three forms of the same force, interact, so that the effect wrapped around each cell of each organism. Plants were removed in their entirety, taking even capillary roots. People and animals were taken whole too, existing from then on only in the memories of the survivors.

Inorganic matter was treated as gently, the effect respecting continuity and wholeness. Cars along the effect lines were taken, but towed trailers or boats were left. Streets ended in neat lines, as if the road had been broken off, but at the break the gravel making up the asphalt was still whole. Brick and wooden structures fared as well, with whole bricks, and whole boards gone, but no severed boards or smashed blocks. Most structures disappeared intact, roof to subbasements, but in some cases huge segments were taken from walls or foundation, and the remaining building collapsed.

As amazing as the effect was, it was not all powerful. The effect could not penetrate deep into the earth, and vessels or structures deep under water escaped. Instead the replacing land was stitched together with the new topography according to some unfathomable physical laws. Grasslands layered over flat surfaces evenly, but on hilly or rocky terrain, it tore or fit loosely, like a rumpled throw rug. Forests that appeared fared the worst, with many trees poorly rooted. Forests deposited on steep surfaces often collapsed like dominoes, the trees bringing one another down. Perhaps the shallow-rooted sequoias fared best, settling into their new home with dignity and majesty.

East of Newberg, Oregon
POSTQUILT: SUNDAY, 6:30 A.M. PST

Cubby and John were sitting in the van waiting for Ripman to return. John was fiddling with the radio, but he wasn't picking up anything he could make out, and he certainly wasn't picking up any of the Portland stations. Cubby was mumbling to himself, with his eyes closed and his head bowed. John guessed he was praying—like he'd been ever since Ripman took off down the hill toward Newberg. John hoped Ripman would return soon. Everything was clearer when Ripman was around. "Of course there hadn't been a second coming of Jesus-what's-his-name. This is just some kind of avalanche, or volcanic eruption," he would say with such certainty that John would believe him. John needed to believe him.

John often found himself between Cubby, the immovable rock, and Ripman, the irresistible force, and not only on metaphysical matters. Their confidence extended to all their decisions, whether it was picking a road to take, or classes to fill in their schedule. John envied their sureness and resented being blown about. Still, he comforted himself knowing that somehow he was the glue that held the threesome together. Cubby and Ripman never went anywhere without him.

John had heard his dad talk about his patients often enough

to know Cubby was experiencing an anxiety attack. Cubby was severely depressed, and scared. He was breathing rapidly and sweating, his only sounds were rapidly mumbled prayers for forgiveness. He wouldn't respond to John and was losing touch with the world around him, drifting into a place no one would be able to reach him. John was scared too, but not immobilized by it like Cubby, who had convinced himself of the worst. John still had hope, or its cousin, doubt.

Now he walked down the road toward town, to get away from Cubby's incessant praying—there was something particularly pitiful when a guy as big as Cubby was so terrified.

It was nearly dawn when John spotted Ripman coming up the road, carrying a big load. He stopped twice on his way up the hill. John met him part way, and helped him. Ripman had three of everything—stuffed packs, bows, quivers of arrows, and canteens.

"Where did you get all this, Ripman? You stole it, didn't you?"

"I midnight requisitioned it from the sporting goods store."

"Jeez, guns would have been better, Ripman."

"You don't run out of ammunition with a bow. Besides, the guns were chained up. How's Cubby doing?"

"About the same, but at least he's not getting any worse. I think that's a good sign."

"Don't you know? Your dad's a shrink, ya know."

"Up yours, Ripman! I'm not my dad."

Ripman ignored him and walked over to Cubby, dropping his share of the booty on the ground. "All right, Cubby, it will be light soon. I'm going to prove to you that this isn't the second coming and there hasn't been any rapture."

Cubby stopped mumbling his prayers and looked up at Ripman, eyes puffy, and tear streaks on his face.

"How are you going to prove it, Ripman? It couldn't be anything else," he said with resignation.

"First of all, Newberg is still full of people. They're in there digging through the wreckage."

"That only proves how ignorant you are, Ripman. God isn't going to take sinners in the rapture, only the followers of Christ. Of course there will still be people around, the sinners. It's my fault, I let you guys down. I knew the path to follow and I didn't even try to follow it myself, let alone show you two. Now we've got to face the tribulation."

Ripman blew out a deep breath. "Cubby, use your head. It's the road that disappeared, not the people."

Cubby looked back at the forest, confusion edging out a little of the fear. Ripman saw the opening and pressed on.

"I'm not saying I believe in this rapture stuff, but if I did I don't think God would want whores and drunks."

"Of course God would want them! Ripman, you really don't know anything about Christianity at all. God wants anyone who repents, confesses their sin, and asks Jesus into their hearts."

"Cubby, do you remember that strip joint we passed on the way here? It had a big sign outside that said NUDE-GIRLS-NUDE. There were pickup trucks parked all around it. Would God take those people? If they were there, they hadn't repented right?"

"No . . . I wouldn't think so."

"Damn right, God wouldn't want them. So let's go see. It's only a few miles from here. If the strip joint's gone then I'm right and you have to shut up about this rapture crapola."

John could see hope in Cubby's face, and some of the tough look started to come back. Hiking into the forest to the strip joint was something to do, and John was pretty sure his dad would approve of occupation therapy. Cubby was already drawing strength from the idea.

Ripman had them divide up the supplies. They all ended up with portions of energy bars and trail mix. Everyone had a hunting knife and sheath, John carried a snake bite kit, and Ripman had a first aid kit. Everyone got a compass, a space blanket, disposable flashlight, and matches. The light from the sun wasn't filtering to the floor of the forest yet, so they spent time practicing with the bows. John had never used a bow like the one stolen by Ripman. As a kid, he'd learned the shooting basics with a fiberglass bow, but these new ones had pulleys on each end, and the string wound back and forth, making three places to notch your arrow.

John wasn't surprised to find that Ripman was proficient with his bow. He showed John and Cubby how to hold the bows, and shoot. The arrows were definitely for hunting, with wicked-looking steel triangles for heads. Ripman pulled his bow back, aimed at a piece of cardboard along the road forty feet away, and shot the arrow smack into the target. John went next and found pulling this bow harder than his old fiberglass one.

"Come on, you wuss," Ripman prodded.

John's arm was shaking, and he still hadn't pulled the bowstring all the way back to his ear. Suddenly his arm snapped the rest of the way back, and he saw Ripman smiling.

"Got easy all of a sudden, didn't it? That's why they have the pulleys, so you can hold the arrow back longer. It lets you wait for the best shot."

John aimed carefully and then let the arrow fly. It disappeared into the grass ten feet short of the cardboard. Cubby didn't have any trouble pulling his string back but his arrow flew way high and buried itself into the hill. They each tried a few more shots, but Cubby and John didn't get better.

The light from the rising sun was sending shafts through the trees when they started into the forest. The beams interwove with the trees creating a fabric of light and wood. Ripman went first, using his hunting knife like a machete, but the undergrowth was sparse and he soon put the knife away. A variety of ferns stood two to four feet in the air, and some clumps of grasses grew head high. The ground felt soft and mushy, as if they were walking through mulch. Occasionally they ran into tall grasses that were stiffer and sharp edged, like pampas grass. They quickly learned to go around these. The trees were all of one type, with coarse fibrous bark. Many were big enough to drive a car through. Ripman stopped by one and cut the bark with his knife.

"Look here, Cubby. This is nothing but a redwood tree, I've seen them in California. Nothing supernatural here."

"Yeah? How did it get to Oregon?"

Ripman ignored Cubby and led off again. John trailed behind Cubby, wishing Ripman had an answer to Cubby's question. John had never heard of giant redwoods in Oregon. As he set a fast pace up the hill, Ripman soon had them puffing with the exertion. Ripman reached the top of the hill well ahead of Cubby and John, and when they caught up, Ripman was kneeling and looking up into the trees.

"Get down you guys, and be quiet."

Cubby and John squatted down next to Ripman. "What are

we being quiet for?" John asked, still gasping from exertion.

"Look around. Do you see them?"

John and Cubby looked around, first at the ground, and then following Ripman's gaze. Cubby slowly lifted his arm and pointed into the tree in front of them. About halfway up, perched on a limb, was a lizard—but like none John had ever seen. It was reddish brown on top and dusky green on the bottom, so it blended in with the tree limb. It had long back legs and shorter front legs, and around its head was a bony flared collar, with short spines protruding from the top. Most striking of all was its size. It was three feet long. John suddenly realized that another similar lizard sat on the branch above the first. As John looked through the trees around them, he realized they were filled with the three-footers, all staring at them.

Ripman leaned in front of the others and whispered, "Toto, I don't think we're in Kansas anymore."

The lizards sat motionless in the trees, seeming confident they were out of reach of the three strange creatures below. The boys sat motionless, staring back, John because he was frozen in fear. Finally the lizard on the lowest branch skittered higher up followed by others on the low branches. That movement broke the stalemate, and Ripman slowly led them off through the trees. Lizards slithered through the branches above them as they walked. No one talked until they were sure the trees were free of lizards.

"Jeez, I've never seen a lizard that size before," John said. "Man, where did they come from?"

Cubby looked like he was going to answer the question, but Ripman shut him up with a glare.

"I don't know, but let's enjoy it while we can," Ripman said.

John watched Ripman's back moving into the lead again, followed by Cubby. He knew Ripman was actually enjoying this. With every step deeper into the forest Ripman seemed more confident, as if he belonged there. But Cubby was badly shaken. He still wasn't saying much, and the panic attack had changed the way John and Ripman thought of him. Silence, always a part of Cubby's personality, had now become a symptom of his vulnerability.

The experience with the lizards sensitized John to his surroundings. Movements, shadows, and noises he had missed before were now acutely important. He began to notice soft rustlings in the grasses, and quick movements in the shadows.

Shortly they came to a fallen tree, its trunk nursing saplings all along its length. Ferns covered the spots between the tree sprouts. Ripman used the stumps of broken branches to climb to the top. Suddenly, something came shooting out from under the tree, running across John's foot and disappearing into a patch of ferns behind him. John yelped and jumped back, tripping and falling to the forest floor.

"What was that?"

"I saw it," Cubby said, speaking with confidence for the first time since they stepped into the forest. "It looked like a weasle but it had gigantic eyes."

"The Bible say anything about weasles with big eyes?" Ripman asked, mockingly.

Cubby scowled, but then followed Ripman over the log. John came behind cautiously, checking the placement of each foot before he put it down. After cresting the hill, they made a slow descent and then a long level trek. Occasionally they came to a section where the trees had fallen or leaned precariously, their roots exposed. In one stretch John could see a whole hillside was covered with freshly fallen trees. It was a crazy quilt forest.

John found the hiking easier when he put his mind into flowing consciousness. One portion of his mind took over the routine task of walking while the higher cerebral matter played with ideas, allowing him to keep up with Ripman and Cubby.

The sun was high overhead when Ripman stopped, dropped his pack and quiver, and sat down, leaning against a branch from a fallen tree. "Well, Cubby? You see any strip joint?"

John looked around. They were standing in a sparse stand of trees no different from a hundred other spots they had walked through. John could not imagine why Ripman thought this was the spot where the bar with the nude girls had been. Cubby looked around trying to confirm their location.

"What makes you think this is the right spot?" John asked.

Ripman started to reply, but Cubby cut him off. "If it isn't this spot, then we're past it."

Again John marveled at their certainty.

"Was I right, Cubby, or what? You see any sinners around

here? You see any topless joint? You think maybe heaven was getting a little boring so God decided to add nude dancing girls?"

Cubby looked lost in thought. "Maybe, Ripman, maybe. But if this isn't the rapture, then what is it?"

Ripman didn't have an answer. Instead he muttered "I told you so" and sat down with his pack in his lap. John broke out some of his trail mix and rested on fern fronds. What had happened? The tornado he could understand. Tornados had happened before, maybe not in Oregon, but they were common enough. There was even a part of the Midwest they named tornado alley. But what about this weird forest? Where did it come from and what happened to the nude girls? What happened to the radio stations? Could this forest go all the way to Portland? Maybe the radio stations weren't broadcasting because they weren't there anymore. And if they were gone what about John's house? What about his parents? Cubby interrupted John's thoughts by standing up and putting on his pack.

"Where you going?" Ripman asked.

"This answers one question," Cubby said, gesturing at the forest around him. "But now I've got to find my parents."

John felt the same as Cubby. John had to know whether he had a home and what had happened to his parents. He just wasn't sure how to go about it.

"Are you going to walk, Cubby?" John asked. "Which way?"

"That way," Cubby said nodding in the direction they had been going.

"Why not head back to the van and try to drive around? If the road is clear we could head out the Wilsonville Highway and try to come in on I-5."

"There was a lot of debris on that highway. I bet it takes two days to clear it. And they'll clear Highway 99 before they work on some back road to Wilsonville. I can walk the rest of the way to Portland before then. Besides, I could break out of this over the next hill and hitchhike the rest of the way—"

"Cubby, for all you know this forest could run all the way to Boston," Ripman interrupted. "Hey, we found the spot where the topless joint was, but that doesn't mean we can find your house."

Cubby thought for a minute and then squatted down. He

ripped some of the grass and ferns out of the ground and cleared a patch of dirt. Then he drew in it with the tip of his knife.

"I can't pinpoint my house too well, but I can my dad's church."

Cubby drew three circles on the ground and a couple of squiggly lines.

"We know the hills and valleys seem to be the same, even though the trees and stuff are all different. We don't know about rivers though. These are the hills I can see from the church. This one's Rocky Butte, this one is Mt. Tabor, and this one is that one that has all the cemeteries on it. My dad's church is right here on this hill." Cubby stuck the knife in a spot just behind two of the hills. "This is the Willamette River and this is the Columbia. After I come down out of the West Hills and drop into the valley, all I need to do is cross the Willamette. Then if I hit the Columbia I'll know I've gone too far east and need to turn south."

Ripman had been studying the map.

"Don't forget the Clackamas and that other river out here," Ripman said adding more squiggly lines. Ripman started arguing over topographical details, but finally they turned to John.

"You going with him?" Ripman asked.

"I've got to find my parents too."

"If I was you, John, I'd head to that cabin your parents have at the coast. They'll look there for you eventually. Besides," he said, his voice softening, "if your parents are in the same place as the nude girls, then you are going to need that cabin. If it stays empty some survivalist is going to occupy it and you won't have a chance of getting him out."

John felt stung. His parents couldn't be gone like the nude dancers, could they? Sure, Ripman was right about the beach house. There was food there, and money hidden away. Still, Cubby was right too. This forest could end a few yards away, and he could hitchhike home by dinnertime. Hitching to the coast would probably take him all night.

"This can't go on much farther, Ripman." John said it without conviction and then added, "I'm going with Cubby."

"Well then I might as well keep you wusses company."

Ripman didn't say anything about finding his father, but

John noticed Ripman had marked his house on the map he and Cubby made.

It was late morning when they started out again, and a warm autumn day. One by one they took off their jackets and tied them around their waists. The forest thinned as they walked and they began passing through small natural meadows. Leafy deciduous trees joined the giant redwoods. John recognized poplars and some trees hung with fruit that looked like figs. There were no ferns in the meadows, and the grass was knee high.

Ripman stopped in a stand of poplars, waved his hand for silence, then unslung his bow and notched an arrow. John and Cubby imitated him clumsily. Ripman whispered to them without taking his eyes off the forest ahead of them.

"Something ran by . . . there."

John looked in the direction Ripman indicated but saw nothing except forest. Suddenly something John had never seen before ran through the trees and disappeared. It was five or six feet high and ran on large black legs, holding its slender tail straight out behind. It had long slim arms in the front and a snakelike neck that ended in a small head. Large yellow eyes were set just above the mouth.

"Did you see—" John stammered.

"Yeah," Ripman replied. "Looked like a plucked ostrich."

Two more ran by, glancing at them. The tails and the necks were striped with wide bands of greenish yellow alternating with grayish greens.

"Come on, let's follow them." Ripman's voice overflowed with excitement.

Ripman led off. John saw the doubt on Cubby's face, but he shrugged his shoulders and started after Ripman.

The boys emerged in a meadow and cut across it, although the animals were out of sight. They had nearly reached the other side when they heard a commotion behind them. Turning to look, they suddenly saw an animal burst out of the forest and come running toward them, bent over and speeding on two powerful legs like the plucked ostriches they had just seen. But this animal was taller and bulkier. Its neck was shorter and thicker and its head larger, with a ducklike bill for a mouth.

Covered with slick-looking skin, with a long tail, it was undoubtedly a dinosaur.

John was staring in disbelief when he felt Cubby jerking on his pack, screaming for John to run. Turning, he started following Cubby's retreating back, his legs pumping away. He felt his heart come up to speed and his breathing quickened and deepened, and now his fear turned quickly to panic. His legs pounded recklessly over the uneven surface of the meadow and drove him into the forest. He jumped grass clumps and ferns that he couldn't run over and followed Cubby's charge even when it led through razor grass.

When John realized he had reached his top speed he glanced over his shoulder. The dinosaur was gaining on him. It wasn't the huge monster that he had expected, but it was big enough to make a meal of him. John's heart was pounding faster than it ever had before, his lungs burned, and his legs were weakening. To his horror John realized that they were now heading up a hill. He could see the ground dropping away to his right. He knew the hill would slow him and tire him more quickly.

A movement down the hill caught his attention. Ripman was weaving his way through the trees. For some reason Cubby had continued up the hill when Ripman headed down, and John had blindly followed Cubby. John, forgetting all loyalty, glanced over his shoulder again in the hope that the dinosaur had followed Ripman.

When John looked back the dinosaur was still behind him, and the head would be within snapping distance very soon. He saw something else. There was a second dinosaur, and this one was huge, with a mouth big enough to bite him in half with its double rows of pointed teeth.

At last John had a plan. He used the remainder of his energy to push up so that Cubby could see him in his peripheral vision. Then when he spotted a large clump of grass a few feet to the left, he headed toward it, noticing Cubby's head jerk in his direction when he broke. Six feet from the grass John dove headfirst, sliding to a stop in the middle of the clump. He pulled his knees up to his chest and waited. As he expected, the smaller dinosaur ran past without stopping. The ground began rumbling then, and the monster that had been following them charged past. Even in the clump of grass John could see the head of the dinosaur towering above him.

He lay in the grass a long time. Slowly his heart rate dropped and he was able to bring his breathing under control. As his adrenalin cleared from his bloodstream, he began to feel the grass cuts on his arms, neck, and face. Before long he risked stepping out. He stood still, listening hard but could hear nothing. His first impulse was to run back the way they had come. He wanted to run back and find Ripman. But what had happened to Cubby?

John started in the direction the dinosaurs had run. It was an easy path to follow, since the big one had flattened everything it stepped on. After a few yards John began to whisper Cubby's name so he could honestly tell Ripman "I searched for Cubby but couldn't find him." Still, John continued looking, to convince himself that he *had* done a reasonable search. He was about to turn back when he heard Cubby's voice, no longer tentative but loud and clear. "Over here, John."

Cubby was sitting on a log unlacing his shoe. Rivulets of red ran down his arms and face. Occasionally he wiped away some of the blood from his face. Overwhelmed by relief, John brightened. "Man, I'm glad to see you. How did you get away?"

"Did the same thing you did. I dove behind this log and waited. Did you see the size of that monster chasing the little one? That little one wasn't after us, it was trying to save itself."

"Come on, Cubby, those things might come back. We've got to get out of here."

"Wait."

John watched Cubby untie his shoe and dump rocks out.

"What's the point of that? Do you really think you could outrun that big one if it decided to make a snack out of you?"

"John, I don't have to outrun him, I only have to outrun you."

John thought briefly, then laughed out loud.

21. Iguanodon

The term dinosaur means "terrible lizard," and terrible they would have seemed had mankind had the misfortune to evolve simultaneously. The naked ape would not have survived to develop into modern man under the onslaught of the giant carnivores.

—Dr. Robert Hampton, *Kingdom of the Dinosaurs*

New York City
PostQuilt: Sunday, 9:37 a.m. EST

The day Mariel spent waiting for the iguanodon to return was a day like no other—a constant parade of surprises. The iguanodon didn't appear, but other dinosaurs did. Mariel sat with her book identifying them as best she could, cursing her eyes and herself for giving away Phillip's binoculars.

A couple of hours after the iguanodon left, she thought the wind had come up because large sections of grass moved simultaneously. But as the movement came closer, she began to see small heads poke up and down quickly. Mariel never got a good count, but she estimated two dozen of the little dinosaurs. They sprinted forward and back in the grass like seabirds running from ocean waves, but Mariel never got enough of a look to identify them. Soon the bobbing heads vanished.

Mariel fell asleep late in the morning, exhausted from the previous night. When she woke it was with a start, to another blast from that air horn. She looked out the window in time to see three big-headed dinosaurs running through the grass, leaning forward on two legs with their tails held straight out behind them. The three ran in formation with one in the front and the other two behind on either side, in a triangle. When they disappeared into the distance quickly, Mariel chided herself for her weakness in falling asleep. Flipping through her dinosaur book again, now familiar with the pages, she found their picture right away. They were deinonychus. The book described them as hunters, probably in packs, and pictured them around the body of a much larger dinosaur, with blood on their huge jaws and with hunks of red meat hanging from their mouths. It made Mariel glad these carnivorous dinosaurs had been chased away, and she worried the deinonychus might attack her friend.

Though she munched on crackers and drank fruit juice, she was about asleep again when she heard someone turning her doorknob. Instantly she was awake. She watched the knob turn back and forth, and then she heard voices in the hall. Mariel knew friends would have knocked first, so she yelled to let them know the apartment wasn't empty.

"Get away from my door! I've got a gun and I know how to use it." She never heard the voices again and her doorknob didn't move after that.

Later she thought she heard the sound of splintering wood somewhere. Now, she suspected thieves were loose in her building but knew she was too old to do anything about it alone. So she sat by the window watching for the dinosaur with the sweet tooth to come back.

A new dinosaur appeared after noon, a funny-looking, dome-headed dinosaur with small spikes sticking up on its snout and ugly green bumps along the back of its head. It ate its way through the meadow, its rounded head coming up frequently to sniff the air and scan the horizon. This dinosaur was nothing like the iguanodon. It was much smaller and obviously much less intelligent. Mariel could tell because it didn't seem surprised by the building—too dumb to know her building wasn't some big rock or cliff. No, this Dome-head had no curiosity like her dinosaur. Dome-head worked through the meadow along the length of Mariel's building, and shortly after it disappeared from her view she heard the sound of the air horn plus car horns. A minute later Mariel saw Dome-head emerge and then disappear into the trees in the distance. Flipping through the pages of her book again, Mariel saw similar dinosaurs but only one with spikes on its nose. She had trouble pronouncing the name, pachycephalosaurus, but didn't care. It was an ugly, dumb dinosaur anyway.

It was midafternoon when Mariel's iguanodon reappeared. He was grazing through the clearing again, but at a much faster rate. Every time he stopped to eat he reared up on his hind legs and surveyed the surroundings, watchful for danger. Mariel hoped the deinonychus were well gone.

Soon the iguanodon forgot all about the grass and fixated his eyes on the window where Mariel stood. The dinosaur swung his head looking left and right. When he was sure there were no lurking predators, he lifted his head and opened his mouth wide making a low "aaaaah" sound. When the sound died, Mariel dropped a paper bag of sugar into his mouth, which immediately snapped shut.

Now the beast made loud smacking sounds and licked his lips. Opening his mouth he started "aaaahing" again. Once more she dropped a bag of sugar into his mouth. When the explosion of sweet faded, the dinosaur raised his head and opened his mouth a third time. Mariel scolded him.

"Two is all you get. Now you get back out there and eat some more of that grass. You'll get sick if you eat nothing but sugar." She had raised three children and knew better than to give in. This dinosaur had to learn that two treats was all and that was final.

The dinosaur stood outside her window "aaaahing" over and over again. But Mariel held firm, and finally the dinosaur dropped his head and walked back into the meadow toward the distant treeline. Smiling, Mariel prepared two more bags of sugar and put them by the window, then picked up her crocheting and waited.

Toward dusk, her iguanodon came back.

This time he wasn't wasting any time eating grass. He walked through the meadow on his two rear legs, headed straight for Mrs. Weatherby's window, lifting his head and "aaahing." Mariel waited again for quiet and then dropped the sugar bomb into the dinosaur's gaping mouth. After a second helping the dinosaur put his head down, turned away, and walked out into the meadow.

"I knew you were smart, Mr. Iguanodon."

Mariel beamed. Back in the kitchen she filled two more paper bags with sugar. She was running low, but it wouldn't be safe to go to a store for more. If her neighbors were home she could borrow some sugar. Then Mariel remembered the splintering wood. "Well, I guess it wouldn't exactly be stealing," she said to herself, and then started down the hall to do her shopping.

---

22. LITTLE ONES

Near Yorkshire, England, eighty feet above the valley floor, we found a cave. If the remains in that cave were to be believed, then reindeer, hippopotamus, lions, and grizzly bear all lived together once in England. What a strange England that would have been.

—William Buckland, 1823

North of Bend, Oregon
POSTQUILT: SUNDAY, 9:45 A.M. PST

Petra and Colter met the rest of the group in Bend and they traveled north in Dr. Coombs's RV, toward Warm Springs. Petra tried to contact Mrs. Wayne and Ernie, but the airwaves were filled with the curious and the panicky. In the back, Colter drifted in and out of sleep, still hung over from the night before.

The road to Warm Springs was clogged with confused travelers, so Dr. Coombs backtracked and found a dirt road angling across the Indian reservation. They drove through arid lands, treeless and covered with sagebrush. Small houses in poor repair sprinkled the low hills. Barbed wire lined the road, the fence held up by a variety of wooden posts. Most posts were well-weathered split rails, but a bewildering variety of replacement posts mingled with the originals. Metal posts were most common, but also axe handles, an oar, a two-by-four, some four-by-fours, and what looked to be the legs of chairs could be seen. Horses gazed near some fences, but there were no cows or sheep.

The dirt road ended in a branch. Dr. Piltcher pointed left and they followed the ruts that led north. Shortly, the road declined sharply, leading to a valley. Dr. Coombs braked to a jolting stop as their mouths fell open in surprise.

They had expected something to happen. They had predicted it—Zorastrus had predicted it, but even he wasn't specific about what would happen. The road zigzagged down the hill and then straight into the valley below, which was bisected by a green line. On one side was the arid land they had been driving through. On the other side was a lush green landscape, thick with bushes and undergrowth. In the distance they could see a lake, and behind that a forest. They sat in silence, trying to understand what they were seeing. Only Colter seemed unimpressed.

"Let's get going, it looks cool down there," Colter said impatiently.

Dr. Piltcher, sitting in the front passenger seat, turned to look at Colter, irritation in his voice.

"Colter, doesn't it strike you as strange that this . . . this tropical forest is sitting here in the middle of this desert?"

"I dunno. Maybe they irrigate."

Dr. Piltcher rolled his eyes and then turned back to face the front, speaking over his shoulder as he did. "They irrigate crops, not jungle. Let's get closer, George."

Dr. Coombs drove down the zigzag road toward the scene below, Petra and Colter bouncing from side to side in the back of the RV. Suddenly Petra cried out.

"Look! There by the lake. Something's moving out there. Something big."

"I don't see it, Petra. Do you, George?"

"No, I'm watching the road."

"I saw it, Dr. Piltcher," Colter cut in.

Dr. Piltcher was exasperated. "And what did *you* see, Colter?"

"It was big, like Petra said. I think it was a tractor. Maybe this is an irrigated farm."

Dr. Piltcher's only answer was a disgusted snort. At the end of the ruts, they found themselves facing a small meadow against a wall of lush greenery seven to nine feet in height, concealing the lake and forest. Dr. Coombs slowly drove up onto the grass to park the RV.

"Petra, try the radio again," Dr. Piltcher ordered.

As she began calling Mrs. Wayne and Ernie, her voice was flat, devoid of hope. She wasn't surprised that no one answered.

Now the others climbed out and walked into the meadow. Dr. Coombs and Dr. Piltcher began examining the grasses and ferns.

"Extraordinary," Dr. Piltcher muttered over and over.

"Exactly so," concurred Dr. Coombs.

The noise of a stream distracted them and they turned to see Colter urinating into the grass. Dr. Piltcher began to stomp toward him, but Dr. Coombs grabbed his arm and began pointing out more of his observations of the flora, temporarily subduing his friend. Petra came out of the RV and shook her head before anyone could ask about contact. Suddenly Colter yelled, "Hey you, come here!"

The others turned to see Colter running in circles through the tall grass, yelling and chasing something through the meadow. Occasionally he stopped abruptly and leaned down with his arms outstretched. Petra began running toward him, though Dr. Piltcher called after her to wait. Dr. Coombs trailed after her, his well-conditioned body carrying him like a younger man as Dr. Piltcher stumbled along behind. Colter bent down again, jerked up and sprinted ahead, and then he dove, disappearing in the grass as a piglike squeal erupted. Then Colter came up on one knee, and then stood holding a squirming animal none of them had ever seen before.

It was eighteen inches in length, its skin a bright green. Colter held it by its thick tail—which was a third of its length—and its thick neck. Its head was a little larger than the neck, and the face resembled a parrot, with a beak that curved over the lower jaw. The eyes on either side of the head were covered with thick lids. Its two oversized back legs contrasted with two thin front ones. The animal was using its clawed front feet on Colter's hand, and from Colter's reaction the claws were sharp.

The others jogged up to Colter, staring openmouthed.

"What is that?" Petra asked.

"It's an ornithopod," said Dr. Coombs, his voice bubbling with excitement.

"Psittacosaurus, I believe," Dr. Piltcher added, just as excited. "But the color seems wrong. I wouldn't have expected it to be this bright green."

"Too bright by far, Chester," Dr. Coombs agreed. "But notice, the color is fading. Like a chameleon perhaps?"

"I do believe you're right, George. It seems to be adapting to the blue of Colter's shirt."

"Come on, you guys!" Colter hollered. "I can't hold this thing forever. Do you want it or not?"

"Yes, of course we want to study it," Dr. Piltcher said. "But what do we do with it?"

Without a better idea they led Colter to the RV, the creature struggling every step of the way. Then they decided to put the psittacosaurus in the back, where the beds were, and block off the front. They used the mattresses to create a wall, and then Colter leaned over and dropped the psittacosaurus on the other side. As soon as it hit the floor it stopped squealing and came up running. The little beast ran through the back of the RV on its two back legs, leaning forward with forelegs outstretched, looking for an escape route. The only way out, however, was past the mattresses, and the four heads peering over them. Still, the beast would not give up and its panic grew.

"The poor thing's scared," Petra said. "Maybe we better let it go."

"No, not yet," Dr. Piltcher pleaded. "I want to study it. Just for tonight. We can let it go in the morning."

Petra's conscience pricked her because the little animal was suffering. "Maybe we should give it something to eat," Petra suggested.

Dr. Coombs suggested fruit or eggs, and Colter came up with a peach. They rolled it across the floor to the psittacosaurus, but it ignored the fruit and continued to search for an escape route.

"What did you call this thing again?" Colter asked.

"Psittacosaurus," Dr. Coombs replied.

"Let's just call it Sid," Colter suggested. "How come I've never seen anything like Sid before?"

"Because," Dr. Piltcher began with forced slowness, "they've been extinct since the Cretaceous age."

"Wasn't that prehistoric times?" Colter asked Dr. Piltcher. "Then what's it doing here?"

With that one question Colter cut right through the fog of excitement that had clouded their thinking. What *was* it doing here?

Dr. Coombs and Dr. Piltcher retreated to the front of the RV and sat in the bucket seats. Colter and Petra followed, Colter a little put out that they hadn't answered his question directly. Despite his naiveté, however, he *had* learned how to fit into the group, and knew it was time for him to fade into the background.

The others assumed their reflective poses and took turns looking at each other, waiting for someone to say what they were all thinking. All except Colter, who stood impatiently waiting. As usual Dr. Piltcher finger-combed his hair, and then spoke first.

"Well, we knew something was going to happen, but I admit I hadn't considered this."

"What *has* happened?" Petra asked.

Dr. Piltcher turned and smiled at Petra. In Dr. Piltcher's eyes she could do no wrong, and he treated even her simplest questions with the same consideration that he gave to scholarly discussions.

"We must investigate further, of course. But from the primitive nature of the flowering plants in the meadow, and of course our friend the psittacosaurus, we seem to be sitting in a piece of the Cretaceous period. We anticipated some temporal dislocation, that fits with the theory, but I rather expected massive amounts of material falling out of the sky. Instead, we seem to have sitting all around us a piece of the past somehow transported to the present."

"There is another possibility," Dr. Coombs added. "We could be in a section of our present that has been transported to the past."

Dr. Piltcher raised his eyebrows but didn't say anything for a full minute. Then he spoke with thoughtful deliberation.

"If we were transported, then a huge portion of land was transported with us. We drove through miles of it, not to mention the radio reports from afar. If that much has been transported to the past, then it makes little difference to us practically. The same would be true if this piece of the Cretaceous period is extensive, but again the radio reports suggest otherwise."

"True enough, Chester, but it raises other interesting questions. If we are sitting on a piece of the Cretaceous period, complete with wildlife, then where is the land that it replaced? In the Cretaceous period? And more important, where are Mrs. Wayne and Ernie Powell?"

Dr. Piltcher was about to respond when a loud crunching sound broke up the conversation. Petra immediately turned and ran to the mattress barrier, motioning for the others to join her. They crowded together just in time to see the psittacosaurus bite down again on the peach pit. Nothing else of the peach remained. The pit broke in two.

"Sid's got quite a bite," Colter noted.

"Good thing he didn't get hold of one of your fingers," Petra said and then retrieved another peach from the refrigerator. "Here, Sid, knock yourself out," she said, and tossed it to him.

Sid ran from the peach, trying to hide in a corner. He looked around fearfully, then defecated, leaving a wet gray pile of solids on the floor, then ran over to the peach. Sid sank his jaws into it and then carried it to a clean corner and began systematically biting off chunks while leaning back on his tail and holding the peach with his forearms. Deftly he rotated it between bites, working efficiently to pick the pit clean. Then, as before, used his jaws to break the pit in two. After breaking the pit into smaller pieces Sid tasted two, then ignored them. Though he remained in his corner he seemed less fearful now and watched his captors with his black eyes. Colter pulled a piece of bread from the bag, tore off the crust, and threw it to Sid, but the animal hesitated, looking around fearfully. Seeing no sudden movement in his captors he snatched up the crust, opened his beak and snapped it up. He didn't hesitate to snatch up the second piece Colter gave him.

"See there, Chester," Dr. Coombs said, "he's blending into the brown of the background."

"I do believe you're right, George. I wonder how many species of the Cretaceous period had this ability?"

"Man, those turds stink," Colter complained. "We should've put some paper down."

Flinching, Dr. Piltcher opened his mouth to speak, but Petra cut him off.

"Outside! Something just ran by."

They all piled out of the RV, scanning the meadow.

"There, that way!" Dr. Coombs shouted, pointing toward the hedge in the distance.

Bobbing up and down in the grass was a greenish, dome-shaped, seemingly disembodied head. They watched it moving closer to the tall bushes in the distance, when suddenly something ran between Dr. Coombs's legs. It was Sid. Colter started after him but Dr. Piltcher called him back.

"Never mind, Colter. I wasn't thinking clearly before. This isn't about one psittacosaurus. This is about a whole new world." Dr. Piltcher waved his arm at the jungle before him. "We need to explore it systematically."

"And look for Mrs. Wayne and Ernie?" Petra asked, timidly.

"Of course, Petra. I didn't mean to sound insensitive."

Petra hugged his arm in response. Reddening, he quickly changed the subject. "Let's make camp here. It's not safe to move into the jungle until we know more about what's out there, and there seem to be animals much larger than Sid."

They jockeyed the RV around until it was level, and set up the canopy, a portable picnic table and lawn chairs. For shade they set up a tarp on poles and anchored it securely with ropes and stakes. Colter and Petra spread out looking for a supply of firewood; there was little wood in the desert, so they walked through the tall jungle grasses picking up branches.

"Hey, Petra, give me a hand with this."

Petra turned to see Colter pushing a large limb up out of the grass. It seemed to be attached to a bigger limb. Colter was rocking it back and forth, judging its weight. If the two of them could move it back to camp, it would supply enough wood for a couple of days. Colter rocked it low and then pulled it up high again, putting his shoulder under the limb. When he pushed up hard, they heard a loud cracking sound, and Colter dropped the limb and dove into the grass.

"Colter? What are you doing?" Petra shouted.

"Here, look at this."

Colter stood up holding something by its tail. Petra approached slowly. It was some kind of lizard, dark green and about eight inches long. Its tail was a third of the body, thick and stubby. It had four long limbs, the front and back pairs about the same length. The neck looked very thin and insubstantial, the head elongated with two large slits at the tip for nostrils. When it opened its mouth it revealed no teeth but white ridges, which it was trying to use on Colter.

"Is this one a baby or what?"

"Maybe it's just a small dinosaur. Let's take it to Dr. Piltcher."

Colter carried the animal by its tail back to the camp, Petra trotting ahead to alert the others. Excited all over again, Dr. Piltcher set the mattresses back up to trap the new find in the back of the RV. As soon as Colter gently set the little dinosaur on the floor, it was off scampering around the enclosure looking for a way out.

"Well, Chester, this one has me beat. It's clearly not local fauna but I don't recognize it."

"Nor I, George. You don't suppose its a mussaurus?"

"I have to admit I'm not familiar with the species. Would this be a full-grown mussaurus?"

"If that's what it is, yes. They didn't get much longer than eight or ten inches."

"Moose, kind of a funny name for a lizard this small," Colter said. "I like it."

Dr. Piltcher shook his head, taxed almost to the limit by Colter's juvenile attitude and his need to nickname each new species. But he kept silent. The mussaurus continued to scramble around looking for a way out. Then it stopped and turned to face them. Dr. Piltcher could see its sides heaving. Suddenly it shot forward and scrambled up the mattresses in three quick leaps and onto Petra's jeans. As Petra screamed, Dr. Coombs and Colter grabbed for the dinosaur. But it was too quick and darted under and up Petra's shirt. Petra gasped as the clawed feet worked its way up her stomach. She clamped her hand down, trying to stop the mussaurus, but gently so not to hurt it.

"Aah! It hurts, help me get it out! It's going around to my back!"

Dr. Coombs shoved his hand up the back of Petra's shirt, embarrassed by the feel of her bare skin and bra strap. Petra kept gasping and flinching at the scratches from the scrambling claws.

"It's going up to my shoulder! Look out everyone!" Petra shouted, and pushed the hands away. Then she reached down, pulling the shirt up and over her head. Suddenly exposed, the lizard froze, and then darted down the front. Now Dr. Piltcher's hand shot out and pinned the dinosaur between the cups of Petra's bra. He flushed but seized the animal. Immediately, Petra pulled her shirt back over her head, noticing the only one without a red face was Colter.

As the dinosaur clamped its jaws on Dr. Piltcher's thumb, the professor dropped it. Free again, the dinosaur scrambled up a wall and onto the small space on top of the cabinets.

"Old Moose is a handful," Colter said. "Copped a feel of Petra and then took on someone a hundred times his size. Want me to get him down out of there?"

"No." Dr. Piltcher said. "It's not worth the risk. Let's just wait outside with the door open. He'll leave on his own accord."

"Don't you want to study him some more?" Colter asked with a smirk.

They worked outside for the rest of the afternoon. When supper time approached they found Moose still on top of the cabinet. They tried catching him again, but this time Dr. Coombs ended up with a nipped finger. Finally they gave up.

They agreed they might attract too many unknown animals by cooking outside, so Dr. Coombs prepared spaghetti and meatballs in the camper. When dinner was ready, they settled down in the cramped RV, but halfway through dinner, something banged against the door. Petra got up and looked out the window but could see nothing. Then it banged again. Petra opened the door slowly, all of them watching curiously. She was about to close the door again when a small dinosaur trotted into view, then out again, and then back. Then another one trotted into view behind the first. One of the dinosaurs was Sid. He had come for dinner, and he had brought a friend.

23. Mountain Mystery

As I approached the Lang farm I could see my friend David working in his field. His family was near the house and waved in greeting. When David turned toward me he suddenly disappeared. The Lang family joined me in the field to search but we found no trace of him.

—Judge August Peck, September 23, 1880

North of Grant's Pass, Oregon
PostQuilt: Sunday, 10:30 a.m. PST

It was a mountain all right, Terry conceded to himself. Even if the word might be a bit grandiose for the pile of rocks in front of him. Rather than towering snow-capped peaks rising above the timberline, Terry was staring at a huge pile of boulders that looked as if they had been poured into the middle of the interstate. It could have been the result of an avalanche, except the pile towered above the nearest hill. Then there was the problem of the vegetation. Leading up to the towering rock pile was a carpet of sparse clump grass, but it didn't match the surrounding vegetation. Would an avalanche have deposited a green carpet of scrawny grass?

Terry and Ellen had been skeptical when they left the parking lot at the Oregon Caves, even as the CB reports of the mountain were confirmed by other motorists with CBs. But still it was hard to believe. They'd driven only a few miles north of Grant's Pass before they realized the traffic in the southbound lanes was very light. The farther north they drove, the lighter it became until the traffic stopped completely. Shortly after that they came to a traffic jam.

The traffic was at a dead stop, and northbound drivers were abandoning their cars and walking forward through the extemporaneous parking lot. Terry and Ellen had to walk nearly a mile before they saw the mountain. It was set a little to the east of the interstate with the mountain tumbled down to the west. A hundred people were milling around in front of it. Many of them were taking pictures or videos. Parents posed their children on boulders or in the clearing, trying to get as much of the mountain in their shot as possible. Other children chased around the clearing or climbed rocks.

Terry and Ellen joined the crowd of happy gawkers, but Terry couldn't share their partying mood. Only here and there were other concerned faces like Terry's. This mountain wasn't just a road hazard that prevented tourists from logging their four hundred miles a day. It represented something far larger, something Terry did not understand. Something impossible.

Terry squatted at the end of the interstate and examined the edge. It was a nice sharp break. On one side you had a four-lane freeway and on the other side coarse grass leading up to the mountain. Terry began looking for a way around the mountain. He certainly couldn't drive around it, but he was curious how big a blockage this was. He was about to suggest a walk to Ellen when he heard a familiar voice, and he looked up to see the towering figure of Bill Conrad.

"If you're wondering if the road continues on the other side, it does. I just don't know how far you have to go. The CB channels are buzzing with southbound truckers and travelers talking about the landslide blocking I-5."

"You read my mind correctly on that one. Now try the next question."

"I don't have any idea where this came from or what is going on."

Terry laughed and nodded. It was reassuring to know Bill was as confused as he was. Bill Conrad had been in his element in the cave, prepared for his role by his training. But out here on the road, standing in front of a mountain that magically appeared on an interstate highway, Bill wasn't any more competent than Terry or anyone else. Terry spotted Ellen talking to Angie. They were laughing and smiling, as if they were old friends.

"It makes you wonder about that kid in the cave, doesn't it?" Bill said. "I mean I wonder if this is what he was talking about?"

Until Bill Conrad had suggested it, Terry had never connected the kid in the cave with the mountain. Now, he was having trouble relating them.

"I don't know, Bill, the kid was delusional, and he was pretty specific about what was going to happen. The world was supposed to end."

"The sister said something about things falling from the sky."

"This couldn't have fallen . . . impossible."

Bill made a noncommittal murmur, but his mind was working. Asserting himself, Terry decided to demonstrate his own specialty.

"I'd guess that kid was paranoid schizophrenic. He exhibited the classic symptoms, the secret knowledge that only he could understand, the certainty that no one would believe him. These types are often pretty successful at fitting into society. They're delusional, though, and their worldview only makes sense to themselves."

Bill was singularly unimpressed by Terry's diagnosis.

"Are you a psychiatrist?"

"Psychologist."

"Mmmm. If someone believes the world is going to end and it doesn't, he's delusional. What if he thinks the world is going to end and it does? That's not delusion, that's prophecy."

"But the world didn't end."

"But *something* sure as hell happened. How do you explain that, doc?" Bill said jerking his head toward the mountain.

Terry conceded Bill had a good point. "I'm not saying I know what has happened," Terry responded. "I'm only suggesting the two events are not necessarily related."

"Mmmm. Peculiar coincidence."

Bill walked over to Ellen and Angie, who were still talking animatedly. The three of them laughed together for a while before the conversation turned serious. Then they approached Terry.

Bill began. "We're thinking of heading back to Medford and finding that kid from the cave. It may be he knows more than people are giving him credit for."

"I told you, Bill, that kid is delusional, and even if he did know something it will be difficult for him to communicate it."

"No problem. We've got a psychiatrist to go with us." Bill winked and grinned cynically.

"Psychologist," Terry answered curtly.

"Whatever."

"If he gives us any trouble," Terry offered more genially, "we've got a marine to shoot him."

"Air force."

"Whatever."

"Come on, Terry, let's go with them," Ellen said. "We can't get through this way anyway, and we'll have to find another way around."

Ellen was right. There really was no reason to stay where they were, and they could hardly backtrack. Terry relented and Bill and Angie led the way back to the cars. Bill, more resourceful than Terry, had driven up the median close to the mountain. They all climbed in for a ride to Terry's car.

Bill Conrad's demeanor worked its magic again at the sheriff's department. The receptionist/dispatcher turned out to be a woman named Karon, who would only say the suspect's name was Kenny Randall, a student at Oregon Institute of Technology, and he had not been taken to the police station. She was reluctant to give any information about Kenny's current whereabouts, but then Bill flashed his military ID, spoke in a clipped, brisk manner, and found out that Kenny was at the community hospital.

The hospital staff buckled just as easily under Bill's demeanor, and the two couples found themselves outside Kenny's door talking to the sheriff and a doctor.

The sheriff turned out to be a refugee from the big city. He had migrated from the Chicago police force to Portland and then to Medford. Well-educated, professional, and not intimidated by big, loud, black air force officers, at six feet two he could almost look Bill in the eye.

"Sheriff, this is official business. You know what's happened to I-5 don't you? Well the air force believes there may be some connection between the two events."

Bill was bluffing, but he was so good at it Terry began to wonder what he did for the military.

"You're talking to the wrong person," the sheriff insisted. "We're only holding the suspect until the FBI can transport him. I don't have the authority to admit you."

"It doesn't matter anyway," the doctor cut in. "He was severely agitated, so we sedated him. He won't be conscious for a few hours. When he does wake up I wouldn't expect much. He isn't responsive."

"Catatonic?" Terry asked.

"Not yet, but that's the direction he's headed."

Bill argued with them until he got a "maybe you can see him" out of them and strode back to the elevator as if he had a sense of purpose.

Terry lagged behind, unsure of what to do next. Ellen was down in the lobby talking to Angie, and Terry supposed he should collect his wife and try to work his way over to highway 101 and head north along the Oregon coast. It would be slower than I-5, but at least there weren't any new mountain detours. Still, Terry had an irrational feeling of unfinished business. Wherever that mountain had come from—and Terry could not even remotely guess—he couldn't move it and had no idea of how to go around it. He might, however, be of some use with Kenny Randall. Paranoid schizophrenia wasn't normally what he dealt with, but his residency had exposed him to most of the psychoses. Still, there were more competent people than Terry to deal with Kenny's problem. Terry had nearly convinced himself to head home when Bill said, "You coming?" Terry followed him, feeling like Tonto.

While Angie and Ellen waited in a coffee shop, Bill and Terry headed south, to search Kenny's dormitory room.

To Terry it seemed that the easiest way to find Kenny Randall's room was to ask the administration. But Bill instead started asking students if they knew Kenny. Everyone did, and everyone rolled their eyes at the mention of his name. The third person they talked to directed them to Residence Hall. Bill had to ask only two people before he found out which room was Kenny's. The reason Bill avoided the administration building became clear as they stood outside Kenny's room and Bill pulled a credit card out and opened the locked door.

"Bill, this is breaking and entering!"

"No, it's only entering."

"Oh, that makes me feel much better. Why are we playing burglar?"

"I doubt the dean would let us in, and as soon as the police or the FBI think of it they'll seal this room. They're probably on their way here now."

"What if someone catches us in here?" Terry worried out loud.

"Don't worry, I'm licensed to kill," Bill said, wiggling his eyebrows.

The room looked much like Terry's son's room. The bed was unmade, and dirty clothes were piled all over the bed, and on the floor. Piles of books and papers were scattered here and there around the room. A desk was buried under more books and papers, a computer sitting in the middle of the clutter. Terry felt skeptical: This was like a thousand other dorm rooms around the country.

Bill settled in front of the computer and began sorting through the disks. Reluctantly, Terry decided to snoop around, not expecting to find anything. The closet was filled with books and more dirty clothes. Buried in the far corner Terry turned up a typewriter case. He found nothing in it but the expected typewriter and two extra ribbon cartridges. He sorted through the books—mostly texts on organizational psychology, systems theory, personnel management, history, literature, and a surprising number of geography books with sections highlighted in yellow and pink.

Terry, who had marked up his textbooks in the same way, reflected how some things don't change about college students. Other books dealt with science, specifically physics, with titles like *Quantum Theory*, *The New Physics*, *Physics in the New Age*, and *Whatever Happened to Newton's Universe?* There were books on magnetism, superconductivity, and nuclear fusion and fission. But the topic Kenny seemed to like best was "time." There were at least a dozen books with the word *time* in the title. So what? Terry wondered. Now we know Kenny Randall likes to read books on management, physics, and time. That does not tell us why a twenty-year-old college student held a group of strangers hostage in a cave. Nor does it tell us how a mountain ended up sitting in the middle of I-5.

Terry thought about the mountain again, and began to wonder if he'd been right in assuming it had been a natural event. He picked up a book titled *Unified Time Theory* and thumbed it. Uneasy now, he tried to remember what Kenny and his sister had said about things falling out of the sky. But why books on time? Wouldn't the mountain be better explained with books on geology?

Bill was still working with Kenny's computer, running programs. So Terry started looking through the books on the shelf above Kenny's desk. There were titles like *Stranger Than Fact*, *The Unknown*, and *Science and the Unexplained*. They reminded him of tabloids in grocery store racks, pulp journals that mixed fact and fiction. Terry thumbed through *Stranger Than Fact* and found a chapter on ghosts, describing how a man bought a house, against the advice of his friends, which supposedly had a haunted room. One night the man went to bed in the room and woke up in the night feeling someone's breath on the back of his neck. He rolled over to find himself inches from the decaying face of a dead woman, her fetid breath blowing into his face. Terrified, the man ran into the street, pulling his hair out.

Other stories were similar, and Terry was about to throw the book back onto the shelf when he noticed some pages were highlighted in pink.

For instance, in a section called "Human Torches" one story detailed how an old woman was found burned to death sitting in a chair in her room on February 5, 1905. She and the chair were burned to crispy charcoal. The floor was charred around the woman's chair eighteen inches in all directions, but beyond that the room was untouched, and the walls were free of soot. The woman did not smoke and the book described it as a case of spontaneous human combustion. There were other similar cases, ranging from 1725 to 1977. The last case was nearly identical to the 1905 one—a woman found in front of her television, her body completely consumed by a fire that left only the head and one foot. Nothing else in the room was burned.

Terry flipped through the book again to a chapter called "Extinct?" A highlighted section described a fish called a "coelacanth" caught in a fisherman's net off the coast of South America. The 120-pound armored fish was half-fish and half–land animal, and thought to be extinct for seventy-five million years.

Terry flipped through the pages to other highlighted sections on Sasquatch sightings in the Pacific Northwest, yeti sightings in Tibet, and dinosaur sightings in Africa. A big section was devoted to things falling from the sky. Fish, frogs, seeds, ice, and rocks have fallen out of a blue sky and pelted people and homes. In Singapore on the morning of February 16, 1861, fish had poured from the sky and the Chinese and Malays had collected hundreds of pounds in baskets. Terry jumped over reports of fish falls in 1920, 1941, and 1968 to a similar report from Kamilla, India, in 1975, when thousands of sardine-size fish poured out of the sky. In this report the fish were dried.

Probably the strangest story told of a group of archaeologists working in the Egyptian desert who were found in the shambles of their camp, dead. They had been drowned. No one could explain how the archaeologists and their workers had drowned in the middle of the desert. There were no signs of foul play, and obviously there wasn't enough water to drown in.

Terry found himself peculiarly attracted to the stories in the book. They had the same kind of appeal that had brought people into freak shows for centuries, and took them to slasher movies today. The excitement wasn't in seeing someone merely killed, but in seeing someone killed in an unusual way.

Despite his affinity for the book and its stories, Terry could not see the common thread that tied the stories together. Spontaneous combustion, Big Foot, and prehistoric fish added up to nothing but a waste of time.

Terry put the book back on the shelf and looked through the stacks of papers and other books. An overstuffed file of newspaper clippings next to the computer told stories similar to those in the books on the shelf. The first was only two paragraphs long, describing a woman walking down a street in Seattle. A man passed her in the other direction. Suddenly there was a "whoosh" and a "pop" and when the woman turned around the man was on fire. Not just flickering with flames, but a human torch that burned so hot the body was nearly consumed. Terry immediately remembered the old woman burned in her room, but still could not see the significance of these events. The next clipping was of an event in Hiroshima, Japan. Several people in a park reported a strange shower of flowers. Not just a few, but thousands; they fell in torrents, burying a woman and a child. Something about the event suddenly tickled Terry's mind, but Bill interrupted his thoughts.

"I can't make heads or tails out of this. Let's go."

Terry started toward the door but Bill began taking the computer apart and putting the pieces into a computer pack—the monitor, the keyboard, and the mouse. There was no place for the hard drive, so Bill stacked it on top of the pack. Then he noticed Terry watching.

"Don't stand there, Terry. Gather up anything and everything."

Not certain enough to resist Bill, Terry gathered up the file folder with the clippings, then the books, using Kenny's bedspread to make a sack. Bill followed his example, and they filled a bedspread, a blanket, and a sheet. When Terry reached up for the last of the books, he noticed a jar at the end of the shelf. He picked it up and shook it. It was full of dried corn.

When Terry and Bill left, dragging their improvised bags behind them, Terry, guilt-ridden, knew Bill felt like they had accomplished something, but Terry was sure only that they had just burgled Kenny Randall's room.

As planned, Angie and Ellen were in the coffee shop. Ellen's face told Terry something was wrong before his wife blurted it out.

"We've got to get home, Terry. We've got to find John."

"What is it, Ellen? What's happened to John?"

"Maybe nothing. I don't know, but Portland is gone."

24. Rogues' Gallery

He was found on the plaza in Mexico City, dressed in his resplendent uniform and carrying a strange gun. He was very confused and thought he was in Manila, Philippines. He said he was looking for the governor's palace, to which he had been posted that morning. We were later to confirm he was telling the truth. In what manner he was so instantly transported no one has yet to explain.

—Mexico City, October 1593

Washington, D.C.
PostQuilt: Sunday, 1:40 p.m. EST

Elizabeth's organizational instincts expanded well beyond the President's needs, and it was no surprise to Nick when she presented him with a schedule of activities. He was only mildly irritated by Elizabeth's intrusion. Nick admitted to himself he was stumbling blindly.

He had accessed the PresNet, the computer network of presidential science advisors. PresNet was Dr. Gogh's achievement. One of his strengths was in organization. He'd managed to negotiate an appropriation out of Congress to fund his dream. Using the prestige of the White House, and the money from Congress, he'd recruited a far-flung group of scientists from all disciplines to serve as the "President's Science Advisor Associates." The networked scientists received the prestige of being part of an elite group, state-of-the-art computer equipment, and perceived access to the White House. More practically they received unlimited database access, on-line supercomputer time, and the means to communicate with colleagues across the country through the sophisticated computer network.

Nick guessed that Gogh never imagined the network would be used in the way Nick was using it. Unfortunately, big chunks of the network were down, and those coming on-line were seeking as much information as they were providing.

The few on the network reported that physical changes had been wrought, apparently instantly, in widespread parts of the country, with no obvious connection. Nick had two assistants working on assessing the amount of affected acreage, and once he had enough data, patterns might present themselves, and theories could be generated. At least that was the idea. But the only pattern Nick could discern was no pattern.

There were now "confirmed" reports of changes in other parts of the world, including Russia. Cannon had sent over these new reports with a note emphasizing that "only confirmed reports were reliable and only these reports should be shared with the President." Nick wondered what criteria the CIA used to decide if a report was "confirmed"? Three reliable witnesses? Ten? Did one of them have to be a CIA agent? Nick also had a copy of the administration's policy on leaking information and an admonition to keep the Security Council discussions to himself. The note ended with Cannon's scrawled signature and a handwritten note stating, "we still have no confirmed reports of dinosaurs."

The schedule Elizabeth imposed on Nick was grueling. She checked with Nick on the hour to see if he had a solution to the problem yet, and at the same time scheduled a series of interviews for him with people who claimed to know what was going on. The list included three psychics who had predicted cataclysmic events, two religious fanatics from cults that preached the end of the world, and a man who had been arrested in front of the Capitol Building for taking off his clothes and masturbating. He later explained that the masturbation symbolized what was soon to happen to the world. Nick thought about it but could see no connection between a public orgasm and time displacement. The last person on the list was a college kid who had been arrested for holding tourists hostage in a cave out in Oregon. He too had anticipated the end of the world.

Each of Elizabeth's rogues' gallery had an individual file. Nick thumbed through them and whistled silently through his teeth. The psychics each had a thick bundle of papers, including faxed air force reports. "Why would the air force keep files on psychics?" Nick wondered. The religious fanatics had FBI files and the masturbator a thick police record. The college kid's file was empty except for a note saying an air force colonel and a psychologist were bringing him out from Oregon. Now that was curious, Nick thought. A psychologist and a colonel;

not a lieutenant, or a sergeant, but a colonel! Nick put the kid's file to the bottom and prepared himself to meet "Madame Sylvia."

Madame Sylvia was large but not fat—instead, what Nick's mother liked to call "big boned." Her hair was a mass of dyed brown ringlets. Fond of makeup, Madame Sylvia used it generously. She was also delighted at being called to the White House. Madame Sylvia's file noted she had a contract with a supermarket tabloid. Nick could only guess what a White House summons would do for its circulation.

"I understand you predicted the world would end?" Nick probed gently.

"I predicted catastrophe, not an end."

"An end to the world as we know it."

"The world as you know it. I am part of a greater world," Madame Sylvia announced loftily.

"A different world than this?" Nick inquired.

"This world is part of a greater world. The essence of my being is part of the greater consciousness that is the spiritual fabric of the universe."

"Is that what allows you to see the future?"

"It is an explanation your mind can grasp?"

"But not all of your predictions have come true, have they?"

"True. My physical self clouds my vision. Once I am released from my body I will see with perfect clarity."

Nick thumbed through the file and pulled out a three-month-old tabloid clipping listing Madame Sylvia's predictions for the next six months. Elizabeth, or someone, had circled one in red: "Earthquakes, floods, and storms will wreak unprecedented havoc."

"Can you tell me more about this?" Nick asked politely.

"New York is gone. There are floods, landslides, hurricanes, tornadoes. These are the catastrophes I predicted and they have come true."

Nick was surprised to hear her say New York was gone. The last Nick had heard the media people were still calling it a blackout. He made a mental note to check Cable Network News.

"What is the source of these catastrophes? Why did they happen all at once and why now?"

"It is part of a larger plan. A plan I cannot explain in terms you could understand."

Nick dug deeper into the pile.

"I see you predicted cataclysms six . . . no, seven times in the past three years. In the last five years you also predicted contact with aliens three times, two presidential assassinations, that California would slide into the sea, and that cancer would be cured . . . you predicted that four times."

"As I told you, my vision is sometimes clouded."

"That physical-self problem?"

"Exactly."

"Thank you for coming."

The religious fanatic was next, painfully thin with a pinched, lined face and dark emotionless eyes.

"Mr. Love? Is that your real name?"

"That is the name I received upon sanctification. Jesus gave it to me," Mr. Love intoned.

"It's a *good* name. Why did you think the world was going to end?"

"Jesus told me. In a vision."

"Something has happened, but the world did not end," Nick countered.

"God has only begun."

"What will happen next?"

"I see hellfire and brimstone. I see the wrath of God poured out from the heavens. Not a stone will be left standing. Not a being left living." Mr. Love stood up, eyes burning.

"Thank you for coming."

"Vengeance is mine, sayeth the Lord . . ." The man leaned forward, gesturing wildly.

"Guard?" Nick turned.

Mr. Love was still speaking as the marine led him away.

". . . turn to Jesus while there is still time."

The masturbator was nothing like Madame Sylvia or Mr. Love. Mr. Gauthier did not seem to take himself, or anything else, seriously. He was a short pudgy man, with a round cherubic face, a ready grin, and long wisps of golden hair combed across a balding head.

"I understand you predicted the end of the world." As soon as Nick said it Mr. Gauthier began to laugh.

"That's good. That's good. I pre-dick-ted it all right. Right there on the Capitol steps."

Nick flushed as he pressed on. "I mean you anticipated that something was going to happen to the world."

"I never said the world was going to end. I jerked off to symbolize what is happening."

"And what's that?"

"We're all getting screwed by the government. Here, let me show you."

Mr. Gauthier unzipped his pants and began fumbling inside.

"I get the point, Mr. Gauthier, you don't have to show me. Thanks for coming."

Mr. Gauthier looked up and chuckled again.

"Well, I haven't come yet but just give me a minute."

He was laughing and masturbating when Nick left the room. After closing the door Nick turned to the marine guard.

"Tell Elizabeth Hawthorne she needs to see Mr. Gauthier immediately."

---

25. CUBBY AND JOHN

So the Lord scattered them from there over all the earth, and they stopped building the city. That is why it was called Babel—because there the Lord confused the language of the whole world. From there the Lord scattered them over the face of the whole earth.

—Genesis 11:8–9

Forest, former site of Portland, Oregon
POSTQUILT: SUNDAY, 4:40 P.M. PST

Cubby and John backtracked until they came to the spot where Ripman disappeared. They called out softly, afraid to shout. They searched fruitlessly until they found themselves deep in a darkening forest.

"Cubby, you think the dinosaurs got him?"

"No way! Not Ripman. Besides, they were following us."

"Then where did he go? Wouldn't he be looking for us?"

Cubby didn't answer, he just flopped down on a clump of grass and took off his pack and bow. John thought Cubby, like him, was worried about Ripman.

"What's going on, Cubby? Those were dinosaurs . . . I mean I've never seen one . . . a real one, but I know that's what those were. What else could they have been?"

"Noah's Ravens," Cubby answered. "That's what they used to be called, that's what a lot of people in our church still call them. It's an old name. It used to be all the evidence of dinosaurs they had were footprints. They make a three-toed track that looks like the footprint of a big bird. Since there were no birds around that make a track like that people thought Noah's flood had killed off all the giant birds, so they called them Noah's Ravens. Even when they started finding bones, many believers refused to accept the idea of dinosaurs. A lot of people still don't accept the idea. Man, what are they gonna say now?"

Cubby picked up a stick and broke it into pieces, flicking them into the grass, lost in his own thoughts. John's mind jumped from the impossibility of the dinosaurs, to his family, to his missing friend.

"I'm gonna go on, John," Cubby said finally. "I don't know what happened to Ripman, maybe he made it to Portland already, but I've got to find my mom and dad. My dad will know what's happened . . . he can explain this . . . Noah's Ravens . . . everything. He has the gift of discernment."

At that moment John realized that if Ripman had wanted to go on, John would have gone with him right away. But when Cubby said the same thing, John lacked confidence, and suddenly Ripman's idea of heading to the cabin sounded better—especially since the incident with the dinosaur.

He didn't exactly understand what Cubby meant by the "gift of discernment," but John already knew what Cubby's dad would say—using words like *judgment*, *sin*, and *repentance*, he'd spiritualize what had happened and Cubby would come away feeling better. But it wouldn't do anything for John, who was betting that Cubby was wrong and that God didn't have anything to do with this. John didn't need his parents in the same way Cubby needed his, John simply *wanted* them.

In the end the prospect of walking through the forest by himself led John to decide to stay with Cubby. Besides, John's confusion about reality scared him. Despite all the evidence of a new, dramatically changed world, John couldn't help but think that just over the next hill, or through the next stand of trees, they would run into a Burger King or a McDonald's, and there would be Ripman with a Big Mac in his hand asking what kept them.

Finally, he just nodded to Cubby and suggested they rest until morning. It was getting dark, so they began looking for a safe place to spend the night. Because of the big tree lizards they were afraid of sleeping in the trees, and besides, they doubted they could climb high enough to elude the big dinosaur. Instead they walked until they found an area where several trees had fallen together and left a hollow underneath. After digging the hollow a little deeper and wider, they wedged themselves inside it, pulled some smaller branches over the opening to hide themselves, and wrapped themselves up in their stolen space blankets.

Cubby muttered urgent prayers for a long time while John listened respectfully. But finally John needed to talk.

"Hey, Cubby, did you ever see that show about those guys who dug down to the center of the earth?"

"I read the Jules Verne book."

"That's different. In the Verne book they climbed down into a cave to get there. In this movie some scientist builds a digging machine that's supposed to be used for mining or tunneling, or something, but once they start digging with it they can't stop it. They end up digging all the way to the center of the earth, and it turns out it's hollow inside."

"I've seen a couple like that."

"Me too. I think they made a couple of sequels. Anyway, I read once there's a bunch of people that really believe the earth is hollow and that there may be a whole civilization inside. Some of them even think that's where flying saucers come from."

"The saucers come from the middle of the earth? How do they get in and out?"

"Caves at the poles. Anyway, in the movie they got down

inside the middle of the earth and there were dinosaurs inside and cave people, and stuff. Maybe Ripman was right, maybe there was a volcanic eruption or something. Maybe this place used to be inside the earth and somehow it got blasted up to the surface."

"Jeez, John. Do you really believe that? This isn't some dumb science-fiction movie. Besides, why are you so hot on *this* idea but you don't believe me when I tell you it's the second coming of Christ? Why is a hollow earth turned inside out more believable than God's judgment?"

John didn't answer right away. He didn't know how. Ever since he could remember he had always preferred to believe in things he could sense. John had always described ESP, and all that paranormal stuff, as crap. He stopped short of calling God's judgment crap, but he still had trouble believing. The forest around him was physical, and that meant *real*—according to John.

Cubby was different. The supernatural came easy for him. Divine intervention, God, the Holy Spirit, sanctification, all fit together like so many pieces of the same puzzle. Together they made a picture of a spiritual realm that was as real to Cubby as the forest was to John. To Cubby the forest was physical proof of a spiritual truth. It was as easy for Cubby to believe that the forest was an act of God as it was for John to believe that it came from the center of the earth.

"Hey, Ripman disproved your theory," John argued. "We didn't find the topless joint, remember. Besides, I thought God was going to use fire or something to destroy the earth. Where in the Bible does it say people are going to be eaten by dinosaurs?"

"Scripture isn't easy to interpret. If you'd ever read any you would know that." Cubby spoke thoughtfully, not in a mean way. After a few minutes Cubby talked again.

"Maybe God did do something like this once before. A couple of months ago my father did a series for his radio show on the Tower of Babel. You remember that story? The people of earth had become arrogant and were trying to build a tower to reach God. To punish the people, and stop them, God gave them all different languages; they couldn't talk to each other anymore."

"Cubby, I can still understand you. I mean I know what your words mean, it's the combination that doesn't make sense."

"Yeah, but if we meet some dude hunting dinosaurs, wearing a skin and carrying a spear, I bet you can't understand him."

"Your theory's thin, Cubby."

"Thinner than UFOs from the center of the earth?"

Because John didn't quite believe his own theory, he couldn't argue it seriously, so he changed the subject. "Cubby, did those dinosaurs look right to you? I mean, they didn't look like any dinosaurs I'd ever seen before."

"Jeez, John, you've never seen a dinosaur before, only pictures."

"You know what I mean. That little one that was being chased, its head was too small and too pointy, and its legs were too big for the rest of its body. And the big one didn't have much of a tail. I thought they fought each other with their tails and stuff."

"I didn't see much of the big one, but the little one did look funny. All those pictures of dinosaurs in books are just guesses. Maybe when they tried covering those dinosaur skeletons with skin they got it wrong? Or maybe the dinosaurs that were chasing us were different from the ones in the museums. They were around for millions and millions of years. Maybe we don't have any bones of ones like these."

John and Cubby didn't sleep or talk much after that. Cubby mumbled prayers most of the night, sometimes loud enough for John to pick out names and words. Cubby was praying not only for his family but also for John's and Ripman's. John wanted to thank him for his prayers. But, reluctant to disturb his friend, instead, John lay silent listening to the sounds of the forest and worrying about his parents.

26. Streets of the New World

Never was there a thunderbolt to match that to come. Italy, Spain, and the English will tremble. And the whole world will never be the same.

—Nostradamus

The disasters came in three waves. The immediate losses of land, crops, buildings, and people were the beginning. Shortly thereafter came the secondary effects. With roads and bridges gone, and sections of track missing, cars and train wrecks piled up all over the country. Along foggy highway 1 in California thirty-two cars drove off a cliff before a slow-moving Winnebago stopped in time. In other parts of the country dams that had disappeared into the night released their waters, and towns and villages were washed away in unprecedented deluges. Fires spread in some areas, growing into firestorms that the survivors were ill equipped to fight. Numerous avalanches of rock, snow, and mud poured down from the hills and mountains, some onto people and houses.

The third wave of destruction was the most frightening. The breakdown of civilization came slowly, but inevitably. Those regions without power were the most dangerous. With no lights, no burglar alarms, and the police needed everywhere, the professionals went right to work, breaking and entering at will. But soon the looters appeared, common folk who blended anonymously into crowds and began to help themselves to the luxuries of life that had eluded them. Other less-noticed tragedies took place with increasing frequency. People died waiting for transplants that never came, or for surgical teams that no longer existed. Blood, at first ample, quickly became precious as those suffering from the disasters were ministered to. Medicines too quickly became as rare as blood. Some pharmaceutical companies were gone, others lost stock or couldn't get supplies. Those that could deliver found the interstate system shredded with precious few alternatives. Deaths from formerly curable diseases began to mount.

Unlike a drought, or storm damage, people were more affected than crops. Concentrated in cities, people were lost by the millions. Some canned and preserved foods were lost with warehouses, but more problematic was distribution. Food shortages, unheard of in the United States, became common as panicky citizens stockpiled. Those with much had to make do with little. Those with little soon faced hunger. Those with nothing faced famine.

New York City
POSTQUILT: SUNDAY, 8:10 P.M. EST

Luis watched his kids sleep. He was using a candle for light, and its flickering gave the room an eerie look. Everything in the room was normal though. His kids were doubled up with their cousins. Ramon was in with Randy. Just the same size, the five-year-olds had giggled for an hour before falling asleep. José was on the floor in a sleeping bag. Though the nine-year-old went to bed with a worried face, he slept soundly now on the floor next to his cousin Nicky. Luis went next door to check on Charlotte, who was in a trundle bed next to her favorite cousin, Mindy. They were still awake and talking about boys. At eleven and ten they were each other's best friend at family gatherings. Katrina was in a sleeping bag near the far wall. She had no cousin to match her three years, but she'd gone to sleep easily enough, listening to her sister and cousin. That left only Cinda, who was asleep in a dresser drawer in the room Luis and Melinda would share.

Luis returned to Melinda in the living room, assuring her about the children with a nod. Placing his candle with the others, he flopped down on the couch beside her, his head on her shoulder. Melinda began stroking his head. They sat silently like that until Melinda's brother and his wife came in with coffee heated on a propane stove and homemade zucchini bread.

"Sounds quiet in there," Steve said.

Luis sat up taking a cup of coffee from Tanya.

"The little ones are asleep. I know ours were exhausted by the walk. It's funny, I thought Charlotte and Mindy would be scared the most, but you know I think José was. He hardly said a word after we saw the dinosaur."

"I still can't believe it," Tanya said. "I mean, I believe you, but I can't believe it happened. You know what I mean, don't you?"

Melinda smiled at her sister-in-law. "Yes. We can't believe it either. You should have seen it, though. First the city out our window was gone and then this huge monster came walking through the grass. It was bigger than any animal I've ever seen. And more terrible-looking than any dinosaur I've ever seen. I mean seen in movies and books."

Steve began munching on a piece of the zucchini bread, then started talking with his mouth full.

"You know, it's almost worth going back over to see it," he said. "If we had some power I could probably see it on TV by now. The only thing we're picking up on the radio is there's been a blackout. Nothing about a big chunk of the city disappearing and especially nothing about dinosaurs."

"If you really want to go, you can come with me," Luis said. "I've got to go back."

"No," Melinda said immediately. "You can't. It's too dangerous. You saw what the streets looked like."

"You know I've got to. Mrs. Weatherby is there. She's got to get out."

"No. You asked her. You tried to help her. You've got no reason to feel guilty. Did Mr. Moreno offer to help? Did the McGregors? No. You did, Luis. God will love you for it. Now God wants you to think only of your family."

"God wants or you want?"

"Luis—"

"Mrs. Weatherby is a nice old lady who is defenseless. How can I leave her there? I'll go, I'll get her . . . carry her out by force if I have to . . . and then I'll come back. Can I bring her here, Tanya? Only until we find her family."

Tanya started to answer yes but Melinda talked over her.

"Luis, you're scaring me. Don't leave me and the kids alone. What if you don't come back? What would we do? Cinda would never remember her dada."

"It'll be okay, Melinda. I'll be extra careful. Just right there and back. I promise nothing will happen to me."

Luis was only stubborn when it came to his honor, and somehow this was the honorable thing for him to do. But she managed one last concession.

"You'll wait till morning? Not in the dark, Luis, it's just too crazy out there."

"Not until morning," he conceded.

Then they snuggled together, both secretly worrying it could be their last night together. Then Steve put out the candles and opened the curtains a little. The street below was empty but in the distance they could see fires.

"Don't go, Luis," Melinda whispered, then took his hand and squeezed it.

Luis put his arm around her shoulder and pulled her close. He never answered. He didn't have to.

Luis left the next morning by himself. The street was sprinkled with abandoned cars, the streetlights off. There were no cars moving on the street but Luis could hear the sound of traffic somewhere in the distance. He didn't bother to try the subway, they'd discovered the day before the trains weren't running.

He walked the streets, watching the shadows and avoiding the alleys and dark doorways, but he made good time. The apartment building's doors were closed and curtains drawn. The corner groceries, video stores, and delis were locked up but intact. The only businesses open were the two bars he passed. Luis gained confidence with each step through the quiet streets until he turned a corner to face unbelievable destruction.

The street was filled with broken glass, pieces of concrete, and goods looted from the stores. In the distance Luis could see a smoldering overturned car. A few people were milling around, looking through the loot in the street or shop windows. Luis thought of finding another way to Mrs. Weatherby's but whatever had happened here was over, and the people in the streets looked anything but dangerous. Besides, he reasoned, he knew what was in these streets but he had no idea what he would find on the side streets.

The wreckage in the streets prevented car traffic, so Luis

walked down the middle of the street. The debris in the streets changed according to the stores. In front of the looted appliance store was a toaster with its sides smashed in, a smashed boom box, and two TVs with shattered screens. Before the grocery lay smashed eggs, vegetables, squashed loaves of bread and various snack foods. The furniture store had produced broken lamps and mattresses, more TVs and crushed stereos. Luis wasn't surprised to find little or nothing in front of the liquor store; its stock was precious.

Luis found himself looking carefully at usable, intact things in the street. When he realized what he was doing he felt shame, but he began to understand how looters felt. If he took the items at his feet, he told himself, he'd be doing the city a favor by cleaning the streets. If he gave into that logic, soon he'd begin to think about items sitting in stores with broken windows, how someone was just going to steal them anyway.

As Luis walked, the streets slowly filled with people, the crowd picking through the debris, looking for overlooked items of value. A few children mixed in, finding treasures in what others discarded. There was no hostility in the crowd, only resignation and dismay. Owners of some shops were looking over what was left of their stock. One old Vietnamese man was tossing what was left of his candy store into the street. A small crowd gathered, scrambling for the few fixtures and sweets.

A burning car served as a marker to Luis: On its far side the devastation reached a new level. Every block contained at least one overturned car. Here the stores weren't merely looted, they were gutted by angry or desperate people, not "shoppers." Luis felt the tension increase palpably. On the first corner beyond the burning car, two ruined buildings sat smoldering. He couldn't remember what had been there before.

Now the people looked sullen and withdrawn. Luis wondered if they were the ones who had destroyed the neighborhood, or the survivors. Then he noticed something else—across the street were two Latino young men wearing colors.

Luis recognized the green jackets of the Diablos, and he paused at a car, checking out the street for others in the gang. Except for their colors, the two leaning on a car smoking were no different from dozens of other young around. Still, passersby gave them a wide berth, and then ignored them.

Luis knew he should do the same; his promise to Melinda to come back safely made him extra cautious. He watched the Diablos a few more minutes and then he started out again keeping to the sides of the street, eyes peeled for green jackets or other gang colors. As he walked, he tried to remember where the turf borders had been. He was getting close to his building now, and he was sure this was Zombie territory. Zombies were a white gang and sworn enemies of the Diablos. Luis turned to look behind him, still checking his bearings, when he spotted three green jackets. He moved on more quickly now, trying not to look scared. Two of them were the same Diablos he passed earlier.

Luis's heart started pounding. He realized his mistake—in a crowd of the poor, he looked prosperous. Luis started walking again, casually at first, but then gradually picking up the pace. It was possible the gang members were simply going the same way as Luis and not following him. He walked a block and then cut across the street to the other side, pausing to pretend to look in a car with smashed windows, but noticing the Diablos on the other side of the street watching him. Luis started off again, wishing Steve had come with him. The Diablos might have passed on two men together.

After half a block, he looked over his shoulder. By now, he and the Diablos knew what was going on. Now they were behind him, and Luis started to jog. He was only about a mile from his building. If he could make it there, he might be safe behind the locked doors. He pumped up to a running speed he knew he could maintain for a while, but when he reached the next block, the Diablos were in pursuit. Already the people in the streets were seeking cover. The hunt was on and the rest of the herd was scattering.

Luis pushed himself to full speed. He didn't bother to look behind him. He was going to run until he couldn't run anymore. He was heading up the next block when he was tackled, landing hard on the sidewalk. He began kicking and flailing at his assailant but soon there were three gang members, their fists pounding him. Luis fought back until something hard as steel slammed into his skull and he was lost in the blackness of unconsciousness.

27. Flowers from the Sky

If you were able to hold a teaspoonful of matter from a black hole, it would weigh as much as the entire earth. Near such dense matter the laws governing time and space are radically different from those we use to describe our universe.

—Dr. Lewis Connors

Heading east at 20,000 feet
PostQuilt: Monday, 6:30 a.m. PST

While Terry's body was in a military jet traveling at 600 mph toward Washington, D.C., his mind was in a different place entirely. He was worried about John. The rumor about Portland being missing was impossible to believe but also impossible to forget. A city can't be missing, Terry told himself over and over. There must have been an avalanche, or an earthquake, or something, he reasoned. Maybe Mount Saint Helens had erupted again and the roads were blocked by ash. No, a city couldn't just be missing, but then there shouldn't be a mountain in the middle of I-5 either. If something had happened to Portland, John might need Terry's help. Knowing that made his decision difficult.

He and Ellen had fought over the course of action. Ellen wanted them to try to get to Portland, to find their son. But influenced by Bill's authority, Terry had finally accepted that he would be of more use in Washington than in Oregon.

"This kid knows something, Terry," Bill had argued. "He's barely hanging on to reality, and we need to know what he knows."

"Our son needs us too, Bill," Ellen retorted.

"You can't even get to Portland. The road's blocked. There is a traffic jam twelve miles long."

"We could try the coast highway or a back road, or maybe fly," Ellen said hopefully.

"I think Ellen's right, Bill," Terry said tentatively. "I've got a boy in Portland. I need to know if he's all right."

Bill was a hard person to disagree with. He didn't use verbal gymnastics. He just spoke with logic and certainty and Terry's own doubts convinced him Bill was right.

"I say the best way to help your boy is to find out what has happened. Help me take this kid to Washington and I'll help you find your boy. We can fly that kid out to Washington and fly back by the time you could find a way to Portland. It's only going to get worse. People will panic soon. Are you ready to deal with looters and people scared beyond reason?"

Terry was weakening and it showed on his face, but Ellen was even more resolved.

"We've got to help our son, Terry, don't let him—"

"What about your daughter?" Bill countered. "What's her name?"

"Carolyn," Angie cut in.

"Yeah, Carolyn," Bill continued. "She's in the Washington, D.C., area, isn't she? What about her?"

"I don't know, Bill," Terry stammered.

"I can get us a helicopter."

That did it. Terry wasn't even sure he could find another way into Portland. Ellen, however, was outraged. She stopped talking to him entirely, and when he left she didn't say goodbye.

Bill used his military ID and three phone calls to get Kenny Randall released in his custody. The same procedure got them a Piper Cub at the Medford Airport and a military 707 at Mountain Home Air Force Base in Idaho. Now Terry found himself baby-sitting a sleeping Kenny as he reconsidered his decision.

Kenny stirred, momentarily distracting Terry. Kenny's eyes moved rapidly back and forth under the lids. Kenny was dreaming, and that meant he'd be awake soon. Terry wondered whether Kenny's dream could be more fantastic than the events of the last two days.

Bill had been up front talking with the pilots and returned with a grim look.

"It's worse than I thought. The pilots are picking up reports from all over the country . . . strange reports. Huge sheets of ice, deserts appearing out of nowhere, floods. There's also another missing city report. New York."

Terry's heart twisted in his chest. One missing city report seemed fantastic; two somehow seemed credible.

"Any response yet?" Bill gestured toward Kenny.

"No. But he's coming out of it. He's dreaming. You have to be in a light stage of sleep to dream. Once he wakes up he'll be lucid for a few minutes. But the more thinking he does, the more anxiety he will feel. He'll handle that anxiety by shutting out the outside world. We better know what we want to ask right when he wakes. We may get only one chance."

"Let him sleep. We're almost to Washington, and I have a doctor standing by to meet us."

Bill and Terry spent the next twenty minutes writing down questions. They decided on a strategy to build Kenny's ego, confirming he was right and then manipulating his paranoid tendencies to get the information they needed.

"Where am I?"

The sound of Kenny's voice rang like a slap across the face. He was looking around the cabin. He seemed generally confused, but not psychotic.

Immediately, Bill employed their plan.

"I'm Bill Conrad and this is Terry Roberts. And you're on your way to Washington, D.C. The President wants to meet you and shake your hand."

Kenny now looked confused and pleased, but disbelieving.

"That's right, Kenny. You warned people. You did your best to save people. How did you manage to figure it out like that?"

Suddenly Kenny lunged at the window, trying to see the ground below. Then he unbuckled his seat belt and ran from window to window, finally settling in a seat toward the rear of the plane, his nose pressed against the window. Terry sat beside him and Bill leaned over from the seat in front. Suddenly Kenny's head snapped around to look at Terry.

"My sister?"

"She's fine. She'll be waiting for you when you return to Oregon."

Kenny looked relieved, and then an emotion Terry couldn't identify reshaped his expression.

After a minute, Terry pressed ahead with his questioning.

"How did you figure it out, Kenny? You must be a genius." Terry tried to say it with conviction.

Kenny pushed his nose against the window again and began to talk.

"I'm not a genius, I just notice things other people don't. Like the corn."

"The corn?" Terry probed.

"Yeah, the corn. Me, Jack, and Robbie went hunting and on the way it started to rain corn. Just poured out of the sky."

Kenny paused and twisted his head, like he had spotted something on the ground behind the plane. Terry was worried about the next question, but Kenny needed to start talking again soon.

"You were the only one who noticed it?"

"You think I'm crazy, don't you!" Kenny's voice was filled with venom. "Of course the other guys noticed it. You think it could rain corn and not be noticed? You're the crazy man, not me."

"What did you mean when you said you notice things other people don't?"

"Jack and Robbie thought it was strange, but I knew it was more than that. I knew it meant something."

"A sign?"

"What do you take me for? Some kind of New Age guru? I just knew that corn doesn't fall from the sky for no reason."

Terry realized he had the wrong point of view. He assumed Kenny would have a mystical interpretation, like most people who prophesied the end of the world. Terry started over. "It must have been more than the corn. You must have had more clues than that."

"Oh sure. I used to read these books when I was a kid. You know, books about strange things. UFO sightings, dinosaurs in Africa, stuff like that. There were even stories about stuff falling out of the sky. Mostly ice, but some animals, frogs, fish, even seeds. It was fun to read about this stuff but I never thought it was true. I always just figured a tornado, or an airplane, or something dropped this stuff. After the corn fell on me I began thinking about these things differently. I started checking. These things really did happen. But I couldn't put it together.

Not by myself. Not until I met Dr. Piltcher. He and Dr. Coombs knew there was something to it . . . and the others. It was Dr. Coombs that found the Zorastrus manuscript. He knew it was coming, he just didn't know when . . . not exactly when."

Kenny paused, lost in thought. His face was still facing the window but Terry could see his reflection and his eyes were unfocused and glassy.

"You finally figured out why it was happening, didn't you? You and the others."

"Not for a long time. We just kept researching all the strange incidents we could find. The regular papers don't report most of this stuff anymore. Used to, though. I found stuff going back over a hundred years, but Dr. Piltcher and Dr. Coombs showed me it had been going on longer than that. Zorastrus knew something was coming and predicted it, but we still couldn't make the model work. Then it came together . . . started to come . . . Phat and me . . . it was the flowers that did it."

Kenny's voice faded out after he said "flowers."

"The flowers . . ." Terry probed gently.

"Flowers—just fell from the sky—" Kenny's tongue began running back and forth over his lips. The seat belt sign came on before Terry could ask another question, but it didn't matter. Kenny was gone. His eyes were fixed and glassy. They maneuvered him away from the window and then lifted his arms to buckle him in. Like a wax model, they remained suspended until Terry put them down onto the armrests.

They were still there when the EMTs came to load him onto a stretcher and wheel him off the plane.

Bill and Terry climbed into a waiting van. When Bill finally spoke, he was clearly disappointed.

"I was hoping for more."

"He caught us by surprise. We weren't quite ready. Still, he gave us something. You ever heard of a Dr. Piltcher or Dr. Coombs?"

"No," Bill said. "Who was that other one? Phat? I'll put some people on it. If they were like Kenny they might be holed up in a cave somewhere, maybe with their relatives. I'll have someone research that name. The prophet. What was his name?"

"Zorastrus."

"Yeah, ever hear of him? Me neither. What was it he said about things falling from the sky? Flowers and corn from the sky? You think Portland and New York were buried by something from the sky? That's not what the reports say. They say gone, and gone is a lot different from buried."

"No, but I remember something about flowers falling from the sky in one of those books of his . . . no, one of those articles. He said the flowers were the clue."

The bags of articles from Kenny's room were in the back of the van, and Bill and Terry opened them, searching for the file folder. They found it in the bundle they'd made from the bedspread.

Terry read the article aloud, but nothing in the article gave them a clue to what had happened. A mother and her five-year-old daughter were sitting in a park in Hiroshima, Japan, when it began to rain flowers—the flowers were wildflowers, with grasses, mostly white flowers, but some of other colors too. Although the shower lasted less than a minute it was enough to nearly bury the little girl. No one could explain where the flowers came from. When Terry finished, he felt the same tickle he felt before in Kenny's room.

Bill shook his head. "I get nothing, Terry. How about you? Read it again."

The van kept starting and stopping in traffic. Reading in a car always made Terry sick to his stomach, but now he felt particularly ill. He ignored the creeping nausea; still, the second reading added nothing; the tickle was still there.

"Bill, let's try brainstorming. We'll take turns saying whatever comes to mind. Don't try to judge your ideas. Let any idea out. I'll start. Flowers from the sky."

"You mean like word association? Tulips?"

"Anything. Park, people, picnic."

"Mother, daughter, family, apple pie . . . make that sushi."

"Japan, Hiroshima . . ."

"World War II, Nagasaki."

The tickle turned to an itch and then into an idea.

"The bomb? You think the bomb did this?"

"That's the first thing I thought of, Terry, but fission bombs don't drop flowers on people. These bombs fry people, not decorate them. If there is a connection then maybe there's an article about something falling on Nagasaki. I wonder—where did that corn fall on Kenny?"

They split up the articles looking for something from Nagasaki but found nothing. They then looked for articles from cities near the now closed Nevada nuclear test site, but to no avail. They were still searching the books when the van stopped.

Terry helped bring Kenny's things into a brick town house indistinguishable from many other such D.C. structures. There was no sign on the front of the building, and no guards stood in the lobby, but Bill had to use an elevator key to get to the floor he wanted. There the doors slid open to two armed airmen who questioned them thoroughly. Bill was given a badge, but Terry had to have his photo ID made on the spot.

Bill knew his way around and led Terry to a conference room. He had the guards spill the bags onto the oversize table and then began sifting through the contents. He found the computer disks, and the hard drive, then led Terry down the hall through another security check and into a room filled with computer terminals and work stations. One station was occupied by a pretty black woman who didn't look much older than Terry's daughter, Carolyn. She smiled when Bill headed directly for her. She wasn't wearing a uniform but Bill called her Lieutenant Gillespie.

"I thought you were on vacation, sir."

"I was, but something brought me back."

"It wouldn't be a few missing cities, three air bases, an aircraft carrier group, not to mention the loss of the ELF system?"

Terry had a sudden urge to run to the nearest airport and catch a flight home. One missing city had become two, and now a "few." Bill must have been equally shocked but merely said calmly, "I need an analysis of these as soon as possible." As always, he was the consumate professional.

"Colonel, I'll give it highest priority, but it will take at least several hours."

Bill and Terry waited while Lieutenant Gillespie copied the disks and the files from the hard drive. When she returned them Bill asked her if she had ever heard of an ancient prophet called Zorastrus.

"I've heard of Zorro," she said with a smile.

Bill thanked her and then led Terry through another door. At the end of a hall Bill turned into a room that was filled with computer parts and repair equipment. He exchanged a few words with the counter man and then led Terry to the back, past shelves filled with parts. In a small room filled with more bits and pieces of computers was an Asian man of about thirty, with thick black hair and rumpled clothes. His nose was six inches away from a computer screen. Several Styrofoam cups of old coffee surrounded him. Monitors, computers, and keyboards were lying everywhere. The beeps of a computer game filled the room.

"Phil, I need a favor."

Phil punched the tab button with his little finger and the game froze on the screen.

"Official or unofficial?"

"An unofficial favor but official business."

"Classified, top secret stuff?" Phil asked eagerly.

"Tip top secret. I shouldn't even be showing it to you."

"All right! Let me see."

Bill handed him two boxes of disks and the hard drive. Phil soon had a screen full of icons.

"What gives? You promised me something secret. This isn't even access protected. No challenge, no deal."

"The challenge is figuring out what it all means. No one else has been able to figure it out."

"No one?" Phil asked hopefully.

"Two CIA cryptographers got canned because they couldn't figure it out," Bill lied.

"Hot damn. I'm on it. What should I look for? A message? Diagrams? Plans?"

"I wouldn't want to send you down the wrong path. I'll check back with you. Call me if you get something."

They started to leave, but then Bill turned back.

"Hey, Phil. You ever hear of Zorastrus?"

"Yeah, the prophet of Babylon," Phil said without taking his eyes from the computer screen. "Pretty astute guy. Not as well known as Nostradamus. Probably because his career got cut short. Some of his short-sighted contemporaries thought he was a little too smart. They put him in a pit and stoned him." Phil looked up at Bill and Terry with a serious face. "Does he have anything to do with what's happened? He made some pretty scary predictions."

"Don't know, Phil. Honestly."

As they left, Bill directed Terry to a phone so he could call his daughter, Carolyn, who was full of questions Terry couldn't or wouldn't answer, but otherwise she was fine. After assuring Carolyn he would call as soon as he found out about John, Terry caught up with Bill.

"You really think that Phil will turn up anything?"

"Terry, there's two ways to pick a lock. One is to work through it systematically. Start with zero right, zero left, zero right, and then try zero right, zero left, one right. Eventually you will open that lock. Lieutenant Gillespie's people will do it that way. Phil—well, he's an unguided missile with an uncanny record of hitting targets, targets he wasn't aiming for. He knew about Zorastrus, didn't he?"

"So why is he fixing computers?"

"Partly by choice, but mostly because he's the biggest blabbermouth in the service. He couldn't keep a secret if his life depended on it, but in this case it doesn't matter. Even God couldn't cover this up."

28. The Brood

The last age of Man will be the great transfiguration and society, and the world, will never be the same. I can see no further ages, not because they will not come, but because the future is confused.

—The Prophecies of Melchi-Zedek

Warm Springs Indian Reservation, Oregon
PostQuilt: Monday, 6:50 a.m. PST

Colter was the first out of the RV in the morning, looking for a place to relieve himself. But as soon as he stepped out he started cussing. Sid and three of his friends were waiting under the RV and darted out when Colter stepped down, nearly making him wet his pants. Still cussing over the scare, he placed his bare foot in psittacosaurus droppings. Colter loosed another barrage of profanity while wiping his foot on the grass. When he finally got far enough away to urinate, Sid and friends ran around harassing him. Colter pissed at them as they ran by but missed them and sprinkled his foot by mistake. He cussed some more and began wiping his foot again. His cussing was so loud and long, the others were up when he got back. Colter intended to climb back into his sleeping bag, but someone had rolled it up while he was gone.

Dr. Coombs cooked bacon and eggs and sour dough biscuits while the others cleaned up the RV and prepared for the morning activities.

The morning was cool but comfortable, so they ate outside under the tarp. Sid and two other psittacosauri circled around the table, darting in and out, snatching up any scraps as soon as they hit the ground. The animals were becoming a nuisance, but the group, despite their better judgment, couldn't help but feed the unusual little creatures. Partway through the meal Petra remembered Moose and took him some eggs and part of a biscuit.

After breakfast they started their study by examining the edge of the meadow. Dr. Piltcher had Colter dig down where the green meadow met the desert. The edge of the turf came up easily, and soon Dr. Piltcher was finger-combing his hair. Dr. Coombs spoke first.

"Everything is intact. There is not a root broken. And look along the edge here. There isn't a broken blade of grass anywhere along the edge."

"Yes, I see," said Dr. Piltcher. "Somewhere a hundred million years in the past is a piece of turf that would match up perfectly with this edge. Very odd. I would have expected something violent. But this seems tender. Not a blade of grass torn or uprooted."

"Yes," Dr. Coombs agreed, "gentle but perhaps too gentle. Look at how easily the roots were exposed. They weren't embedded in the soil. They need to take root again or these grasses will not survive, not to mention the bushes or trees."

Petra had been listening silently, absorbing each word. Since she rarely broke into their discussions, they listened when she did.

"They won't live anyway. This is tropical vegetation, or at least subtropical. This climate won't even support a pine forest, let alone a jungle. These grasses are going to start drying up soon, and when the vegetation dies, so will Sid and his friends, and any other animals we might find in here."

"She's right," Dr. Piltcher said. "We need to identify as many species as we can as quickly as possible. Once we know what we are dealing with we need to get help to relocate the plant and animal life."

"What?" Colter cut in. "Moose is okay, we can't seem to get him out, but if you're thinking of carrying Sid and his friends along, think again. Did you smell that mess he made in the RV?"

Petra quickly stepped in to smooth things over.

"It may happen again. You know how badly Sid reacts when he feels trapped."

"One way or another they will move," Dr. Coombs said. "When the vegetation dries up they will start searching for another food source. This land barely supports the little livestock we've seen. When these animals start to move, they won't survive long. If the local vegetation doesn't kill them, the local ranchers will."

"Well then," Dr. Coombs said. "Let's see what we're dealing with."

They loaded day packs with lunch and water and then spread out along the lush clearing, walking through the knee-high grass. Sid and friends circled them, chasing ahead and then dropping behind and blending into the bright green of the grasses so quickly it was hard to spot them. Dr. Piltcher's frustration grew with each fleeting glance of something disappearing into the grass, and he began whispering about setting snares and traps to get a better look at the fauna. They were near the taller bushes when Colter dove into the grass again, wrestling with another animal.

"Colter, the last thing we need is another psittacosaurus," Dr. Piltcher warned while he stomped through the turf.

"This one's different . . . bigger. Hey, ow, ow, ow! You little bastard."

"Don't hurt it!" Petra shouted.

"I'm the one getting hurt. *Now* I've got you!"

Colter struggled to his feet with something wriggling violently in his arms. This time Colter stood holding an animal a foot longer than Sid. The animal had a large bony collar around its neck and a head that was a third of its body size. The parrotlike snout curved over the lower jaw, but the overhang was much less than Sid's. The animal's short, stocky legs were all the same size, clearly indicating a quadriped. Its body—bulky and ending in a thick tail—was covered with gray-green skin.

"It looks like a baby stegosaurus," Petra said.

"I don't think so, wrong suborder. More likely a ceratopsian," Dr. Coombs replied. "I believe this is full grown." Dr. Coombs paused, looking concerned. "We better hope so, I'd hate to be holding a baby if the mother showed up."

Colter glanced around quickly, and then looked as if he might put the dinosaur down.

"Don't let it go just yet," Dr. Piltcher said. "It's beautiful."

"It's heavy," Colter responded.

"It's not a baby stegosaur," Dr. Piltcher corrected. "I believe it is a microceratops."

"This one's not much bigger than Sid," Petra said.

"It's heavy," Colter reminded them.

"Put it in the RV, Colter," Dr. Coombs said. "We'll look at it later."

As Colter walked off he shouted over his shoulder, "This time I'm putting down some papers."

When he was out of earshot Dr. Piltcher turned to Dr. Coombs and said in a low voice, "I bet he names it Mike."

Overhearing, Petra snickered and then walked off toward the hedge, Dr. Coombs and Dr. Piltcher following. Creatures continued to dart through the grass, and soon Dr. Piltcher's frustration returned. Even though he didn't like Colter, he found himself envying him. He was turning out to be a crackerjack dinosaur catcher, too dumb to know there was any danger.

The tall bushes were too dense to pass through, but soon they came to a narrow opening and prepared to walk through single file. Petra was about to enter when Dr. Coombs held her arm.

"What do you think made this path?"

As Petra looked she saw the branches of the bushes were broken and the grasses trampled. Dr. Piltcher knelt, studying the grass. Then he looked up at the others.

"Something bigger than Sid," he said.

Their curiosity was greater than their fears and Dr. Coombs led the way. As the undergrowth thinned, the movements below ended, and they began to walk more casually. The doctors paused occasionally, examining various bushes and arguing over classification. Petra continued to be amazed by their range of knowledge but wondered if a real specialist would quickly spot holes in it.

Now they could see the lake shimmering in the distance. They were about to move toward it when Dr. Coombs motioned them into the shadows of an overhanging bush, where they squatted expectantly. Something about six feet high was moving ahead of them, through the bush and across their path. The animal was hard to see but it seemed to have a long thin neck and walked upright. It moved slowly, apparently unaware of their presence. As it drew close, the explorers involuntarily held their breaths, but it continued its easygoing stride. It was just about out of sight when the bushes behind them parted and something came through. They all jumped up, spinning to meet the threat—Colter.

Petra gasped, and then pounded her fists gently on his chest. "Don't *do* that," she whispered.

Dr. Piltcher and Dr. Coombs were as relieved as Petra.

"Is the microceratops secure?" Dr. Piltcher asked.

"Sarah is as secure as I could make her. She may be slower than Sid, but she's a lot stronger."

"You named the microceratops Sarah? Not Mike?"

"You don't call a girl by a boy's name."

"How do you know it's female?" Dr. Piltcher asked.

"Because when it peed all over the floor of the RV, it squatted."

Dr. Piltcher shook his head at Colter's logic, but didn't argue.

"Did you give the poor thing something to eat?" Petra asked.

"Two apples, and a pile of Ritz crackers. I gave Moose some—" Colter paused, looking over their shoulders. "And who's this?"

The others spun around to see a six-foot dinosaur standing thirty yards away. It wasn't anything like the other dinosaurs they had seen. Much larger, it had a huge head that was nearly all mouth. Two small black eyes were set on either side of its face and large nostril holes tipped its protruding snout. It stood on two large back legs, leaning forward with its thick tail trailing out behind. Two thinner forelegs ended in three-fingered hands. The body was covered with loose, wrinkled, gray-green skin, and the most noticeable feature was the wicked-looking curved claws on each finger and toe. Colter leaned over Dr. Piltcher's shoulder and whispered in his ear, "If you want me to wrestle this one to the ground, forget it."

Suddenly the dinosaur cocked its head to the side, as if it was listening. The group froze, angry at Colter, while the dinosaur stared at them curiously. There was no menace in its eyes, only interest. Then it turned, leaned forward and trotted off through the brush, its long tail held straight out behind it. It stopped once to look back over its shoulder. The others remained silent until the dinosaur was out of sight.

"Maybe we better rethink this, Chester," Dr. Coombs said. "That was a deinonychus."

"No, I don't think so," Dr. Piltcher said too quickly. "More likely a stenonychosaurus." He didn't say it with any conviction.

"What aren't you telling us?" Petra asked.

Dr. Coombs finally spoke reluctantly.

"Deinonychus is a carnosaur."

Petra fell silent trying to think through the implications, but Colter spoke up.

"What the hell's a carnosaur?"

The others remained silent, so Petra turned to Colter.

"It's a meat eater."

"So? I mean you guys didn't expect them all to be like Moose or Sid, did you?"

Colter seemed unconcerned by their close encounter with the predator, and in many ways he was right. Colter, who had not believed this was a piece of prehistoric past in the first place, now accepted the reality of it and the accompanying dangers the others had been denying.

Dr. Piltcher, embarrassed, defended his actions and his ego.

"No, I didn't think they would all be like Sid . . . the little dinosaurs. But there was no reason to think this little patch of the past would contain any predators at all. After all, there were no more predators then than there are today. Only about two percent of the dinosaurs were carnivores. That's about the same ratio as modern mammals. How often, Colter, when you walk in the woods do you meet a bear, or a cougar? I'd wager never."

"How sure are you about the two percent?" Colter asked.

Dr. Piltcher looked uncertain and Dr. Coombs stepped in.

"The two percent number is educated guesswork, although based on what we've encountered in such a short piece of time . . . I suppose it could be inaccurate."

"Hey, we need a rifle. Want me to drive back to town and get one?" Colter offered.

"No . . . no," Dr. Piltcher said. "I wouldn't want to kill one . . ."

"Deinonychus were thought to hunt in packs, Chester," Dr. Coombs reminded him, seeming to accept Colter's idea.

Dr. Piltcher hesitated. "Let's think about it. Perhaps we should head back and talk it over. Let's circle back this way."

Dr. Piltcher pointed in the direction opposite the deinonychus's route. They walked in silence, vigilant now for larger dinosaurs as well as the smaller ones. They continued through the taller brush, curving back toward the RV, relieved when the brush thinned again and they could see farther ahead and behind. At a section of overlapping bushes, they pushed themselves through the thick brush to a small clearing filled with a mound of leaves. They started across, but found the mound soft, so they skirted around the outside—except for Colter, who continued on his way, his feet sinking into the surface.

"Man, this stuff is hot," he complained.

Dr. Piltcher ignored Colter's complaint for a few steps and then stopped abruptly. Petra, following close behind, bumped into him.

"Colter, is it just warm from the sun, or hot?" Dr. Piltcher asked.

"It's hot. Come here and feel this."

Dr. Coombs pushed his hand into the leaves.

"It is inordinately warm. It must be from the decay."

Dr. Piltcher pushed his hand in too.

"Well, Chester, shall we dig?" Dr. Coombs asked.

"I can't find any reason not to, but let's not dillydally. Colter, dig down, will you? Carefully?"

"What for?"

"Colter, dig! Petra, you help watch."

Dr. Coombs was already moving handfuls of leaves to the side. Colter bent over at the waist and began digging dog style, throwing leaves between his legs. Soon Dr. Coombs adopted the more efficient posture. They opened the top of the mound and spread out, enlarging the hole. While the leaves on top were dry and crisp, underneath was moist decaying matter, with a pungent odor.

Colter complained about the smell but his arms never slowed until he gave another shout.

He'd found an elongated egg, eight inches in length. Dr. Piltcher immediately held it out to Dr. Coombs. They turned it slowly in their hands, feeling the smooth soft shell.

"It's very warm," Dr. Piltcher observed.

"Yes, because of the decay," Dr. Coombs added. "Very clever, really."

"Hey, there's lots more."

They turned to see Colter holding an egg in each hand. When Petra and the men completely uncovered the nest they found three concentric circles of the eight-inch eggs, each one pointed toward the center of the nest.

Dr. Piltcher sketched the layout of the eggs and then directed that the eggs be reburied while he took custody of the first one. When they finished, the mound looked different. It was higher now, and lumpy.

Dr. Piltcher stopped at the edge of the clearing and put the egg on the ground, wrapped it in a sweatshirt borrowed from Dr. Coombs, placed it inside his shirt, and then led the way out of the clearing and toward the RV.

Forty minutes after the humans left, an animal twice the size of a rhinoceros shuffled into the clearing. She had a short thick tail and a large bony collar around her massive neck. A long curved horn protruded from her large snout, and two smaller horns protruded from the neck collar. Her head was huge, easily a quarter of her enormous body. She walked on all fours, her back legs longer than her front legs, so her rear hips were higher than the front, and her head was held close to the ground, where her nose was busy smelling. Something was wrong in the clearing.

Her eyes were weak, and she relied on her sensitive olfactory organs for most of her information. She had smelled the mound twice a day since laying the eggs and each time the smells had been the same. Today there was a new smell, one she had never encountered. She pawed the center of the mound, quickly removing enough material so she could check. They were still there. Sweeping with her tail, she refilled the depression and smoothed over the surface. Now she put her head to the ground and began sniffing, spiraling down the mound and toward the periphery. She was working along the outside edge of the clearing when she smelled that one of her eggs had been there. The smell was faint but distinct, and it was mixed with the strange smells of the mound. She discovered her nest had been robbed. Then she followed the smells out of her clearing.

29. Life in the Forest

Oh, that I could live to see the time of two times; to walk with the ancients.

—*Zorastrus, before the King of Babylon*

Forest, former site of Portland, Oregon
PostQuilt: Monday, 7:05 a.m. PST

Cubby automatically assumed the leader's role, now that Ripman was gone, and as John trod behind, he regretted his decision to stick with his friend. He thought about the beach cabin. He imagined his parents were probably headed there now and would soon be sitting around the fireplace eating crab or tossing bread crusts off the balcony to the seagulls. Lost in thought, he nearly stumbled into Cubby, who had stopped and crouched down.

"What's the big—"

"Shhhhh." Cubby put his fingers to his lips. Then he pointed over the clump of grass in front of him. They were at the top of a long slow grade. John stood up slowly until his eyes cleared the bush. Their hill dropped off sharply into a little valley, with few trees but rich with the same deep green grasses and ferns beneath their feet. Here and there in the valley, boulders stuck above the grass. John didn't understand Cubby's caution until one boulder raised its head and looked around.

"They look like rhinos."

"More like a giant armadillo. See, it's covered with armor plates and it doesn't have a horn like a rhino. Look over there."

One of the animals was moving through the clearing, and they got glimpses of its body and tail. It walked on all fours with its head down, its dragging tail ending in a bony sphere.

"Did you see that tail? It looks like a—a *mace*, one of those heavy-duty weapons the knights used."

Cubby shushed him again, and nodded, and whispered softly, "Let's work our way around the valley."

"Good idea," John whispered back. "Let's head due west and when we get to the Pacific we'll turn left."

Ignoring John, Cubby turned and led off through the trees. As John followed, he tried to remember the map Ripman and Cubby had drawn in the dirt. They worked their way around the little valley by going uphill, and John wondered whether this was one of the hills near Cubby's dad's church.

The big dinosaurs in the valley were the first they had seen since being chased, although many smaller lizards scuttled out of the way as they passed. John kept thinking of the beach cabin.

The trees thickened, and as the giant redwoods once again dominated the forest the underbrush thinned to soft ferns. As they climbed a steep slope, John decided to conserve his energy, and he lagged behind, hoping Cubby wouldn't notice. When Cubby disappeared through the trees ahead, John was motivated to pick up his pace. Suddenly he heard Cubby yell.

"John! It's here. It's here!"

Pushing his aching legs harder, John pumped up the hill, dodging trees. The ground steepened and then leveled and John burst out of the forest onto a bald peak. Cubby was shouting and pointing. Another valley lay below them, and another hill behind that sloped down to meet the valley. After a gap another hill sloped up out of the valley. John followed Cubby's finger, pointed between the hills. He had to stare hard, but there in the gap was Portland—a shimmering misty image, but undeniably Portland.

"We found it," John said out loud, "we made it."

Cubby picked John up in a bear hug and spun him around. After they danced and whooped, they sat on the rocks and rested, eating more of their trail mix, and drinking from their canteens. Bursting with excitement, they planned delightedly how to get into the Willamette Valley where Portland lay. John was still talking when Cubby fell silent, staring at Portland. Concerned, John followed his friend's gaze. Portland was there in the gap, shimmering and shifting. Then John saw something else—the hills on the other side of Portland. No—the hills through Portland.

"I can see through it," he said aloud.

"No you can't."

"Cubby, I can see through those buildings."

"It's an illusion. You can't see through a building."

John didn't argue with Cubby, but he was sure the image was transparent. How could it be? he asked himself. But then there couldn't be dinosaurs either.

Cubby led off down the hill without speaking, John following, but his enthusiasm dampened.

The trip downhill was more difficult than it had seemed from the bald peak. The sparse forest suddenly gave way to a section of trees crisscrossed in every direction, and Cubby and John had to climb over and under them.

Suddenly, a high-pitched roar pierced their ears and rattled the trees. They turned in time to see two dinosaurs racing out of the woods. The one in front had a domed head and a short thick neck. Bipedal, pumping hard to get away, it was easily fifteen feet high, and the biggest dinosaur John had seen. Until he saw what was behind it. Towering ten feet above the domed head were massive gaping jaws John recognized as belonging to *Tyrannosaurus rex*. Blood was running down the side of the dome-headed dinosaur, and it ran out of the forest with a limping gait. When it reached the edge of the fallen section it slowed its pace. John could see it was weakening; the tyrannosaurus would have it soon.

John and Cubby ran for a pile of fallen trees and crawled underneath. The ground began to shake, and the smaller dinosaur began to scream. Cubby, peeking between the logs, jerked on John's sleeve. Scared to look, but too scared not to, he pushed himself up into a squat and peeked out. The dinosaurs were fighting seventy-five yards away, the tyrannosaurus crunching the neck of the dome head. The dome head was screaming in pain and struggled violently to break the grip of the tyrannosaur, swinging wildly with its tail. The tyrannosaur rotated away from the blows and repeatedly slammed its own tail to counterbalance its victim's moves. Chunks of turf and debris were kicked up and rained down on the boys as the dinosaurs struggled.

Blood streamed down the neck of the dome head, across its chest and legs, making its skin a slick red. The tyrannosaur kept its lock on the dome head's neck as dome head's struggles weakened and its screams softened. The dome head collapsed to its knees and then to the ground. The painful screams of the dome head became a mournful whine, and then the whine died with its last breath. The tyrannosaur kept its jaws tightly clamped on the still form for another minute and then shook the body several times. Only then did it release the still form. John expected the tyrannosaur to raise its head and bellow in triumph, but instead the tyrannosaur took a long lingering lick across the neck of the dead dinosaur, soaking its tongue in blood. Then it slurped in its tongue and smacked its jaws loud enough to echo through the forest. When Cubby whispered "God protect us," the dinosaur's head snapped around and it stared at their hideaway, as if it heard.

"Don't move," Cubby whispered.

John wanted to shout at Cubby to shut up but instead he froze. After a long hard stare the tyrannosaur turned back to its meal. John slipped silently to the floor, Cubby next to him. John watched his hand shake, thinking he couldn't get any more afraid. Then the sounds of eating echoed through their hiding place. The tyrannosaur made great smacking and slobbering sounds, but the worst sounds of all were of flesh ripping and bones crushed in massive jaws.

30. Debris

Towns will be turned upside down and the below ground will become the above ground.

—Zorastrus, Prophet of Babylon

Off Naples, Florida
PostQuilt: Monday, 10:15 a.m. EST

Saltwater, thick with sticks and leaves, washed over the family, shocking them awake. It was late morning but the dense cloud cover and fog made it as dark as night.

"Put down the sides to keep the waves out," Carmen said. "Rosa? Can you sit up?"

Ron looked at Chris. His eyes were open, but he looked groggy. The gash on his forehead was surrounded by a large swelling. "Chris, are you okay? Can you move down, opposite Rosa?"

Chris didn't speak, but he nodded and scooted. Ron worked opposite Carmen to drop the sides of the raft, which were tied up at the top of the canopy. It wouldn't keep out an entire wave, but it would cut down on the sea spray. When Ron stretched up to unite the top he spotted another large wave coming toward them.

"Everyone hang on!" he yelled.

They all grabbed for the cords strung around the inside of the raft. Carmen wrapped an arm around Chris and Ron hooked Rosa's arm with his. They all hunkered down, and the wave broke over them—another muddy one, and full of debris. Leaves and twigs slapped them on their heads and arms. The raft tossed and rocked violently. After the wave had passed, Ron broke out a bailing cup and went to work while Carmen and the others lifted out the branches and the other debris.

Rosa was having trouble lifting her left arm over her head, and finally gave up and used only her right one. Ron suspected cracked or broken ribs. Chris was helping too, scooping up handfuls of leaves and twigs and dropping them over the side, when he stopped, staring into the gloom.

"Hey, there's a lot of smoke out there."

Ron turned to see a cloud bank broiling toward them. "Everyone hang on again."

The family ducked down as the raft rocked violently, hot moist steam enveloping them. The steam was sulfurous and they coughed, their noses and throats burning. The pitching slowed and the air cleared slightly. Ron looked over the side but could see nothing in the dense fog.

"It's just steam," he said reassuringly. "Nothing to worry about." He didn't add that they had enough to worry about already.

Ron helped clear debris and bail out the raft. Then he checked the supplies. There were cans of water, food, a pocket knife, four flares, fishing tackle, and a paddle. He was repacking the supplies when something rammed the raft.

"It's a log," Carmen yelled. "Help me push it away."

Ron used the paddle. The branches were thick and Ron had trouble getting a solid push. Finally, the raft drifted off only to spin around and butt up against the bare trunk. Ron wedged the paddle again and pushed. Suddenly, something came running the length of the trunk. Green, lithe, and frantic, it was a foot-tall lizard. Ron instinctively swung with the paddle, knocking it off its feet. The lizard hung over the side of the log briefly, its tail in the water, then it launched itself again. Ron was ready and hit it with a full swing, knocking it into the water. The lizard churned the water, trying to reach safety. Ron pushed off from the log, and then paddled furiously, leaving the log in the haze.

"What was that?" Carmen asked.

"I'd never seen one before. Its head was huge." Ron didn't add it had a wicked set of teeth. "It's gone now. We're fine."

The kids settled back but Carmen and Ron exchanged worried looks.

Exhausted from the night before, the family rested silently, worrying privately. Chris soon leaned over the edge, watching the waves.

"He looks better," Carmen said.

"His color's good. I wish we could get him to a doctor."

Helpless, the parents fretted.

"There's another lizard out there!" Chris suddenly shouted.

Rosa popped up next to him and confirmed it. "It looks like more than one."

"Switch with us, kids," Ron ordered. Quickly, Ron realized the creatures were coming toward the raft. "Hand me the paddle, Rosa."

Paddling furiously, Ron futilely tried to move the raft away. A thick soup of debris made paddling difficult. Looking back, Ron could see the bobbing heads gaining, but there were more than two. Carmen appeared next to him armed with the knife.

Paddling only slowed the inevitable. The bobbing green heads were mostly jaw, with small black eyes—eyes fixed on the raft. Finally, Ron raised the paddle for battle.

"Ron! There's a dozen of them!"

Ron drove the first one under with one blow, but it came up snarling. Two more blows sent it down for good, but others were taking its place. Ron struck violently, delivering blow after blow.

"Over here!" Carmen screamed.

Ron spun, batting one off the lip of the raft. As it fell it slashed an air cell. Chris's scream brought him around to see the other side of the raft suddenly dip. A head appeared and Ron fought to keep his balance, swinging with all his might. The blow stunned the beast, but its claws clung to the side. Turning the paddle sideways, Ron cracked its skull with the blade, the lifeless form slipping into the water.

Ron knocked two more off from behind and then heard Chris scream again. Another animal was crawling up his side.

"Duck, Chris!"

Chris flopped into the bottom of the raft just as the paddle cleared his head, catching the lizard just under the jaw, snapping the neck. Ron swung recklessly now, smacking head after head, driving them back into the sea and away from the raft. The assault ended when another log floated near, and the remaining lizards scrambled aboard.

Quickly paddling away, they soon found themselves alone in the fog again.

"What were they, Dad?"

Shaking his head, Ron said "I don't know. They came from the island, I guess."

Suddenly a clawed arm reached over the side, tangling Rosa's hair.

"It's got me!" she screamed.

Another claw appeared, followed by a head. Rosa sank lower, her hair still tangled in the claw.

The jaws opened, exposing wicked teeth. Ron struggled to his feet, the soft bottom rocking from his efforts. Grabbing the paddle, Ron struck just as a leg flopped over the side, splintering the paddle on its skull. Stunned, the animal hung briefly, then screamed in Ron's face. Instinctively, Ron brought the handle up and jammed it down its throat. The jaws snapped shut just missing his fingers. Its forelegs frantically clawed at the handle embedded in its throat, as it tottered on the side. Then Carmen jammed the knife in its neck. Without another weapon Ron lunged, shoving with all his might, pushing the lizard back into the sea. It squawked and splashed noisily until it slipped beneath the waves.

Exhausted from fear, the family flopped in the bottom of the raft, Carmen still holding the bloody knife. Ron stroked Chris's head and hoped they wouldn't need the knife again. Soon everyone was asleep.

"Uh-oh! Something's coming again," Chris shouted, waking the others.

Carmen and Rosa instinctively moved to see.

"Don't move!" Ron shouted. "We don't want to capsize. Carmen, you look, and Rosa, stay where you are for now."

Carmen scooted a little closer to Chris to see what he'd seen.

"I think he's right. It's splashing through the water a couple of waves away."

"Is it like the others?"

"I can't tell, but it's bigger. Ron, you better take a look at this."

Ron and Chris changed places. Ron had trouble spotting it in the fog. Like the others, it looked monstrous, with a human-sized lizard head, and a partially opened mouth lined with sharp teeth. It was having trouble in the water as it splashed inefficiently with small legs.

Ron turned, looking for another weapon. There was nothing but the knife; a pitiful weapon.

"Ron, it's here! Oh it's big. Real big!"

Ron turned to see Carmen backing up, motioning for the kids to move to the other end of the raft. Suddenly the raft wall was pulled down violently, and the massive head appeared. Chris screamed and stumbled back into Ron. The lizard was snapping its jaws, and at the same time scrabbling with its clawed forearms to pull itself into the raft. As the claws shredded the raft, the air emptied from cell after cell. That lowered the side and the lizard pulled itself forward. The raft flooded, but the lizard continued to scramble. Then a huge rear leg appeared.

"We've got to get out," Ron said. "Over the side."

But Carmen was already helping Chris into the water, and Rosa rolled off backward like a skin diver. Ron looked back to see the lizard struggling into the raft. It didn't look vicious, it looked scared—just trying to survive like Ron and his family.

Ron was about to jump when he remembered the survival supplies. Quickly, he grabbed a net bag and jammed four plastic quart bottles of water in it and jumped over the side. They had to push debris out of their way as they swam. When they were far enough away to feel safe, they turned to see the raft had collapsed, the lizard's weight pulling the sides in over its head. As they watched, the lizard continued to struggle frantically, succeeding only in wrapping itself more and more tightly in the shredded fabric. Finally it sank from sight, the raft as its shroud.

The family bobbed in the water in stunned silence. With no life jackets to support their weight, Carmen and Ron soon began to tire. The family formed itself into a ring, the parents using the children's life jackets to support as much of their weight as possible. It was at best a temporary solution.

The wind was still strong, but the sea had settled some. They were still riding a roller-coaster ocean, but the dips were smaller. The sky remained black, and the fog thick and sulfurous.

"Hey, Mom," Rosa said. "There's something over there."

Ron looked at the same time as Carmen. Something dark was moving slowly through the water—shaped like the inverted hull of a ship, about twice the size of the *Entrepreneur*'s.

"It looks like another capsized boat," Ron volunteered. "Swim for it."

They angled toward the moving mound, gently brushing up against it. Carmen tried climbing up the side first, but the movement of the mound made it difficult.

"Ron, this doesn't feel like Fiberglas."

"Just climb, Carmen. We've got to get out of the water."

Finally, Carmen lay spread-eagled on the side of the mound and reached down and managed to pull Chris up next to her, but Rosa and Ron found themselves falling behind. Ron struggled to get Rosa up on the side, but she could only use one arm effectively, and the net bag with the bottles was heavy. Ron realized the mound might pass them by and he panicked at the picture of Carmen and Chris floating off, out of sight.

Desperately, he pushed on Rosa with little strength. Then his foot hit something. He planted both feet and heaved Rosa up, hearing her gasp from pain as she flopped on her side. Ron pushed her higher and then inched up next to her, repeating his efforts until they joined Chris and Carmen. The four linked hands and lay flat against the surface.

Ron was so exhausted it took time to realize Carmen was right; this was not the surface of any boat he had ever seen. It was smooth, but still rougher than a fiberglass or painted surface. He put his cheek to it and felt definite, almost mechanical rhythm. A right-and-left rocking motion. He was still trying to figure out what it meant when he heard a splashing behind him.

Ron turned to see another lizard angling toward them. This one was much smaller but had the same large head and a bony collar around its neck. About a quarter the size of the larger one, it looked like it was going to climb up on the mound with them.

As the lizard used razor sharp claws to climb its way up the side, Ron thought he felt the mound shudder. The lizard was twenty inches long with a triangular head, bony neck collar, and fat stubby body. A foot of tail trailed behind it. Ron kicked the lizard full in the side with every bit of strength he had left. But the lizard was quicker than it looked. As the blow knocked it back into the water the claws raked across Ron's leg leaving three gashes. Though the lizard came up swimming, it fell behind, and Ron could see it wouldn't catch up. He felt sad. He had just condemned it to a fate he and his family were fighting to avoid.

Ron returned to his family and lay back down again, totally exhausted. He fell asleep only to be shaken awake by Rosa.

"Wake up, wake up! But be quiet. Mom says we're in trouble."

He started to sit up but Rosa held him down.

"Move very slowly."

Ron was confused. Why move slowly? Had another lizard scrambled aboard? He lifted his head and chest gradually. The sun was finally cutting through the gloom and Ron could see the sea around him a little more clearly now. Rosa whispered in his ear again.

"Mom says to look forward."

Carmen was in front of Rosa, and Chris was sitting between Carmen's legs. Ron looked past them to the sea. Something was rippling the water. In the weak light Ron saw a thick snake-like form emerging. On top of the snake shape was a head. It looked like a sea serpent to Ron and it took him a few seconds to realize the head was connected to the mound they were on. They were on the back of some kind of animal.

31. Luis

Some have said the age of dinosaurs ended because it had all been a mistake in the first place. Perhaps someday the same will be said of us.

—Robert Winston, *On Things Gone By*

New York City
PostQuilt: Monday, 12:02 p.m. EST

Luis woke in darkness. His eyes were heavy and blurred. He felt terrible; his head ached and he found blood crusted in his hair. Melinda would be angry. He had broken his promise; he was injured. Luis's eyes wouldn't focus but he could see a soft glow. He felt around. Touching a wall behind him, he sat up and leaned back. He didn't need a mirror to know his face was swollen and purple.

Luis pushed himself up, keeping his back against the wall. The light got brighter as he stood and found himself in a diner behind the counter. Smashed dishes and silverware were everywhere, and the cash register was upside down in the middle of the floor. The light was coming through the—window? Luis shook his head and tried focusing again. The light was coming through the empty frame where the window had been. He stumbled out through the broken dishes to the street, looking around to get his bearings. It was too far back to his brother-in-law's, and he didn't want to return looking like this. His own building was close, so he turned toward home and staggered down the sidewalk. He didn't bother calling for help he knew would never come.

When Luis neared his building he suddenly encountered people. Some looked at him curiously but no one offered to help. They were standing behind cars parked three deep in the intersection at his corner. Luis realized the cars were parked fender to fender on the sidewalks as well as the street. Finally, he understood: The cars provided a barrier between the buildings to keep the dinosaurs out.

Silently, Luis walked up the stairs to his building, feeling for his keys and then his wallet. Both were gone. When he realized the lock had been jimmied, he pushed open the door and went up the stairs. Weak and exhausted he paused often to rest. At the third floor he sat down again, his head hanging, but suddenly he heard a voice.

"Luis? Is that you?"

Luis looked up to see Mrs. Weatherby holding a bag of sugar.

"Oh, Luis, you better come back to my apartment with me. Whatever happened to you?"

"Diablos," Luis managed to mutter.

"Those horrid young men. What their mothers must think of them!"

Mrs. Weatherby took Luis by the arm, helped him to his feet, and then guided him down the hall.

"Are Melinda and the kids safe? Oh, thank goodness. What are you doing back here? You didn't come back for me, did you? I told you I would be fine and now look at what's happened."

Mrs. Weatherby scolded Luis all the way down the hall to her apartment, but Luis was comforted by it. She directed Luis to her couch and then removed his shoes and covered him with a crocheted bedspread.

Luis and Melinda slept under a larger, similar bedspread—crocheting incessantly, Mrs. Weatherby had turned out a queen-size bedspread for the Ibarra family in less than a year, made up of squares of intricate yellow flowers and green leaves. Mrs. Weatherby had beamed when she saw it in their home and then promised spreads for the girls' beds too.

Now she returned with a plastic tub of warm soapy water and began washing the blood from his face with a washcloth.

"How did you heat the water, Mrs. Weatherby?"

"Don't talk, Luis, until I get you cleaned up. When you talk your face wrinkles."

Luis lay quiet while Mrs. Weatherby cleaned his wounds. While she worked she talked.

"I heated the water with a propane stove I found in the Santinis' apartment. I know you think I stole it, but I didn't. I was looking for some sugar to borrow when I found it. Besides, someone had already broken in anyway. All the apartments have been, even yours I'm afraid, Luis. I don't know what else they took, but your TV and stereo are gone."

Luis grimaced and groaned but Mrs. Weatherby ignored him.

"By the way, I borrowed the sugar out of your apartment. I left a note for you and Melinda. I'll repay you when I can get to a store."

"Don't go near a store, Mrs. Weatherby. They've all been looted anyway—" Mrs. Weatherby hushed him.

"You lie still. I'll go up to your apartment and get you a change of clothes."

Luis didn't bother to protest. Too tired and sore to manage an argument, he lay on Mrs. Weatherby's couch with his eyes closed and was soon sound asleep.

When he woke, his mouth was dry. When he was sure he could stand without fainting, Luis walked to the kitchen sink, took a glass from the cabinet, and turned on the faucet. Nothing came out. Then he remembered Mrs. Weatherby and the pan of soapy water. Where had she gotten it? And where was she now?

Luis went back to the living room and spotted a neat pile of his clothes on an end table. Mrs. Weatherby had picked out a pair of blue slacks and a white dress shirt. Luis smiled at her choice and decided to use the bathroom to change, in case Mrs. Weatherby came in. He found the bathroom down the hall and closed the door behind him. When he turned, he noticed the top of the toilet tank had been removed and was sitting on the floor. There was a cup on the countertop next to the toilet tank, which was only half full. Luis said out loud, "Very clever." Convincing himself it was clean water, he took the cup, scooped up some, and quenched his thirst.

When he was finished changing, the apartment was still empty. He was about to start searching the building when he heard a strange sound. "Aaaaah," loud and hoarse. He followed it to the living room window. When he looked out he couldn't believe what he was seeing. Mrs. Weatherby was on her knees in her garden, working with her flowers. Luis had seen this a thousand times but never seen it in this setting. The dinosaur that had scared the Ibarras out of their apartment was walking toward Mrs. Weatherby with its head down and its mouth open. "Run, Mrs. Weatherby! The dinosaur, run!" Luis yelled out the window.

Mrs. Weatherby looked up and waved. Then she stood and turned toward the approaching dinosaur, which went down on all fours, its huge head still coming directly at her. Luis yelled again but to no avail. Then, the head stopped with its mouth open wide, "aaaahing" louder as Mrs. Weatherby dug in a big satchel. Then she pulled out a bag and stepped forward and dumped the contents in the dinosaur's mouth. The mouth immediately snapped closed and the jaw began to grind. Next the lips smacked and its massive tongue slipped between the lips, first cleaning the lower lip and then the upper. Then the mouth opened again and the "aaaahing" started all over.

With another bag, Mrs. Weatherby produced the performance again. When the dinosaur opened its mouth a third time Mrs. Weatherby spoke to it sternly. Luis couldn't make out the words over the "aaaahing" sound. Then to his surprise Mrs. Weatherby put her hands on the animal's huge jaw and pushed the head away from her. The head barely moved. Mrs. Weatherby slapped the jaw with her hand and pushed again. This time the dinosaur pulled its head up and stood, then turned and walked into the clearing, pausing twice to turn around and "aaaah" softly at Mrs. Weatherby. Then it pulled up a mouthful of grass and walked off chewing into the distance. Behind the retreating monster Luis saw a misty shimmering cityscape. It was an unsettling sight—a dinosaur as tall as a two-story building walking off toward a shimmering city skyline.

Too stunned to speak, Luis stood in the window, not knowing what to say anyway. Mrs. Weatherby called up to him and waved. Numbly Luis waved back and then went to the couch to lie down. Soon he couldn't tell if he was awake or asleep. Was he hallucinating? Had the Diablos cracked his skull? He couldn't have seen Mrs. Weatherby hand-feeding a dinosaur, could he? Luis was still trying to sort reality from fantasy when consciousness folded into sleep.

32. Puglisi

The theory that the Cretaceous-Tertiary mass extinction was caused by a meteorite is gaining credibility. It's not a good theory, but the best there is to explain what happened to the dinosaurs.

—Cindy Wong, *The Cretaceous Mystery*

Honolulu, Hawaii
PostQuilt: Monday, 9:30 a.m. AHT

Emmett Puglisi reclined in Professor Wang's new blue executive chair and gently rocked and swiveled, admiring the smooth motion and the deep blue padded armrests. He wondered vaguely if he would someday have this chair too. He'd inherited Dr. Wang's old chair. When the new one had been delivered, Emmett happened to be walking down the hall. Emmett had asked for the old chair, and she gave it to him. Of course jealous colleagues claimed he kissed up to Dr. Wang for the chair, but it had been a matter of timing, not brownnosing. Dr. Wang had taken pity on him, even though half a dozen associate professors, with seniority on lowly Assistant Professor Puglisi, would have liked the chair. But Emmett had been in the right place at the right time. It had been like that for much of his life.

Emmett had been wait-listed for the graduate program in astrophysics at the University of Hawaii, and only been admitted late in August, just two weeks before the start of the semester. He fared well in his studies, but as graduation approached his efforts at finding a job had not gone well. He received two phone interviews for instructor positions on the mainland, but no offers and had serious prospects until one of the faculty at the University had taken ill. Then Emmett agreed to fill in on a one-year appointment. That appointment was followed by another to fill a vacancy created by a sabbatical. Another sabbatical followed and another appointment. That year Emmett won a teaching award and co-authored a successful National Science Foundation grant. When a tenure-track position opened up for the next year Emmett had advance information and successfully campaigned for the position.

That was two years ago, and now he found himself in the right place at the right time again. Although this time he wasn't sure it wasn't the right place at the wrong time.

Dr. Wang had disappeared along with four of their colleagues. Now there were five empty offices on Emmett's floor, but only Dr. Wang's was part of PresNet. Emmett had resisted at first, but the news reports of widespread disaster didn't ring true to him, and his thirst for understanding grew until he could no longer resist.

Emmett wasn't authorized to access the PresNet, but he knew Dr. Wang's computer was networked and would automatically access the system. Once into the system he could read the posted messages, but to send you needed a security code. He had ransacked Dr. Wang's office until he found it taped to the bottom of her new chair. The little news the islands were getting was confused and impossible to believe. Floods, avalanches, disappearing cities; none of it made sense. As far as he knew, Hawaii had been spared a disaster like those described on the network.

Emmett had hoped the PresNet would have more information, something that could make sense of it. He was disappointed. It was filled with the same kinds of reports being carried on the news, but with more detail and in more variety. The mystery was only getting bigger.

So he sat in total frustration, watching the scientific parade pass him by, his self-pity interrupted only when he heard a tapping at the partially closed door.

Associate Professor Carrollee Chen-Slater came through the door holding two paper cups of coffee. Emmett had his usual mixed reaction. He was happy to see her again, but also a little apprehensive.

She was the only woman in the botany department and was highly regarded for her competence. Carrollee was also valued because of her multicultural background. Her mother was half Nez Percé and a quarter each of Polish and Hispanic, and her father was a mix of Chinese and Swedish. The Slater name came from his stepfather, who adopted him. On her office desk was a sign that read simply MELTED POT.

Carrollee was as popular with students as Emmett was. She'd won a campus teaching award and two departmental awards. Carrollee was also popular among the faculty. She was friendly toward everyone, and everyone appreciated her ready smile and sense of humor. The faculty was also generally amused by the outlandish clothes she wore. Today her brown curly hair was pushed to the right side of her face and held in place with a large silver barrette. Under her unbuttoned lab coat, Emmett could see a one-piece black jumpsuit with an oversize silver belt with a huge oval buckle. He often wondered if those cover-up lab coats weren't keeping Carrollee on tenure track.

"You know, Emmett, it's customary to wait until a person is declared dead before you move into their office. Have you no respect?"

Emmett took Carrollee's coffee and comments as she meant them, good-naturedly. Carrollee was as amiable a person as Emmett had ever met. He knew she had personally called the families of the missing faculty, and visited some. She was respectful and somber when proper, and genuine tears of empathy came readily. But Carrollee preferred to live her life with a smile and rarely lost it when she was with Emmett.

"I respect the dead, but I covet the position and power of this office."

"I wouldn't say that to too many people. The way it looks you'll become department head by default. They start putting two and two together and you could end up at the top of the suspect list."

"Suspect? You think some lowly assistant professor wreaked worldwide havoc to become department chairman? I'm flattered you think I have the wherewithal to accomplish this."

"I don't think you have the wherewithal to remember to keep your fly closed. Others just don't know you as well as I do."

"Thanks, Carrollee," Emmett said, surreptitiously checking his zipper. "It's nice to know that no matter how bad things get, you can always make them worse. Of course this time I may have made things worse by myself. Take a look at this."

Emmett swiveled the monitor around to make it easier for Carrollee to read. Her eyebrows went up when she realized he was on the PresNet. Then she clucked her tongue and shook her head.

"Let me summarize the situation," she said, plopping down into one of the visitors' chairs. "You've broken into a private office, accessed a computer network you are not authorized to use—that's theft of services, I think—and are in possession of sensitive information you're not cleared for. And now you are impersonating someone with enough brains to be part of PresNet. Did I leave anything out?"

"Yeah, I ate a package of Tic Tacs I found in Dr. Wang's desk."

"Of course. I was wondering why I could get this close to you. I don't suppose a busy lawbreaker like you has time to lend a hand to a lady? I had a proposition for you."

"You really shouldn't make a habit of propositioning people."

"Hey, it keeps me from streetwalking." Carrollee looked around the room. "Does Dr. Wang have a radio in here? No, then you may not have heard the news."

Emmett rocked forward. Had something new happened?

Carrollee began. "First, there have been some ugly incidents at grocery stores throughout the islands. I drove by a Safeway on the way in and they've got police stationed all around it."

Even a big island like Oahu was overstocked with people and understocked with resources. Without supplies from the mainland there wasn't enough food to last thirty days. Pineapple, sugar, and fish would only go so far among a million people. Gas and oil would dwindle just as fast. The implications of being cut off from supplies were staggering, and the consequences could be ugly. But they weren't cut off completely, were they? Only interisland flights were still operating because of what had happened to the three flights from the mainland, but for how long? What of shipping? Emmett realized he needed to come back to reality.

"You want me to help you get stocked up on food?"

Carrollee briefly looked hurt, and Emmett regretted his suggestion. She was one of the most capable people he knew.

"Not a problem. Richard's navy, remember? But thanks for

the offer," she continued. "No, there's another thing you might be interested in. You know how we thought Hawaii had been untouched by what happened? I mean by all the disasters. Well something strange has been drifting ashore. Mostly plants and a few dead fish. Nothing spectacular, but a friend of mine said it wasn't the usual kind of seaweed and grasses. Thought you might like to come along."

"You need an astrophysicist?"

"You don't have to come, it's just for company."

Carrollee made no attempt to leave and sat uncomfortably. Maybe there wasn't chaos outside of the campus, but Emmett knew Carrollee, and he understood her request wasn't for company, it was for safety. Emmett wasn't a big guy, actually only five seven, so he wasn't being asked to come along for muscle, only numbers. He realized he might need to make the same request of her one day.

"How long will we be gone?"

"A couple of hours, tops. You'll be back to committing crimes in a jiff."

Emmett hesitated, turning toward the computer screen with the PresNet messages still displayed. This trip with Carrollee might give him something to put on the network, if he had the nerve.

Emmett turned back to see her looking at him quizzically.

"The computer will still be here when we get back. Besides, it's not like you can use the network. You need a code to get on it."

Emmett tried to stay stone-faced, but he blushed slightly.

"You didn't break into the network, did you?"

"Absolutely not. I found the code."

"Where?"

"On the bottom of Dr. Wang's chair."

"Her chair just happened to fall over and land upside down? Emmett, you're shameless."

They took Carrollee's car to the beach. Too busy looking for signs of looting or other potential danger, they didn't talk much on the way. The stores they passed were untouched, however. A convoy of military vehicles on Kalanianaole Highway they took as a bad sign, and then realized they were becoming paranoid—military vehicles were common on the highway.

Wailupe Beach turned out to look as serene and inviting as it always had to Emmett. It took him a few seconds to realize what was wrong. People were not on the beach but milling around in the park. When they pulled in the parking lot they spotted two squad cars, evidence that the police were guarding the beach.

As they approached the beach Emmett realized there was an abnormal amount of debris there. A policewoman stopped them before they got to the shore. She looked Carrollee's outfit over.

"Sorry, beach access is restricted," the policewoman said.

"We're from the university. We were called to come down and check things out," Carrollee answered authoritatively as if the governor had called her.

Emmett bit his tongue to keep from smiling and dug his faculty ID card out of his wallet. It was really just a glorified library card, but his name, picture, address, and official faculty ID number undoubtably impressed the officer, who then examined Carrollee's.

"Thanks for coming, Dr. Chen-Slater and Dr. Puglisi. I can't believe you got here so fast, but we appreciate it. We'll be here if you need us."

The officer walked off. After she sealed the entrance to the park she came back with two shotguns and handed one to the other cop.

"Is there something you're not telling me, Carrollee?" Emmett asked.

"No. I don't think so. My friend called and said there was some unusual marine flora washing ashore. That's all I know."

Carrollee lead the way down to the beach and immediately began examining the seaweeds, grasses, and other materials. Emmett saw only a dark green mass of smelly plants quickly dehydrating in the sun. Carrollee's interest in the material, however, seemed intense.

He watched in silence for a while, then announced abruptly, "Take a couple of samples, and let's get out of here."

"Don't rush me. We've only been here a few minutes. This is very strange. Take a look at these," Carrollee said, pointing to four pieces of seaweed laid out on the sand. "These are all varieties of *Laminaria. Laminaria* is a kind of seaweed that attaches to the bottom with roots and then has one principal blade responsible for photosynthesis." Carrollee pointed to the bottom of all four plants. Emmett noticed they all had similar rootlike ends.

The tops of the plants were distinctly different. One looked like a fluorescent tube attached to a cord that ended in roots. One was a large flat blade that looked like a canoe paddle. A third had a long stem that ended in three clumps of whitish material that looked like cauliflower. The fourth had several thin strands that looked like elongated lawn grass.

"I see four different plants. What's got you so excited?"

"These are all laminaria. There's no doubt about that. But these are four laminaria I've never seen before. This one," Carrollee said, pointing to the one shaped like a canoe paddle, "might be one I've seen in marine taxonomy books. Maybe this one too," she said pointing at the overgrown lawn grass. "Maybe. But these two . . . I don't think they've ever been recorded." Then, glowing like a kid on Christmas, she said, "I think I've got a new variety here. At least two. I'll get tenure for sure."

Happily, she went back to sorting through the beached seaweed. Emmett felt useless and saw the cops watching him with puzzlement. Uncomfortable, Emmett started up the beach along the line of seawood, but soon he heard the policewoman yell.

"Look down by the water, that's where they saw it. At least that's what the tourists said."

The hair on Emmett's skin stood erect at the word *it* and he knew the police officer wasn't talking about seaweed. Looking back, Emmett saw Carrollee still on her knees, sorting out specimens, unaware of anything else. To buy Carrollee more time, Emmett walked slowly to the shore, watching the waves rhythmically washing the sand. As he approached, the surf seemed to be one great green mass of seaweed.

The police were still watching him, so he squatted as if he were examining vegetation. Instead, he watched the waves and thought about the PresNet. A new variety of seaweed was hardly worth the risk of illegally using the network.

Emmett was still feeling sorry for himself when something

surfaced to his left, but by the time he turned his head it was gone. He stood, staring at the spot to see if it would surface again.

Suddenly Carrollee was next to him, staring into the surf. Then she unhooked her big silver buckle and unzipped the front of her black jumpsuit. Emmett was both shocked and aroused. She stood in a one-piece swimsuit—black with a few oversize silver sequins. Emmett realized it matched the jumpsuit, which she handed him along with her shoes.

"What are you doing, Carrollee?"

"I'm getting samples. These will be a lot fresher."

She waded knee-deep into the water while Emmett looked up and down the beach nervously, still trying to spot what he had seen in the surf. Then he heard footsteps and turned to see the two police officers approaching with their shotguns.

"You think that's a good idea? Her getting in the surf like that."

"She's just getting some samples of the seaweed. She wants fresh samples."

The two police officers were looking at each other in confusion.

"Why is she getting seaweed?" the policewoman asked.

Overhearing the conversation, Carrollee turned to answer, standing in the surf in her swimsuit. For the first time, Emmett saw her as an attractive woman.

"I'm selecting specimens for identification. That's what marine botanists do."

"You're a botanist?" the policewoman said, clearly surprised. "Why would they send a botanist to—"

The policewoman broke off her sentence when a head popped through the surface behind Carrollee. Slowly, the head rose higher out of the water—it was large, shaped like a turtle's head, but elongated and covered with gray lizard skin. The mouth opened silently, revealing uneven rows of triangular teeth, and the head continued to rise, revealing a snakelike neck that thickened as more of it appeared above the waves. As it rose above Carrollee, it seemed smaller, dwarfed by the length of the neck. When its ascent stopped, the head was fifteen feet above the surface.

Both Emmett and the two police officers were speechless.

When Carrollee spoke to Emmett, breaking his trance, he looked down to see her staring at them with a comical look. Her back was still to the monster.

"What are you people doing? If you could see the way you look—"

Then three things happened at once. The policewoman raised her shotgun to her shoulder and shouted to Carrollee to get out of the way, and Emmett bolted into the water, racing to reach Carrollee in time. At the movement, Carrollee turned to look behind and said, "Magnificent."

Then the monster screamed a sound like tearing metal. The cops couldn't fire until Carrollee and Emmett were safely out of the way, but Emmett feared they might panic. He was nearly to Carrollee when the monster turned its head to the side, staring down into the sea, and Emmett realized it was farther out to sea than he'd first thought—he wasn't used to animals of that size. He grabbed Carrollee and pulled her toward shore.

"Stop yanking me. Don't you know what that is?"

"I know it's not Flipper! Now let's get out of the water."

"It's a plesiosaur. Can you believe it? A plesiosaur. Everyone thinks they're extinct . . . extinct for millions of years. Let go of me!" Carrollee yelled, jerking her arm away from Emmett. Then to Emmett's horror, she turned and dove into the water toward the animal, disappearing beneath the waves. Suddenly the head stabbed down into the sea and the cops, startled, shouted a warning. Emmett screamed, "Carrollee!" Near panic, he kicked off his shoes in preparation for swimming after Carrollee and had pulled down his pants when she resurfaced.

"It's too far away. I can't see its body, but I'll bet its got four flippers and a ten-foot tail."

Emmett zipped up and dragged Carrollee out of the surf, looking fearfully over his shoulder at the monster. The plesiosaur's neck looked like a huge piece of curved pipe. Then the neck straightened and the head appeared again, a fish in its mouth, and it used a snapping motion of its head and jaws to work the fish lengthwise and swallowed the fish whole. Then it turned to look back at the people on the beach. By now Carrollee and Emmett were clear and the police raised their shotguns again to fire.

"Don't shoot it. Don't shoot it," Carrollee shouted. "It's not dangerous. It only eats fish."

"It's big enough to swallow a dolphin whole," Emmett responded, "or a person."

"It's not that big. Well, even if it is, it eats fish, not people."

The police were confused. They had a strong desire to shoot the plesiosaur but believed Carrollee was an authority on the creatures, and a representative of the university. The police were indoctrinated into taking orders and shooting only as a last resort, so Carrollee's protest stopped them from firing. But they didn't take their eyes off the beast. Emmett, meanwhile, was trying to hurry Carrollee away from the water. The police walked backward behind them, their guns trained on the animal's head.

"There must be a colony of them living deep in the ocean," Carrollee hypothesized. "There was probably an underwater volcanic eruption or avalanche that drove this one to the surface. That would account for all this unusual laminaria. It was probably sent up with the plesiosaur." Then Carrollee paused and looked back. The plesiosaur was still staring at the beach and screeched its metal-tearing sound again, rattling Emmett and the police. Carrollee didn't even pause in her speculation. "Except," she continued when the screeching died, "this is a reptile. It couldn't live deep in the sea without coming up for air. And if they keep coming up why haven't we seen one before?"

Even safe on the beach, Emmett was still nervous. The plesiosaur seemed fixated on the beach and very disturbed by the people there. Emmett picked up Carrollee's jumpsuit and handed it to her, but she was too lost in thought to put it on. Instead she held it and free-associated for everyone to hear.

"How about this? An egg is frozen in the antarctic ice. It breaks free in an iceberg and heads north. The iceberg melts, freeing and warming the egg. The egg hatches and a baby plesiosaur is released." Then she frowned again. "That is too far-fetched even for me to believe." Carrollee fell silent and stared at the plesiosaur. Emmett watched it too, stunned by its size. Then Carrollee turned and looked Emmett in the eyes. "What do you know about this? What aren't you telling me?"

"Let's get back."

"This has something to do with all the disasters, doesn't it?"

"Here're your shoes, Carrollee. I really don't know what's going on, that's what I was trying to find out in Dr. Wang's office."

Carrollee still looked suspicious, but she let the matter drop. "Help me get my specimens then."

Obligingly, Emmett was picking up her seaweed when he heard a cop shout a warning.

"Look out, it's coming!"

Emmett's head snapped up. It *was* coming—the plesiosaur was moving through the water toward the beach. As it approached it screeched again. The cops raised their guns again but Carrollee ran out onto the beach in front of them.

"It's harmless. I'm telling you, it doesn't eat people!" she screamed urgently.

The expression on the cops' faces told Emmett they were losing confidence in Carrollee.

When Emmett turned back to the plesiosaur, its movement had changed. Instead of gliding toward shore, it was now swimming jerkily, its head rocking back and forth.

"Carrollee," Emmett said. "I think it's beaching—"

"No it isn't!" Carrollee shouted, loud enough for the cops to hear. "It lives in the sea. It can't get around on land. It has only flippers."

The cops heard Carrollee, but they kept their guns on the beast. Slowly its body began to emerge from the water, the fifteen-foot neck attached to a huge lump of a body with gray skin, like the head, but speckled dark green along the spine. It became clear the plesiosaur was dragging itself along the sea bottom and coming ashore.

"Dr. Chen-Slater," the policewoman said without lowering her shotgun. "I'm no expert, but that dinosaur is headed this way, and it's not swimming."

"It's not a dinosaur," Carrollee argued. "It's a reptile. It shouldn't be coming ashore. Really. It's probably curious about us. Maybe we should back up."

The plesiosaur screamed, seemingly at the people on the beach and in the park.

"It sounds angry to me, not curious," the policewoman answered. "I think backing up is a good idea. But if it charges I'm going to kill it no matter what you say."

"It can't charge . . ." Carrollee began, but gave up. She had already lost most of her credibility. Besides, she really didn't know if it could charge.

The plesiosaur dragged its body out of the water using four huge paddle-shaped fins, dragging a long tail. The flippers worked in unison, the front and back ones rotating forward, to dig into the sand, dragging the animal's body toward the shore. The police pushed the tourists, Carrollee, and Emmett back into the park away from the beach, but still the animal kept coming, dragging itself across the sand. When it reached the embankment edging the park it stopped, swinging its head back and forth, screaming at the people, pushing them back farther. But suddenly it turned its back to the bystanders and stopped. Everyone waited for it to return to the sea, but it didn't move. Instead the rear flippers folded together under its tail and pushed outward, throwing sand to both sides again and again.

"What's it doing?" Emmett asked Carrollee.

"I don't believe it. It can't be."

"What? What?"

"Wait, Emmett. You'll see."

After digging for some time, the animal stopped again. A few minutes later it began breathing hard and swinging its long neck back and forth, seemingly oblivious to the people in the park behind it. Its breathing became ragged, but still it didn't move.

"Come on, Emmett," Carrollee said, pulling his arm. "Let's see what's happening." She moved forward before Emmett could protest, so he followed. He'd seen the slow gait of the beast and felt confident he could outrun it. A puzzled look on her face, the policewoman also followed. Carrollee led them directly behind the plesiosaur, whose head occasionally swung left and right, freezing them in their tracks. However, it seemed oblivious of their presence.

Carrollee reached the edge of the park and looked down into the hole the dinosaur had dug, then she signaled Emmett with a frantic motion of her hand. He approached carefully and peered into the sand to see three eggs. Emmett turned to say something to Carrollee, but both the cop and Carrollee put their fingers to their lips.

As Emmett watched in silence, suddenly the rear of the plesiosaur pulsed rhythmically and another egg emerged wet from the animal and fell into the hole, bouncing off the others, its shell soft and pliant. They waited in silence until another egg emerged, and then they backed away slowly.

When they were out of hearing range Carrollee babbled ecstatically. "Can you believe this? A plesiosaur laying eggs on our beach. I hope there's a male in that clutch. That species could be reestablished."

The plesiosaur stayed on the beach another hour, slowly drawing a big crowd of people behind it in the park. When cameras started clicking, the cops decided the crowd might upset the plesiosaur, so they backed them up again. Shortly after that the animal began burying its clutch, the back flippers covering the eggs with huge scoops of warm sand. When the hole was completely filled the plesiosaur turned and moved up onto the mound it had created, screaming a warning at the people. Then it turned, moving toward the sea, stopping again twice to scream warnings. Finally it disappeared into the sea again. Emmett was sure it wouldn't go very far.

Carrollee immediately talked the cops into posting a guard on the eggs until she could arrange people to protect the site. Emmett knew she would have no trouble rounding up faculty, graduate students, and environmentalists to mount a twenty-four-hour guard until those eggs hatched.

Only after the cops agreed could Emmett pull Carrollee into the park and past the gawking bystanders. He complained when his bare feet met the hot pavement of the parking lot.

"Where are your shoes?" Carrollee asked.

"In the surf."

"Scared right out of them, eh?"

"Not at all."

"Then let's go back for them."

"That's okay. They were a month old anyway."

After they swung by Emmett's apartment for shoes and dry clothes, they headed for the university again. This time they passed a grocery store that was being looted—though not by an angry crowd, at least not yet. Three blocks away they passed four police cars going in the other direction. Without saying anything to each other, Emmett and Carrollee both knew things would only get worse.

Carrollee dropped Emmett at the university and then left to arrange for protection for what she was now calling "her babies." As she drove away she promised to call Emmett.

When Emmett got back to Dr. Wang's office he immediately called up the PresNet, scanning the network looking for something about plesiosaurs, but there was nothing. Knowing about the plesiosaur was too important a piece of knowledge to keep to himself, and he typed in a report about it. After he finished it he felt a pang of guilt and added Carrollee's name. Then he reread the report several times, trying to get the nerve to send it. Finally, he typed in Dr. Wang's access code and punched the send button. A few minutes later Emmett's terminal was flooded with requests for additional information. Emmett's ego swelled with each request. He was a player now. If only he knew what the game was.

---

33. HUNTED

A great horned beast came terrorizing the villages. It walked on two legs like a man, and had a great tail. Our spears could not penetrate its skin. One hundred warriors died before we drank its blood and ate its heart.

—Legend of the Toltecs

North of Bend, Oregon
POSTQUILT: MONDAY, 12:05 P.M. PST

Dr. Piltcher carried the egg inside his shirt all the way back to the RV, where he wrapped it in a blanket and placed it in the sun in the front window. Sarah, the microceratops, was still in the back of the RV and whining irritatingly. Petra tossed her an apple, and she immediately attacked it, crunching and slurping; then Petra split another apple between Moose and Sarah.

Dr. Coombs and Dr. Piltcher decided to rotate the egg every half hour during the day, keeping it in the sun. At night they would have to use the oven, or even sleep with the egg. Dr. Piltcher kept unwrapping the egg, looking at it and feeling the shell.

"It's nearly hard," he said. "That probably means it's ready to hatch."

"I agree, Chester," Dr. Coombs said. "Of course it will hatch sooner if you stop unwrapping it."

From then on, Dr. Piltcher checked on the egg every few minutes but he didn't unwrap it. Instead he perched himself on a bunk in the back and sat studying Sarah, who wandered around her enclosure sniffing, and snorting. Occasional small amounts of mucous sprayed from her nose. Excited by this, Dr. Piltcher wondered aloud whether she might have a cold. Colter's only response was to put down more paper.

Then Dr. Coombs called Dr. Piltcher outside, where he found Dr. Coombs and Petra kneeling in the tropical meadow looking at the grass.

"What is it, George? I believe the microceratops has a cold . . . wouldn't that be interesting? Not surprising, for sure, but an interesting subject to study."

"Very interesting," Dr. Coombs agreed. "But something more serious is happening. Look at the grass here, notice how it is drooping. The meadow is drying out; it won't last long without rain. And when the snow comes in a couple of months, everything will die, animals and all."

"Yes, we expected this. But so soon? We've only begun to explore."

Petra cut him off by putting her hand on his arm and then slowly standing and pointing across the meadow. The others looked in that direction to see the biggest animal they had encountered yet. Its huge head was shaped something like a rhinoceros and was tipped with a long horn and surrounded by a large collar. Two smaller horns protruded from its collar above its head. It was five feet at the shoulder, and taller at the back, its head hanging low to the ground.

"What do you think, Chester?" Dr. Coombs asked. "Is it a triceratops?"

"No, the horns are wrong. But it's similar."

"Maybe we better get inside," Petra whispered quietly. "Please, let's go."

"I don't think we should all go at once," Dr. Coombs said. "Petra, you go first."

Petra slowly backed up several steps, before turning to walk toward the RV. When she was nearly to the door, Dr. Piltcher turned to follow. As he turned, the dinosaur raised its head, moving it back and forth slowly, then dropped and lifted it quickly again—and came up roaring. As the group watched, the head dropped again and the dinosaur broke into a run, right toward the group.

Dr. Coombs and Dr. Piltcher bolted toward the RV. Petra dashed the last few yards to the door and then shouted for the others to hurry. Colter came up behind her and watched silently. Petra was sure her friends would win the race—the humans had too much of a head start. Petra felt relief as she and Colter made room for Dr. Coombs and Dr. Piltcher. When they were safely inside she stepped down, grabbed the door, and pulled it closed behind them. When she locked it, Colter laughed.

"It's not going to make any difference, Petra. Look at the size of that mother."

As they looked out the window, they saw it looming larger and larger, not as big as the RV, but close enough.

"Everyone get down!" Colter yelled. "Get down or fall down!"

They all sat down on the floor and against the back wall of the RV. Watching the charging dinosaur had been terrifying, but sitting on the floor, unable to see, was worse. Petra linked arms with Colter and Dr. Coombs, who linked his with Dr. Piltcher. Colter pushed his legs straight out against the cabinet opposite him, wedging himself in as tight as he could, the rest copying him. They were all tightly packed when the dinosaur hit. It did little good.

When the curved horn on the snout slammed into it, the door of the RV crumpled, ripping from its hinges in a scream of metal. As the huge mass of the dinosaur continued forward the head forced itself through the door and into the RV. The neck collar, too wide for the opening, crumpled the wall on both sides of the door. Now the impact turned loose objects in the RV into shrapnel. Pens, and paper, a flashlight, apples, and peaches ricocheted all around, drawers flew open and silverware bounced around. Cupboards opened and dry goods poured over the four heads.

The impact of the collision drove the RV backward across the clearing, rocking the occupants forward and then throwing them back as the RV absorbed the rest of the force and jerked to a stop. When their heads cleared, those inside realized the vehicle was tilted at an angle.

They held their breath waiting for it to fall over or rock back onto its wheels. Neither happened. Then they realized why. The dinosaur's head was still jammed in the door, and it was looking at them with a huge angry eye.

They were all frozen in fear except Colter, who reached down, picked up a spatula, leaned forward and slapped the dinosaur on the nose.

"Get the hell out of here!" he yelled.

The dinosaur went crazy and began thrashing its head. Its power was stunning. The RV shook back and forth with the wrenching head, the thin metal of the doorway screaming with each motion. Then, with a powerful jerk, the head withdrew from the doorway. Suddenly the beast slammed against the side of the RV, again and again. The powerful shocks reverberated inside, making it impossible to stand. The dinosaur was systematically crushing the full length of the RV. A particularly vicious slam shattered the window farthest back, showering the inside with glass. Sarah's fearful squeal could be heard above the din. Then the attacks stopped, and only Sarah's squeals continued, eventually dying to a whimper.

When the group managed to get their own breath under control, they heard the dinosaur breathing outside. They sat paralyzed with fear, afraid to move lest a sound would bring another attack. Colter, the spatula still in his hand, started to move to the window, but Dr. Piltcher grabbed his back pocket.

"Whatever you do, don't hit it with that again!"

Colter smiled reassurance and handed the useless weapon to Dr. Piltcher. Then the dinosaur screamed. Colter dove to the floor just before another slam shattered the window.

The dinosaur continued crushing the side of the RV, deafening the cowering occupants. Then it stopped again. They waited fearfully, afraid to move. The dinosaur slammed the vehicle twice, then took up a station outside the RV, its wet, ragged breathing sounding menacing. Soon, it was clear, the animal wasn't going to leave until it had what it came for.

---

34. TIME WAVES

I can foretell what is coming because I know what has been.

—Zorastrus, Prophet of Babylon

Washington, D.C.
POSTQUILT: MONDAY, 3:58 P.M. EST

Frustrated, Phil stared at the piles in front of him. Kenny's disks were divided into three categories: "software," "useless," and "what the hell is this?" The software category contained commercial programs for word processing, drawing, or spreadsheets. The "useless" pile included data storage files that contained Kenny's term papers, book reviews, class outlines, and letters home. Bill snagged the disks with the letters on them. The "what the hell is this?" category were the programs Phil was concentrating on.

"Why don't you tell us what you know so far, and maybe we can help a bit," Bill suggested.

"There's a dozen programs here but they seem to be of three types." Phil pulled down menus with the mouse, then three columns filled the screen. The first column was labeled DATE, the second was labeled PLACE, and the third EVENT. The first entry was July 22, 1879; London; frog fall. The second entry was August 19, 1881; Kiev, Ukraine; woman burns. The third entry was March 2, 1882; St. Augustine, Florida; ice fall. Terry scanned the list. These were the kinds of events Kenny's books and files were filled with.

"There's five hundred and twenty-two entries on this list. There's three other lists too. One of the lists isn't in any kind of order. It's kind of a hodgepodge of things like Sasquatch and yeti sightings, UFO reports, junk like that. Most of it's garbage except the report about a prehistoric fish caught off the coast of South America. I saw a picture of that fish so I know it's true."

Terry understood. He'd never have believed the I-5 mountain either, if he hadn't seen it in person.

"Some of this stuff is pretty old. I found a file labeled with Zorastrus's name. It's got the really old stuff in it."

Bill and Terry exchanged glances. The name Zorastrus kept coming up.

The screen now filled with programming commands.

"This is the second kind of stuff. He's got several versions of this program. You can see what he was trying to do. Most of this stuff is just display instructions—commands to read his data array, complete some calculations, and display the output. The important part is here." Phil scrolled the program until his finger came to rest at a particular spot. "This is where his formula starts."

"Formula for what?" Bill asked.

"I ain't no mathematician," Phil protested, but then he yielded. "It looks like he's trying to fit a curve to three sets of variable data. Okay, it's like this. Let's say I draw a line on a piece of paper through points A, B, and C. Then I want to know where that line will be if I add an inch to A, an inch to B, and an inch to C. That's what he had the computer doing. He wasn't using inches though, and he wasn't always adding the same amount to each reference point, and sometimes he subtracts."

"If he wasn't using inches what was he using?" Bill asked.

"The only one I've figured out is this one." Phil reached up and tapped the third column. "It looks like it varies between 1 and 200,366. One set ranges from 1 to 366 and the other from between 1 and 200. It works something like an odometer.

Once this column reaches either 365 or 366 it rolls over a number in the next column."

"It's counting days and years?"

"Yeah, it even corrects for leap year."

"Umm . . ." Bill began. "That makes sense. Kenny thinks these events in the past have something to do with what's happened. What's the third kind of stuff?"

"Graphics. Here, watch this." Phil opened another file using the mouse. "This is still a piece of crap, but it's the best thing this bozo programmed." The screen was split with a line marking off one third of the screen. The larger portion had two small circles, one in each upper corner of the screen. Phil punched a key and the two circles slowly expanded. When they met the screen froze and the letter A appeared at the point of contact. Another letter A appeared in the left-hand column with three sets of figures. Phil punched another key and the circles expanded again. As soon as the circles finished crossing each other the screen froze again. This time two more letters appeared, a B and a C, marking the two new contact points between the circles. There were now three sets of three figures in the left-hand column. Terry noticed that the A figures had changed. Another key punch and the circles began to expand again. Terry watched the A, B, and C columns of figures change as the circles expanded. When they reached the edge of the screen the program stopped.

"That's it?" Bill asked. "That's all it does?"

"I told you it was a piece of crap. Part of this stuff is dates again." Phil pointed to the columns of figures on the left side of the screen. "Hard to tell though because he ran all the numbers together, course I could fix it in a jiff."

"No, Phil. What about the rest of the numbers? Counting the dates, it's really four sets of numbers. I haven't figured out the other three yet. Here, look at this one." More work with the mouse and another set of commands filled the screen. "This one's a little different."

Punching more keys, Phil called up another program. It was like the other program but instead of two expanding circles, these began to pulse, repeatedly sending out expanding waves. As one circle expanded, another circle formed within it, chasing the first circle to the edge of the screen. When the expanding circles nearly reached each other, the image switched to show smaller multiple circles expanding within each other.

"He adjusted for scale, it's the same circles," Phil added.

The circles continued to expand, but one by one the inner circles overtook the outer circles and merged until only two circles remained. Then the image froze. Terry looked over at the numbers on the left.

"Phil, what's the date count?"

"You have an idea, Terry?" Bill asked.

"Remember our idea about Hiroshima and the bomb? Maybe these circles start with the bomb?"

Terry and Bill looked at Phil expectantly, but he just shook his head.

"Counts wrong. If we subtract the count from yesterday then we miss Hiroshima by seventeen years . . . still . . . that's an interesting idea."

Phil drifted inward, reminding Terry of Kenny's drift into a catatonic state. But Bill urged Phil on. "These other numbers, do they have something to do with the frog falls, avalanches, and other events on Kenny's list?"

Phil seemed reluctant to come back from wherever he was.

"You're thinking latitude and longitude, aren't you? That's what I was working on when you got here. There's too many numbers, though." Phil looked lost in thought again. "All right, maybe you guys can help me—I think I'm getting it. Colonel, I need some more data."

Bill agreed to get him whatever he needed.

"Hot damn," Phil laughed, "some of it's classified."

Modern communication systems are made up of radio, television, phone, and computer networks. To keep this system functioning, there must be transmission and reception facilities, copper cables, fiber optic lines, broadcast towers, dish antennae, translators, boosters, switching stations, and satellites. Lose a part of this system, and backup systems automatically come on-line. Lose the backup systems and computers will automatically reroute signals. Lose those routes and the system fails.

Like everything else about the effect, the losses were uneven. Some satellites were lost, and others lost their ground communication facilities. Other ground stations reestablished contact where possible.

Underground transmission lines were left intact, as were transatlantic and transpacific cables. Cities untouched by the effect kept local phone, TV, and radio, and some long-distance, while those in or near cities sliced by the effect were hardest hit. Some lost everything, others kept some local radio or TV. Military bases were similar but reestablished satellite communication sooner, then commandeered civilian lines, further snarling civilian communication.

As a result some sat riveted to TVs witnessing the bizarre unfold before them, while others only heard rumors and half truths. Still others in rural pockets continued their lives completely unaware of the drama unfolding across the face of the planet.

Nick Paulson's encounter with the masturbator left him wary of any more of Elizabeth's prognosticators. Additional psychics, religious fanatics, and nuts were still being rounded up, but Nick delegated the interviewing to the CIA. Instead, Nick combed the PresNet.

Nick used the directory to get a rough map of which parts of the network were lost. The northeastern part of the country was mostly off-line, although a terminal at the University of Delaware and one in New Hampshire were listed. The Chicago area was well represented as were the states surrounding Illinois. The southeast was another near-total loss. There was nothing from Georgia, Mississippi, and Louisiana, and precious little from the rest of the South. There were three terminals listed from Florida State University but none from the University of Miami. There were few advisors in the far West except for California, but functioning terminals were listed in Houston, Galveston, Reno, Cheyenne, and several in the Southern California basin. Only Seattle was represented in the northwest, with terminals at the University of Washington and Boeing. Nothing was showing for Alaska, Puerto Rico, or Guam. Three stations were listed as on-line in Hawaii. After his survey Nick estimated only a third of the network was still functioning.

The reports on PresNet described the kinds of impossible topographical changes Nick heard described on the radio. One posted message was from a scientist named Robert Cory in Houston, who was bounced off the highway when his car was hit by a pressure wave. Back on the road, he rounded a curve to find a red hot lava field. Fires were spreading along the highway. Another report came from a Mavis Farnsworth in Minneapolis, who described a loud whooshing sound in the middle of the night, and opened her drapes to find herself staring at a jungle. The network was filled with these kinds of reports, but Nick was frustrated with them. They were too descriptive and not analytical. The PresNet advisors were acting like tourists, not scientists.

Nick sent an all-points message requesting direct analysis of any topographical changes the associates had access to. He also asked for continued reports on "unusual events," but to look for common denominators. Nick hoped this would begin to focus the work of the network scientists. At first he had been tempted to ask for reports on dinosaurs or other prehistoric lifeforms, but he knew if he suggested what to look for, that would limit the observations.

The phone beeped several times before Nick picked it up. A guard announced an insistent air force colonel named Conrad was at the gate with a psychologist, and a sergeant, claiming they had vital information. Nick remembered that the college kid from Elizabeth's list was to be accompanied by a psychologist and a colonel. Frustrated by the lack of information on the PresNet, he agreed to see them but swore he'd personally castrate any of them that started masturbating.

That wasn't necessary. The men were all-business. None of them was wearing a uniform, but the colonel's military bearing and demeanor set him apart instantly. The other two seemed to wear rumpled casual clothes, although on closer inspection it appeared the taller man wore rumpled clothes, and the shorter Asian was a rumpled man in well-pressed clothes.

The colonel took charge and ordered Sergeant Yamamoto to set up their computer equipment. The sergeant, protesting, looked lustfully at Nick's console, so Nick invited the sergeant to help himself. After brief introductions, the colonel said abruptly, "I think we know what's happened."

Nick's hopes sank. The colonel was as confident as the psychics, and experience told Nick that no one that confident was ever right. His explanation made a good story though. A psychotic college student, hostages in a cave, the mountain in the middle of the freeway, and then the search of Kenny's room.

As Bill described what they had collected, Terry handed examples of articles and showed sections of books to Nick. Dr. Paulson showed none of the skepticism Terry had expected.

"You think these events have something to do with what happened?" Nick asked.

"Kenny Randall certainly did and he worked out a model . . . Phil, you ready?" Colonel Conrad asked.

"Yeah, here we go. Remember though, this thing's a piece of crap and I had nothing to do with the programming. The colonel here won't even let me clean it up." Phil shook his head and punched a key.

As they presented it, Nick's own ideas were confirmed and expanded. Yet when they were finished he was left wanting to know more.

"There must be something else. Weren't there equations or notes somewhere?"

Colonel Conrad described the rest of the materials and then named a Dr. Piltcher, a Dr. Coombs, and someone named Phat as colleagues of Kenny's. He also spoke of a manuscript from a Babylonian prophet named Zorastrus, which wasn't among Kenny's things. Colonel Conrad's people were already searching for Kenny's friends, so Nick made a mental note to get a copy of the manuscript. It was a long shot, but no more impossible than what was happening in the streets. Nick asked a guard to bring the rest of Kenny Randall's possessions. He was going to take this to the Security Council, and if he was going to convince them, he first needed to convince himself.

"Okay, let's start with the computer programs. Show me everything," he said.

Nick found out how efficient government could be when a young marine delivered a cardboard box containing the complete known works of Zorastrus, the Prophet of Babylon. There were copies in multiple languages. Selecting the English copies, they scanned them. Colonel Conrad found what they were looking for.

"Here, in this one called the Apocrypha of Zorastrus. He writes about things falling from the sky: water, fish, rocks, and a whole tree. There's one about a strange animal appearing. He describes it as a huge beast that came walking on two legs and ate whole cattle."

"Is this in the program?" Nick asked.

"I don't think so," Colonel Conrad said. "The dates on most of this stuff are too vague to work in the program. Here, let's check it against the list." While Phil, Terry, and Colonel Conrad worked with the program, Nick dug out a copy of the Zorastrus text in a German translation. Nick found Zorastrus had done more than just list the strange events, he had tried to explain them. His predictions were specific and described events much like they had experienced. Zorastrus believed the things that fell from the sky came from the past, and that they were the debris of a collision of eras. As Nick read, his respect for this prophet grew. Nick could find no specific predicted date, but it didn't matter. There was plenty of proof the ancient seer had been right. Now if only Nick could convince the Security Council.

---

35. Ellen and Angie

The Eilean Mor light went out ten days before Christmas. When the provision ship reached her on the 26th, the three lighthouse men were missing. All was in good order; the wicks were trimmed, the lanterns filled with oil, and the beds made. Three good men, gone to God-only-knows where.

—David Rose, Scotland, 1900

Carlton, Oregon
PostQuilt: Monday, 3:11 p.m. PST

Ellen's back and bottom ached. Looking for a way into Portland, she'd been bumping down back roads filling with people trying to find some way around the mountain on I-5. Most of them were tourists trying to find a way home to the city or north of it. Mixed in were other travelers and rubberneckers, going to see what had happened, and more had happened than Ellen had realized.

She had spent several fruitless hours trying to phone friends in or near Portland, ones who could check on her son, but the phone system was a mess. Many of the interstate long-distance lines were still accessible, but the limited intrastate made calls to Portland impossible. Ellen's frustration at that, combined with her anger at Terry, reached critical mass late that night. She couldn't just sit in a motel doing nothing, and since Terry wouldn't help find their son, she decided to do it herself. Loyally, Angie had started packing her own suitcase as soon as she realized what Ellen was up to. Ellen protested, but only politely; privately she was relieved to have Angie's company.

They were now about ten miles southeast of Portland near a wide spot in the road called Carlton. The traffic on the road was once again at a standstill. They waited, listening to the CB and switching channels, trying to pick up someone at the head of the line. They finally picked up a woman who knew something, and from the sound of her voice she was angry.

"There's some smart ass cop up here who's barricaded the highway. He says there's no place to go. Says the town's already full of people and there's no road on the other side. Over to you, Hot Rod."

Angie flipped off the radio.

"Looks like we walk from here. Maybe this cop knows what's going on."

They pulled the Jeep to one side, locked it up, then started walking through the parked cars. There weren't as many cars here as on I-5. But because the road was two lane, and the cars were backed up only on the right side, the hike was longer. Angie and Ellen hiked around curves and over hills listening to other people talking. Many were walking forward too, but some had unpacked picnics, lawn chairs, or blankets. Kids ran around the cars playing tag.

Angie had suggested cutting cross-country; the Willamette valley was thick with farms, and she reasoned they might be able to use the four-by-four to cross them. But on this side of the city there were fewer farms, and lots of forest. There must be logging roads or fire district roads, Ellen thought, but they had no idea how to find them.

At last they came to the barricade, four sawhorses with two-by-fours stretched across them, with a hand-lettered sign reading:

Nearby, two uniformed men stood. One was surrounded by a mob of people. It was clear he was in charge. The mob around him was a mixture of the angry, the frustrated, and the curious. The cop kept repeating, "One at a time, one at a time."

Angie gave Ellen a look that said "I'll take care of this" and then plowed into the crowd and struck a provocative pose near the cop.

"Hey, darlin', why is the road blocked?" she drawled loudly.

The cop turned, looking angry until Angie's voluptuous figure softened his response.

"Listen," he began, then he spread his voice to cover the crowd, "listen to me, everyone." The crowd of people quieted. Looking at Angie he said, "The road is blocked because there is no place for you to go. The road continues on the other side of town for only a mile and then it ends. There are cars and trucks abandoned all over that road. There is no room in town left for you to park and no place to stay. You can walk down the road if you don't believe me."

Disappointed voices rang out: "But we've got to get to Portland," moaned someone from the back of the crowd. "I've got relatives waiting for me. When's the road going to be clear?"

"Everyone here has the same problems," the officer said. "I can't clear the road for you. Go take a look for yourself if you don't believe me." Then he shook his head and shooed the crowd away.

Grudgingly the people dispersed and wandered off, telling new arrivals what they just heard.

Angie sidled up to the cop, looking as sexy as she could after a twenty-hour drive, and Ellen was impressed with how sexy *that* was. The cop seemed to agree, and it irritated Ellen, but she told herself she was merely annoyed, not jealous.

"Yes, what can I do for you?" the officer asked while trying not to stare at Angie's cleavage.

"My friend here has to get home, officer," Angie said sadly, nodding repeatedly toward Ellen. "Her son is home all alone and she's afraid something might have happened to him." The officer, enthralled with Angie, gave Ellen only a brief glance.

"There's nothing I can do!" he said with exhaustion. "The road isn't just blocked, it's gone. There used to be houses up there and stores. Bill Brandt, the guy who owns the hardware store, he lives . . . lived just on the other side of where the road ends. He had five kids. Where are they? I don't know! There's nothing there now but trees." His tone was a mixture of fear and anger. "Nothing but trees and ferns," he repeated.

Ellen had heard stories like this on the CB all the way to Carlton. They still frightened her, but that fear created only a stronger need to find her home and her son. She had no idea when Terry and Bill would get back, and she was still angry with Terry for going in the first place.

Angie blinked worriedly, stepped closer, and slid her hand through the officer's arm. "I know it's been tough on you. Officer . . . Peters? I'm not asking you to let us through, but maybe you could tell us if there are any other roads into Portland from here? Any other way we could get in to look for her son?"

The cop's voice softened as Angie's charm took effect.

"I do sympathize," he said, giving Ellen a quick look and a nod of his head, "but this isn't just the road that's gone, it's everything. Portland isn't there anymore. Every road we've checked just ends."

Ellen was tired of being ignored.

"We've been listening to the CB and some people say Portland is there," she said defensively. "Besides, how do you know the city isn't there, you can't see it from here can you?"

"Ladies, I'm tired of people not believing me. I've talked myself blue. I don't give a damn what you do, just don't try to bring a car into this town."

With that Officer Peters walked off a short distance and began to attract another crowd of people as Ellen felt hope leave with him. They were so near, yet miles from her home. The Jeep might take them closer, but all the fields they had seen were ringed by either forests or fences. If they had to cut their way through with a chain saw and wire cutters it would take days. The only option left was to walk.

" 'Scuse me, ladies."

Ellen turned to see the other officer staring at Angie, or more precisely at Angie's cleavage. Tall and thin, he had a small head, and his nose and chin poked out too far. He wore a pair of glasses with one of those straps basketball players wear, to keep them from falling off. Other generations would have called the man geek, nerd, queer, square. He seemed to be all of those and more.

"I couldn't help but overhear your situation and I might just be able to offer you some assistance. I happen to know a group of off-road recreational enthusiasts who are planning a little excursion into the Portland area. I'm sure they would be willing to help you once I explain your situation."

Ellen didn't know what to make of the offer. The name tag on the uniform said STANLEY COOPER and the look in his eyes suggested sincerity. Still, the man seemed decidedly strange and made Ellen uncomfortable. Angie was looking him over, too. Now he wasn't staring at Angie's cleavage, but he was sneaking occasional glances.

"Could this excursion take us into southeast Portland?" Ellen asked.

"If it's there."

Apparently Angie had made up her mind and accepted for both women as she slipped her arm through the cop's and leaned into him so that her breasts were pressed firmly against his arm.

"Could you really help us?" she asked in her little girl voice. "We'd feel so much safer if you could take us, Stanley."

"Call me Coop."

"Okay, Coop. Coop, that's cute," Angie giggled. Ellen didn't know whether to laugh or throw up.

"Coop, we can't thank you enough," Angie said squeezing his arm in her hands and giving him a peck on the cheek as Ellen nearly gagged.

Coop used a police car to lead Angie's Jeep up the left side of the road, getting them closer to town. The women ended up spending the night in the Jeep. It was uncomfortable and they slept fitfully. Ellen spent the night alternating between worry about her son and daughter and anger at her husband. Mostly she wondered about her son; she knew where her husband was and knew he was checking on their daughter, but she had no idea where her son was or what had happened to him.

---

36. JAWS

I deployed 3000 reinforcements across the Yangtze River to defend the bridge and the town. The next morning only a small pocket of 100 could be found. The sentries stationed on the bridge reported no crossings during the night, and when we were overrun the Japanese claimed no contact with my troops. Perhaps my vanished army could have saved Nanking from the rape that followed.

—Colonel Li fu Sien, December 1937

Forest, former site of Portland, Oregon
PostQuilt: Monday, 4:10 p.m. PST

It was late afternoon when the *rex* finished and wandered off down the valley.

"Thank God he went the other way," John whispered. Cubby whispered, "Amen," then urged his friend, "we've got to move, John."

"No way. We're safe here."

"That carcass will attract scavengers all night long. They could find us too."

John desperately wanted to stay where he was. He didn't even know how to deal with bears, or lions, let alone dinosaurs. Now if Ripman was here, he might know what to do. After all, he knew about survival, he knew about animals, he knew about being elemental.

But Cubby persisted. "John, every dinosaur from ten miles around heard that *rex* make a meal out of that other one. They're probably already thinking about the leftovers. Let's get out of here before they get here."

John was nearly persuaded when a noise outside distracted

him. It grew louder, stopped, and then something started sniffing at the opening. John cringed and backed into Cubby, and they both fell back against the logs that made up the back wall. Suddenly a three-toed claw appeared in the opening, each toe tipped with curved spikes, ripping away chunks of dirt, first on the left, then on the right. To John's horror the opening was already doubled. The claws dug methodically several more times, then disappeared, and Cubby and John froze in fear. Cubby feverishly whispered a prayer. Then they both screamed as a giant triangular head jammed its way into the opening.

John was about to be eaten. The head in the opening strained forward, trying to get at Cubby and him. The gaping maw, blood red with a double row of jagged teeth, exhaled, filling the small enclosure with the smell of rotting flesh. Both boys were paralyzed with fear and indecision. Suddenly the head pulled out, and the paws returned to make the opening larger. John turned in panic and started pushing through the spaces between the logs, trying to find a way out. The biggest space would accommodate only his arms and his head. Try as he might, he couldn't push his shoulders through the opening. If he was going to die he didn't want to be eaten from the bottom up. He'd rather have his head go first and get it over with.

John pulled back in to look, but he saw no other way out except where the giant claws were diligently excavating. Cubby knelt on the ground and began fumbling with his bow and quiver, notching an arrow and preparing to use his bow . . . his weapon. Seeing him, John did likewise, pulling an arrow out of his quiver. There wasn't enough room to stand, and he tried to figure out a good position to shoot from—assuming he could, because his hands were shaking terribly.

Cubby held the bow diagonally, because he couldn't hold it vertically without hitting the roof.

With a wham and a roar the animal's head was back. The roar stretched every nerve in John's body to the breaking point. The head roared again, its warm sour-smelling breath in John's face. It wriggled back and forth in the opening, shifting the logs. From a few feet away, Cubby let his arrow fly into the green scaly flesh above its eye. The dinosaur didn't even flinch. It just kept wriggling and coming closer and closer. Shaking,

John fumbled an arrow into place. Unable to stand, he put his feet on the bow and pushed until he felt the compound bow give into its ready position.

"Shoot it, John, shoot it!" Cubby shouted, fumbling with another arrow.

The dinosaur lunged again, and this time the logs shifted. John suddenly slipped, rocking onto his back. He shook his head to clear it and looked between his legs. Inches from his feet was the biggest eye he had ever seen. Screaming, he let go of the bowstring.

Twelve inches away, the razor sharp arrowhead penetrated the eye of the dinosaur, who screamed and reared. The roof gave way under the pressure and the back wall collapsed and rolled away. Cubby yelled a warning and pointed to an opening behind John, who scrambled out. Cubby followed him and they started running, the dinosaur screaming behind them.

In John's blind panic he tripped over a root and sprawled flat. Cubby literally ran right over him. A short distance later Cubby fell and John passed. They continued running and tripping until they could go no farther.

John and Cubby found themselves in a patch of ferns, gasping for breath, and holding their aching sides. Slowly their breathing grew normal and they began listening for sounds. They'd made so much noise running and panting, they were afraid they'd attract flesh eaters.

They sat for more than an hour without speaking, each lost in his own thoughts. John was worrying about his family. He knew his sister was safe in Washington, D.C., but were his parents at the beach cabin or in Portland? John knew Cubby would keep looking until he found his parents, and John would keep following Cubby. John couldn't go back now. He was closer to Portland than to where they had left the van. He still worried about the way Portland had looked, but what choice did he have? After a while Cubby lay down in the ferns. John soon followed, pushing his back up against Cubby, and fell asleep listening to Cubby's prayers.

37. SEA MONSTER

In my visions I see the shadows of great beasts. Before them flee the shadows of man.
—Zorastrus, Prophet of Babylon

Off Naples, Florida
POSTQUILT: TUESDAY, 6:50 A.M. EST

Dawn broke, bringing them the clearest view yet of the monster's head. It was perched on a neck rising fifteen feet out of the water and wasn't much larger in diameter than the neck. The skin appeared to be the same color as the mound they were sitting on, a deep green. The neck and head undulated rhythmically. Ron looked behind where the mound curved down to the water. He knew there was a tail under there somewhere, and from the swirls behind them he could tell the tail was moving. Undoubtably the animal was swimming and making slow steady progress.

Chris was still in the front sitting between Carmen's legs with Carmen's arms around his waist. Rosa was sitting behind Carmen, her left arm folded across her body and held in place by her right arm. Ron was in the back, staring around the others.

Ron heard Carmen's whispered voice.

"Ron, back down. Let's get off here."

Ron started to move but then hesitated. They had spent the night on the animal, too afraid to move off, and with no place but the lizard-infested ocean to go to. The beast had shown no awareness of their presence during that time, let alone hostility. The few hundred pounds of weight they added to its bulk would be insignificant, like a bird riding the back of a rhino. Ron also guessed the animal was preoccupied with saving itself. The animal was heading straight toward the sun, and that meant they were traveling in the right direction. If it kept going in a straight line it would eventually reach the coast of Florida. Estimating its speed, Ron calculated that it would take maybe two days to get to the coast. Otherwise, Ron and his family had no chance of swimming to shore, and no boat or raft to take shelter in. He agreed they had to get off, but thought maybe they should wait for a good-size log or some other wreckage to come by before abandoning their ride.

"Carmen," he whispered. "I don't know . . . maybe we should stay. It's going in the right direction."

"Are you kidding?" she whispered back. "Do you know what this is? It's a brontosaurus."

Ron had been shocked too many times in the last few hours to be surprised now. All he could do was mutter numbly, "A brontosaurus? You mean a dinosaur brontosaurus?"

"It's not called a brontosaurus anymore," Rosa whispered. "It's an apatosaurus."

"Yeah," Chris said in a normal voice, "it's a potosaurus."

Carmen visibly cringed at the volume of Chris's voice and hushed him. Ron found the strength of Chris's voice not frightening, but reassuring, confirming that Chris was alert and strong.

"I don't care what it is, I want off," Carmen whispered harshly.

"Mom, they were herbivores, they only eat grass and leaves," Rosa said.

Rosa said it as if she were an authority, and Carmen seemed to listen. Ron had to admit that it looked like a dinosaur, but he also knew such a thing couldn't exist. Dinosaurs were long extinct. But there shouldn't have been an island at that longitude and latitude either. It seemed likely this animal and the other lizard things had come from the island, but he couldn't make the jump to calling them dinosaurs. There had always been stories of large animals in the ocean, even in lochs. Of course this one didn't seem to be a sea mammal. It showed no intention of diving below the surface, and had no blow hole. It might be a relative of dinosaurs, Ron rationalized, but dinosaurs were extinct. They could call it a brontosaurus or apatosaurus if they wanted to, but Ron suspected any big animal would be an apatosaurus to the children.

"Besides," Rosa continued, "I don't think I could take that water much longer."

"Hey look," Chris said, in an even louder voice. "There's another one."

Ron looked to their left to see a smaller shape in the water, a miniature version of the one they were sitting on. It was swimming just off the shoulder of the big one.

"It's got a baby," Rosa whispered.

"Yeah," Chris said in a normal voice. Then after a shush from Carmen he continued softly, "It's got a baby."

Ron estimated the baby was bigger than a full-grown elephant. Its neck was proportionally much shorter than the mother's, but even then it cleared the water by six feet. The baby didn't seem to be having much trouble keeping up, but Ron suspected the mother was holding back considerably. It made him wonder about the bone structure and anatomy of these animals. They seemed to be using all their energy to move through the water and little or none to stay on top. If the bone structure was light enough, the fat content high enough, and there was enough lung capacity, they could float. Ron suspected that was the case, and it was another reason to stay onboard. They wouldn't find a better raft, or one easier to spot from the air.

"Carmen," Ron whispered, "maybe we should stay here for a while. There might be more in the water, or those other things—at least until we find a log or something."

Carmen looked around fearfully. Ron knew she was thinking of the lizards they had fought in their raft. After thoroughly scanning the surrounding ocean, Carmen whispered back, "All right, but only for a little while."

Somehow staying on the monster had become the safe thing to do, although everyone except Chris was cautious enough to sit perfectly still until their bodies ached. When the pain finally forced them to move, Carmen made sure they moved one at a time, and very slowly. Ron found the sun on his bare back and the rhythm of the animal restful, and soon, like the rest of his family, fell asleep.

38. Friends

We often refer to civilization as a thin veneer, but the constant violence in our country suggests it might be better characterized as a net, with great gaping holes that people are constantly falling through. As the net fills with population growth, the net stretches, making the holes bigger and more people slip out of civilization's control. God help us if the net should ever tear open.

—Dr. Charlene Hall, *The Violent Society*

New York City
PostQuilt: Tuesday, 7:30 a.m. EST

The sounds of Mrs. Weatherby in her kitchen brought Luis back to consciousness. He was feeling better. The headache was finally gone. The lump on his scalp was still there, but the swelling in his lip was down noticeably. He sniffed the aroma from the kitchen and realized with a start he had slept through the night. Mrs. Weatherby was fixing breakfast. Luis could pick out the smells of coffee and frying bacon; they reminded him of his family. Melinda must be out of her mind with worry; Luis knew he had to go and he wanted Mrs. Weatherby to come with him.

Luis sat up slowly. When he was sure he wasn't going to faint he walked to the kitchen and leaned against the door frame. Mrs. Weatherby, wearing a red and white checked apron, was cooking a pan of eggs and bacon over a propane stove. When she saw him she flashed him a grandmother's smile and motioned to the table.

"Sit down, Luis. You're just in time. I'm afraid there's no toast this morning. The toaster is out, you see. I do hope the electricity comes on again soon. I know, I'll toast a piece of bread over the flames of the stove. That just might work you know."

"No, Mrs. Weatherby. This is fine. More than I ever hoped for."

"I'd be happy to try toasting the bread."

"I'm fine, really."

Luis sat down at the table and ate greedily. When he was about halfway through, Mrs. Weatherby clucked her tongue and began frying the last two eggs in the carton. He felt guilty. "Mrs. Weatherby, you're feeding me the last of your eggs. There won't be anymore, you know. At least not for a while. There's no law out there. Take a look at my face if you don't believe me. Let me take you to Melinda's brother's place. The kids are there. You could really help us out. You know, you watch the kids while Melinda and I look for a new place. The kids would love it. Especially Katrina. You know she loves you."

"Katrina is a dear, Luis, and you give her a hug from me. But this is my home and I see no reason to leave it; I can do without a few eggs. As for food, I have everything I need to last me a month right here in this apartment, and when that runs out I've got lots of neighbors to borrow from. I've been through blackouts before, Luis, and they're no problem if you're prepared."

"But, Mrs. Weatherby, there's a dinosaur out there."

"Many dinosaurs, Luis. It's been a constant parade. Some of them I haven't learned the names for yet, but I know I saw a polacanthus and a pachycephalosaurus and those awful deinonychus. They're terrible killers! And of course there's my iguanodon friend. A vegetarian, you know. He has a sweet tooth."

She scooped the eggs onto Luis's plate, then took apple juice from the refrigerator and filled a glass for Luis. "I don't know why I keep the apple juice in the refrigerator. It isn't working, of course. I guess it's just habit."

Luis sighed. "That big dinosaur, he doesn't have to eat you, you know. Stepping on you would turn you into a pancake."

"He's really quite careful." Then Mrs. Weatherby looked thoughtful. "Would you like some pancakes, Luis? I could whip them up real easy. I've got lots of syrup. I've got one of those mixes that doesn't use any eggs. Of course—"

"No, please no. This is fine. I'm already full. I said that dinosaur will turn you into a pancake, I didn't mean I wanted any. He's not smart enough to be careful. He's going to hurt you. He won't mean it but it will happen."

"He is *so* smart," Mrs. Weatherby replied defensively. "You should see how quickly he learned that sugar trick. Now I'm teaching him to stay away from my garden. Why I think I could—"

Mrs. Weatherby was interrupted by the now familiar "aaaah" sound drifting in from the living room window. She immediately took two paper bags from the kitchen counter and walked through the door, calling back over her shoulder as she left, "Finish your eggs, Luis. I've got to see to the iguanodon's sweet tooth or he'll never leave us alone."

When she walked out the apartment door, he realized she was going down to feed her dinosaur by hand. She was impossible. Luis had nearly lost his life trying to rescue her from something she didn't want to be rescued from. He couldn't drag her all the way back to Steve and Tanya's apartment. He was going to have to leave her here, and if that dinosaur got her it wouldn't be his fault. He had tried.

When he looked out the living room window, the dinosaur was there with Mrs. Weatherby. He was down on all fours getting seconds, his massive mouth wide open as little Mrs. Weatherby poured sugar inside. It was a strange and wonderful relationship, but Luis knew it couldn't last. Mrs. Weatherby would have to leave eventually. The electricity wasn't coming back easily this time, and even if it did it wouldn't matter. The police would evacuate these buildings when the looting ended, and they would seal off the dinosaur meadow.

Luis finally conceded defeat. He had to leave. He had a family worrying about him and he should have been home long ago.

Mrs. Weatherby had finished feeding her dinosaur, who was walking off into the meadow chewing a mouthful of grass.

Luis called out the window to her. "Mrs. Weatherby, I've got to go to my family. Won't you come with me?"

She smiled up at him. "Go take care of your babies, Luis. Stop worrying about an old woman. Please don't worry about me. I haven't been this happy in years."

Luis nodded and waved good-bye. She might die, he thought, but she would die happy. Could anyone hope for more than a long life and to die happy? Then he stepped out the door.

The streets were worse than Luis remembered. He figured

that earlier the pain in his head helped blank out his memory. The area near the dinosaur field was nearly a total loss. They hadn't burned the buildings yet, but every window was broken, and anything of value had been hauled away. The leftovers from the looting filled the streets, which were haunted by the scavengers, who were mostly male. The families were long gone and the elderly were holed up like Mrs. Weatherby.

Luis stood in the doorway of his building studying the passersby—young and male, and a mixture of races. The whites had been moving out of Luis's neighborhood for the last few years, but it wasn't clear yet whether the neighborhood would go Latino or black. That was partly why the gang problems were worse here. The white gang called Zombies was losing control over their turf and becoming increasingly violent. The Zombies were on their way out, but they were taking some of the Diablos and Kimbos with them. Still, Luis couldn't spot any gang colors among the crowd. But something else about the crowd bothered him. Why was the crowd still here? Why weren't they where the pickings were better? What kept them here? The dinosaurs surely kept them penned in on one side, but what about the other sides? Luis wondered if the police weren't slowly taking back the streets.

Luis started out cautiously. When he first heard the faint popping sound in the distance he instantly knew it was gunfire. The sounds came closer, more furious. He looked left and right, but the firing was coming down from the street, so he melted into a doorway and waited, peeking out occasionally. Men were running down the street toward him, and Luis recognized the red jackets of the Zombies. They slowed and then spread out, hiding behind cars and in doorways. A minute later they began firing down the street at something Luis couldn't see. Then they began running toward him again. It was time for Luis to hide.

Luis looked around and found he was in front of Mr. Choi's grocery store; he shopped there occasionally and he knew the old man who owned it. Mr. Choi and his wife lived above the market. When Luis first moved to the neighborhood Mr. Choi had two sons who worked in the store with him. They were gone to college now and Mr. Choi used neighborhood kids in the store. He was a gruff old man, but his wife was as sweet as Mrs. Weatherby.

The store's windows were gone like every other window nearby. Because the glass doors were smashed, Luis stepped through the frame. The store shelves were empty and many overturned. Luis walked toward the back, looking for a good place to hide. Only a few cans of beets were scattered on the floor—and Luis kicked at them, realizing there were some things not even looters would steal.

Gunfire sounded outside, closer now, and Luis hurried toward the back of the store. As he passed the last of the overturned shelves he saw a foot sticking out from under the case. He kicked it but got no reaction. It was a brown work shoe like so many others, except that it was small. Luis lifted the fallen shelf until he could see the face of the man underneath. It was Mr. Choi. He was on his back, his eyes wide open in a dead man's stare. A pool of blood made a red halo around his head. Luis set the shelf back down gently. Mr. Choi had died trying to defend his store. Luis knew it was all Mr. Choi had—his livelihood, providing for his family and his children's college education. Luis guessed if he were Mr. Choi he would have died trying to save it too. Then Luis remembered Mrs. Choi.

Luis forgot about the gunfire and found a stairway in the storeroom to the apartment above, which looked untouched. The television and VCR were still there, as were the Oriental trinkets and paintings that decorated the apartment. Luis searched quickly, afraid of what he would find in each room, but it was empty. Filled with relief, he sighed. Mrs. Choi could still be downstairs somewhere under one of the overturned shelves, but he didn't have the heart to look for her.

More gunfire sounded, this time much closer. Luis dropped to the floor and kept his head down until he was sure he wasn't the target. He crawled to the windowsill in the living room and stood slowly with his back firm against the wall and peeked out into the street. At first he saw nothing. Then he heard the pop pop pop of a handgun. Someone ran by below him on the sidewalk wearing a red jacket. More firing sounded. This time Luis was sure it was rifle fire. Two more Zombies ran by and then men not wearing colors—the street was silent for a minute and then another figure, wearing a uniform and carrying a rifle, ran up the sidewalk and crouched behind a car. He stood, leaning the rifle on the roof of the car, and fired up the street. From the distance Luis heard the pop of small arms fire. The soldier fired twice more and then another soldier ran past the first and up the street.

Luis pulled back and leaned against the wall. Elated and scared, he realized it had to be the National Guard taking back the streets. Soon Luis could stop worrying about Mrs. Weatherby—the Guard would make her move, or at least protect her. It also meant Luis would make it home to Melinda and the kids.

Mariel missed Luis. He had been gone only a short time and already she missed having someone to care for and someone to talk with. Luis would never take the place of Gertie or any of her friends from her early and middle years, but he was nice and so polite, not like most young men today. He was one of the few people in the building ever to visit her, and the only one to check in on her to see if she needed anything. She had been touched by his concern for her over the years, and now coming back for her like that made him someone special. That was something a son would do for a mother. Yes, Mariel would miss Luis.

The gunfire started a few minutes after Luis left. Mariel had heard it before, of course, but not this close and not this loud. She wasn't really frightened by it, really just annoyed. All that racket would scare away the dinosaurs. Worse, it might keep the iguanodon from coming for his treat.

Finally, the sounds were so faint Mariel became hopeful that the meadow dinosaurs would return. But although she watched diligently, she could only spot fleeting movements in the grass; nothing she could identify. Then it happened again. Mariel looked down at her crocheting for a minute to check a stitch and then out the window to see the city was back. More distant this time, and shimmery and pale like some reflection in a pond. Leaning out her window, Mariel looked down. She could see the neat line where the meadow met the asphalt, but when she looked into the distance she saw the shimmering city. Mariel took off her glasses and cleaned them on her apron. When she put them back on the city was gone.

"Well I'll be. I must get my prescription checked."

Mariel looked again to make sure and then decided it was time for a cup of the orange spice tea she'd found in the McGregors' apartment when she was looking for sugar.

Luis listened as the gunfire slowly moved up the street and faded into the distance. He stood and peered out at the empty streets. Then gunfire sounded again up the street somewhere near his building. Luis thought again of Mrs. Weatherby, and how he'd eaten her eggs, and felt guilty.

He ducked down and crawled across the floor to the Choi's kitchen. There was an old-fashioned white refrigerator against the wall, with rounded edges and a huge handle. He opened the refrigerator and felt a soft rush of cool air—not cold air, but cooler than the room temperature. The light was out of course, but on a middle rack Luis found two cartons of eggs. One carton was full and one half full. Luis took the eggs and dug deeper into the shelves. He found a quart of orange juice, which he placed with the eggs. If he'd taken anything from downstairs he would have felt like a looter, but up here it was borrowing. He and the Chois hadn't exactly been friends, but they were at least acquaintances.

In the cabinets he found two six-packs of juice boxes and canned fruit, including peaches and pineapple tidbits. In the last one he found an unopened ten-pound bag of sugar. He was loading a box when the sound of the shooting changed.

Now the burping of automatic weapons met his ears. Luis crawled to the window and inched up, peering out. The street was empty, but the sounds of battle were coming closer again. He watched the soldiers appear. They were retreating, running from cover to cover, spraying the streets with automatic fire from their M-16s. Then they were gone and the street was empty again. Luis waited, knowing what was to come. Soon a red-coated Zombie came into view, carrying a weapon whose rapid fire told Luis it was a machine gun. Another Zombie appeared, firing with a machine pistol. More automatic fire sounded. Still another Zombie shot up the far side of the street, and Luis could hear weapon fire surrounding the Chois' store.

Luis shrank back, despairing. He knew the soldiers would be

back eventually, armed to handle the Zombies, but it could take days.

As the gunfire faded into the distance again, Luis realized most of the Zombies and their allies were busy driving the Guard off of their turf. Figuring the odds, he decided now might be a good time to risk it. The box of groceries he had gathered for Mrs. Weatherby would make him look like a looter scurrying home with a few extra spoils. If anyone stopped him he could offer the food to buy passage.

The streets looked empty, but Luis could feel eyes on him. He didn't mind as long as the eyes stayed in the buildings. Heading away from the gunfight, he kept a close watch on the barrier of cars between his building and that across the street. He couldn't see anyone near the cars now. But coming down the street was a small group with two men wearing red. Luis turned to go the other way but spotted men in doorways a half a block off. They looked at him, and Luis felt panic. He had only one choice—to turn and walk between the cars and down the street to dinosaur land.

When the street ended abruptly and the meadow began, Luis hesitated. It was too unnatural, too surreal. The sound of voices behind him forced him forward. He carried his box around the corner of the building. Afraid to step on the meadow grass, he set the box down and peeked back around the corner. Three men were standing by the cars talking. When one of them pointed between the buildings where Luis had gone, Luis folded back around the corner, pressing his back against the wall.

He stood staring at the meadow and thought of the dinosaurs Mrs. Weatherby had described. How many were there, he wondered? What had she called the ones? Terrible killers.

He stood undecided. He had killers on all sides of him and wasn't sure which were the most dangerous.

Now he peeked back around the corner. Six men stood by the cars now, seemingly content to wait Luis out. They're afraid of the meadow, Luis realized. Afraid of the dinosaurs, just like me.

Looking back across the meadow, he saw something moving in the distance—something big, walking on all fours with a huge frilly spiked collar, moving parallel to the buildings. Soon it disappeared into the grass.

Luis quickly scanned the meadow looking for other dinosaurs. There were none, but in the distance he saw the faint image of buildings. Hadn't he stood in Mrs. Weatherby's window, seeing similar buildings? Then, just as before, the shimmering image faded away. He shook his head in confusion. His cracked skull must have scrambled his brains. It was too much for Luis. He wanted out of there and could think of only one way to do it.

Luis dug the bag of sugar out of his box, walked to Mrs. Weatherby's garden and then into the meadow—Luis walked gingerly, expecting the meadow grass to disappear like a mirage at any second. When he saw movement ahead he froze in his tracks—the tops of the grass were moving. Luis watched carefully, and when he was sure it was gone, he ripped open the top of the bag and poured a pile of sugar in the grass. Then he retreated quickly out of the meadow, poured another pile by Mrs. Weatherby's garden and three more piles leading to the corner of the building. At the corner, with part of the bag still left, Luis sat down to wait.

Mariel rocked in her chair, occasionally sipping her tea. The meadow was still, and she made good progress on her crocheting, quickly finishing one square and starting another. Time passed pleasantly and soon a familiar figure appeared in the distance.

The iguanodon was coming straight toward her window, and it was time to get his treat ready. Mariel walked to the kitchen and measured out two sacks of sugar, reminding herself to search the rest of the apartments for more. Still, she had quite a supply now, brown sugar, powdered sugar, Karo syrup, and molasses, anything she thought might please a dinosaur's sweet tooth.

Mariel took her bags back to the window to wait for the dinosaur's "aaah" sound. She hadn't been able to break him of the noise and had finally given up. It had been irritating at first, but now she thought it kind of cute—a big monster like the iguanodon singing for his supper. Mariel thought about that late-night show where people brought their dogs on TV to do stupid tricks. What would they think of the iguanodon and his "aaahing"? She chuckled to herself while she pictured the look on the host's face when the iguanodon walked out onstage and chuckled again as she watched the dinosaur striding through the meadow. He would scare any audience to death. They wouldn't know he was a gentle giant.

Mariel watched the iguanodon approach in his usual way until he neared the edge of the meadow. Suddenly he stopped and bent to sniff the meadow grasses. Then he backed up and began eating something. It wasn't grass, because when he ate grass he ripped it up and then stood to chew it, looking around. Then he did something strange again. The iguanodon sniffed the air and then turned away from Mariel's window, stopping to eat something off the asphalt. Mariel leaned out the window and spotted Luis standing by the corner of the building. What was Luis doing here? Mariel wondered. Why wasn't he home with his family? She pulled her head in, picked up her bags of sugar, and left the apartment.

Luis stood with his back to the wall, watching the dinosaur walk to the next sugar pile, which it devoured eagerly. From the window, Luis had been afraid of the dinosaur, but up close it was terrifying. Its head was massive, bigger than an elephant's, and covered with thick leathery skin. Its mouth contained rows of huge teeth; its back legs were gigantic and its front legs thick and powerful. Worst of all its forelegs carried thumb spikes large enough to skewer a human being. Luis gained a new respect for Mrs. Weatherby.

When it finished the sugar it stared quizzically at Luis, who poured another pile by the corner of the building. When the dinosaur moved toward the new pile Luis ducked around the corner and walked toward the cars.

Mariel stepped out of the building by her garden just in time to see Luis disappear around the end of the building, the iguanodon following him toward the corner. He shouldn't be there, Mariel knew. That's where all the horn blowing and some of the shooting came from. She hurried down the side of the building toward the iguanodon, who was busy eating something off of the ground at the corner. When he finished he lifted his head and sniffed the air. Mariel was afraid he was going to step into the alley, so she shouted to him.

"Wait, wait!"

The dinosaur turned its head and looked her over. Then he walked toward her, his head lowered. When he reached her his mouth opened and the "aahing" sound began. Mariel poured the first bag of sugar into his mouth and then waited while he went through his slurping and lip-licking routine. After the second bag, Mariel pushed on his jaw, told him to go back to the meadow, then left him and walked to the corner to find Luis.

Luis poured another pile of sugar halfway down the street and then walked up to the car barrier. The men behind the barrier—one wearing a red coat—were staring at him. Two of the men held pistols. One man spat something over the car he was leaning on and yelled at Luis.

"Whatcha doin, asshole?"

He wasn't wearing a red jacket. Luis, while relieved, still ignored him and poured more sugar.

"I'm talking to you, asshole!"

Luis looked up slowly and feigned ignorance. "You talking to me? Oh, I'm feeding my pet dinosaur."

The man came around the car and walked toward Luis, who could see a pistol in his belt. He leaned near Luis with an icy stare, and reached up, revealing a tattoo on the back of his hand—a shrunken head, the symbol of the Zombies. His voice was as cold as his stare.

"I don't like smart ass assholes."

Luis stepped forward holding out his bag of sugar.

"Really, I'm feeding my pet dinosaur. It's sugar, see."

He poured the sugar at the man's feet, careful not to get it on the man's shoes.

One of the Zombie's friends suddenly yelled, "Hey, Barton. Ain't ya gonna charge him the toll?"

Barton never took his eyes off of Luis. He merely rubbed his tattooed hand across his stomach just above the butt of his gun.

"Give me your wallet," Barton ordered.

"I haven't got one. Really, I was mugged yesterday."

"You better have something, man, if you want to get out of

here alive." The Zombie pulled his gun, pointing it at Luis's stomach and stepped closer.

"I'm telling you the truth, I haven't got anything but this sugar."

"Yeah, you told us. Your pet dinosaur and all that shit."

In a flash of lights and pain, the gun slammed into the lump on Luis's head and he collapsed to the street. Even after his pain was gone, Luis continued to writhe, trying to convince Barton he couldn't respond to threats. Then, someone behind the car hollered to Barton that something was coming down the alley.

When Mariel turned the corner she saw Luis at the end of the street, talking to some men by the cars. They looked dangerous, not like the kind of men Luis should be associating with. Mariel walked down the street, intending to get Luis back to his family where he belonged. She also wanted to ask him why he was feeding her iguanodon. Suddenly the man closest to Luis hit him, knocking him to the ground. Luis held the left side of his head, the same place he had been hit before. Mariel was angry now, angry and reckless. She strode down the street to help Luis and tell those men what she thought of them, with words she seldom used.

The men behind the cars saw her and shouted to the man leaning over Luis. The man who'd hit Luis looked up and stared blankly at Mariel, irritating her. She wanted him to be afraid or ashamed, and she certainly didn't want to be treated as if she weren't even there. Her face flushed, and she set her jaw. This man needed a slap. Suddenly the man's eyes went wide. Now he was afraid and Mariel felt satisfaction, until she saw he was looking past her. Then he turned and ran around behind the cars to where his friends were hiding. Mariel was puzzled. Now they were all pointing down the street and jabbering. Mariel turned to see what all the excitement was about and saw the iguanodon coming between the buildings, walking upright, taking long powerful strides.

Mariel remembered the men had guns and she turned to warn them not to fire.

"He won't hurt you. I'll take care of him. Let me send him back to his meadow."

Her words fell on deaf ears. The men were so terrified by the size and fearsome appearance of the iguanodon, they weren't listening. Still, they held their fire.

Mariel knew the iguanodon was in danger, and she pushed out her arms trying to send him back. On he came, however, oblivious of the danger. As he approached Mariel he began to bend, coming slowly over and lowering his head until he was down on all fours just behind her. Still the men held their fire.

Mariel stepped forward and pushed on the dinosaur's jaw, telling him to go away. The dinosaur held its ground, then slowly the huge jaws opened to their full expanse. Mariel found herself staring in the iguanodon's cavernous mouth as a deep rumbling began and out came a loud "aaaaaaaaaahhhhhhh!"

From the far end of the barrier a shot rang out. A hole appeared just behind the dinosaur's jaw. His mouth snapped shut at the impact and he stared into Mariel's eyes for a few heartbeats. Then he reared, rising to his full height and screaming at the same time. Every pistol behind the barrier fired and Mariel watched bloody holes pepper the thick skin of the iguanodon's neck.

Mariel's heart ached and she screamed for the shooting to stop. It didn't. More holes appeared along his neck and chest. Sobbing, she ran toward the shooting men waving her arms. Then just as quickly as it began the shooting ended. Mariel turned to see the wounded dinosaur walking down the street toward his meadow. He was walking upright, but slowly, his head hung low. A low rumbling groan came from his throat with each jarring step.

"Oh, no. Don't go!" Mariel called after him. "Please come back." But he didn't. She went after him, hurrying to catch up. She heard Luis shout something behind her, but she ignored him. All she could see and hear was her injured iguanodon friend.

The dinosaur strode out into the meadow. Mariel chased behind, trying to catch up, but even injured, the iguanodon's giant stride kept him moving ahead.

At the meadow she found a new horror awaiting her. The crushed grass that marked the iguanodon's trail was smeared with blood. Her tears began to flow again. "Oh no," she whispered over and over, "oh no!" Then Mariel wiped her eyes and followed the bloody trail.

Groggy, Luis got to his feet, but he staggered when he stepped toward his building. He heard laughter behind him. Barton and the others were bragging about how many bullets they put into the dinosaur.

"Pow, man, right in the jaw. Did you see my shot, man?"

"Your shot? Sheee-it. My shot. Believe it."

"Believe shit, man."

Inside, Luis sat on the stairs to rest. When his head cleared a little and the spinning subsided, he climbed the stairs slowly, pausing on each one. He made the third floor and staggered down the hall into Mrs. Weatherby's apartment—to her rocking chair by the window. He collapsed and rocked gently. When his head stopped throbbing he opened his eyes and looked out the window into the meadow. The last thing Luis saw before sleep took him was the iguanodon walking slowly into the meadow followed by a small figure.

---

39. Black Ripple

The weakest force in nature is gravity. It takes the entire mass of the earth just to make a leaf fall to the ground. But condense the mass of the earth to the size of a marble, and you have a black hole, where the laws of time and space, as we know them, cease to exist.

—Merlin Constantine, *Of Time and Space*

Washington, D.C.
PostQuilt: Tuesday, 8:00 a.m. EST

The President was more than tired. He was afraid, and he was desperate.

Nick had taken the President's alien theory as a naive attempt to cover all possibilities, but Nick wasn't as sure now. He saw the President as a drowning man, grasping at straws.

The President would be open to Nick's new theory—but perhaps too open. The President spoke calmly and in a controlled manner, but his fingers told another story as he reflexively twirled a twisted paper clip. Nick looked up to catch Elizabeth Hawthorne's eye. Normally inscrutable, now she looked worried—about what had happened, or about the President? Nick wondered.

The order of reports on the agenda was the same, and Nick had to wait through the military assessments again. There was still no identified strategic threat, so the reports focused on losses. In addition to the loss of the ELF system, contact had been lost with seven military bases in the United States, including one SAC bomber base, several bases on foreign soil, an aircraft carrier group, and several other individual ships. There were also communication problems with some Landsat and civilian weather satellites and loss of contact with some military KH 13 satellites. Until contact could be reestablished, the military was substituting aerial reconnaissance of the affected areas.

Samuel Cannon's report included a confirmation that all of the black bag projects were suspended, as the President had ordered. The CIA's report also included a surprise: no confirmation of the dinosaurs in Oregon, but a confirmed report of dinosaurs in Quebec, with photos. The CIA director's aide passed around copies. Nick had trouble believing what he was seeing. The heavily armored animal walking past a barn was five feet at the shoulders and fifteen feet in length. Its body was bulky, but the head was small for an animal this size, and its tail was as armored as the rest of the body and tipped with two spikes. It looked like an overgrown armadillo. Cannon reported their experts identified it as a living ankylosaur—an animal extinct since the end of the Cretaceous period.

Everyone at the table turned to look at Nick with new respect—except Gogh, who kept his eyes on the photograph.

The report on the civilian situation had new dimensions of horror. Part of Mobile, Alabama, was a lava field now, and the rest a firestorm. An avalanche of steaming mud had buried Aspen, Colorado. Omaha was inundated by a wall of water roaring across the wheatfields. Lake Tahoe had overflowed its banks, drowning the cities of South Tahoe and Stateline.

U.S. military bases also were reporting on overseas effects. Part of Paris was forest, and most of Rome, including the Vatican, was missing. London was untouched, but there were severe tidal wave losses along most of the English coast. Scotland was gone. Russia and the Ukraine were the only East European countries still communicating, and their reports had a familiar ring. Countries all over South America and Africa were pleading for help. From Central America came reports of missing cities and villages and strange animals roaming the countryside. The Panama Canal would have to be redug.

The reports were bleak, endless, and repetitive, and soon, under Elizabeth's urging, the President cut it off with a curt "thank you" and then moved down the agenda.

When Nick's turn came he asked that Colonel Conrad, Dr. Roberts, and Sergeant Yamamoto be admitted. The first two took seats against the wall while Yamamoto went immediately to the computer. Colonel Conrad looked comfortable, every inch the confident professional. Dr. Roberts looked ill at ease but Yamamoto appeared almost gleeful. The chance to sit with the Security Council and hear the secrets of the secret was his fantasy become reality.

Yamamoto's computer was linked to a special overhead projector, which enlarged the computer images and projected them on a wall screen. Now he called up the list of events and dates.

Nick began, "Mr. President, we have a theory that may help us explain what has happened. If you remember my earlier report I said that what appears to have happened could best be described as time displacement. I still believe that to be true, and the photo of the ankylosaur and other evidence support the theory. I also said that it might be a natural phenomenon. I was wrong about that."

Heads turned and mumbling filled the room. Elizabeth leaned forward and whispered in the President's ear. He nodded and then spoke.

"If it was not natural then was it an attack?"

"No, sir. Nor were aliens involved. Take a look at the screen. The list you see represents unexplained events that have occurred over the last century. Most of these are objects falling from the sky, like boulders, ice, huge amounts of water, grain, even unidentified plants. Sometimes animals have fallen from the sky, like frogs, tadpoles, and rabbits. There are also mysterious intense fires, floods, and rock falls. We believe that all of these events were real and that they were caused by the same force that caused our current problem."

Gogh cleared his throat for attention and then spoke, looking back and forth from Nick to the President as he did.

"Ice falling from the sky is hardly the same as a city disappearing. Frogs from the sky we can handle, but ankylosaurs roaming the countryside suggests a completely different kind of problem."

"Different problem but the same source," Nick dismissed Gogh curtly. "Run the next program, Sergeant." The program with the two circles appeared on the screen. "These two circles represent nuclear explosions. You know when nuclear weapons are detonated several waves of destruction spread out from ground zero. There is a pressure wave, which does the blast damage. There is a wave of thermal radiation—essentially a ball of hot gas that expands rapidly; that's about a third of the released energy. There is also an electromagnetic pulse, which induces current in power lines and electrical equipment. There was an EMP accompanying the time displacement we've experienced. Then of course there's the ionizing radiation, neutrinos and gamma rays." Nick looked around, making sure everyone was with him. "We're proposing that another kind of wave is also created, a time wave, which radiates out not only through three-dimensional space but also across the fourth dimension." Murmuring filled the room.

"We have no evidence of such a wave, Dr. Paulson." Gogh said it with an air of dismissal. "We would have detected it long before now."

"Detected it with what? What instrument? The only evidence is that list I put on the screen."

Dr. Gogh pursed his lips as if he was going to say something but kept silent, his eyes focused intently.

"We believe that when a nuclear device of sufficient size is detonated, it sends out a time wave in the same fashion that it sends out heat and pressure."

"And how does that drop frogs from the sky?" Nick turned at the President's question in time to see Elizabeth lean back.

"It doesn't, sir. Not by itself. Sergeant, run the program." The circles appeared, then expanded until they intersected and froze with the *A* showing. "It appears to take two waves in conjunction. Where the two waves contact, the time displacement takes place. Say two bombs were detonated, the first bomb one hundred kilometers east of Washington and the other simultaneous detonation one hundred kilometers west. If both waves traveled at fifty kilometers per hour they would contact each other over Washington two hours later."

"And drop frogs or something?" Gogh suggested derisively.

"Possibly drop something, but more likely pick up something. People walking down the street at the contact point might find themselves . . . displaced." Nick nodded to Yamamoto and the program continued until *B* and *C* appeared on the screen. "The displaced person would find themselves along the line marked by *A*, *B* and *C*."

"Say, in San Francisco," the President offered.

"Possibly," Nick conceded, "but you can't just speak of where, you also have to ask 'when?' This wave is four-dimensional. If the waves travel at fifty kilometers per hour and one year per kilometer, then the person would disappear one hundred years from now and reappear someplace along this line in the future."

"So how do we get frogs falling out of the sky?"

"If the contact point is a wetland on a summer evening you could pick up a pond full of frogs and drop them fifty years later on tourists at Fisherman's Wharf."

"I assume that you checked the dates of the events on that list against the dates predicted by the model," Gogh said.

"That was the most difficult part. We tried using Soviet and American test sites, and Hiroshima and Nagasaki, but the model didn't fit well and it did not account for many of the events. We tried various starting dates for the model, and different rates of geographic and temporal spread. Various combinations of blasts do seem to predict the events on the list, but the best fit comes if you assume a starting date of October 31, 1952."

"Halloween?" the President said. "You're not suggesting a supernatural source, are you?"

Defense Secretary Natalie Matsuda lifted her hand to catch the President's eye, and then turned to Nick.

"It's Mike, isn't it?"

"Mike marks the beginning of it."

Matsuda turned to the President to explain.

"Mike was the code name given to the first hydrogen fusion bomb tested. It was an above-ground test . . . everything was then . . . we set it off on Eniwetok Atoll." Then turning to Nick she asked, "Is it the fusion or the tonnage that causes the effect?"

"We suspect tonnage. Mike was a ten-megaton device. The fission tests before that approached a thousand kilotons and maybe exceeded it. Anyway, the effect seems to be rooted in a series of tests carried out by us and the Soviets, which ranged from fifteen to sixty megatons. It was the combination of Soviet and U.S. tests that gives us the best model fits."

Gogh tried another tactic.

"I still say that frogs and wholesale topological change are not the same thing."

"I agree with Arnie," the President said, nodding his head toward Dr. Gogh. "It's a good theory but it seems inadequate."

"Yes, sir, but there's another piece of the puzzle," Nick explained.

Yamamoto pulled up the next program without being asked. The pulses of circles began and raced toward the edges of the screen, the screen changed and the circles merged into two larger circles and then contacted each other.

"One more time, Sergeant," Nick explained. As the circles expanded he explained. "As you can see, the time waves that follow the earlier waves travel at a faster rate. We think this may be for two reasons. It might be that the earlier waves somehow alter the time/space relationship. Each wave would clear the path for the wave following it. Just like the first snowshoer does most of the work and the tenth snowshoer in line has a well-packed path to follow. This also might explain why the effect does not begin until the fifties. The earlier fission explosions might have cleared the way for the effect to occur.

"The second explanation may actually depend on the first. The earliest explosions may have been insufficient to cause the effect. We don't know what the minimum explosive power would be for such an event, but we moved from the fifteen kiloton warhead used on Hiroshima to sixty megaton devices during that time. The speed of the wave may be a function of the megatonage of the device. Larger explosions could send out a faster wave . . . and by faster I mean in terms of time and space. The faster later waves from the sixty megaton warheads would eventually catch the waves in front of it."

"And pass it," the President offered.

"Let's assume for now they merge to form a larger wave. When the smaller waves contact each other you pick up some frogs here, apples there, chunks of ice in the antarctic, water off of lakes and oceans, possibly the heat of a blast furnace in Pittsburgh. In the future frogs and ice fall from the sky and people and buildings burst into flame, all events that have been recorded. Now picture several of these waves merging into two larger waves . . . two superwaves. What would happen when two superwaves contact?"

Nick paused, and let the idea sink in. There was silence around the table, although Gogh was scribbling furiously on a yellow tablet. After Elizabeth whispered again, the President had a question.

"It takes two waves, you said. The other wave comes from Soviet testing?"

"Yes, sir. The model assumes a Soviet wave and a U.S. wave meeting. I have some people working on contact points using French, Chinese, and British waves, but their programs may have been insufficient in terms of frequency and megatonage to create the effect."

Admiral Chelsea asked the question Nick had expected Gogh to ask.

"Some of those dates you had up there were before the first bomb was ever tested. How do you account for that?"

"Two ways. First we assume that the time wave travels in both directions, forward and back. We've tried to fit the earlier events to the model, and some events are when and where they should be, but there is little accurate data to work with. The best data we have from before the turn of the century is more than two thousand years old, but it too isn't specific enough. A second possibility would be natural events. Mount Saint Helens exploded with the equivalent of ten kilotons, and there are other more powerful explosions in history—Krakatoa, the Siberian explosion, Pompeii. They aren't regular enough to produce a superwave but perhaps could have combined to produce some events."

The room filled with silence, the only sound the hum of the fluorescent lights. Then Gogh started scribbling on his notepad again. Others around the table started asking questions, and Nick handled each of them within the parameters of the theory. Then the President asked the question he was dreading.

"Dr. Paulson, how did you come up with this theory and these programs in so little time?"

"I didn't, sir. Colonel Conrad and Dr. Roberts obtained the computer models, and Sergeant Yamamoto helped decipher them." Grinning, Yamamoto waved his hand at the mention of his name.

"Who created the original program?"

As Nick started into the story of the hostages, the I-5 mountain, and how a college kid and some mysterious group of friends in Oregon had predicted the end of the world, he watched for reactions, knowing that some would judge his theory on its source and not its merits. He decided partway through not to mention Zorastrus yet, or his predictions. This group was more likely to put its faith in technology, not in the analytical abilities of an ancient scientist. At some point Gogh stopped scribbling and began listening. The President's eyebrows raised when Nick mentioned Kenny's current mental state. Nick quickly added the fact that a psychologist had been with him in the cave and on the trip to Washington.

"Dr. Roberts," the President asked, turning toward the psychologist, "is Kenny Randall insane?"

Nick watched as Dr. Roberts rose shakily to his feet. He was pale and perspiring and his voice wavered.

"Kenny is in a catatonic state. However, the psychosis is reactive, not chronic, and there is a good chance he will recover. But what I think you are really asking is whether this theory is real or the product of a delusional mind. My best professional judgment is that Kenny's condition resulted from two factors: the knowledge that something terrible was going to happen, and the inability to get anyone to believe him. He was sane when he began this work. We don't know anything about his friends yet, but we assume they all couldn't have been insane."

Nick paused, studying the President's face. He looked unconvinced. Nick had only one other card to play, and it looked like this was the time.

"Sir, what has happened was predicted—but not by those psychics Ms. Hawthorne rounded up. It was predicted by a man called Zorastrus . . ."

"The Prophet of Babylon," the President said, surprising Nick and the others at the table.

"Yes, sir. Even in his day things did fall from the sky, or strange animals appeared. He documented them and measured the time between events. He knew something would happen, and he predicted it, unfortunately he was executed before he could finish his calculations, otherwise we might have had some warning."

Nick paused again, waiting for some response from the President. When it came, it surprised him.

"I know of Zorastrus, but I never connected his prophecies with what has happened. It gives the theory a certain credibility."

"I'm not so sure," Gogh interrupted. "Time displacement is not a part of any theory I've heard of, ancient or modern. Time travel has been speculated on, but the conditions for time travel are not met in this instance." As he habitually did, Gogh talked only to the President, then occasionally remembered others were present and made a quick head sweep to include [illegible]m. The President seemed interested in Gogh's opinion and [illegible]ged him with a nod.

[illegible] travel can be accomplished in only two ways, neither [illegible] practical. One way is to travel through a wormhole, [illegible]les exist only at the center of black holes, since [illegible] conditions of infinite density and gravity to warp [illegible] waved his hand as if to sweep the idea away. [illegible]eory of travel in time involves cosmic strings— [illegible]n strings of pure energy left over from the big bang. These strings would need to have a density of a thousand trillion tons of mass in each cubic inch. Two such strings moving past each other would warp space/time and allow an object, say a spaceship, to loop around the nearer string and arrive in the past of the farther string. You may or may not understand the theory underlying what I am saying, but you can note that none of the conditions for time travel are met with Dr. Paulson's theory."

"Dr. Gogh," Nick cut in, "there is a common thread in your time travel theories. Both theories require dense matter, either a black hole or a cosmic string. An uncontrolled fusion event does condense matter. Some have theorized that such explosions create black holes."

"There is insufficient mass to create a black hole."

"There is insufficient mass to create a cosmic black hole, but what mass there is may be condensed to a level similar to that of a black hole or a cosmic string. You need a black hole for a wormhole, but this is something short of a complete breakdown of the laws of physics. There may be other effects produced by dense matter."

"Dr. Paulson, if such effects were possible then cosmic explosions, say a supernova, should produce these time waves. We have no evidence of such effects. And what of the big bang itself? Shouldn't it have produced such a wave?"

"Dr. Gogh, I think the evidence is there . . . has been there. We just didn't have a theory that properly accounted for it. For example, take the lumpy universe problem and the problem of missing mass." Nick paused and saw the President and the rest of the council staring at him blankly. He turned to the President and tried to explain in simple terms.

"The big bang theory hypothesizes that at the beginning of time, all matter was collected . . . existed in a state so that the laws of physics as we know them would have ing. Then, for a reason we cannot know, this mass creating the universe as we know it. If we accept beginning, we explain much of what we observ verse, like the intense background radiation, a ing nature of the universe. But the big b weaknesses. One of these is the problem of mi version of the big bang theory hypothesizes that the exp of the universe is slowing and that gravity will eventua all matter back together. The problem is that there cient mass for either the big bang to have occurred universe to pull itself together again, and we can't find the missing mass."

"There is dark mass—" Gogh began, but Nick cut him off.

"Yes, Dr. Gogh," Nick said turning back toward Gogh. "But even that is insufficient." Nick turned again to the President. "The second difficulty with the big bang theory is the lumpy nature of the universe. If the universe did begin with a big bang, then why isn't mass evenly distributed throughout the universe? Instead we find lumps, galaxies and solar systems. Why the uneven distribution? Our theory offers an explanation. If the big bang created a time wave, mass could have been time displaced. The lumpy universe could be created when mass that is time displaced suddenly appears in a region of space occupied by matter traveling in normal space time. These clumps would then coalesce into galaxies and solar systems. The missing matter isn't really missing, it has only been time displaced and has been, and will continue, to appear. What we have experienced is a smaller version of what is a natural cosmic event."

Gogh frowned darkly, immediately rejecting a theory he had considered for only a few minutes. "The mass is insufficient to produce the effect you claim." He shoved his yellow pad across the table toward Nick. It was covered with computations. Nick ignored it but Gogh continued, "There are theories to account for both the lumpy universe and the missing matter."

"But no unified theory that takes into account both, plus the unexplained historical events and the time displacement we have experienced. As to the insufficient mass to produce the effect, you're looking for enough mass to produce a black hole and a complete disruption of the laws of physics. My theory doesn't require a wormhole, only a ripple in the space/time continuum . . . a black ripple," Nick argued.

Silence returned as every mind in the room tried to digest the ideas presented.

Then the secretary of defense leaned forward to make eye contact with the President. Natalie Matsuda was a listener, not a talker, but when she talked, she used such force and seriousness that her few words had enormous impact.

"Mr. President, I've read reams of reports on what has happened, but I've seen only two theories to explain it. One is supernatural punishment, which I'm not prepared to accept. So I suggest we accept Dr. Paulson's theory as our working assumption and move on from there."

"I agree, Natalie." The President looked relieved and seemed anxious to move on. "Arnie, I appreciate your input. It's important for us to get all perspectives on a problem, but please put aside your concerns for now and work with this new theory. I want all of you and your respective departments to go to work on a way of reversing what has happened. Let's get our people back."

As the President broke up the meeting he whispered to Elizabeth, who moved to Nick and held him back until the others left. This time the President spoke without waiting for a whisper from Elizabeth.

"Nick, when time displacement takes place, what happens to the people displaced? Where do they go?"

"I'm not sure, sir. I believe they are displaced into the future or the past."

"The past? I thought everything was pushed forward. We don't have any reports of people from the future appearing, do we?"

"No, sir. But if we assume that the sections of land displaced are swapped with sections of land in the past or the future, and this happens in a predictable way, then in the future we would avoid building on these sites. We should be able to determine this by examining the flora and fauna, but it hasn't been done yet."

"So one of our cities could have ended up in a prehistoric period?"

"Yes, sir." Nick wanted to add there was a seventy percent chance the city had ended up in an ocean, but the President seemed pained enough.

The President thanked Nick and urged him to get to work on a solution. Nick didn't bother to protest. As they were leaving, Elizabeth turned and slipped Nick another worried look.

40. First Kills

The extinction of the Cretaceous terrestrial vertebrates was one of the five greatest extinctions in history. The cause of such a mass extinction, and its nature, has long been debated, yet remains a mystery.

—K. Carmen Sontag, *Nature's Lost Species*

Forest, former site of Portland, Oregon
PostQuilt: Tuesday, 7:03 a.m. PST

The sun was peeking through the trees when something moving through the ferns woke John. He bolted upright and came face-to-face with a dinosaur, its head about half the size of John's and its mouth full of greens. When John screamed with the shock, the dinosaur's mouth dropped open and the half-chewed ferns dropped in John's lap. Spinning around, it took off in the opposite direction, its long tail whipping around behind and toward John's head. He rolled with the blow, but even so the tail knocked him sideways and out of the fern patch. He jumped to his feet and looked around wildly, scanning for other dinosaurs, but saw only the tail of the little one disappearing into the underbrush. Then he heard Cubby laughing.

"Jeez, John. You kill a tyrannosaurus one minute and then you're running from a baby the next. My hero!"

"I was just surprised, that's all," John argued lamely. Then [illegible]ing to hide his embarrassment said, "Anyway, I don't think [illegible]t was a tyrannosaurus last night. It was too small and its [illegible]nt legs were too long. Besides, I didn't kill that dinosaur, I [illegible]st made it mad."

"Maybe. But a needle in the eye ain't bad. Maybe it'll die of infection? Maybe it's on its way for a tetanus shot right now."

Cubby laughed at his own joke and John joined in.

"Wait'll its mom finds out what happened. I can hear its

mama now. 'I told you not to play with sticks, and if I've told you once I've told you a hundred times you'll put your eye out.' "

Cubby and John laughed together. It was the first time John had felt good since Ripman disappeared. Sitting in this weird forest, and laughing at stupid jokes, John understood why he was friends with Cubby and Ripman. This was the feeling they had shared riding in Cubby's van, sipping Big-Gulps, and insulting each other. They were too different to be lifelong friends, John had always known that. Someday Cubby would follow his dad into the ministry, John would go off to college, and Ripman . . . well, Ripman would be Ripman. They would keep in touch for a while, but eventually, John thought to himself, we'll be so different that we'll even stop sending Christmas cards. Knowing that made John even more determined to enjoy the feeling while he could.

Cubby and John still had their packs, so they ate the last of their energy bars and emptied their canteens, then took stock of what they had left. There was still a little trail mix but it wouldn't last the day. They both had their hunting knives and packs and John still had the snake bite kit. John had been so afraid the night before, his hand had frozen around his bow, and they found it in the fern patch. Cubby's bow and their quivers of arrows, however, were back in the forest.

"I'll tell you what, John," Cubby said, pulling a coin out his pocket. "We'll flip to see who goes back for the arrows. Heads, I stay here and you go back, tails, you go back and I stay here."

"Screw you, Cubby. Maybe we can make some arrows?" John pulled out his hunting knife and started looking for a straight branch.

"Maybe Ripman could, but you and I will be lucky to keep ourselves off some dinosaur's menu," Cubby said. They both knew it was true. "Even if we could make some arrows, you saw how much good my arrow did with that one last night, and [illegible] had a steel tip. What do you think a sharpened stick would [illegible] Besides, do you want to sit still long enough to make so[illegible] arrows? We're almost to Portland, and I say we keep goi[illegible] Hey, we get to my house and my mom will cook us up hash browns and eggs, and some of that thick bacon you like. Ripman's probably already there laughing at us because we're taking so long."

Cubby was sniffing at a make-believe plate and rolling his eyes. John had eaten at Cubby's before and it was always a feast. His mother, a transplanted southerner, was the best cook in Portland. John's mom was a good cook, but her beans tasted like beans. Cubby's mom's beans had bacon bits and two or three spices, making them a full meal. Now John's stomach was doing his thinking for him.

They left the useless bow behind and started off through the jungle. As John followed Cubby the good feeling was lost, replaced by fear. The arrows hadn't been much more than a security blanket, but now even they were gone. They had already been chased by dinosaurs twice. He wondered what the odds were of getting away three times. They walked on in silence, working their way downhill and to a creek bed with pools in it. From the look of the banks, the creek was once a foot or two deep.

"Wonder what happened to the water?" John asked.

"Maybe some dino got thirsty and slurped it up." Cubby meant it as a joke, but that started both of them looking around cautiously.

They found a clear pool and dipped their canteens in, watching the bubbles break on the surface. Cubby ran his fingers around the edge of the pool a couple of times, then his eyebrows went up and he jerked his canteen out of the water and fumbled the cap back on.

"What's up, Cubby?"

"Take a look at these pools. Notice anything?"

To John, they seemed just ordinary water. Then it hit him. The pools were in pairs, two straight lines, one on each side of the creek bed. He saw Cubby disappearing into the trees and followed, nearly running into him. John looked down and saw Cubby's footprints—two impressions in the grass side by side—and remembered those in the creek bed. The boys kept running.

Ellen and Angie met Coop's "off-road recreational enthusiasts" early the next morning. The group turned out to look like a backwoods motorcycle gang—the five men besides Coop all looked as if they made their living with their hands. Only Coop had bothered to shave, and their clothes looked as if they had never been washed. All of them were wearing leather work boots, jeans, and flannel shirts topped with sweatshirts or down vests. When the women approached some of the men started clapping and howling at Angie. Even in a coat and jeans Angie had an aura of sensuality. Coop stepped forward as they approached and introduced them.

"These are the ladies I was telling you about. This is Angie." Two of the men whistled in appreciation. "And this here's Ellen. Ellen has a young progeny somewhere in the Portland vicinity, and she needs assistance in reconnoitering the area. I said we would facilitate." Ellen didn't mention that her little boy was seventeen years old.

As Coop spoke Ellen noticed two things that bothered her. First, the group was heavily armed. The motorcycles were fitted with rifle sheaths, and every sheath had a gun sticking out of it. Two of them were also wearing holsters. Why would cross-country motorcyclists need weapons?

Second, one of the men wasn't staring at Angie, he was staring at Ellen with the kind of look the other men were giving Angie. Angie may be used to that kind of look, Ellen thought, but I don't like it. Coop had introduced the man as Carl. He was as tall as Coop but muscular, with dark hair slicked back on both sides of his head and curls hanging down covering his forehead. His face was covered with a dark stubble and his eyes were staring at Ellen.

Looking straight back at Carl she asked, "What do you need all those guns for? Expecting to run into a gun show?"

Carl smiled. "The big city's a real dangerous place, right guys? Country boys like us can't go into town unprotected. Besides, we've got you women folk to look out for. Right guys?"

The others snickered.

"The guns are for hunting," Coop said. Then he paused, as if he were thinking about telling them more, but he merely shrugged and muttered, "You never know what you might run into."

There was something going on here that the "guys" weren't telling the girls, making Ellen uncomfortable. But the only remaining option was walking into Portland, which could take days, and she was concerned about her son.

Angie and Ellen followed the motorcycles in their Jeep, winding through the small residential section of the town. Officer Peters had been right. Cars packed the streets, parked in every nook and cranny. They came to what looked like a dead end but instead of stopping they drove down a long driveway around a house and to a dirt road. That road led up over a hill and down into another patch of forest. At the bottom of the hill they came to a small one-lane bridge that crossed a creek. Before crossing, Carl and the guys stopped and gathered together talking. Finally, Carl and Coop returned to the Jeep. Ellen noticed that Coop came to Angie's window and Carl to hers.

Coop said, "You'll have to abandon your vehicle here. We're going to follow the creek bed. You can go double with Carl and me."

The thought or riding with Carl made Ellen shudder. "What about the road? Why don't we just stay on the road and follow it?"

Carl leaned in Ellen's window to speak. When he did, she smelled stale beer on his breath and flinched back in revulsion. Her reaction made Carl smile. Carl was missing an eye tooth, and from the brown crust between his other teeth, she judged he'd be missing more soon.

"Hey, what's a matter? Don't you trust us? We're gonna get you to your boy. There just ain't more road to use. Coop and I been down there," he said nodding over the bridge. "You can get another half mile and then nuthin' but forest. You'd never get this mother through those trees," he said as he banged the door of the Jeep with his knee. Carl smiled sweetly and then turned serious. "Better to come with us. We'll follow the creek bed and use it like a road. It'll get us closer to where we'll jump off and head through the forest."

"Okay," Angie said, "we'll get our stuff together."

Carl and Coop drifted back up with the guys and started talking with them. The guys kept looking back at the Jeep and laughing as Carl gestured obscenely. Angie then turned to Ellen.

"Honey, I'm getting a bad feeling about this. I trust that Coop, I can handle him, but Carl and the guys are a different story. And what are they doing with all those guns? Did you notice two of them are carrying assault rifles? I'm not saying I won't go with you, don't think that for a minute," Angie was saying. "I just want you to know what we're getting into. Carl and his buddies are just having a good time now, a chance to get away from some mill or factory job, and cat around. Maybe Coop can keep them in line—probably he can."

"Angie, you've done enough. You've brought me all the way across the state on back roads, spent your time and money when you could have been lounging around a motel pool waiting for Bill. Go on back, I can handle it from here. I don't trust them either, but I'd make a deal with the devil to get to my son. I've got to know if he's there, if he's somewhere."

"You want me to ride with Carl."

"Angie, I said you didn't have to go."

"I heard you honey, now who do you want to ride with?"

Ellen smiled at Angie and then leaned over and hugged her. "I'll ride with Carl. You work your magic on Coop."

"He'll be horny enough to hump a tree by the time this motorcycle ride's over."

Ellen was sure about that. She only hoped Carl wouldn't feel the same way.

When she and Angie climbed on the bikes the other guys grunted their approval with "all rights" and "way to go"s. All of them were looking at Angie and Coop except Carl, who made a disgusting "smacking" sound and then winked at her. Ellen hated riding behind Carl. When she spread her legs wide to squeeze in beside him, Carl pressed between her legs and made another disgusting sound.

The other bikers led off across the bridge and then turned and dropped down the sharp bank to the rocky creek bed. Ellen tried hanging on to the seat, but the terrain was rough and bouncy. She hated putting her arms around him, so she grabbed his coat, only leaning against him occasionally to keep her balance. Ellen noticed that Angie wasn't as picky—she had her arms around Coop and her chest pressed up against his back.

After a while Ellen relaxed a little. She began to trust Carl—at least his riding skills.

After what seemed like hours the lead rider, a big man called Bobby, stopped and rode back to talk with Coop. Bobby had powerful-looking suntanned arms, and scraggly blond hair, with a half-grown beard on his boyish face. Bobby asked about something being "around here somewhere?" and Coop pointed up over the bank. Bobby rode out into the creek a little way, then the motorcycle jumped forward and roared up the bank, actually becoming airborne as he cleared the rim and he disappeared over the top. After a while he reappeared and signaled the others to follow. One by one the bikers launched themselves over the edge.

Coop and Carl waited for the others, and then Coop leaned back and said something to Angie, who wrapped her arms tighter and leaned into him. Coop too roared up the bank, the bike fishtailing and then straightening as it continued up over the edge.

Carl turned to Ellen and said, "Do it like Angie did, hang on tight and lean into me as we climb."

Ellen wanted to get off and climb the bank herself. It would make more sense than making a risky climb with two on a cycle built for one. But she knew the bikers didn't care. This wasn't about climbing a hill, it was some sort of macho thing, and all the guys were waiting to see if Carl could make the climb. The fact that Coop, the nerd, had done it with Angie on his bike made it imperative that Carl do the same.

If Ellen was to handle Carl, she could not risk damaging his ego. Being married to Terry meant picking up bits and pieces of psychology whether you want to or not. Ellen knew that the best way to turn someone violent was to wound his ego.

Carl gunned the engine and pointed the fork of the bike at the lowest part of the bank. Swallowing her revulsion, she wrapped her arms around Carl's waist and leaned into him, hoping he was too preoccupied to feel her breasts flatten against his back. Then Carl released the clutch. The bike flew forward and suddenly the front end of the bike tilted up at a sharp angle. The speed of the bike fell quickly and the engine began to strain. Just as they slowed to a near stop, the front of the bike dropped back flat, and they were over the top.

The other bikers were watching them clear the bank. Carl raced down the line of bikes for a victory lap and then turned around and stopped in front of the line. Bobby and the rest of the bikers applauded and yelled, "All right." Then Bobby stared right at Ellen.

"Looks like she's coming round, Carl."

Ellen realized she still had her arms wrapped around Carl. She let go and sat back, giving Bobby a piercing look. He just smiled.

They cut through a sparse stand of Douglas fir to a field of strawberry plants. Running along the far side was a forest. Ellen had heard about it on the CB, but seeing it made it even more unbelievable. The trees were not the expected fir or yew, and she realized they were huge. As the forest loomed above her she identified the trees as redwood, as big as any she had seen along the Avenue of Giants in California. The guys stopped their bikes at the edge, staring at the trees in awe. The undergrowth was sparse but oversize. Some ferns grew nearly as tall as Ellen, and big patches of grass climbed nearly six feet in height. Elephant grass? she wondered.

Ellen thought back to the kid in the cave. It seemed like a hundred years ago. "The end of the world," that's what he had said. Ellen looked at the forest and wondered if he had been talking about this. Mountains on I-5, a redwood forest dropped on Portland? Is this how the world was to end? In confusion?

Even the guys were surprised by the forest. When they started off again Coop led, with Carl right behind. They rode across the strawberry rows, crushing the plants as they followed the edge of the forest. Worried about the damage, Ellen looked around for a farmhouse but saw no buildings. She was so close to her son now, she didn't want to get stopped for trespassing. Finally, Coop cut into the forest and Ellen could see what he had been looking for—a clearing on the other side. They rode to the middle of it, where Coop stopped. Carl pulled up next to him and the guys pulled up on both sides.

"I saw him right over there," Coop said, pointing.

Ellen wondered what "him" they were talking about.

"Bullshit," said the one called Kishton. He was the shortest of the group but probably the strongest; his upper arms and chest were muscular, forming a body builder's classic V shape. He also had the only full beard in the group.

"I still say it's bullshit."

"Coop wouldn't lie to us, would you, Coop?" Carl said.

Kishton shut up and looked around.

This is the classic adolescent friendship pattern, Ellen thought. How had Terry described it? "A like-minded group of males loosely associated for the purpose of fellowship, with no formal leader." As Ellen remembered it, the individuals of the group would adamantly deny there was a leader, yet to an outsider the leader was clearly discernible. Carl was the leader here. Ellen knew leadership depended on having something the other males prized—being the strongest, having the best car, or making it with girls. Ellen studied Carl and decided he wasn't the toughest. Kishton probably was, or maybe Bobby. Carl didn't look that tough, yet he was clearly the leader. Why? Kishton started talking again.

"All right, if he's here, how do we find the mother?"

"Coop'll find him, won't you Coop?"

It wasn't really a question. Carl was telling Coop to deliver what they were looking for, or else.

They seemed to have forgotten about Ellen's son, so she spoke up. "I thought you were going to help me find my son. What about us?"

Carl turned to Ellen and smiled broadly, revealing his missing eye tooth.

"Oh, don't worry. We'll be getting to you. Lead off, Coop, I'll pick up the rear."

Angie pulled Ellen to one side and put her arm around her shoulder.

"How you doing with good ole Carl? You want me to switch with you?"

"No. You're doing a great job with Coop. Just keep him under your spell."

"Don't you worry about that. He's mine," Angie giggled.

Coop led them once around the perimeter of the clearing and then headed through the trees. The ferns and grass were thick and tall in the clearing, but once under the canopy of the giants the undergrowth thinned. The going was slow but steady. Carl kept cussing and kicking at the clumps of vegetation as they worked their way around and through the undergrowth. Once Carl rode close to a patch of grass that brushed Ellen's arm, leaving three painful, bleeding slices, like paper cuts.

They broke out of the trees into another clearing, and Ellen looked around Carl in time to see Coop and Angie drop over an edge and disappear. One by one the other cycles followed. Carl went over the edge last, into a soggy creek bed with a small stream running through the middle. The going was slippery here, but they made better time. There wasn't much of a bank, and Ellen could watch the scenery. The forest thickened and thinned in no particular pattern, but it was becoming clear that Portland was no longer here. Ellen realized if Portland was gone, so was her son.

Coop led them back up a bank into a clearing and stopped, turning off his motor.

"Looky there," Coop said, pointing into the clearing.

Ellen could see nothing but grass and clumps of ferns. Suddenly a head popped up over the top of the ferns, with a dome, perched on a long thin neck, and covered with a gray-green skin. Ferns were hanging from its mouth and its eyes were fixed on their group. Ellen had never seen one before, at least not alive, but it was a dinosaur.

"Hot damn!" Carl screamed. "That mother is mine."

"Holy shit, deputy dawg wasn't lying."

"I told you. I wouldn't prevaricate about something like this."

Ellen watched as the men pulled their rifles and checked the load.

"Leave it alone!" Ellen shouted. "If that's a dinosaur, it's the last of its kind. You can't kill it. Let's just leave it alone."

"Who asked you?" Kishton snapped. "I say whoever nails it gets dibs on its head."

The rest of the guys cheered and yelled, "All right."

"I don't *know* about this," Coop added. But he looked nervously at Carl and the other guys, and wh[illegible] e was going to say withere[illegible]

"She's right, [illegible] aur is worth a lot more alive th[illegible]

The mention of money slowed them down until Carl spoke. "Hell, there's more where that one came from."

Excited, the men jump-started their bikes and were off,

bumping across the rough terrain. Only Coop and Carl hung back, Carl fixing Coop with a piercing stare.

"You one of us or not, Coop?"

"You know I'm with you, Carl," Coop said weakly. But it was becoming clear to Ellen that Coop had bought his way into this group with his knowledge of the dinosaur.

Poor, nerdy, Coop was beginning to look like Ellen felt. The deeper they got into the forest, and further from civilization, the less civilized the "guys" were.

The dinosaur hunt was on. Briefly, the creature watched the cycles coming toward it, then it bolted in the other direction. As it ran, Ellen watched intently. Running on two legs, it was faster than a man—about eight feet tall with long forelegs and a domed head.

The cyclists split up, racing to each side of the running dinosaur, trying to cut it off before it reached the forest. One cyclist, burly, balding Butler, who seldom spoke, skidded to a stop and fired his rifle. The shot missed, but the sound made the running dinosaur bolt to the right, forcing Kishton to swerve. As he did he clipped a clump of ferns, and the front wheel of the bike buried into the patch, launching him over the handlebars.

Butler fired again, and this time the dinosaur dropped to its knees, skidding and then bouncing onto its long neck. Now Butler jumped on his bike and raced after the remaining cyclists as they closed in, but before they could shoot him again the dinosaur was up and racing toward the trees. Too far away to see the action, Coop started up his bike, Angie climbing on behind him. But Carl made no move to follow, and Ellen had no intention of squeezing up behind him unless she absolutely had to.

The motorcyclists cut the dinosaur off again, and it raced toward the center of the clearing. Anguished, Ellen could see blood running down its right rear leg. She gave up hope of saving it and wished now they would kill it and get it over with. But the bikers were enjoying the hunt.

The dinosaur circled back toward Carl and Ellen, coming straight for them. Ellen had a good view now as the dinosaur closed on them, but suddenly another shot rang out, and the dinosaur went down, dropping onto its right side and struggling to get up. Its back legs seemed to be working but the front ones could not support its weight, and they collapsed, creating a pivot, and the dinosaur went into a spin.

The animal's blood soaked the ground as it flattened a circle of grass, going round and round. The hunters gathered, pointing and laughing at the spectacle—until Coop joined them.

Coop got off his bike, angrily confronting Bobby, who pushed his face within inches of Coop's and began shouting. Angie wrapped her arms around Coop's waist and pulled him back, then Bobby said something that made the others laugh. The hunters went back to enjoying the dinosaur's struggle. After Angie and Coop talked for a second, Coop turned, pulled his revolver, and emptied it into the dinosaur.

The hunters jumped back at the sound of the revolver and watched—then they turned on him.

Even from this distance Ellen could feel their anger. Ellen started forward, fearing for Angie's safety, but a rough grip on her arm stopped her.

"Let 'em party," Carl smirked, pulling Ellen toward him.

Ellen put her hands on Carl's chest and pushed. Leering, Carl wrapped his other arm around her waist and pulled. He was strong and could have pulled her flat up against him, but the cruel look in his eyes told Ellen he was enjoying her struggle. Then Carl began to exert more pressure, drawing Ellen toward him. Suddenly, he dropped his hand, wrapping it around her bottom and pulling her hips tight up against his. He held her there briefly and then began grinding his hips against hers.

"Stop it, Carl! Let me go."

"Where you going? They're done huntin'. Nuthin' left to see."

"I've got to find my son."

"Lady, ain't it clear to you yet? There's nuthin' here. It's all gone, the city, the people . . . your son. Looks like you're gonna need another. I'll be glad to help you make one."

As Carl shifted his weight, bending her over backward, he tripped her. Ellen crashed to the ground with him on top. She could smell the liquor on his breath again. His eyes still looked cruel and his lips still sneered. Now Ellen began to struggle again and pounded on the sides of his head. As he yelped and jerked back to protect his face, Ellen pounded harder.

"Get off me!" she screamed.

Carl wasn't laughing now, he was dodging blows—then Ellen heard someone else laughing.

"Carl, looks like you bit off more than you can chew there."

Ellen stopped pounding and Carl dropped his hands to see Kishton watching them. He'd fallen in the sharp-edged grass and bled from dozens of cuts. His face, shirt, and pants were torn and blood soaked.

"Beat it, Kishton, I'm busy," Carl snarled.

Ellen realized Carl's ego was wounded. After all, Kishton had seen him getting slapped around by a woman. Now Carl would retaliate. Before Kishton could decide whether to leave or watch, Coop came roaring up. Angie immediately jumped off and helped Ellen off the ground. Without a word to Carl, she just pulled Ellen off to one side, asking if she was okay.

Coop looked angry. "What the hell were you doing, Carl? We're here to assist her in locating her boy, remember? You perpetrate something like that again and I'll . . . I'll . . ."

"You'll what? Arrest me? You see any fuckin' jails around here? Shee-it, you're not even a real deputy."

"Am so. I'm a reserve officer—"

"Coop, you ain't nuthin' but a pain in Sheriff Peter's ass. The only reason he keeps you around is cause me and the boys won't work for the slave wages he pays you. Are you that stupid, Coop? He's offered me, Kishton here, and nearly every one of the others your job at one time or another. Ain't that right, Kishton? I'll tell you something else, Coop, I'm thinkin' we don't need you anymore. We got the dinosaur. Just what else are you good for?"

His tone sounded final, and Angie and Ellen pulled each other closer. Coop had never had much authority, and even that was eroding fast. If they sent Coop back, or worse, nothing would keep Carl from Ellen. Coop was watching nervously to see if Kishton would intervene. They were interrupted by the grisly sight of Butler roaring up with the head of the dinosaur strapped to the back of his motorcycle. The others followed, each with a dinosaur leg strapped to the back of his bike.

"You call that baby a dinosaur?" Ellen asked. All heads turned toward her.

"Baby?" Butler said, jerking his head toward the head on the back of his bike. "You call this mother a baby?"

"That's right," Ellen continued, "they grow much bigger than this. Some of them are as big as a three-story building. They come so big, that I doubt you're man enough to bring one down. Isn't that right, Coop? I bet you could find us a bigger one, couldn't you, Coop?"

Angie chimed in. "I've seen these things in movies and I know they come bigger than this. Did you ever see that *King Kong* movie? Think they get that big, Coop?"

No one was listening to Coop's answer. The men were talking among themselves. Someone dug a bottle of Old Crow out of a saddlebag and they started passing it around, reliving the hunt and planning the next one. As they talked Carl gave Ellen a look that said there was unfinished business between them.

After the men fortified themselves they were back on the cycles. Ellen had only two choices, and she swallowed back her fear and climbed up behind Carl. Angie gave her a look that said she would trade places, but Ellen couldn't do it to her. Besides, Ellen thought, Angie seemed to be handling Coop quite well, and they needed whatever control over the guys he had left.

John felt as if they had been walking for hours when Cubby finally stopped again.

"Something's not right, John. We should be to Portland by now. This is where we saw it."

John looked around but recognized nothing. He could tell they were down in a valley, since hills were visible to the right and left, covered with tumbled-down trees. The forest was thick, but it looked level. Was it the Willamette valley? Cubby was sure of it, and John, as usual, trusted Cubby's instincts better than his own.

"Maybe it's just a little farther ahead," John suggested. Cubby pursed his lips considering.

"I don't know, John, we should at least be able to see those skyscrapers." Cubby looked around intently. Then he pointed up at the hill to the south. "Let's climb up to those fallen trees. Maybe we can get a look around from up there."

John hesitated, then followed Cubby, though his stomach

was rumbling, and his muscles complaining. After another crested hill, he was just about to quit when they came to a clearing amidst fallen timber. Trees lay every which way, and their roots and crowns towered into the air, blocking the view. They worked their way to where the hill dropped off sharply, then climbed the jagged roots of a big tree and stood on the top of the trunk. They had an unobstructed view of the valley, its floor a forest with clearings sprinkled here and there. In the middle of the valley was Portland, wispy and still shimmering, but undeniably there. Cubby and John shouted and whooped and jumped up and down. Then Cubby gave another shout and whoop and pointed to the south of the city. John looked, at first seeing nothing but buildings and trees. But then he spotted it. Separated from the city by a stretch of suburbs was a hill, and shimmering and flickering on its crest was Cubby's church. John stared, then looked for his house. He knew there was no way he could see it from here but he looked anyway.

"Thank you Lord Jesus for delivering us," Cubby prayed aloud. John whispered an amen silently to himself. Enthralled with the feeling that something good was about to happen, they stood there staring at the church. Soon, John's thoughts were interrupted by a roar—not the roar of a dinosaur, but the distant roar of a jet.

Spotting it, he watched it arc across the sky above Portland; then it was gone. John tried to estimate the distance to the church and then looked at his watch. It was nearly eleven o'clock. He was sure they wouldn't make the church by nightfall, but like Cubby, he was willing to give it a try.

They rushed into the forest, recklessly hiking toward their destination. Still tired and hungry, but like racers nearing a finish line, they found reservoirs of strength. The forest on the valley floor was thin, with little underbrush. They still had to dodge razor grass and walk around giant clumps of ferns, but they made good time. At one point when they heard something big moving through the trees, they hid in the undergrowth, lying flat and praying that dinosaurs have a poor sense of smell. Soon the sound moved off in another direction, and the boys quickly got back on track.

John watched the sun sinking lower and lower as they walked and began to get nervous. Here the vegetation was sparse. They'd have difficulty finding a place to hide for the night. John heard the distant roar of another jet and looked at the sky, but couldn't spot the plane. As the roar of the jet engines faded he heard the familiar sound of motors. Someone was driving through the forest.

"People, Cubby. Listen, I can hear people."

"You're right. Maybe we're near the edge of the city."

They listened, trying to locate the sounds, which suddenly died. Cubby pointed in their direction and led off through the trees at a quick pace.

They stopped in the creek bed while Bobby climbed the bank again. The rough terrain had made Ellen's sore bottom burn with pain, and she was glad Carl finally stopped. Bobby had just disappeared when they heard a shout.

"I'll be damned. You've got to see this. Come on up here."

Following Bobby's track up the bank, they found themselves in a large clearing. There, shimmering faintly in the background, was the Portland skyline. Ellen felt hope flood her body. She had been slowly reconciling herself to the loss of her son—but maybe, just maybe, there was hope.

Now John felt better. If they were near the edge of the city he could catch a ride to his house and spend the night there. John and Cubby found themselves climbing yet another hill, a gradual one so the climbing was easy. On the other side, the trees thinned, and they found themselves staring into a large clearing.

Near the far edge were parked several motorcycles. Eight people stood near the bikes, and even from this distance, John could tell two were women, and one seemed familiar. When she moved he knew it was his mother.

"It's my mom," he said, starting past Cubby into the clearing. Cubby's hand on his arm stopped him.

"Wait, John, something's not right."

Maybe it was the motorcycles—John and Cubby had seen many biker movies—or maybe they'd developed natural caution in the forest. But John and Cubby just stood and watched.

* * *

Ellen and Angie were excited by the presence of the city, but the guys seems disappointed, and even angry.

"Thought you were going to find us a mama dinosaur, Coop," Carl said in a threatening tone.

"Yeah," Kishton added menacingly. Ellen could see that some of the razor grass cuts were still bleeding. "I missed out on the first hunt, and I came out here looking for some excitement."

He was off his bike and approaching Coop, who urged Angie off, then confronted Kishton.

"I found you one dinosaur, I didn't say I could find you two."

"Well that's not good enough, Coop. If you can't find dinosaurs for us, just what the hell are you good for?"

"Coop didn't let us down, Kishton," Carl said, walking up in front of Coop. "He found us a dinosaur. And not only that but he brought us some more fun." Then he chuckled.

Coop's face was drawn, his lips tight, his eyes fearful.

"Good buddy Deputy Dawg brought us Ellen and Angie. Two of the hottest babes in the county."

"At least Angie is," Kishton said, walking up behind her.

"Hey, Kishton, you and the others can have her. Ellen straightens out *my* pecker."

"Knock off that kind of talk, Carl," Coop said, his voice trembling. "They might think you're serious."

Carl grabbed his crotch and gave it a shake. "Don't I look serious, Coop?" The others laughed.

"Don't touch them, Carl." Coop dropped his hand to the butt of his gun.

"You gonna stop me, Deputy Dawg?"

"I'm the law—"

"Coop, you weren't much law back in Carlton and you sure ain't the law out here. I'm the law here."

Then, without any warning, Carl dropped his hand to his gun, pulled it and fired it into Coop's chest. Coop dropped to the ground, twisting left and falling into the deep grass. Ellen knew he would never move again.

The other guys stood still, shocked. Ellen imagined they would have willingly beat up Coop, de-pantsed him, tarred and feathered him, or even tied him to a tree naked and left him. But she believed only Carl would have killed Coop in cold blood. Carl's ruthlessness was probably what made him their leader. But now that he'd murdered Coop, how much further were they willing to go? Kishton answered the question by grabbing Angie's arms, and pulling them behind her back.

"Give me a hand here, will you, Butler?"

Butler hesitated. Then a big smile crossed his face, and he stepped forward and grabbed Angie's breasts.

"Oh mama," he said, "we're going to have some fun."

With that Butler tore Angie's blouse open. She didn't scream or cry out, but she began to struggle and kick. Butler jammed himself up close to Angie, so she couldn't kick him between the legs, and tore her blouse down to her waist.

Ellen, frozen in disbelief, now saw Carl's face turn toward her and took off running. Heavy footsteps behind her urged her to run faster. She headed for the treeline, hoping to lose herself in the underbrush. In the twilight she might be able to hide herself.

Halfway to the trees Carl tackled her. She went down hard on her stomach, her chin striking the ground, her teeth aching from the impact. Still, she kicked and pushed to keep Carl from getting a solid grip on her. He laughed, enjoying her struggle. When Bobby arrived, the two men flipped her onto her back. Carl sat on her, pinning her solidly to the ground, and then timed his grabs to seize her flailing arms. Then Bobby pulled them above her head. Carl leaned back, putting more weight on her stomach, staring at her breasts, smiling in anticipation. Thinking quickly, she relaxed a little, encouraging Carl to lean back some more, then she jerked her knee sharply upward, cracking Carl in the back. Carl yelped with the pain. His eyes flashed and he slapped Ellen hard across the face, twice. Suddenly she felt Carl's hands on her chest, tearing her blouse open.

"Hot damn!" Carl said. He looked up at Bobby. "I think we made the right choice. Besides, we can always have a go at Angie later."

Carl reached down, trying to pull off Ellen's bra. The straps held, cutting into Ellen's back. Finally, the clasp gave, and she felt Carl's rough hands on her breasts. Bobby was giggling uncontrollably by now, and Carl rocked back and forth, inching his way down so he could get at Ellen's pants.

Then Bobby screamed.

He reached around to his back and stood, almost falling into Ellen and Carl, his mouth opening and closing. But the screaming had stopped, replaced by short gurgling breaths. He collapsed to his knees, then fell sideways onto his face. Ellen could see an arrow sticking out of his back. Carl leapt to his feet, pulling his gun. He was looking past Ellen into the trees when another arrow flew over Ellen's head and buried itself into his calf. Now he too fell to the ground with a scream, dropping the gun and grabbing at his leg.

Ellen rolled to her stomach and then came up onto her feet running. She bolted toward the darkness of the treeline, listening for pursuit but heard only her own blood pulsing through her system. She made the trees and ran wildly, not looking where she was going. Bushes and branches swiped at her face as she ran. When she stumbled to her knees, gasping for breath, she looked behind her. Someone was crashing through the trees, a strange half-naked figure. Ellen realized it was Angie.

"Thank God," Ellen sobbed. "I'm sorry, Angie, I'm sorry I left you." Ellen felt guilty for getting Angie into this mess in the first place, and for thinking only of herself when a chance to escape had come.

"Nonsense," Angie said briskly, "you did what I would have done. Now let's get out of here."

They were about to head off again when they heard a voice.

"This way, Mrs. Roberts."

Ellen looked to see a man—no, a boy—emerge from behind a bush. He was wearing a camouflage jacket. A bow with three strings was in his hand, and a pack and a quiver of arrows was on his back. Ellen searched her memory. The face was familiar; it was Robert, John's friend. Except, she remembered, he liked to be called by his last name, Ripman.

41. Pursuit

The careful arrangement of eggs in a nest, and the close proximity of adult fossils and that of their young, suggest dinosaurs may have had a maternal instinct similar to mammals.

—Gregory Hale, *Dinosaur Dreams*

North of Bend, Oregon
PostQuilt: Tuesday, 7:13 a.m. PST

They spent the night huddled in the RV, afraid to move or even make a sound. Occasionally the dinosaur could be heard moving around outside, and twice it sounded farther in the distance. Both times the creature returned within an hour, snuffling around the outside of the RV. As morning broke the dinosaur could be heard moving off into the distance again. After twenty minutes, Colter stood to peer out.

"It's gone," he whispered. He walked through the RV checking the other side and the front and back. "Yeah, it's gone for sure."

The others stood slowly, each checking separately that the dinosaur was gone. Only when they were all sure did they speak, and then only in hushed tones. Incredibly, Dr. Coombs and Dr. Piltcher immediately fell into another debate.

"Are you sure it's not triceratops?" Dr. Coombs asked.

"Certainly a ceratopsian, but the horns are wrong for triceratops. More likely monoclonius," Dr. Piltcher countered.

"I can't agree," Dr. Coombs argued. "The curved nasal horn would be typical of monoclonius, but the frill horns seem exaggerated for this particular species. *Mono* means one after all. Perhaps it is an intermediate form—"

"What difference does it make?" Petra shouted. "Triceratops! Monoclonius! What matters is whether it is coming back or not!"

Dr. Coombs and Dr. Piltcher looked sheepish.

She found Colter outside looking at the RV. Its entire length was crumpled or dented. He tried to pull a crushed fender away far enough to free one tire, but failed.

"Help me, Petra," he urged, straining.

Petra reached in next to him and grabbed the edge of the wheel well just below his hand. Bracing one leg against the side of the RV, the two of them pulled on the metal. It barely budged. More hands reached in; Dr. Piltcher and Dr. Coombs jockeyed for position. Moose appeared in the broken window above them, startling the group; he was balanced on the edge and staring down. His mouth moved open and closed, but no sound came out. When he made no move to jump down and run away, the others went back to their task. When they all had a firm grasp they pulled and the metal began to move. Suddenly Moose screeched, then spun and dropped back in the RV. Then something bellowed behind them.

They turned to see the dinosaur charging down on them. Scrambling to get in the door they automatically paused to let Petra go in first. She dove into the RV as the others realized there wouldn't be enough time to get in before the dinosaur rammed it again. Hesitating, not willing to be either first or last into the opening, the three men stood in the doorway paralyzed with indecision while behind them loomed the on-rushing dinosaur.

"Move!" Petra screamed.

Colter was the first to break and ran to his right, the dinosaur's head jerking in his direction. Dr. Coombs broke next, running left and pulling the dinosaur's attention back from Colter. Left alone in front of the door, Dr. Piltcher struggled to climb in before the dinosaur crushed him in the opening.

When Dr. Piltcher disappeared inside, the dinosaur turned toward the escaping Dr. Coombs. But it turned too late, crashing into the wall of the RV. Instead of pushing the RV back with the blow, the dinosaur's snout horn penetrated, peeling the metal wall away followed by its massive head. The snout horn drove deep into the RV, demolishing cabinets, and only the massive collar of the dinosaur prevented the head from completely penetrating the wall. Dr. Piltcher, knocked backward by the force of the blow, bounced off the back wall, falling forward. As he put out his hands to stop his fall, he found himself slamming against the snout of the dinosaur. The dinosaur and Dr. Piltcher froze, startled at such close contact.

Then the massive mouth opened and screamed, nearly deafening Petra, and Dr. Piltcher and he pushed back with his hands, throwing himself away from the opening mouth. When the dinosaur screamed again, Dr. Piltcher and Petra scrambled to the back of the RV to hide with Sarah.

The dinosaur roared its anger again and then began violently shaking its head and pulling back with its massive legs. With every swing of the monster's head the jagged edges of the torn metal sliced deeper and deeper into the thick skin of its head. Blood began to stream in rivulets at the base of the collar, dripping inside the RV. Oblivious to the pain, however, the dinosaur continued to swing its head. As the opening enlarged, the head moved back, and with a final powerful tug the head wrenched free, leaving a gaping hole in the side of the RV as Dr. Piltcher and Petra watched with relief from the back.

The collision stunned the dinosaur, but once free it smelled the nest robber. The dinosaur backed two steps and then spun left, toward a figure racing through the clearing in the distance. Then putting its head down, it charged again.

Petra, horrified to see the rapidly retreating dinosaur was chasing Dr. Coombs, turned to her mentor.

"We've got to help him, Dr. Piltcher. What can we do?"

Dr. Piltcher stood numbly, frozen into inaction. Theory and speculation were his forte, or the recall of fact after fact, but creative problem solving on the spot was alien to him. Sensing this, Petra bolted out the door and began calling for Colter.

He popped up out of the grass at Petra's shout. He'd tried to draw the dinosaur off by giving it a running target, but when it slammed into the RV he took the opportunity to disappear into the grass. Colter now saw her pointing at the retreating dinosaur and yelling.

"Colter! It's after Dr. Coombs! Help him! Help him!"

Colter spotted Dr. Coombs zigzagging in front of the dinosaur to keep it from closing. Colter knew of only one option—give the dinosaur another target. He sprinted through the grasses, angling to put himself into the dinosaur's peripheral vision. If he could get close enough to seem threatening, the dinosaur might slow to assess the new threat. That would give Dr. Coombs enough time to make it to the hedgerow where he could hide.

When Colter's plan became clear, Petra raced for the other side to create a third target. The couple sprinted through the grass shouting. But the dinosaur was singleminded and continued to close on Dr. Coombs, who was nearly to the taller brush. In desperation Dr. Coombs turned sharply to the right, almost running toward the onrushing behemoth. Like a charging bull, the dinosaur lumbered past Dr. Coombs before it could turn.

Colter shouted out encouragement.

"Do it again, Doc! Just keep turning tight circles, it's too big to get you that way."

As he did, the dinosaur turned after him again. Dr. Coombs prepared to run right again around the back of the dinosaur. But then it happened.

In midmove, the dinosaur swung back the other way just as Dr. Coombs jumped its tail. As he landed he saw the head coming toward him. He turned to race the other way, but it smacked him in the back and sent him tumbling across the clearing. As soon as he stopped rolling he struggled to his feet, moving his bruised body as fast as he could. It wasn't fast enough. Dr. Coombs turned just in time to take the dinosaur's charge full in the chest.

Miraculously, Dr. Coombs struggled to his feet again. Now the dinosaur lowered its head, took two steps, and brought its head up into Dr. Coombs's stomach, tossing him up and impaling him on the two horns protruding from its crest. Petra froze in horror, then turned away in disbelief. It took all her willpower to look back. When she did the horror was still there.

Dr. Coombs's limp form was impaled on the upper horns. One of the horns was buried in his thigh and one somewhere in his back, and he was held across the head of the dinosaur. The confused animal shook its head trying to dislodge Dr. Coombs's limp body. Petra watched helplessly as the dinosaur's efforts became more violent, but still the body hung on the curved horns. Petra saw no way she could help. She spotted Colter doing something in the grass. Then he stood, holding a long stick in his hand.

The dinosaur was still struggling with Dr. Coombs's body

when Colter approached stealthily, keeping slightly behind the head of the dinosaur. Then, out of the corner of her eye, Petra saw Dr. Coombs move. It was just his arm, but it moved up, and then dropped again. He's alive, Petra thought. Then she ran forward to draw the dinosaur's attention away from Colter.

Colter was getting close now, so Petra shouted and waved her arms. This time the dinosaur turned toward her. Its huge eyes flamed with anger, but it only stared at Petra defiantly. As soon as Petra had it distracted Colter broke into a sprint.

Colter ran the last few steps to the dinosaur and plunged the sharpened stick into one of the wounds in its neck. To Petra it looked as if the stick barely penetrated, but the dinosaur screamed in pain. It shook its massive head, forgetting about Dr. Coombs's still-impaled body. Colter, shaken loose by the dinosaur, grabbed the stick again, then plunged it back into the beast. This time the dinosaur began to run. Colter tried to keep up but soon stumbled and was left behind. Petra followed the retreating dinosaur toward the tall brush. Just as it disappeared, Dr. Coombs raised his head again and opened his eyes. Then the dinosaur crashed through the brush and out of sight. Petra stumbled to a halt at the hedgerow. The grass was sticky with a mixture of human and dinosaur blood. Colter came up next to her, and behind him she could see Dr. Piltcher walking through the grass, his face pale and drawn.

"He's alive, Dr. Piltcher," Petra said.

Dr. Piltcher shook his head.

"Petra, I know you want him to be . . ."

"He is, Dr. Piltcher. I saw him move."

"Petra . . ." Dr. Piltcher began, but Colter cut him off.

"I saw him move too."

Dr. Piltcher's eyes went wide and some color returned to his cheeks. Then he turned to the forest and shouted.

"George, we're coming. Don't you die on me, George!"

Dr. Piltcher turned to follow the blood trail, but Colter's hand on his arm stopped him.

"Without a weapon?"

"You can go to town for a gun if you want, Colter. George will be dead by the time you get back. I'm going after him. He's my friend."

Colter looked past Dr. Piltcher to Petra for help, but she

looked as determined as Dr. Piltcher. Colter dropped his eyes and shook his head.

"All right, all right. Just give me a minute, will ya?"

Colter trotted off toward the mangled RV, pausing long enough to retrieve the stick he used on the dinosaur. Dr. Piltcher watched him briefly and then started to follow the dinosaur's trail. But Petra stopped him, and the look in her eyes persuaded him to give Colter a few minutes. Dr. Piltcher paced anxiously looking vainly for signs of Dr. Coombs in the brush ahead.

Colter returned with a knife securely wired to the bloody end of his pole. To Petra it seemed a flimsy weapon to use on a dinosaur, but Colter led off confidently.

Crushed grass, broken limbs, and sticky red smears showed them the way. A short distance into the brush, a four-foot bipedal dinosaur turned down the trail ahead of them. Colter signaled a halt, and they watched its mottled green tail disappear down the trail. Colter was about to move off again when a dinosaur, walking on all fours, moved through the grass and down the trail. Colter waited again to give the smaller one some space. They followed the trail only a short distance when once again something moved through the grass toward the trail—a dinosaur similar to the first one, trotting upright down the trail. Colter turned in frustration.

"It's like rush hour on the freeway. They're scavengers, you know."

They were about to strike out again, but something moved through the grass ahead of them. Too small to see, it too was following the scent of the blood.

Petra stood defiantly and walked back the way they had come. When the others caught up, she said simply, "I know where the dinosaur's going. She's going home."

Petra led them back to the clearing and then back into the brush toward the nest of eggs. After a short distance Colter turned and whispered to the others.

"You hear something weird?"

Petra and Dr. Piltcher heard only the wind rustling the leaves. Still Colter hesitated and only led off after Dr. Piltcher threatened to. Colter crept forward, his pace slow and deliberate. He paused often to listen and his eyes moved constantly.

Dr. Piltcher became impatient and tried to push past Colter, who pulled him to the ground.

"Listen! Don't you hear it?"

Dr. Piltcher pushed Colter's hands away, but looked to see Petra squatting, her head tilted back, listening intently. She turned to Dr. Piltcher, her forehead creased.

"Listen, there is something," she whispered.

At first Dr. Piltcher could hear only the wind, but slowly his ears filtered it out. New sounds came: a mixture of tearing, slurping, and crunching.

When Dr. Piltcher realized he was listening to tearing flesh and crunching bones, he sagged to his knees and began to sob. "Oh, George, what have I done to you?"

---

42. THE PRESIDENT AND GOGH

The rhythm of civilizations is written in the fabric of the universe by the gods. But that rhythm speaks of an age when the fabric will be torn.

—Zorastrus, Prophet of Babylon

The developed countries, self-absorbed with their own suffering, offered little to the Third World. With only basic transportation and communication networks, Third World countries were thought to have suffered less, but what they had was essential, and the loss of dams, power generators, phones, bridges, and population was devastating. Life on the farms went on virtually untouched, but the overcrowded and undercivilized cities that suffered from the effect were plunged into darkness and anarchy. Separatists, liberation armies, and the politically disaffected seized the opportunity, and war spread. Ethnic cleansing quickly became a norm, as peace-keeping forces were withdrawn to see to the needs of their home countries.

Without the support and resources of their patrons in the developed world, governments fell and civil war spread like wildfire. Soon, even the cities and regions untouched by the effect were infected with the spreading disorder.

War would kill the most for a while, but without facilities for exports, medicines, and imported food, disease and famine would soon displace war. Peoples dependent on U.N. feeding stations would soon find them empty, and regions battling famine would face new horrors. A new order would eventually displace chaos—political maps would be drastically rewritten. But the new order would be different, for it would include the new wildlife.

Washington, D.C.
PostQuilt: Tuesday, 10:35 a.m. EST

The President put down his reading and leaned back, staring at the ceiling. So many bizarre reports had left him numb to new horrors. The report on his lap summarized the situation in South America. Elizabeth kept insisting a worldwide catastrophe opened possibilities a President couldn't ignore, but his interest was in the domestic situation. Agreeing finally to read the summaries, he read with one part of his mind while the rest worried about Sandy. The Secret Service had lost touch with the first lady's escorts, and although he knew they were working frantically to reestablish contact, every second without word turned his hope to despair.

The President turned back to the report. It described an incident in Argentina near La Plata where a herd of cattle was attacked by an "unknown carnivore." A rancher and his son were killed trying to drive off the beast—killed and eaten. The locals fled, and the army was called in to kill the animal, which so far had eluded them.

There were dozens of detailed stories like that one, as well as general descriptions of disappearing dams, avalanches, and missing cities. Power outages were widespread in Argentina, Chile, and Brazil, and virtually no news was coming from the rest of the continent. The reports were identical to what had happened in his own country and only reinforced his feelings of helplessness.

Arnie Gogh knocked at the open door.

"Hello, Arnie. Come on in. I need the relief from these reports. It's as bad everywhere else as it is in our country. None of our allies escaped."

"I know, Scotty. I'm afraid I didn't come to make things easier for you."

"Sit down. Let's get it over with."

"First, we have an unusual request. Are you familiar with our antarctic research station? There are about two hundred personnel at the site. When the . . . it happened, they found their camp sitting next to a tropical jungle. It's a familiar story, but it had to be particularly stunning in a barren landscape like Antarctica. They went exploring, naturally, and soon ran into something pretty nasty. They lost a couple of personnel. They retreated to camp to prepare themselves better, but it turned out to be unnecessary. The dinosaurs—which we can assume they are—were sluggish and stuporous. They were freezing to death and soon most of them slipped into a state like hibernation. Being enterprising scientists, and not knowing the same thing had happened all over the world, they began capturing the dinosaurs and dragged them to their port. They want to ship them to a warmer climate."

The President was exhausted from worry over his wife, and the survival of his country, and had little patience for a group of eggheads trying to save dinosaurs.

"Arnie, we don't need any more dinosaurs. If half of these reports are true . . ." the President said without finishing.

"I know. I know. But it's a bit more complicated than it seems. There's a political side to this. What if things turn out to be better than we thought? What if we can reverse this? Then what will people think if we let these dinosaurs die?"

"Arnie, do we need dinosaurs?"

"No. There's no niche for them in the ecosystem. I can't imagine any of the developing countries will want to deal with them, and I have no idea where they could be kept in our country. But that's not the point. If we let the dinosaurs in Antarctica die, and they could have been mating pairs for dinosaurs elsewhere, then the environmental lobby will blame us. Better to let the antarctic scientists risk their lives trying to save them. We can always shoot them later."

The President hated politics and political thinking, but Arnie Gogh was good at it, and he always found his judgment reliable.

"What's the downside of this decision, Arnie?"

"When those dinosaurs warm up on that ship they could be uncontrollable. There could be personnel losses, Scotty. But given the losses nationwide the losses on the ship would be insignificant."

Arnie's cold analysis was disturbing, but correct. The President had little to lose by letting them try to save the dinosaurs, and there was some potential for political gain. "These dinosaurs could be vegetarians, right?"

"They could be. They didn't specify. That's quite useful, now that I think about it. If something does go wrong then we can always claim we didn't know they were going to move carnivores."

"All right. Give them permission, but don't bring them here."

"I already have a port in Panama picked out. It's a good climate for dinosaurs."

The President watched Gogh as he made a notation on the outside of the folder he was carrying. When he was done he sat silently. The President appreciated his old friend's company. The two of them had been friends since their first university days, and even when Arnie had been forced to resign the President had retained his respect for him. But Arnie wasn't sitting there for the company; there was something else on his mind.

"What is it, Arnie? News about Sandy."

Arnie averted his eyes when he spoke, "Atlanta is gone, and Sandy with it. We haven't given up yet, but there's no place to look for her—the city isn't there."

The President turned and looked out the window, and twirled a paper clip crank. After a minute he turned back and said, "What did you think of Dr. Paulson's theory?"

"Highly improbable—no foundation."

"What else do we have, Arnie? I want Sandy back—I need Sandy back. Will you look at his idea, for my sake?"

"I've looked at it."

"I mean really look at it." The President leaned forward and put the paper clip down. "Arnie, I know how badly it hurt to lose your position here. You and I—we worked half our lives to get here. It wasn't fair to you to lose it all just because of one mistake." The President paused as Arnie shifted in his chair uncomfortably. "Arnie, look at the theory. See if you can find some way to get Sandy back. If you'll do this, I'll name you science advisor again—or any job you want."

Arnie's face was impassive, but his pupils dilated.

"I can't promise—" he began.

"Just do your best."

"Yes."

The President picked up his report and then dropped it and reached for a new paper clip. Quickly absorbed, he never saw his friend leave.

---

43. Unfinished Business

This is what the sovereign Lord says: When I make you a desolate city, like cities no longer inhabited, and when I bring the ocean depths over you and its vast waters cover you, then I will bring you down with those who go down to the pit, to the people of long ago . . . You will be sought, but you will never again be found.

—Ezekiel 26:19–21

Washington, D.C.
PostQuilt: Tuesday, 11:15 a.m. EST

Speaking to the Security Council had terrified Terry. He considered himself a good counselor on a one-to-one basis, and good with small groups of parents or teachers, but he was never comfortable as a public speaker. And nothing in his experience had prepared him to speak to the movers and the shakers of government. Now he realized he'd made the last meaningful contribution he could make in Washington. It was time to call in Bill's promise and get to his son.

As they left the White House in the van, Terry turned to Bill and said simply, "It's time." Bill turned his face to the window and watched the buildings race by, then leaned forward to whisper in the driver's ear.

Terry sank back into his seat and reexamined his decisions. He had been only minimally helpful with Kenny Randall. Of course he couldn't have known that when he decided to come, but in retrospect, Ellen had been right.

Nick was exchanging information on the PresNet when Elizabeth Hawthorne appeared at his door. It wasn't like Elizabeth to show up without an appointment. She was carrying a bright blue file folder filled to overflowing and leaned against the doorway trying to act casual. Unfortunately, "casual" was not in her vocabulary of body language. However, she spoke with characteristic bluntness.

"They're going to blame the Russians for this."

"Excuse me?"

"You said that it takes bombs of a certain megatonnage to produce the effect. They're putting together a press release claiming only the old Soviet Union detonated enough of these bombs often enough to produce the effect."

Nick didn't know how to respond. Politicians specialized in covering their asses, so why should this case be any different, and why would Elizabeth bring this piece of news to him? Did Elizabeth care who got blamed for the disaster? Did she think Nick could do something about it?

"It's not true, Elizabeth. Either everyone involved in nuclear testing is to blame, or no one is."

Elizabeth nodded and finally entered the room, walking closer to Nick and watching the messages scrolling across his computer screen.

After another full minute she stopped reading the messages and turned to leave.

"Oh, is that psychologist still around?"

"Dr. Roberts? No, he left with Colonel Conrad after the meeting."

Elizabeth's face showed just a hint of disappointment. Then she took the blue folder out from under her arm and handed it to Nick.

"These are the satellite photos you wanted."

As she walked out the door Nick began to understand what had happened. The satellite photos normally would have been delivered by a staff member. Elizabeth, Nick realized, had actually come to ask about Dr. Roberts. Why would Elizabeth Hawthorne want a psychologist? It seemed so unlikely. Elizabeth Hawthorne's life had focused on getting and exercising power. She thrived on crisis management. But if Elizabeth did not want to see the psychologist for herself, then who? The President? Nick thought back to the Security Council meeting. He had noted a change in the President. He still functioned, he ran the meeting, with Elizabeth's whispered help, but he seemed uncharacteristically single-minded. He wanted to know what had happened and what could be done about it. Still, wouldn't any President respond the same way?

Nick pushed his concerns about the President to the back of his mind and opened the folder. The top photo was from Landsat of the North American continent, zoomed in on the United States. The continent looked like a quilt. Contrasting topological colors were sprinkled from the East Coast to the West Coast, and the sprinkling continued into the sections of both Canada and Mexico that were visible on the photo. Other photos showed similar effects in both eastern and western Europe. There were no photos of the Southern Hemisphere, but Nick had no doubt the effect was worldwide.

Deeper into the pile of photos and analysis reports, he found a photo taken off the Florida coast. An attached report noted that a tidal wave had washed over part of Florida's gulf coast. The photo of the ocean showed massive amounts of debris in the water. The water itself looked more like mud, and there were whole evergreen trees mixed in the muck, their roots and crowns jumbled together. Wherever this land had been displaced from, it had the bad luck of being displaced into the ocean. Whatever animal or human life it had held was lost now.

There were three sealed envelopes at the bottom of the pile marked SECRET and stamped with a red top-secret seal. One envelope was labeled New York City, the second Atlanta, and the third Montreal. Each envelope carried a label with the obligatory warning against unauthorized access to the information inside and the requisite listing of penalties. The first envelope included an aerial photo of New York City—a picture worth a thousand words, showing what Nick had only read about. At first glance it looked normal, but scribed across one edge of the city was a neat line. On one side was a dense urban setting, on the other side, nothing. Nick had heard the devastation described as "prairie" in some reports, but from an aerial photo it looked like a void. A second photo showed more of the city and the surrounding urban area. The shape of the void approximated an oval. Pulling the Landsat photo out of the stack again, Nick held it close to his eyes. Most of the quilt pieces seemed to be oval.

The third photo confused him. It was the same photo of New York, but in this photo the section of missing city was there. He looked closely at it, noticing that part of the photo—where the quilt section had been—was fuzzy. There were time notations in the bottom corner of the photos, indicating that the third was taken after the photo with the void. Nick examined the photos again. The third photo showed the city in the center of the quilt section that became fuzzy toward the edges. Was the city coming back? Nick turned to the accompanying report and began to read. When he finished he immediately began composing a message for the PresNet, the top secret classification quickly forgotten. While he typed, a message appeared at the bottom of the screen. As it scrolled up Nick realized it was essentially the message he was about to send. It was from Dr. Gogh.

44. Ocean Ride

People of all ages will become prisoners of the unseen. Good times will become times of misfortune; bitterness will replace sweetness: The wealth of nations will float in the wind.
—Zorastrus, Prophet of Babylon

Off Naples, Florida
PostQuilt: Tuesday, 12:00 noon EST

Ron woke at midday to find everyone else asleep on the back of the beast. He was thirsty, but the water had to be rationed. Even with a deep tan, the sun burned his back. He tried rolling over, but the sun was too bright. Sleep eluded him, and he found himself studying the baby.

It was a magnificent animal. It had a long neck like an elephant's trunk. A triangular head was covered with slick gray-green skin, and it had large black eyes, with eyelids that blinked occasionally, clearing away the salt spray.

Ron was staring into the water looking for the legs when he realized the baby was moving toward him. It swam closer and fell a little behind the mother and then swung its head to look at Ron square on. His heart started to pound, but not from fear, from excitement. There was curiosity in those huge round eyes, maybe even intelligence. Ron slowly raised his head and smiled at the face, almost ready to talk to the baby, when the mother turned her head in a slow pendulous motion and made a bleating sound. The baby immediately returned to its position in the mother's peripheral vision. Ron felt sad when it left.

They passed out water in the early afternoon, each taking a little. It couldn't be more than eighty degrees, yet with so little to drink it seemed like a hundred. Ron hoped his estimate of distance was correct because if it took more than a couple of days, they would be dead of thirst.

As Ron took his turn at drinking he noticed the baby had dropped back again and was watching him. The baby's face was nothing but taught gray-green skin, but Ron imagined he saw sadness in its eyes. Then he realized the baby and its mother had been churning through the ocean with nothing to drink. Was it as thirsty as he was? he wondered. Surely it had to be. Ron and his family had been riding while the dinosaurs worked, and they were very thirsty. Ron knew some animals could go long periods without water but doubted a dinosaur was like a camel.

Later that afternoon Ron was awakened from a light doze by Rosa talking to Chris, saying something about the dinosaurs eating. Ron sat up in time to see the mother's head dip down into the ocean and up. Her back rolled gently when she did. A few seconds later the baby's head dipped into the ocean and came up with seaweed hanging from its jaws. The baby chewed the seaweed slowly, working the drooping strands into its mouth. Ron worried about the salt content. He suspected they would last longer if they didn't ingest the salt. Still, he found his concern about the dinosaurs ironic. They were all hungry, thirsty, and exhausted, but they also felt secure on the great animal's back. In a few short hours the dinosaur had been transformed from a mere vehicle to their friend and savior.

By late afternoon they began to talk again, their fear of the animals forgotten. They named the big apatosaurus Patty and the little one, Pat. They all agreed Patty was a good mother. Somehow she had managed to save Pat from the sinking island and get him to sea. Ron speculated with Carmen and the kids about what it must have been like on the island. There had been a noise like a sonic boom, and then the island had just started sinking—relatively slowly, fortunately, because anything faster would have created a much bigger wave.

Patty and Pat must have found themselves in a landscape quickly flooding with water. The trees would have been pushed around or toppled by the rising sea. The animal life would have panicked, fighting for higher ground, ground that would become crowded with terrified animals, and then, in turn, flooded. Big animals like Patty could have kept their heads above water longer, but eventually they would have had to swim for their lives to solid ground that was miles away. Patty would have had a better chance of saving herself without Pat, but she stayed with him, like a good mother would.

"Dad," Chris asked. "Do you think there were people on that island?"

"I don't think so," Ron said to reassure Chris, but there was no way to know. That island shouldn't have been there at all. It just appeared; with animals like nothing Ron had ever seen on PBS or a National Geographic Special. If people knew about that island, it certainly would have made the news.

When Ron next passed water to the family, he noticed Carmen only wet her lips, so he did the same. When Ron had the water bottle back in its net bag he noticed Rosa staring at Pat.

"Hey," Rosa said. "I think Pat is having trouble."

Ron watched the baby for a while, but it seemed to be moving steadily, even after more than a day of swimming. Ron shrugged his shoulders at Rosa.

"Listen to it," Rosa ordered.

Ron listened and realized he could hear its labored breathing. It was in trouble, and he wished there was something they could do to help it, but there wasn't. No one talked after that, instead they spent the time watching Pat and listening to his breathing grow deeper and more ragged. Patty regularly swung her head around to look at Pat with one eye. At first that unnerved them, but Patty paid no attention to them, only to Pat. Patty also slowed her pace, but it didn't seem to help.

"I hope you make it, little one," Ron whispered. "I really hope you make it."

45. Contribution

The Bible, and other authorities, record that God made the sun stand still in the sky, so that Joshua could defeat his enemies. Astronomically this is impossible. It is no more difficult to believe Joshua and his men were somehow sent back a day in time.

—William Renfro, *Space, Time, and History*

Honolulu, Hawaii
PostQuilt: Tuesday, 11:07 p.m. AHT

Assistant Professor Emmett Puglisi was sitting in Professor Wang's executive chair brooding. Since he and Carrollee encountered the plesiosaur, he hadn't seen the botanist again. She had been busy organizing people to protect the buried plesiosaur eggs and with other activities she wouldn't tell him about. Emmett had been just as busy. At first he spent his time answering the many questions about the plesiosaur on the PresNet. He'd gotten his fifteen minutes of fame, but then other reports of dinosaurs began to appear on the network. Emmett wanted the attention back, but he wasn't a biologist, and he had little to offer. He felt like a bystander once more.

Emmett found himself both frightened by and drawn to the network, especially to models proposed to explain what had happened. Hour by hour, day by day, he sat there, downloading the complex data and models, spreading them across Dr. Wang's desk and struggling to understand them. Slowly the equations came into focus, and Emmett began to see how the models evolved. Still, he remained a spectator. He longed to play in the big leagues but could see nothing original to add. His frustration only grew as other scientists proposed new models, richer, more detailed, or unique in structure, models just out of the reach of his comprehension.

Creativity came only when he stopped struggling toward it.

Emmett reconstructed the latest variation of what was being

called the Gomez model using the equations provided on the PresNet. He was looking for some variation that hadn't occurred to others, working diligently until he realized he had extended the model too far, projecting it into the space/time future. He was about to quit when he noticed something about his solutions. The time displacement varied with the distance from the mass. Near the mass of the earth the time distortion was clearly affected in a proportional way, but, at least mathematically, the temporal displacement decreased with distance from the earth.

It was at that point Emmett had his insight. He knew the effect was hypothesized to weaken with distance from the source, but he wondered what a significant mass besides the earth would do to the effect? Specifically, what effect would the moon have on the space/time disruption?

Although only a sixth of the earth, he calculated that the moon was of sufficient mass to influence the time distortions. What he hadn't anticipated was the inversion of the effect. He knew his model was speculative, and none of the respected names was theorizing in this direction. So he hesitated at sharing them on PresNet.

He hadn't originated the theory, or the model he had used. He merely extended it. He wasn't sure it was a contribution sufficient enough to put on the PresNet with his name on it. Besides, the problem was here on earth, now; what happened to the moon paled in comparison.

In the end, the insignificance of his speculation overcame his fears of charges of plagiarism. He believed those on the network would pay scant attention to his model, so he sent it. Emmett was soon shocked to find that not only someone had noticed it, but someone at the top.

46. Operation Mend

It happened as we were boarding the coach. Benjamin went to check the horses and never came back. The coachman says he never saw my husband, and we have not seen him since. It's as if God lifted him off the face of the earth.

—Lucy Bathurst, November 29, 1809

Washington, D.C.
PostQuilt: Tuesday, 5:00 p.m. EST

Nick had to admit that Gogh had a better grasp than he did of the mathematics that physics required. Gogh had been exchanging ideas with a physicist at the Fermi particle accelerator complex in Illinois over the PresNet—but the physicist, Dr. Gomez, had almost immediately rejected Nick's model and substituted one of her own, which involved complex equations. He could only follow the math to a point, but to Nick it seemed both to confirm and disconfirm his theory.

He considered another factor: Maria Gomez had somewhat of a reputation in physics. She wasn't known for her contributions to the field as much as for her ability to show the weaknesses in the contributions of others.

Nick admitted to himself that the Oregon model, as it was now being called, was inadequate. It had good predictive validity but it lacked proper theoretical underpinnings. Like Zorastrus, Kenny Randall and his friends had observed peculiar phenomena, detected a pattern, and used the pattern to predict a future event. He would receive well-deserved recognition for his accomplishment. But also like Zorastrus, Kenny, and whoever the others were, had not really understood what caused the effect. Kenny had correctly traced it to the nuclear detonations, but that was not the same as explaining it. Nick had been influenced by Kenny's ripples-in-a-pond idea, attracted to its predictive power and its theoretical simplicity. Gomez, however, had shredded the idea mathematically and substituted her own.

The Oregon model assumed the time displacement occurred sequentially and was a function of time and distance from the source. It was an assumption rooted in the human experience of linear time. The Gomez model assumed that all time displacement events occurred simultaneously, in all the affected times and locations.

Because four-dimensional thought did not come easily to Nick, he struggled with Gomez's idea. However, when Gomez also hypothesized the existence of transient superdense matter as the root of the phenomena, Nick felt some satisfaction in having his contribution to the Oregon model supported. It was the coexistence of these dense strings of matter that created the time/space disruption, the black ripples. Apparently Gogh was hypothesizing that the effects radiate out from the source much like a field around a magnet, except, in this case, the field radiates four dimensionally. The fields are created at the moment of detonation, but Nick, and the rest of the people on the planet who must experience time sequentially, have to live through the effect. The major time displacement they had just experienced had been there since the explosions in the sixties, waiting for the human inhabitants to live through the event.

As the exchanges between Gomez and Gogh continued, Nick became uneasy. Gomez continued to talk about the original detonations and the time displacement as concurrent events. Gomez was supplying equations to support her theory but cautioning Gogh that the theory was little more than speculation at this point. Gogh, however, ignored the cautions and pushed Gomez to speculate further. Nick did not like the direction of Gogh's pushes, but knew that intruding would only make Gogh more protective of his convictions.

Other physicists tried to break in on the discussion, but Gogh only responded to those who seemed supportive of the model. Nick corresponded with some of the others but lacked the expertise to follow the arguments.

He was about to turn off the network when he noticed a new flag. The name E. Puglisi was unfamiliar to him, but what caught his attention was the description of his model variation: "Projects temporal disruption to near space, and hypothesizes a temporal inversion." Nick called up the file and was pleased to see the sophisticated mathematics were represented with a model. Nick skipped right to it and was impressed with the graphics. The model showed a ball labeled as the earth surrounded by an ovoid made up of a tangled web of lines, labeled with a mathematical equation Nick recognized as the time waves. After another page of graphics Nick scrolled on. This following graphic showed a slice of the previous page, with the earth apparently in a cone. On top of that cone sat another cone with a smaller sphere sitting in it. The two cones were point to point. The second sphere was labeled the moon. Nick stared at the model for a minute and then scrolled back to the equations. It couldn't be right, could it? The model projected the time disruption into the space around earth; that was the first cone. Then Puglisi's model showed another cone indicating a reversal of the time flow, and the moon was in the second cone. If this Puglisi was right, any time disruption on the moon would be in the opposite direction of that on the earth. On the moon the future came to the past, not the past to the future.

Nick checked his list of PresNet advisors, but there was no Puglisi. He checked the access code of Puglisi's computer, and it showed it was coming from the computer of Dr. Connie Wang, of the University of Hawaii. Whoever Puglisi was, he was not authorized to use the system. Nick realized he was beginning to judge the worth of Puglisi's model on the unknown person's credentials, yet Kenny Randall's own lack of credentials had kept his warnings from being heeded in the first place. Nick vowed not to repeat that mistake. Instead, he typed in a message to Puglisi and sent it.

Elizabeth appeared in Nick's office again, just before he was about to leave for the Security Council meeting. She didn't try to look casual this time but came right to the point.

"The President's not himself."

"In what way?"

"When he makes a decision, he normally listens to all points of view, and even solicits dissenting opinion. Ever since I've known him, he has insisted on having all alternatives before him before he makes a decision. But he isn't listening now—"

"To you?" Nick was sure that part of Elizabeth's concern involved her personal loss of influence with the President.

Elizabeth looked stung by Nick's suggestion but didn't deny it.

"Not to me, not to any of his advisors. Even Samuel Cannon, who's been a friend for years, can't get through to him. He only listens to one person, Dr. Gogh."

Nick's stomach knotted at the mention of Gogh's name, remembering the messages exchanged on the PresNet system. He didn't like the direction of Gogh's reasoning—even less so now that the man had direct access to the President.

"The President respects you, Nick. He and the others were impressed by the way you figured out what happened."

Nick swallowed back a protest. A college kid from Oregon and a mysterious group of others had seen what scientists with multiple degrees and decades of grant-supported research had overlooked. Nick had no intention of taking credit for the discovery.

"I know what Gogh has in mind, Elizabeth, and I'm going to argue against it."

"You should know that Sandy McIntyre is in Atlanta—was in Atlanta. The Secret Service can't contact or locate her. She apparently was in the part of the city that is gone. The President isn't thinking clearly, Nick. He only wants to get her back, nothing else matters."

Now Nick understood: The President's rapport with his wife was legendary, and a big part of his success in politics was due to his wife. Sandy McIntyre was witty, attractive in a motherly way, and the warmest person Nick had ever met. So wide was her appeal there had been half-serious talk of putting *her* on the ticket.

Nick realized he felt more of a loss for Sandy McIntyre than for the millions lost across the country. He understood why: partly because for the first time he had thought about the loss of a particular individual. But mostly he grieved at losing the first lady's personal magnetism. If Nick mourned, the President must be devastated.

The agenda had undergone radical change. At its top was a plan of action from Dr. Arnold Gogh. As Gogh began, Elizabeth leaned forward to whisper to the President, but uncharacteristically he dismissed her with a sharp wave of his hand.

"As the President directed we have been working on a solution based on the time displacement theory," Gogh stated.

Nick noted he did not give any credit for the theory to Nick or to anyone else. At Gogh's direction the lights came down and a slide was projected on the screen. It was the photo Nick had seen of the quilted New York City.

"As you can see from this photo, approximately one third of New York City has experienced time displacement. The segment is grassland and is probably from the Cretaceous period."

Gasps and expressions of disbelief rippled around the table.

"Cretaceous period? Impossible!" Natalie Matsuda answered loudly, ignoring the mounting evidence.

Dr. Gogh looked irritated but ignored Matsuda and called for the next slide.

The next slide was blurry but it was an overhead shot of an animal. That photo had not been in Nick's packet, and he realized he had been partly cut out of the decision loop, just like Elizabeth.

"This is a blowup of one of the aerial photos. As you can see there is an animal in the photo."

"Is that another dinosaur?" Cannon asked.

"Yes, but one much bigger than the ankylosaur in your Quebec photo."

Gogh said it with pride, as if he were in a competition to find the biggest dinosaur. "Professor Struthers of the PresNet has tentatively identified this as an iguanodon. It's hard to scale this photo, since there are no familiar objects near the dinosaur, but Professor Struthers tells me iguanodons can be twenty-five to thirty feet in length, and when standing they might be fifteen or twenty feet tall."

Gasps and soft whistles filled the room as the occupants launched impromptu discussions. Some wondered if the animals were aggressive. Others speculated on what would happen if one wandered into New York City's midtown streets. Nick listened to the voices around him and then asked that the previous slide be put back up. Looking disgusted at the interruption, Gogh nevertheless reversed the projector.

"What's along the line where the prehistoric segment meets city?"

"Buildings, of course," Gogh replied abruptly.

"Buildings with people inside!" Nick pointed out. "How close are these animals to the residents? We already know some of the animals in the Quebec displacement are wandering out of their natural environment. What about here? There's a human factor to consider here."

Nick was embarrassed he too had never considered the human factor. But now, that attention was long overdue. He turned and looked at the President, who studiously ignored him.

"Shouldn't we take steps to protect the residents near the displaced segments?" Nick prodded.

Still the President ignored him. Nick caught Elizabeth's eye, and she shook her head briefly, indicating they had done nothing about this.

Finally Gogh spoke. "I'm sure the local authorities are taking care of that problem, but as you will see there may not be any need for federal action. Next slide, please. This slide shows New York an hour later. Notice that the missing segment is back."

Instantly the room erupted into a mixture of relief, disbelief, and hope. For a minute Gogh enjoyed the effect of his pronouncement, then pushed on.

"Notice the fuzzy sections around the displaced segment. This next slide shows a blowup of the fuzzy section."

Another picture Nick had not seen appeared on the screen. It was an aerial shot of buildings, but they were transparent and the golden color of the grassland showed through them. More discussion rippled around the room, though the President sat quietly lost in his own thoughts. Elizabeth tried to whisper to him again, but he dismissed her with another wave.

"Notice the indefinite state of this section." Gogh walked to the screen and pointed at the transparent section. "Notice also this ring." He traced a thin golden section. "This is a section of grassland around the outer edge of the displaced segment. The next photo was taken two hours later, and the next was taken an hour after that."

The next slide showed a New York City with a clearly missing section. It was quickly followed by a slide showing New York with the piece back. It took Nick a minute to notice the change.

"You will see," Dr. Gogh said, pointing with a pen, "that the amount of city in the displaced segment is smaller and the indefinite area has pulled toward the center. Notice also that the ring of grassland has grown larger." Again he traced the golden ring around the oval. "This phenomena tells us two things. First, that the effect appears to be in an indefinite state. Second, that the effect is reaching a state of equilibrium, and doing so rather quickly. The oscillations between city and prairie are irregular, but the growth of the stabilized time-displaced sections is increasing logarithmically. We have little time to act. Fortunately, we have developed a plan of action to deal with the problem."

Everyone at the table leaned forward at that point except the secretary of defense, who kept her eyes down and looked distinctly uncomfortable.

"We have accepted the theory that the time displacement occurred as a result of time disruption created by the detonation of nuclear devices. However, the idea that waves are sweeping across the surface of the planet has been rejected. Instead, in conjunction with Dr. Gomez, at the Fermi Institute, I have developed a model that shows that the current effects and the originating explosions are actually connected."

"Connected how?" the CIA director asked. "The bomb testing you are talking about happened in the sixties, maybe even the fifties."

"The explosions created an effect that crosses space and time. The effect we have today is happening because the explosions are happening right now in the sixties."

Cannon shook his head in confusion but kept quiet.

"Since the events in the past and the current event are linked, it means we have an opportunity to manipulate the event. We intend to disrupt the effect before it has a chance to reach equilibrium by creating another time wave to counteract the effects of the one that produced our current problems."

Nick was confused for a moment. He knew of no way to create a time wave except with dense matter, and the only human way to create dense matter was with a nuclear explosion. Then he realized what Gogh was planning and a sick feeling swept over him. A moment later Gogh confirmed what Nick was thinking.

"We intend to use a nuclear detonation to create another wave."

As chaotic discussion followed, Gogh and the President waited it out. Most of the questions directed at the President were the "Why wasn't I consulted?" type. When order returned Nick managed to get the floor.

"We don't know this will work. We don't even know for sure this is caused by the nuclear explosions. For all we know, it could be some factor interacting with the detonations to produce the effect. Besides, what's happened to us wasn't produced by a single bomb, it was the accumulative effects of hundreds of explosions."

"That's why we intend to use more than one device." Gogh waited, making Nick ask the obvious question.

"How many more than one?"

"One hundred."

Even the stoic military officers gasped at the thought of detonating a hundred hydrogen bombs. Nick was stunned by the thought but slowly realized if you were going to take this course of action you had little choice but to use such megatonnage. The time wave that had disrupted Nick's present and sent millions, if not billions, of people spinning off into time wasn't caused by one or two bombs. There had been nearly a thousand British and American bombs tested at the New Mexico test site alone. From that perspective a hundred bombs was even conservative, but no human or natural event could match the power of one hundred warheads detonated in the atmosphere. Krakatoa and Mount Saint Helens would pale in comparison. Nick recalled the nuclear winter concerns of a few years ago. Even if they got the missing people back, they could lose them again to starvation. Nick quickly assessed the benefits and costs and took his stand.

"You can't do this. We don't understand what we're dealing with yet. All we have is a rudimentary theory and there is no evidence that this will return things to normal. At best all you will do is create more time displacement and at worst . . . who knows? We know it will cause vast destruction, and may have long-term effects. You have heard of nuclear winter?"

"A discredited theory."

"It won't be theory if we detonate that many warheads, and then it could be too late."

Nick was surprised to find the President and not Gogh responding. "We know what will happen if we don't do anything. We will lose millions of our citizens, billions of dollars in property, not to mention the cost of rebuilding. This country already has more debt than most of the rest of the world combined. How will we rebuild from this? You see, Dr. Paulson, I *am* thinking of the human factor. The human factor on a worldwide scale."

"Mr. President—" Nick began, but found himself cut off by the President.

"We've considered the risks, Dr. Paulson, as well as safety and other issues." The President motioned for Gogh to continue, then picked up a paper clip and began twisting it into a shape he could twirl.

Gogh returned to his presentation with a new air of confidence and self-importance. "As the President indicated we have considered the consequences of this action and have taken steps to reduce risk. First, we must select a displaced segment suitable to our needs. The potential detonation sites are limited by several factors. They must be U.S. territory and must not require an overflight of another country to reach the site. We have too little time to pursue diplomatic channels for overflight permission. Second, the site should be located as far west as possible. The effect spread from the east to the west, so there will be more instability in a western site."

The east-to-west spread was a new idea to Nick. He hadn't seen that on the PresNet, and Gomez had not mentioned it. Did the idea originate with Gogh?

"Third, since the detonation will take place in our past it must be in an era that will not disrupt our present. So far all the confirmed data suggests the displaced segments are from the Cretaceous period, but we can't be sure of all. Some could be from more recent time periods and possibly even the future."

"Dr. Gogh," Nick interrupted, "what do you mean the detonations will take place in our past?"

"We will select a displaced segment that is clearly not from the future, or the near past."

"But all these segments are in the present now."

"When the bombs go off they will return to the past."

"What do you base that prediction on?"

"I've been in consultation with colleagues who agree that a new ripple could return the time segments back to where they came from. Therefore, the explosions will take place in the past and remain in the past, and not affect our present."

"Isn't it more accurate to say that your colleagues agree that time displacement is likely to occur again, but they are not sure whether the displaced segments will return to their own time or whether new displacement will occur?"

"There is some disagreement, yes. However, it is a course of action with little or no risk and the potential of great gain."

"No risk to you . . . to us . . . only if you're right about the detonations taking place in the past. But what about whoever is at ground zero?"

"No one will be at ground zero. Perhaps some animals, yes, but unless you're a radical antivivisectionist I can't believe you would exchange the lives of a few animals for millions of people."

Gogh's last sentence was spoken as if from a pulpit. The President's eyes looked glassy and he seemed to be uninterested in the discussion, as if he'd expected some disagreement and was letting it run its course. Elizabeth looked encouragingly at Nick, so he took another approach.

"It won't work. You won't be able to identify enough identical time periods to drop the bombs into. Besides, even if you could, the time displacement would end up taking place sometime in our future and past, depending on how far apart the detonations are at the various sites."

"True. That is why we intend to detonate all the bombs in the same displacement at the same time. The simultaneous explosions will create the effect immediately."

"Immediately in our *past*," Nick corrected.

"Yes, but with immediate effects in our present."

"On what do you base that conclusion?"

"On an improved version of a theory you endorsed just a short time ago."

The President's loud slap on the table broke the exchange. "Dr. Paulson, there is no place for professional jealousy in my administration. You will receive appropriate credit for your contribution to solving our problem, but don't attack Dr. Gogh for taking your idea a step further than you were able to yourself. I asked for solutions and I got nothing from anyone except Arnie. You had your chance. Now unless you have something constructive to contribute I suggest we move on."

"Mr. President, perhaps no one offered a solution because there is no solution."

"That's defeatist. Let's move on."

"This won't bring your wife back, sir."

"I said move on!"

Tears filled the President's eyes and Nick regretted mentioning Sandy. He knew if he pushed it any further now he would risk losing his seat at the Security Council and his chance to influence the outcome.

The rest of the meeting was a discussion of possible detonation sites. The one chosen could not have any evidence of human presence, or any signs of civilization. They did not want to risk killing people from the past, since that might set off a chain of events that would alter the present. Since communication across the country was disrupted, they had very little information to work with, and as a result the list of potential sites was small. There was an Alaskan site southeast of Nome described as having sparse vegetation. It was on the list because of unconfirmed reports that a pack of dinosaurs was attacking a herd of elk there.

The second site was in northeastern Washington, where a huge glacier now covered parts of Washington, Idaho, and Canada. However, the detonation site was uncomfortably near the Canadian border. The third site was what had been Portland, Oregon. Gogh announced that they were expecting aerial photos any minute to confirm the eyewitness reports, but so far it appeared to be a displacement populated by dinosaurs.

The discussion moved on to the preparation efforts. The military was using overflights of the potential sites to develop the bit maps that would guide the cruise missiles to their target area. Since the missiles would be launched by both ships and B-1 bombers and would have to travel different distances over a variety of terrain, timing would be tricky and need highly accurate maps.

Nick felt dazed. His mind had not switched over to the practical side of the plan; he couldn't get the image of one hundred bombs going off at once out of his mind.

Nick paled at the thought of the impact on any site, but especially Portland. Bombing uninhabited sections of Alaska or eastern Washington was horrifying, but the thought of its effect on a metropolitan area sickened him. Abruptly, he decided to risk expulsion from the council and broke in at the first pause.

"Since the sites are unstable, sometimes they are the present and sometimes the past. How will you be sure to deliver the bombs to the past?"

Gogh smiled at the question. Clearly he had thought of this and prepared an answer.

"The missiles are terrain guided. They will be programmed with the terrain from the past. If they do not identify the terrain as matching their program they will not arm their warheads. Instead, the missiles will harmlessly pass over the site," Gogh said, and then swept his audience with his eyes. "Thus guaranteeing the detonations will occur in the past."

Nick conceded to himself that it could work. Still, from what he knew of the programming of cruise missiles Gogh wasn't telling the whole story.

"Dr. Gogh, isn't it true that under combat conditions cruise missiles often arrive at their target after previous attacks have significantly altered the terrain?"

Gogh looked at Nick suspiciously, as if he knew where Nick was leading him.

"Can you tell the council how the missile's programming handles that contingency?" Nick continued.

He glared at Nick, leaving uncomfortable silence in the room. Finally, Dr. Gogh answered in a monotone. "When the missile nears its termination point, and the terrain ceases to match the digitized map, the missile can exercise an option to use the last confirmed position to estimate distance and direction to target."

Many of those at the table began murmuring, but Nick

wanted to make sure everyone knew full well what Gogh's missiles would do.

"In other words, Dr. Gogh, if the missiles get lost, they will guess."

This time everyone murmured.

---

47. Death for Dinner

Our decoys were bringing the flock down and we were ready to fire, when there was a flash. Suddenly, we were pelted by roasted ducks—burned, feathers and all.

—Reuben Black, Winston, Maine, 1972

Warm Springs Indian Reservation, Oregon
PostQuilt: Tuesday, 2:25 p.m. PST

The sounds of the feeding were horrifying, but the thought of who was being eaten was worse. Dr. Piltcher sat in a crumpled heap, broken by the thought of the fate of his friend. Petra kept her arm around his shoulder while he stared at his hands in his lap. Her words were no comfort to him, but Petra continued speaking softly, as if to soothe herself. Colter stood nearby, holding his spear like a talisman, but soon he returned to the others and squatted.

"That's not Dr. Coombs. I mean what we're listening to."

Dr. Piltcher continued to stare at his hands, but Petra looked up.

"What? How would you know?"

"Well . . . there's just too much eating going on. Don't take this wrong . . . but if that was Dr. Coombs he would have been gone a long time ago. Know what I mean?"

Petra was sickened by the logic, but it made sense. The dinosaur that terrorized them was so big, Dr. Coombs would have provided just a snack, and the gruesome sounds ahead indicated several feeding dinosaurs. Dr. Piltcher remained oblivious to

Colter's suggestion until Petra took his hands in hers. He looked up then, his eyes puffy and red. Petra was going to speak but Colter cut her off.

"Doc, Dr. Coombs would be an appetizer, and whatever's up there is eating a six-course dinner."

That brought Dr. Piltcher to his feet, his cheeks reddening, but he turned to Petra, not Colter. When he spoke his voice trembled.

"Monoclonius was a herbivore. It wouldn't eat my friend, it would only kill him." Dr. Piltcher paused to control his grief. When he spoke again it was with anger. "If you want my opinion, somewhere in there," he said, pointing toward the noises, "is a pack of small scavengers making a meal of my best friend."

"Uh-uh." Colter argued. "Whatever is up there is big, and they're having a feast, not a snack. Let me make it plain for you. If that was Dr. Coombs, those mono-monsters would be picking their teeth with his bones by now."

Petra watched as Dr. Piltcher's face flushed again. This time he turned to face Colter, staring him in the eye. When he found his voice it came in a near shout.

"What do you know, Colter? In all the time I've known you, you've shown an interest in only one thing." He turned and pointed at Petra, opened his mouth to speak, but then turned back to Colter. "Colter, you are what you are, an ignorant young man who's biggest accomplishment will be seducing a young woman I admire . . . and love. Why she chose you . . . chose to carry you, I'll never know. But I'm telling you, George . . . Dr. Coombs, is dead."

Colter flushed this time, but when he spoke it was in a whisper.

"He may be, Dr. Piltcher. I never said he wasn't dead. I'm just telling you what they're eating up there isn't him." Colter paused, collecting his thoughts. He wasn't angry, but he was hurt. "As for being ignorant, I guess I am when I'm back in the city. Sitting around discussing all that crap you guys think is so important, I probably looked pretty dumb. I admit it, I wouldn't have been there if it wasn't for Petra. But you tell me, Dr. Piltcher, who's the ignorant one out here? Who wouldn't let me go get a gun? And who is whispering and who was shouting when there's a pack of dinosaurs about a hundred yards away?"

Dr. Piltcher stared back defiantly, but had no answer. In the city his vast storehouse of the arcane had given him cult status and a circle of followers who marveled at his knowledge and wisdom. But here in this strange world, book learning meant nothing. It didn't matter whether it was monoclonius or triceratops that had impaled and carried off his friend. What mattered was having the knowledge to keep it from happening again. If Colter had his way they would be walking through the brush with rifles and George would still be alive. Instead George was dead, and their only weapon fashioned by the one he had called ignorant. As if to confirm it, Petra turned and spoke to Colter.

"Is there any chance Dr. Coombs is still alive?"

"Slim. If we want to know, we need to see what's going on up ahead. Why don't you wait here while I scout it out."

Petra looked at Dr. Piltcher and back to Colter, and then shook her head.

"I think we better stick together. But as soon as we know for sure one way or another, let's get out of here."

Colter shrugged and led off, resuming his slow, stealthy approach. The sounds grew louder and more terrible. The gurgling and growling repelled them, and they had to force themselves forward against their natural inclination to run. Suddenly, Colter bolted several feet and then knelt behind a dense bush. He stared straight ahead for a minute and then signaled to the others. They quietly crept up behind him, but the sounds of the feeding were so loud now that they could have driven a car up and not been heard.

When they were all together Colter reached out and gently pushed a limb aside, revealing the clearing where they found the egg. On the far side of the mound was the dinosaur who had attacked the RV and carried off Dr. Coombs. She had returned to her nest, and then finished bleeding to death. Her lifeless form was lying on its side and its body was nothing but shredded, bloody meat. Half a dozen bipedal dinosaurs were tearing off huge hunks of flesh, or gnawing on ribs torn from the carcass. The biggest ones were fifteen or twenty feet high. Smaller bipeds, no more than two or three feet high, circled around the outside, darting in to grab dropped pieces of flesh, or bits of bone. The larger carnivores snapped and snarled at the little ones, but were too slow to stop them. There was more than enough meat anyway.

Something moved through the brush near them and they froze in fear. One of the smaller dinosaurs darted through, then ran into the clearing and began circling the dinner party, looking for a chance to snag a helping. They sighed with relief when it passed and then backed away slowly until they felt safe enough to talk softly. Petra spoke first.

"I didn't see Dr. Coombs's body there. Maybe he got off somehow."

"If he did," Colter suggested, "he'd be back along that blood trail. It may be risky to search there. We don't know if any more of these things are following it to supper."

Dr. Piltcher and Petra understood the implications. Every second they spent among the dinosaurs was a risk, but walking along a blood trail could be suicidal. Still no one wanted to be the first to give up on Dr. Coombs. Colter took the now familiar role of leader.

They backed well away from the clearing before circling around to the trail, which was heavily trampled by the gathering scavengers. Though the blood was drying, it was still crimson on the green grass. Quickly, before they met another predator, they backtracked toward where they left the trail originally. But suddenly something cut across the path, and they gasped in fear. The three were about to start off again when Colter turned, looking to where the little dinosaur had disappeared. He took a couple of steps off the path and then squatted. Petra knelt next to him as Dr. Piltcher looked over his shoulder, and they saw blood on the grass.

"More blood. So what, Colter?" Petra asked.

"How did it get here? The trail's back there." Colter stood and walked a few more steps. "Here's more of it."

Then, without another word, Colter trotted off through the brush. Petra and Dr. Piltcher looked at each other, suddenly realizing it was another blood trail. A hundred yards away they found him staring at a pack of small dinosaurs in the grass ahead.

It took Petra and Dr. Piltcher a minute to recognize Dr.

Coombs's remains. The small dinosaurs had shredded his clothes and picked his bones nearly clean. Even his skull had been peeled of its flesh, although his eyes were still intact in the sockets.

When the small pack of dinosaurs spotted them they froze, heads up and tails held straight out. As Colter screamed and then charged the pack, thrusting at the closest dinosaur with his spear, the pack scattered, some with meaty bones still in their mouths. Colter stood looking down on Dr. Coombs's remains, Petra's mind was overflowing with horror, and Dr. Piltcher was once again lost in his grief. This time he had no doubt about his friend's death.

Colter returned to the others, his face impassive.

"Want me to bury him? There's still quite a bit left. I don't know, though. They'll probably just dig him up again. Maybe we could cover it . . . him, with rocks."

Dr. Piltcher was about to reply when the branches behind him began to snap. The three turned to see a fifteen-foot-tall carnivore coming through the brush, towering above them. Its head and jaws were huge. It walked on two well-muscled back legs, but its forelegs looked smaller and useless. A long thick tail dragged behind.

"Run," Colter yelled, and the others obeyed. Colter took the lead, breaking trail through the brush. He ran a straight line, dodging only the thicker stands or those with thorns. They pounded through, oblivious to the blows from the branches. Dr. Piltcher, soon exhausted, began to trail behind. When Petra noticed she shouted to Colter, who shot a quick look over his shoulder, and then trotted off to the side, motioning for Petra to take the lead. When Dr. Piltcher plodded past, Colter fell in behind, watching over his shoulder for the dinosaur.

Petra set a slower pace than Colter so Dr. Piltcher could keep up, but something was wrong. Petra had seen him jog for miles before. He was stumbling along now, head down and breathing raggedly. The brush thinned, and then they broke into a clearing that led down to the lake, where the grass was short and looked well grazed. They were moving at a slow jog around what Petra realized were huge piles of animal droppings. Dr. Piltcher stumbled over one pile but kept his feet. Petra dropped back to jog next to him, setting a pace. Dr. Piltcher's chest was heaving and his breathing was irregular.

When Petra looked back for Colter, her feet caught in something and she fell headlong into the grass, just missing a pile of dried dung. Dr. Piltcher stopped when she fell and dropped to his knees, desperately trying to catch his breath. Petra found herself lying in the grass on an uneven surface, the turf beneath her looking like a badly laid carpet with huge wrinkles. Petra rolled to her knees, looking for Colter, but he was nowhere in sight. Neither was the dinosaur. Dr. Piltcher was still on his knees, his breathing labored, one hand was pressed tight against his chest, and his face red and sprinkled with sweat. Looking up at her, he shook his head, and began puffing rapidly through his nose, trying to control his breathing. He spoke finally, in a hoarse whisper.

"Petra, I'm sorry, but I . . . my chest . . ."

"It's okay, Dr. Piltcher. Don't speak. I think we're all right here," Petra answered reassuringly, but not believing it.

Petra scanned the meadow looking for Colter or signs of danger. If she hadn't been so scared she might have noted the details in the landscape—the still, blue lake in the middle, surrounded by clumps of towering leafy trees along its shore. The bright green sea of swaying meadow grasses hid the wrinkled turf.

Taller, forest green bushes dotted the clearing as far as Petra could see. She looked from left to right for a hiding place or a way back to the RV. The lake narrowed on the south end and a finger of the lake ended in a stream. Whether it fed the lake or drained it, Petra couldn't tell. But along that stream were large moving shapes—quadrupeds like the one that destroyed the RV and killed Dr. Coombs. They were still a long way off, but it was clear they were coming closer. Petra felt trapped. She feared running back into the brush because the dinosaur that had chased them was there somewhere. She was too afraid to head toward the approaching herd, but if they cut across the meadow away from the herd she could be inviting attack. Besides, Dr. Piltcher wouldn't be running much farther today.

Petra could see only one choice. She urged Dr. Piltcher to his feet, took his arm, and led him toward the trees along the lake. They would climb a tree if they could. Otherwise they could swim for it, although she had no idea whether dinosaurs could swim or not.

Dr. Piltcher padded along next to her, Petra supporting him when he stumbled. As they ran, Petra kept watch on the approaching herd. They showed no signs of attack, or even of notice. At the first tree, Dr. Piltcher sat with his back against the trunk, his hand on his chest and his head down. He was breathing easier now, although still ragged.

Petra walked around, trying to find an easy tree to climb. Similar to poplar trees, these had branches covered with thousands of round leaves. When she found it she returned to help Dr. Piltcher to his feet. He let her guide him, his strength and spirit left behind with Dr. Coombs.

Petra's tree was on the edge of the clearing near the lake. The lowest limb was just out of her reach. She knew she could jump to it and pull herself up, but Dr. Piltcher couldn't, even if he was feeling well. She tried boosting him up, but he was too weak to grip the limb. After their third try Petra let Dr. Piltcher slip to the ground and rest while she trotted along the edge of the small stand looking vainly for signs of Colter. At the far edge of the little wood, she was shocked to see the dinosaurs had nearly reached the lake and were fanning out along the shore, coming closer. Hiding behind the tree trunks, she shrank back when she saw them. Petra's eyes riveted on the massive set of horns—images of Dr. Coombs impaled flashed through her mind. Urgently, she dodged from trunk to trunk back to Dr. Piltcher. She had to get him in the tree somehow, or it was the lake.

She pulled the professor to his feet again. His breathing was better now, though his hand was still pressed to his chest, and his face had regained some color.

"We've got to climb this tree, Dr. Piltcher," she said. "More of those dinosaurs are coming, like the one that wrecked the RV."

"Monoclonius," he managed to whisper.

"Yes, monoclonius. They're almost here. I want you to stand on my back."

"I'm sure George was wrong about them being triceratops."

"Dr. Piltcher, you must climb on my back."

"I don't want to hurt you, Petra."

"Don't worry, you won't hurt me."

Dr. Piltcher continued to protest, but Petra shushed him and got down on her hands and knees. The professor stepped up on her gingerly, but his full weight was soon on her back. His boots seesawed across her spinal column, and she had to bite her lip to hold back a gasp of pain. She could feel the older man trying to pull himself up, but he had no strength.

"I can't do it, Petra. Leave me. You climb up, I'll be okay."

"No. Don't you move, just hang on to the limb," Petra nearly shouted, and Dr. Piltcher stood still, his hands drooped over the top of the thick limb. Then Petra inched her legs forward and began to push. Suddenly the weight was removed from her back and she collapsed to the ground. She rolled over, expecting to see Dr. Piltcher sitting in the tree. Instead, she found him hanging from the limb, his arms wrapped over the top, and his legs dancing below.

"I'm going to fall, Petra."

"No!" she shouted, leaping to her feet. She knew she wouldn't be able to lift him again, so she put her hands on the professor's bottom and pushed. At the same time Dr. Piltcher used his arms to hitch himself higher on the limb. Finally, his chest worked its way up, and then he was lying on his stomach on the limb. Petra watched him turn toward her, a slight smile on his face—then the smile evaporated.

"Petra, behind you," he whispered.

Petra turned carefully to see a monoclonius looking down its snout horn at her. Two smaller monoclonius were behind, both with their horns pointed directly at her. Petra was afraid to move. She was pretty sure she could pull herself up, but pretty sure wasn't good enough. She might not get that second chance. The monoclonius weren't moving, or acting aggressively, but something that size would petrify Hercules.

The standoff continued for a full minute, then the closest monoclonius walked deliberately forward, keeping its eyes on Petra. She retreated until her back was against the tree trunk. Petra looked right and left, trying to decide on which way to run. The monoclonius was only twenty feet away when it stopped. Then it raised its massive head, pointing its three long horns at the sky. After several sniffs the dinosaur dropped its head, pointing the three mighty horns at Petra, sniffed again, snorted out a spray of mucus, then walked past Petra and out into the clearing. The two dinosaurs behind it followed suit, each pausing to sniff at Petra. Petra held her breath until they were well gone and then jumped up, grabbed the branch, and pulled herself onto the limb. Dr. Piltcher managed to sit up.

"I told you, Petra, they're vegetarians." He smiled weakly.

Petra smiled back. She hated to see him like this, weak and dependent. For the last two years he'd been her father figure. It was a symbiotic relationship. He needed his ego boosted by a young admiring female, and she needed some older charismatic man to make up for the father she never really knew. She also knew children eventually become parents to their parents, but she never expected it to happen with a mentor, and not in such a bizarre fashion. Dr. Piltcher was still smiling at her so she shook her head in disbelief and whispered back to him. "So a vegetarian did that to the RV? Needed a little iron in its diet, so it decided to eat an RV."

Dr. Piltcher returned her smile, seeming to have more energy now.

"Let's try to get higher," Petra suggested.

They spent the next half hour working their way higher into the tree. Dr. Piltcher could manage to climb, but only if Petra boosted him. She was exhausted and Dr. Piltcher complained of chest pains again. He urged Petra to continue climbing, but she refused. Now, they sat in silence.

Petra planned to wait in the tree until the dinosaurs moved on and she was sure the big carnivore wasn't going to show up. In the meadow, she could see the monoclonius grazing, just outside their stand of trees. Smaller monoclonius were mixed into the herd, obviously much younger—the chest and hips narrower. Trying to pick out mothers and offspring, Petra watched the smaller dinosaurs, but they showed no preference for particular adults. Several larger animals stood off from the main herd, distributed around the outside. Petra decided the larger monoclonius were males doing picket duty, and the dinosaurs herding together were the females, with young mixed in. What she didn't understand was why the young showed no preferences for a female. There didn't seem to be any evidence of imprinting. She wanted to discuss the lack of bonding between mother and offspring with Dr. Piltcher, but suddenly every head in the herd snapped up and pointed toward the brush. The monoclonius were combing the wind with their nostrils. Something was happening.

---

48. BIG BIRD

Not far from the great year, the old ones will come out of their tomb.

—Nostradamus

The I-5 Mountain, Oregon
POSTQUILT: TUESDAY, 3:09 P.M. PST

Chrissy Watkins chased after her brother through the rough grass. He was being mean and wouldn't play what she wanted to. He kept running off, too fast for her. He wasn't supposed to do that. He was supposed to play with her. Mom said so. And he was supposed to watch her too while Mom found out why they were stuck in traffic.

Rita Watkins was standing with a group talking to a policeman. Chrissy pulled on her mom's pant leg, but her mom shushed her and pushed her hand away. Chrissy tried listening, but what they were saying didn't make any sense to her.

"Clear the road? Are you kidding?" the cop asked. "That's a mountain. It would take a year to dynamite a level grade through that. I'm telling you they'll have to build around it. They'll take I-5 right out there into the valley. Just go around this damn thing."

Some man with a big stomach and no hair did most of the talking.

"You can't tell me there's no way through? I've got to get to Eugene, and I mean today. Now are you going to get me through or aren't you? Don't make me go over your head."

"I'll say it again, but this is the last time. You've got to head back down the other side of the interstate. Go on back to Medford and wait. We're checking on the roads to find a way around. You might have to head over to the coast."

Another man, with a big mustache, came running up.

"Hey, look up there. Everybody look up there."

Chrissy looked up too. The big people all started talking about how neat it was, but at first Chrissy couldn't see anything. Then she saw a big bird flying in the sky. At least she thought it was a bird. It was really just a shadow in the sky.

"Is that a bird, Mommy? Is it? Huh?"

"Yes, honey. It's a big bird. Probably an eagle."

"That's no eagle," the policeman said. "It's too big. Funny shape to the wings too."

"I'll say it's big," the fat man said. "That's got to be a condor. Must be one of them California condors they released in the wild. Wonder what it's doing up here?"

"Are you sure that's a condor?" the mustache man asked. "I've never seen a silhouette like that."

Chrissy's neck hurt from looking up at the bird. All it was doing was flying around in circles at the top of the mountain. She was bored and wanted Matt to play with her.

"Mommy, mommy, mommy!"

"What?" her mom said impatiently.

"Matt won't play with me. And he's not watching me like you told him."

"Honey, I'm trying to find out what's going on. You go tell Matt I said he has to play with you or he won't get his M&Ms."

Chrissy was satisfied. Matt wanted his M&Ms. The grown-ups were still talking when she ran off. The last voice she heard was from the man with the mustache.

"I think that condor is circling down."

She couldn't see Matt but knew he was somewhere in the rocks hiding. She ran along the edge of the boulders, peeking around the big ones and looking in cracks. She worked her way along the edge of the rocks and away from the crowd. "Matty," she called. "Matthew Broderick Watkins, where are you?" she yelled. "Mom says you have to play with me. Play with me or you don't get your M&Ms." Matt still wouldn't come out.

Then she heard the grown-ups yelling. She turned to see them pointing up at the sky.

"Look at that. It's huge!" someone yelled.

The only thing Chrissy could see was the big bird. It was coming closer and closer. Chrissy was good at picking out shapes. The bird had a long skinny triangle for its head, and two big triangles for its wings. It didn't have a body, the wings just seemed to come together. As it circled closer Chrissy could see long feet hanging down, with sharp claws.

Rita Watkins watched the condor circling down. As it got closer she realized she had badly underestimated its size. She estimated the bird had a wingspan longer than her living room. She watched it riding the air currents down, never flapping its huge wings, just riding the breeze and the updrafts.

"Geez, will ya look at the size of that thing?" the fat man said. "It could pick up a calf."

With that, Rita's emotion changed from admiration to panic.

"Where are Matt and Chrissy?" she asked the strangers around her. Then directly to the policeman she said, "Where are my kids?"

"I don't know, lady, but maybe we better get all the kids out of the clearing. Birds don't attack people, but just in case . . ."

The group broke up and began rounding up children and shouting for others to do the same. Rita ran toward the boulders looking for her own. When the shadow of the bird passed over her she broke into a run, screaming for Matt and Chrissy. Matt popped out behind a rock and yelled, "Boo." Rita grabbed his arm, barely slowing her stride.

"Where's Chrissy?"

"I dunno. She wanted to play dumb games."

"You were supposed to watch her," she scolded, feeling guilty she'd delegated her responsibility to an eight-year-old. She jogged along the edge of the mountain with Matt in tow stopping periodically to look between rocks and up onto ledges, all the while shouting Chrissy's name. Then she saw Chrissy, in the clearing ahead walking away from the rocks, her head tilted back looking into the sky.

Then the shadow of the bird passed over Rita again. This

time she felt the breeze from its wings. To her horror she saw that the shadow was heading directly toward Chrissy. Then the bird swooped down, flexed its huge wingspan slightly, and dropped onto her daughter, knocking her to the ground.

"Chrissy!" she screamed.

Other people were screaming too and bolting across the clearing to reach the bird and the little girl. Then the bird floated, pirouetting around to face the angry crowd and again landing on Chrissy's back and shoulders. It was a bird like none Rita had ever seen before. It seemed all wing and head, its body no bigger than Chrissy's. The head was almost all beak, with huge black eyes. It had no feathers, just taut skin. A long rigid crest ran along its head and extended out far behind. From the crest on its head, sinew stretched out to its spine. The underside of its wings were a light gray, and the back so deep green it was nearly black, with tan splotches. Then it opened its mouth, revealing a set of sharp teeth, and screeched, stopping would-be rescuers in their tracks.

"Go hide in the rocks, and don't come out until I come to get you!" Rita screamed at her son.

Shoving Matt toward the rocks, she ran toward her prostrate daughter. Chrissy moved beneath the bird, which danced to stay on top of her. Then it dug its claws into the child's shirt and shoulder. Chrissy screamed and wriggled beneath the bird. It floated in the air again and then came down, seizing Chrissy's arm as well.

Then twenty feet of wing stretched taut, the huge surface area—as big as the sails on a small yacht—trapping every bit of the gentle breeze. The bird flexed its wings, curving them slightly to direct the captured breeze and floated upward—but the bird couldn't lift Chrissy, who struggled to get free.

Then the wing tips bent and then flapped, and to Rita's horror, Chrissy was lifted into the sky. In response to Chrissy's weight the bird's clawed feet dug deeper into her shoulder and arm, and Chrissy cried out again, breaking Rita's heart. More of the wing tips bent in another flap, and the bird carried its prey higher into the air.

Rita put every bit of energy she had into a last sprint. But as she approached everything happened in slow motion. Chrissy was dangling beneath the giant bird, screaming and crying, floating higher and higher. Rita approached, raising her arms to grasp her daughter's legs and rip her away from the bird.

Just then the bird's full twenty feet of wings pushed down in a slow, powerful motion, and Chrissy and the bird shot beyond Rita's reach.

Rita watched helplessly as the bird pumped its wings again and Rita felt the rush of air. Above the sound of the breeze she heard her daughter's voice.

"Help me, Mommy, help me!"

The words brought Rita to tears, and she fell to her knees begging God to help her daughter. Still the bird spiraled upward, floating on air currents close to the mountain where it caught the updrafts. It glided out away from the hillside, dropping slightly, and then circled back where it would catch another updraft. It gained altitude on each pass.

Rita had never felt so helpless. Her baby was floating ever farther out of her reach to a horrible fate and there was nothing she could do. In desperation she picked up the nearest stone and threw it into the sky only to watch it fall well short of its target. Once again she dropped to her knees, sobs wracking her body. Then she heard the shot.

Rita turned to see two men wearing jeans and flannel shirts standing with rifles at their shoulders. She watched as one of them fired. She turned to look at the bird, but it continued to climb, seeming oblivious of the rifle fire. Another shot rang out, but the bird still climbed. Rita suddenly felt panic. What if they shot Chrissy by mistake? Then she admitted to herself that it wouldn't matter, a bullet would be kinder than the bird. Another shot and another miss. The bird was getting too high. Soon there would be no chance for Chrissy to survive the fall, even if Rita could catch her. Rita turned to the men with the rifles and shouted, "Either save her or kill her!"

The men looked at her in surprise, but then their faces turned grim. They both raised their rifles again and took aim, but they didn't shoot. What were they waiting for? The bird was on the outward swing of its spiral and turned to float back toward the mountain. Still they did not shoot. "Shoot!" she said out loud. The bird drifted toward the rocky mountain, then turned to catch the updraft, its wing tip barely scraping the edge of the nearest rock. Then two shots rang out.

There was the slightest pause when nothing happened—a tiny piece of time just big enough for hope to die, only to be reborn an instant later when one wing buckled and the bird collapsed against the mountain, sliding down the smooth rock face and disappearing behind an outcropping.

Pandemonium broke out. The people in the clearing cheered and shouted their approval and Rita felt waves of relief sweep over her. But where was her daughter now? Rita looked to see if the bird or Chrissy appeared anywhere below, but nothing but a trickle of gravel came tumbling down the mountain. Rita ran back and forth under the mountain looking for any sign of Chrissy, but found none. Other bystanders helped her in her search, and others appeared with binoculars, but no sign of Chrissy or the giant bird was found.

Then, when the noise of the crowd died down, Rita heard something else. She shouted for quiet, others taking up her cry, and soon she could hear her daughter's distinct crying. It was the happiest sound Rita had ever heard, and she laughed out loud with the hope. Others came to her, reassuring her, telling her that her daughter would be okay, and she believed them. She needed to believe them.

She believed them right up until she heard the shriek. All heads in the clearing snapped up. There, just above where the bird and Chrissy had disappeared, was movement. The people in the clearing all pointed and gasped at once when the head of the bird appeared briefly above the rocks and screamed at them. The men with rifles raised them again, but the head bobbed back and forth behind the rock, preventing a clear shot.

The bird's screeching drowned out Chrissy's crying. At least that's what Rita hoped, because they could hear nothing of Chrissy now. The screeching continued and then suddenly sounded weaker. The louder screech sounded again, quickly followed by a softer one. The pattern repeated, the second screech growing louder and louder. Then above the mountaintop appeared the silhouette of a second giant bird-thing.

49. Prehistoric Shore

After a hundred years of collecting specimens, we have but a small record of the vast dinosauria. How many thousands of other forms might have existed, we will never know.

—K. Carmen Sontag, *Nature's Lost Species*

Warm Springs Indian Reservation, Oregon
PostQuilt: Tuesday, 4:25 p.m. PST

Petra stood on the limb and leaned out, one hand firmly grasping the overhanging branch. She could see through the leafy overhang, but couldn't see why the dinosaurs were reacting. In the herd, the pickets were moving. The large males on the forest side of the herd were pawing the earth, while those along the lake side were trotting to take position next to their brothers. Finally, the large males were spaced evenly along the side of the herd facing the jungle. The females formed a ring within that, encircling the calves. Petra was impressed with their instinctive wagon-train behavior. The males made a formidable barrier with their long snouts and collar horns, and their huge bony collars. The females made an equally impressive wall, standing shoulder to shoulder to protect the young. Petra couldn't imagine a dinosaur that would dare attack such a defense.

A crashing sound drew her attention to the brush. Something was moving through the brush recklessly, heading straight toward the herd. Petra held her breath, waiting to see the source of the ruckus. Suddenly it broke into the clearing at a dead run. It was Colter.

Petra laughed out loud. She shouted his name, happy and relieved at the same time. Colter was only a short distance across the clearing when he saw the dinosaur wall ahead of him and he turned, angling toward the clump of trees. Petra shouted to him again and waved her free arm. Colter seemed oblivious though, and kept looking back over his shoulder. Petra followed his glance back to the brush.

Then she nearly lost her grip. Coming through the brush was the biggest dinosaur they had seen yet. It towered above the vegetation, walking on two huge back legs, and had a massive head with immense gaping jaws. Loud enough for Dr. Piltcher to hear, she said, "I don't think we climbed high enough."

Petra was afraid to shout now and instead prayed silently that Colter would make it to the trees. She watched the race in silent horror, images of Dr. Coombs's ravaged body drifting through her mind. The monster was in single-minded pursuit of Colter and seemed oblivious to the monoclonius in their defensive position. Colter was losing the race and Petra knew it would happen soon. The dinosaur would lean down and snap Colter up, swallowing him down in two bone-crushing bites. Petra couldn't watch, and she started to look away, unprepared to lose two friends in one day. Then Colter bolted left.

Colter ran right toward the circled monoclonius. The pursuing dinosaur heeled over and followed, its tail swinging through the clearing, throwing up turf and dust. Petra screamed at him.

"No, Colter, no! They'll kill you!"

Petra could see no hope for Colter now, but she was riveted to the scene. The monoclonius pickets were closing ranks, the males coming shoulder to shoulder, their heads down, ready to impale the threat. Colter raced on, the pursuing dinosaur gaining. He was trapped between a wall of horns and a set of jaws well practiced in bone crushing.

But Colter didn't slow. Instead he hit the wall full speed, squeezing between two of the large males and out behind them. Then he turned, avoiding the wall of females, and raced between the males and females, curving around to the end of the picket line, and then out toward the clump of trees holding Petra and Dr. Piltcher.

The pursuing monster pulled up just before the horns of the males, who stood their ground, prepared to take the full charge of a carnivore with twice their mass. The monster screamed in frustration, blasting its breath at the monoclonius, who stood silently but defiantly. Suddenly, one lowered its head and then charged forward, thrusting its horns up at the monster's side. The newcomer turned left to avoid the charge, screaming in rage, but another monoclonius charged forward, jabbing it on the right. The monster trumpeted in pain this time, but backed up and then began walking along the defense line, looking for an opening.

Petra watched Colter run into her clump of trees but lost sight of him when the leaves obscured her view. She yelled to him again, but the roars of the dinosaurs drowned out her voice. Turning back to the standoff, she saw the monster walking along the defensive line toward her tree. Suddenly she felt naked.

"Dr. Piltcher, we've got to climb higher. Now!"

Dr. Piltcher struggled to his feet, and reached for another limb. Even though the limbs were smaller and closer together at this height, Dr. Piltcher had only half of his normal strength. The dense foliage made it hard for Petra to help him. The best she could do was lean into the trunk from her side and steady him with one hand while he tried to pull himself up.

The monster was continuing along the picket line, which moved in front of it to keep the largest males in front of the enraged carnivore. It paused to roar at the monoclonius occasionally but made no attacks. It was close to their tree now, and Petra signaled Dr. Piltcher to freeze while it passed. Its head moved along the treeline at eye level, and Petra found herself mesmerized by one huge eye. How could something that big be alive? But it passed and Petra watched its back move toward the lake and to where Colter had disappeared. Whispering a prayer for him, she signaled Dr. Piltcher to try again.

When the giant carnivore reached the lake its frustration boiled over. Obviously, there was no opening in the line of monoclonius, only a solid line of horns and armor. From experience, it knew the three horns could be killed, but only if caught alone. In a pack they worked together, jabbing over and over, and exposing nothing to the carnivore's jaws except horn and bony collar. But the giant's hunger was great today, almost as great as its frustration, so it screamed again and then charged.

The carnivore's scream nearly shook Petra from her limb. She could hear its rage. Petra turned to see the carnivore thrust down, clamping its jaws on the collar of one of the monoclonius, its teeth squalling on the bone like fingernails on a blackboard, and Petra flinched. The monoclonius roared back defiantly, trying to shake the carnivore from its collar, but the massive jaws kept their grip and the carnivore jerked the monoclonius briefly off its feet.

The monoclonius roared again, but in anger, not in pain. Petra realized there were probably no nerves in that protective collar. Suddenly another monoclonius shot forward, burying its snout horn into the thigh of the carnivore, and then quickly pulled out and backed away. As the carnivore's jaws released, and its head snapped up and turned toward its tormentor, another male jabbed it from the other side. It trumpeted in pain this time, snapping its head toward the new threat. Again it was attacked from its left. Petra silently cheered the monoclonius.

The carnivore, bleeding from the thigh wounds, began backing up, bellowing out its pain and outrage. Now the monoclonius advanced slowly, heads down, pawing the ground, threatening the carnivore every step of the way—Petra realized it was backing straight toward their tree.

She turned to signal Dr. Piltcher to freeze only to find him hanging upside down, with one leg over the overhanging limb, trying to get still higher. Petra turned to see the back of the carnivore's head coming toward her. Yelling for Dr. Piltcher to hang on, she wrapped her arms around the trunk of the tree and buried her face in the bark.

At the last second, the carnivore turned and backed into the tree next to theirs. With nowhere to go, the monster bent and snapped its jaws at the advancing monoclonius, who stopped their advance and backed away. When the monoclonius had given it enough space to retreat, it released its anger in another deafening roar, and then turned—spotting Petra and Dr. Piltcher.

Petra's strength melted away when the giant's eye fixed on them. Then the head turned, showing both its eyes, and its huge flaring nostrils. The head leaned into the tree, snapping off limbs in its way. When Petra saw the jaws opening slowly she turned away, and jumped to a limb below. She caught it, but her weight pulled her free, and she fell again. She hit another limb with her hip, ricocheting off and onto another. This time she wrapped her arms around it and managed to hold on. Her legs were still dangling, but she looked up.

Dr. Piltcher had dropped back to the lower limb and was standing facing the monster's head, flinching back, turning to jump, when the jaws reached him. They crushed both the professor's feet and the limb. Dr. Piltcher screamed and fell headlong, his ankles still trapped in the jaws. With a mighty shake of its head, the professor was thrown to the ground. Still he remained conscious and lay screaming, his ravaged legs spurting blood.

With more terror than she'd ever felt, Petra turned away when the dinosaur bent and clamped its jaws over Dr. Piltcher's head and shoulders. She closed her eyes, but knew that if she lived she'd spend her life seeing that image every day. As the dinosaur worked at its meal, tearing the body and crunching the bones, Petra saw her chance and carefully dropped onto a lower limb on the other side.

Then she climbed down recklessly. She'd rather die from a fall than in the jaws of that monster. A rumbling sound brought her head around to see that the monster was back, and its head sniffing the tree where she had been. Now she dropped, barely looking to check her footing before moving to the next limb. Another rumbling above her, this time closer—she didn't bother to look but swung out and dropped to the ground. Her knees buckled—she crumpled, looking up to see the legs of the monster move toward her. She didn't have to look to know the jaws were coming down.

When Petra stood to run the monster roared, its hot fetid breath knocked her to the ground. Petra rolled over to see the monster's towering head swing away toward something behind it—Colter, running through the trees, holding his spear, the tip bloody. Petra was on her feet when he reached her and they ran through the trees side by side. Futilely, the monster tried to follow. Branches snapped and bent, but the trees proved too much for the awkward behemoth. Finally, it turned and moved to the edge of the woods, trying to catch them when they entered the clearing.

Colter, running on Petra's right, reached out, pushing on her shoulder. Petra stumbled left, turning to glare at Colter, thinking his push might cost her life. But he reached out pointing left and he shouted, between gasps, "Run for the lake."

Petra didn't bother to answer. Dodging bushes and trees, she headed where he'd directed her. Colter ran abreast of her. When they reached the treeline they stopped to catch their breaths, trying to spot the dinosaur. They could hear the dinosaur bulldozing through the brush, but it was nowhere in sight. Colter kicked off his shoes, pulled off his shirt, and began unbuttoning his pants; Petra, exhausted, followed suit but kept her bra on.

Glancing at Colter's body, she saw it was cut in a dozen places with dried blood covering his chest and legs. His white underpants were stained with blood too. As Petra watched bewildered, he took her pants and zipped them up and buttoned them, then tied the legs in knots. Colter looked up, his forehead creasing in concern.

"Are you all right?" he asked.

"What do you think?" she snapped.

Then Colter wiped a finger across her forehead. When he pulled it away it was covered with blood. Petra started to check her head for wounds, but then realized that when the monster blasted her with its breath, it misted her with Dr. Piltcher's blood.

"I'm okay," she whispered. "It's not my blood."

Colter didn't ask whose blood it was.

"I'm ready," he said instead. "Let's go."

Colter got up, holding their pants in one hand and trotted toward the lake. It was a warm autumn day, but they were wearing nothing but their underwear, and their sweat-coated bodies cooled rapidly in the breeze. Halfway to the lake the monster came around the treeline. It spotted them instantly and charged. They sprinted the rest of the way to the lake across rock and weed, unmindful of the little creatures skittering away from their feet. Petra and Colter hit the water full speed, but the water slowed them. Waist high and barely moving, they saw the monster was turning into the lake, splashing toward them.

Colter and Petra began stroking as fast as they could, pulling for deep water, realizing the lake would have to be thirty feet deep to force the monster to swim. They heard it splashing behind them, creating deep waves that rolled Petra, making it difficult to swim. She turned her head back with the next stroke to see the dinosaur behind them, very close to Colter who dove, disappearing beneath the waves. Bellowing, the monster turned toward Petra. She too dove, kicking and stroking furiously, holding her breath until her lungs were ready to explode. Then she surfaced, blowing out the stale air, and breathing in new.

She heard the monster roar behind her and dove again, now angling away from her last position. This time she couldn't stay down as long, but when she came up again she found the monster turned away from her and looking down into the water. She took several quiet breaths and then dove again, stroking away from the beast. When she came up the dinosaur was staring helplessly into the lake.

Now she breaststroked away from the beast, looking back frequently to make sure it wasn't following. Well out into the lake, safe from the dinosaur, she was tiring quickly. The monster watched her from shore but still didn't move to follow—she hoped it couldn't swim. Colter was struggling through the water, swimming with one hand. Petra worried that one of his arms had been injured but then realized he was still dragging the jeans. When Colter splashed up close to her he reached out and thrust a pair of jeans at her.

"Here, hold these."

"What for?"

"Just do it," Colter yelled breathlessly.

Petra took the jeans and found her arm immediately pulled toward the bottom of the lake. Colter was struggling to stay afloat by using only his legs, while he fiddled with the jeans. Then he took the pants by the waist and swung them up and then down into the water, inflating the legs. Petra grabbed them at the waist and held it in the water and found the makeshift float supported her. Colter inflated the other pair, then side by side he and Petra floated.

The lake was silent now. The bellows of the frustrated carnivore retreated into the distance and then faded away. The only sound was the sound of the air slowly leaking through the fabric of the jeans, which they had to reinflate every few minutes. Small ripples in the water caught Petra's eye. Still watching the surface of the water, she saw dozens of bumps appear on the surface of the lake. When the closest set of bumps blinked, she screamed and smacked the water.

"Petra, stop, stop. Here, look at this." Colter held out his hand.

Something was sitting in his palm: a little brown fish with huge bulging eyes. It had two fins and four little legs.

"What is it, Colter?"

"I don't know, but it's breathing. It's kind of a fish and kind of a frog or something. I don't think it's dangerous."

Colter dropped the little creature in the water and swam closer to Petra, then floated by her side. They rested together until they began to shiver, then they knew it was time to move. Kicking through the water, across the lake and away from where they entered, they reached the middle of the lake and turned toward shore. They moved slowly, not wanting to attract attention. The monster was gone, but as tired as they were, even the three-footers would be more challenge than they could handle. The shore remained empty though, and they gained confidence as they neared. Then something brushed Petra's leg. Something big.

Whatever it was, was armored with bony scales and scraped a few inches of skin off of her calf. She yelped when it hit and Colter immediately swam closer.

"My leg! Something hit my leg. I think I'm bleeding."

"That's bad. Trailing blood is like ringing the dinner bell. Make for shore as fast as you can."

Petra frog kicked herself forward, keeping both hands wrapped around her jeans float. Colter settled in behind her, zigzagging across her wake. The shore crept closer at a painfully slow pace.

"Petra, to your left. In the water."

Petra turned following Colter's instructions. There was something swimming alongside of them, matching its pace to theirs—a dark mass six or eight feet long. It looked like a fish to Petra, but without putting her head in the water there was no way to tell what kind. If only Dr. Coombs or Dr. Piltcher were here, they could tell her what kind of fish to expect in a prehistoric lake.

Petra sifted through her own memories, but the only images that came to mind all had long thin necks and huge flippers.

This mass didn't look like that. Instead it looked like something the size of a shark. Freshwater sharks? Realizing she was only scaring herself, she saw it wasn't attacking, and the only thing more important than that was the approaching shore.

"Colter, it's gone. Do you see it?"

"No. Man, I wish I knew if that was good or bad. Just keep swimming."

Petra gritted her teeth against the pain in her aching muscles and kicked even harder. As she swam she watched left and right, vowing not to give herself up to some fish when she had beaten a monster like the one that killed Dr. Piltcher.

Not just killed, she reminded herself, but eaten. Why did being eaten horrify her more than just simple death? Surely it didn't matter to Dr. Piltcher and Dr. Coombs, they were both beyond caring. But to Petra it did matter. Maybe she wanted something to bury and mourn. But most of all she was repulsed by the idea of humans being used as food. Humans weren't food. At least they weren't in their own world. Here the human place in the food chain was still being worked out and the humans hadn't done well so far.

"It's back, Petra," Colter announced. "It just cut between us. I think it's trying to separate us. Just keep going, I'll stay close behind."

Petra tried, but she had no more energy. She was making her best possible speed—a snail's pace. Suddenly Colter gasped, and Petra turned to see him struggling back up onto his float. He was coughing and sputtering.

"I'm okay. It scraped me too. I think it's tasting us."

"Shut up, Colter, and swim!"

Petra turned toward shore again and forced herself back into her rhythm. Something rushed by her legs, creating powerful swirls around her dangling feet. Petra kept up her pace, but then it rushed by again, closer this time.

Petra could feel the attack coming and then Colter shouted, "This is it! Swim for it, Petra!"

Confused and scared, Petra wanted to shout she *was* swimming but had no energy. Colter was facing the other way. She couldn't see the fish but its wake was rushing toward Colter, whose float, she realized, was gone. She turned, let go of her float, and began arm stroking toward shore, finding her rested arms had more energy left than her nearly useless legs. Despite her loud splashing, she heard the attack behind her; violent thrashing in the water. Petra was too afraid for herself to think about Colter. Instead she repeated to herself, left, right, left, right. Soon, her arms tired and her speed dropped off.

A new sound came behind her now, a rhythmical splashing. Petra began to cry. Her arms moved mechanically, and with every stroke she lost a little speed. Her vision was blurring. Before she had seen the blue murk of the depths. Now a greenish fuzz hung before her eyes, drifting up to meet her, and then on her next stroke she hit it. It was the bottom.

She folded at the waist trying to get her legs under her, but she was too near the shore. Now she found herself kneeling in the water, chest deep. Still, she felt as if she were onshore, safe from the lake's menaces. Then she heard splashing behind her.

She spun to see Colter wading through the water, spreading his arms as he approached. Petra stood to take his embrace, but instead Colter turned her toward shore. With his arm around her they walked along the lake bottom toward the meadow beyond.

As their bodies met the cool air, they began to shiver. Petra wanted to run to shore and into the grass of the meadow for warmth, but Colter held her back.

"Let's make sure something's not waiting for us."

The breeze was chilly, so Petra squatted in the water to warm herself.

"What happened back there, Colter? I thought that fish had you for sure."

It almost did. I stuffed my Levi's into its mouth. It tore them up something bad, but while it was wasting its time I took off."

"I'm sorry I didn't stop to help you."

Colter turned when she said that, anger flashing across his face.

"Don't be sorry. Petra, everything I've done, I've done for you. Dr. Piltcher is right . . . was right. I'm not that smart, not like you. I didn't really belong in the group. I was only there for you. Now all I want is to get you out of here."

"Get *us* out of here," Petra corrected. "Let's get out of here and see if my dorm room is still there."

Pushing herself out of the water as she spoke, she stood in

her soaking bra and panties, holding out her arms. Colter, nearly naked himself and covered with wounds, stepped into her arms. They hugged, enjoying the warmth of each other's bodies, and rocked gently against each other, their eyes closed, lest something distract them from their internal sensations. The released libido warmed them slightly, giving them comfort and pleasure.

Then Petra pushed her hips against Colter and leaned her head back. Colter bent his head to kiss her, but never got the chance. When Colter moved to kiss Petra he saw something coming out of the water behind her. It was the fish.

This was like no fish he had ever seen. It had a fish shape, but it was armored from head to tail, with four flippers it used like legs to run along the lake bottom. Colter started to push Petra aside, but it was too late. The fish hit her from behind, clamping its jaws down on her left leg. The blow knocked Petra into Colter and he stumbled back, falling into the shallows. Screaming from the shock and the pain, Petra's leg was jerked out from under her as the killer fish pulled her toward the depths. In vain, Colter charged after them.

"Kick at it, Petra," he shouted in desperation.

Petra mouthed something Colter never heard and then her head was pulled beneath the surface. Diving into the water, Colter saw Petra pulled deeper into the lake, her arms outstretched, reaching for him. He stroked and kicked after her, reaching out to grab her retreating hands, but it was no use. He watched her pleading eyes and reaching hands fade into the murky depths, until she was gone.

50. Rescue

You have confessed your prognostications of doom. Have you forgotten I am a god? Would not I know the future if it was to be known?

—King of Babylon to Zorastrus

Forest, former site of Portland, Oregon
PostQuilt: Tuesday, 5:20 p.m. PST

They were running through the trees away from the camp. Ripman led the way, moving through the forest with a familiarity that was natural, not acquired, and Ellen and Angie struggled to keep up. Both women still had on their shoes and pants, but Angie's blouse was completely gone and Ellen's had no buttons. Branches and tall grasses scratched tender skin unaccustomed to exposure.

When they first followed Ripman into the forest, Carl and the guys fired recklessly. Ripman had darted from one giant tree to the next, Angie and Ellen mimicking his moves. The crack of gunshots and the whine of bullets—sometimes slamming into nearby trees—covered the sounds of their movements. Ripman angled them up the hill and away from the guys, and soon the gunfire became distant thunder.

He kept the pace long after the gunfire ended. Ellen's fear was diminishing as was her adrenalin-fed strength. Exhaustion filled her body. The sun was gone now and the forest had become one unending shadow. Their eyes adapted to the dark but Ripman's pace meant stumbles and falls. Ellen was about to ask him for a rest when his hand came up, signaling for them to stop.

They were near the crest of the hill by a rocky outcrop. A huge fallen tree lay there and disappeared into the forest in a tangle of broken limbs. Ripman circled the tree, climbing toward the massive exposed roots. When he disappeared over the rocks, suddenly Ellen's fear returned. Ripman had been their savior and protector. Though no older than her son, John, his competence was evident in every move he made.

He soon reappeared at the top of the outcrop, motioned them up and then signaled for quiet. Angie and Ellen pushed and pulled each other up the rocks. Around the exposed root of the tree, they could see fresh dirt, as if the tree had fallen that morning. Ripman led them down and under the overhanging roots, into a hollow.

Ellen and Angie collapsed against the dirt walls, enjoying the womblike security. Temporarily safe, Ellen began to think about what had happened to Angie and was plagued by doubt and guilt. Angie's friendship, which had made it possible to look for John, had resulted in disaster. She had no idea how far the rape had gone before Ripman interrupted it. She also knew she would never ask and doubted whether Angie would ever say.

Now Ellen and Angie were hiding in a hole, in a forest that couldn't possibly exist, and being hunted. Ellen thought about the forest around her and hoped she had been wrong about the possibility of other dinosaurs. But why would two dinosaurs be more impossible than one?

Perhaps if they had found John their situation would be easier to accept, but it was hopeless. Portland was gone. Their home was gone, and her son. With that admission Ellen began her grieving. She cried softly in the darkness, muffling the sounds with her hands. After a few minutes she felt Angie's arm around her shoulders. Then she remembered that John's friend Ripman was sitting in the hole with them.

"Ripman! You're here! Is John here? Is he alive?"

Moonlight filtered into the hole, and Ellen could see Ripman's face. He looked uncomfortable and turned away, visibly ashamed.

"I don't know. Last time I saw him he was alive."

"When was that? Why didn't you stick together?"

"We did stick together at first. We were out in Newberg when it happened. John and Cubby wanted to find their moms and dads . . . you . . . so we headed into the forest to look." Ripman paused and looked down again. "I couldn't believe those two . . . complete assholes. They were clueless about what to do. Made every mistake possible. They talked, stumbled, wandered off the trail. Didn't know when to be quiet and when not. If it hadn't been for me they would have been dead a hundred yards in." Ripman brought his eyes up to meet Ellen's. "Finally I had to ditch them. They were stumbling along behind me making a racket I couldn't believe. Some dinosaurs heard it and came after us. We took off running. I was leading, but when I looked back they were running off on their own with the dinosaurs right behind them. I couldn't do nothing so I just kept running."

"Oh no!" Ellen gasped. Angie pulled her closer.

"Those dinosaurs didn't get them. I heard them calling my name later. Walking through the forest yelling my name. So stupid. I knew they would only get me killed so I just let them keep looking. They're still looking as far as I know."

"You should have stuck together."

"What for? They almost got me killed. If I stuck with them I'd be dead now. It's every man for himself in here. They needed me. I didn't need them, I can take care of myself. I don't need anybody."

Angie, whose arm was still around Ellen's shoulder, had been listening to the conversation, watching Ripman's eyes.

"So why did you help us?" Angie asked.

"For the fun of it. I didn't like what they did to that dinosaur. They didn't kill it for food, they did it for fun. I decided to have the same kind of fun."

"You could've left us."

"I may still."

"And you don't need anybody?"

"Nobody."

"Then why do you keep looking at my breasts?" Angie challenged him.

It was too dark to make out colors, but Ellen was sure Ripman's face reddened. He turned away and didn't say anything. Angie obviously knew what men needed—especially teenage men. Suddenly self-conscious, Ellen pulled her blouse together in front. The absurdity of her sudden modesty struck her: one minute running through the forest dodging bullets, and the next minute embarrassed that a teenager was peeking at her bosom.

Then she realized Angie was naked from the waist up.

"Ripman, give Angie your coat," Ellen told him crisply.

Ripman turned back defiantly. He sat tight-lipped, making no move, facing the same crisis he'd faced with John and Cubby. He didn't want anyone to become dependent on him. Finally Angie spoke up.

"If you're cold, go ahead and keep it, I'm fine."

Ripman snorted softly and mumbled, "I don't get cold," then removed his coat and tossed it to Angie.

"Get some sleep," he ordered. "I'll keep watch."

When he left he took his backpack and canteen with him. Ellen wasn't sure they would see him again. Eventually Angie slept fitfully, but Ellen spent the night worrying about John and damning her husband for leaving her.

They were drunk, but the party atmosphere was gone, replaced by fear and anger. John was glad that one of the men was dead, one of those who attacked his mother. Another one was hurt, but not hurt bad enough to suit John. It must have been Ripman, John thought, who put those arrows into the men and helped John's mother escape.

Cubby and John had watched as the men fired after his mom and the other woman. It was a long time before the bikers gave up searching.

Then the men built a fire away from the body of their friend and passed bottles around. Cubby and John crept through the forest until they could hear the men talk of their fear and plans. The injured man, Carl, listened for a while before cussing their stupidity and throwing the fiberglass arrow from his leg in their faces. After that he led the discussion.

"We can't let those women get away," he argued. "They saw Deputy Dawg get it." No one dared point out that Carl had done the killing. "What about what we did to the women? Hey, Miller, what's your wife's old man gonna say about that? Think you'll still be workin' at his mill after that? Butler, Chief Peters hates your guts already. He's been looking for some reason to get your parole pulled. He finds out about this and your ass is back in the can. He didn't like Deputy Dawg better'n anyone else, but what's he s'posed to do when one of his deputies gets killed? He'll pin it on all of us, not just me. And what about Bobby? Kishton, you were a better friend a his than the rest. You gonna just let someone murder him like that? Shot him in the back . . . in the fuckin' back! It ain't right."

Carl wheedled and worked on all of them till they agreed. They couldn't let the women get away, and whoever killed Bobby was going to pay for it.

Cubby and John slipped away after that for their own discussion.

"We gotta help them, Cubby. Ripman helped my mom. You know he'd help us if we were in a jam."

Cubby agreed and so they decided to disable the motorcycles, giving Ripman and the women a chance to get away. It also gave Cubby and John a better chance if they came after them. They then worked their way through the forest to a spot well away from the camp. It wasn't close to the bikes, but a shorter crawl wasn't worth the risk.

John had listened to the men long enough to pick out their voices. There was Carl of course. One of the others was Miller, one Kishton, and Butler, who seldom spoke—that worried John. As John crawled he listened, checking the voices against his list. They were around that fire—except Butler, who could be anywhere.

John had been inching through the grass on his stomach for what seemed like hours and was almost to the motorcycles. The last stretch would be the most dangerous, because the grasses and the ferns were trampled down and even on his belly he would be visible. John knew the roaring fire the men were staring into would help. Their constricted pupils would find it hard to pick out shapes in the shadows.

He heard Cubby crawling through the grass to his left. They'd started toward the bikes at different spots, but were angling toward the targets. But another noise came from his right and he froze. Someone was walking through the grass. He pulled his knife from its sheath and slowly rolled over. He was angry about what they had done to his mother, but he was also afraid.

There was a burst of shouts from the fire and he picked out Kishton's voice, then Miller's. This one near him was either

Carl, or Butler. He listened to the approaching steps. There was no hint of a limp, and Carl had been limping badly. It must be Butler. It wouldn't matter, they were all bigger than John, and all with biceps twice the diameter of John's skinny ones.

The footsteps were almost in John's ear when they stopped, replaced by fumbling and then the sound of peeing. John could smell and hear Butler's loud whizzing. Soon, John's knee felt damp. John silently cursed him.

A loud splintering crash rolled through the meadow startling a gasp out of John, who trembled, afraid of being heard. Butler took two steps forward and uttered a "What the shit?" John could now see him through the grass, but Butler's eyes were riveted on the far side of the meadow. John heard the sounds of running men.

Butler shouted, "What the hell is that?"

"You see anything?" an approaching voice asked.

"Damn. Maybe Coop and the bitch was right. Sounds like there are more of those things around. Maybe bigger ones."

The sounds of splintering and thumping continued but gradually drifted off. One by one the men judged the noise to be far enough away and then turned and walked back to the fire. Butler was the last to go. John waited until Butler had enough time to walk to camp, and then pulled his leg out of the puddle.

He worked his anger back up so he would have the courage to continue and then crawled forward, inch by inch, as silently as possible, trying not to sway the grasses and ferns. He reached the trampled-down portion and pushed his head out far enough to see down the newly created path. The men still circled the fire. When John looked to the left Cubby poked out of the grass, gave him a thumbs-up sign, and crawled to the nearest bike as John did the same. The plan was to cut a fuel line and the spark plug wires on each one—otherwise they could cannibalize one bike to fix another.

Ripman's stolen knife was sharp and the fuel line cut easily. The spark plug wires, however, were deep in the engine and John had trouble reaching. He switched from the smooth edge to the serrated edge and sawed more than halfway through the wire, seeing no point in cutting any further. On the second one the spark plug wires were easy to cut. He found some tubing—the fuel line?—and cut through it. He approached his last bike, the one closest to the fire, slowly on his hands and knees. The men were talking softly now, poking at the fire with sticks, and passing around a bottle.

John sawed through one spark plug wire, and then another, but he had trouble reaching the remaining wires from this side. However, the cut fuel line immediately began dripping gas.

He turned to crawl back and realized Cubby was gone, his earmarked destruction apparently complete. John was debating whether to follow Cubby's path back, or his own, when he heard a "pssst," and turned to see Cubby's face poking out of the grass on the other side of the bikes. Checking the men again, John crept across the makeshift parking lot. Cubby disappeared into the grass as he approached, and John followed. A few yards away, Cubby waited. Putting his mouth to John's ear he whispered, "Help me find that man they killed. He's around here somewhere. But be quiet."

John was too scared to risk asking why. They split up but kept each other in sight. After a few minutes Cubby motioned John over, a pistol in his hand.

"They forgot about this," he whispered. "See what else we can find."

John looked reluctantly at the body, and his stomach rolled. He was glad that it was dark because the body was being consumed by the small inhabitants of the forest. John tenderly patted at the dead man's many pockets, avoiding the crawling insects. The pockets on his chest were sticky with partially dried blood and John could only poke at those. They found a package of blood-soaked Camel cigarettes and a Bic lighter in one shirt pocket. A wallet, comb, and loose change were in the pants, with a huge set of keys that jingled when they pulled them out, freezing John and Cubby in a minute of panic. They found two spare magazines for the pistol in a vest pocket, and cartridges for his rifle were in another. They also found three block-style Hershey bars and a roll of mint Lifesavers.

"You think they left his rifle on his bike?" John asked, in a barely audible voice.

"No, I checked. I think his bike was that blue one."

Then they took the shortest path back to the trees. The splintering and roaring returned as they faded into the forest.

"You know who that is, don't you, John?"

"I know what it is."

"It's your old buddy One Eye. He's looking for you, John. Wants a little midnight snack."

"Up yours. Give me one of those Hershey bars."

"Let's find a good hiding spot for the night first."

They looked for a high spot this time, remembering their experience in the fallen trees, but couldn't find a tree they could climb. Instead they found a fallen tree that had sprouted a mini forest of its own, with young trees twelve inches in diameter forming a semicircle. The boys hid in the middle of the enclosure and filled the gaps with branches.

They ate the Hershey bars and drank from their canteens, talking briefly about the success of their mission and sharing the good feeling that comes of managing one's fear—they had ridden the most dangerous roller coaster in the world and walked away with bragging rights. It was hours before they fell asleep.

---

51. The Mean Bird

Therefore, hear what the Lord has planned. . . . The young of the flock will be dragged away; he will completely destroy their pasture. . . . Look! An eagle will soar and swoop down, spreading its wings.

—Jeremiah, 49:20–22

The I-5 Mountain, Oregon
PostQuilt: Tuesday, 10:05 p.m. PST

Chrissy woke up hurt and crying for her mommy. But Mommy didn't come. No one came. She finally controlled her tears, but couldn't keep sobs from wracking her body. When she sat up her arm ached, and she screamed and then began to cry again. But when she screamed something big moved behind her. It was dark, but she could see the big bird staring at her. She instinctively froze, and tried very hard to hold in her crying. She remembered the big bird. A mean bird, not like the one on TV.

Chrissy remembered the bird knocking her to the ground and then hurting her arm and shoulder. The mean bird wouldn't leave her alone and kept hurting her. Then it picked her up into the sky. She remembered seeing her mommy running to get her, and being lifted out of reach and floated up in the sky and her arm and shoulder hurting worse and worse. She remembered yelling at the mean bird to put her down, to let her go. But the bird just lifted her higher and higher. Round and round they went, getting farther and farther from Mommy. The bird kept flying close to the mountain and then away from the mountain. Chrissy remembered yelling down to her mommy, yelling for help. Then she remembered falling. The bad bird had fallen too. They had fallen down toward the mountain. She didn't remember anything after that.

Chrissy stifled another sob and stared back at the bird. It was a few feet away from her, lying in a pile of its wings. She could see the bird was hurt. There was blood on its wing. Then the big bird opened its mouth and screeched. Chrissy screamed and tried to crawl away from it, but her arm hurt her. Instead, she put her good arm down and pushed herself up. She looked back to see the bird struggling to get up too, trying to get its wings out of the way, so it could get to its feet. Suddenly the bird lunged at her, its big beak poking toward her face. Chrissy screamed again and backed farther away as the bird struggled once more to get up. She looked for a place to get away from the bad bird, and ran to the edge of the ledge and looked over. It was so far down she got dizzy. She looked back at the bad bird. It would be up again soon.

Chrissy wanted to run, but there was no place to go. She wanted to hide but there was no place to hide. Chrissy ran to the wall of the mountain and tried to climb up. But there was no place to climb to even if she had two arms. Turning, she saw the bad bird stand up. Then it stumbled toward her, dragging the hurt wing. Chrissy tried scrambling up the wall again but couldn't get up. When she looked back again the bird was right behind her, and it jabbed at her with its beak. She tried to run out of the way but tripped and fell. Her hand and arm went deep into a shadow at the bottom of the rock wall and she landed on her sore arm. It made her hurt bad again. The bad bird was hopping and fluttering around. Chrissy knew it would hurt her again. She felt with her good arm in the shadow. It was a crack that got bigger ahead of her. Chrissy wriggled forward and down until she got herself all into the hole.

The bad bird was outside. Chrissy could see it looking at the hole. It jabbed its beak into the hole, making Chrissy scream and cry. She wriggled deeper into the hole. The bad bird jabbed again and again. It was like some mean game that her brother, Matt, would play. Chrissy finally learned the bird couldn't reach her. Then she refused to play anymore, and lay quiet, out of its reach. It stayed outside her hidey hole and looked at her. Sometimes it opened its mouth and screeched at her.

"Go away, you bad mean bird!" she yelled back.

The bird jabbed and screeched some more, but finally it hopped away, dragging its hurt wing across the hole. Now Chrissy couldn't see.

"You mean bird!" she screamed again. Then she wondered how she'd see her mommy when she came. Chrissy cried again. "You mean bird," she said. "I hate you." She lay there holding her hurting arm and crying for her mommy until she fell asleep an hour later. When she woke, it was pitch black in her hidey hole.

52. Tropical Snow

We was watching Lucy on TV when, crash—a naked body came through the roof. If that wasn't strange enough, the police said it was frozen.

—Josh Hinson, Jacksonville, Florida, July 15, 1959

Hilo, Island of Hawaii, Hawaii
PostQuilt: Tuesday, 8:15 p.m. AHT

The streets of Hilo were strangely quiet, the tourists and residents glued to the news. Debris in the street announced every grocery store as they drove their rental car out of the city. Just like on Oahu, those stores with goods left had armed guards. They had expected vandalized grocery stores, but they soon encountered looted department stores and electronics stores. Most disturbing of all were the gutted liquor stores. But the countryside was quiet and dark, with few vehicles on the road, and Carrollee resumed her usual animation as they began the climb to the observatories on Mauna Kea.

"Let me see if I can remember her name," Carrollee teased. "You only dated her two or three times, I believe. Scored right away, though, didn't you? Your ear is turning red. I'll take that as a yes. What was that name? Barbie? No, I'm thinking of her figure. Bunny? No, now I'm confusing her name and sexual tendencies. Fluffy? No, that was her personality. Floozy? No, now I'm thinking of her moral character. What was her name? Oh yes, Bree-geet."

"Bridgette."

"That's what I said, Bree-geet. What makes you think Bree-geet will let you use her telescope? As I remember it you two didn't part as friends."

"We were friendly. We split because, well, she didn't think I was ambitious enough."

"Oh yeah, that was it. She waited . . . I think it was a week wasn't it? . . . before moving in with that Canadian. He had better prospects, *oui? Comprenez-vous?*"

"She waited a month. Anyway, it's not her telescope. Dr. Paulson was supposed to contact her and authorize the photos. If everything went right she should have it set up by the time we get there."

"*Très bien.*"

"*Clampee votre* mouth shut, will ya?"

"*Oui.*"

Carrollee turned and looked out the window, pleased with the pins she had poked into Emmett in just a few minutes. Now they slowly left the lush tropical forest behind as they traveled to the higher elevations.

When Emmett had received the PresNet message from the President's science advisor he had nearly panicked. But Dr. Paulson said nothing about Emmett's unauthorized access, he was only interested in Emmett's model.

"You do understand the implications?" he asked.

Emmett assured him he did.

"And have you thought of verifying your theory?" Emmett had confessed inadequate math skills, but Dr. Paulson had something much simpler in mind. Emmett quickly agreed with the idea; after all, he was a player now.

Emmett had feared he wouldn't be able to break Carrollee away from her incubating eggs, but it had been easy. Nearly an army of volunteers was protecting the site now, and nothing exciting would happen until the eggs hatched. Emmett explained the purpose of the trip vaguely and then emphasized it would take only a few hours. Carrollee quickly agreed to come along and even seemed eager to spend more time with Emmett, who was surprised and glad.

The interisland flights were operating, so they flew from Oahu to Hawaii. They left their lightweight tropical clothes in an airport locker in exchange for the heavier clothes the cooler climate demanded. Carrollee came out of the airport rest room wearing the least outlandish thing Emmett had ever seen her wear, but it was still gaudy. Her Levi's were held up with bright red suspenders and she wore a long-sleeve red blouse and carried a red checked sweater. On her feet were hiking boots with red socks folded neatly over the tops, and her bright red lipstick matched her sweater and blouse. Emmett had chosen Levi's too, and a University of Hawaii T-shirt. He carried a matching hooded sweatshirt. He wasn't a hiker though and was wearing his Nikes instead of boots.

He was about to compliment Carrollee on being circumspect when she pulled a giant red and white checked bow out of her bag and clipped it to the back of her head.

"Did that outfit come with a red rubber nose?" he asked.

Carrollee let a smile flit across her lips, then feigned confusion.

"What did you say about coming with a rubber?" She said extra loudly, turning heads at the airport.

Emmett blushed, opened his mouth to speak, then changed his mind. He wouldn't get the better of Carrollee.

Their conversation in the car alternated between somber and silly but avoided the issue of the time quilt. They discussed the plesiosaur and the unusual seaweeds, but Emmett held back what he knew about other dinosaurs from the PresNet. Then they discussed who would succeed Dr. Wang as department chair, and who might be recruited to replace the missing faculty. They recognized that issues of hiring, tenure, and promotion were part of the old world, but they refused to acknowledge the new order.

As they climbed the extinct volcano Mauna Kea, the air cooled and Emmett soon turned on the seldom-used car heater. Mauna Kea towered over Hawaii, the peak reaching 14,000 feet above sea level. At half the height of Mount Everest it was a nearly ideal location for the university to build an observatory. Several instruments sponsored by a variety of nations now speckled the lunarlike landscape that made up the peak. Emmett and Carrollee's destination was the Canada-France-Hawaii telescope, but any other optical instrument would serve their purpose.

The wind picked up as they climbed above the last of the vegetation into the broken lava fields that made up the mountain's dome. The car was warm enough, but outside it was cold enough to snow, and indeed frost speckled the ground. Emmett knew blizzards were frequent here in winter, and that somewhere in a maintenance shed was the only snowplow in the islands. Even in the controlled climate of the car they began to feel the effects of the elevation and cold. The dry air made them lick their lips frequently.

"I've heard the air's so dry up here, they have trouble with the electronics. Sometimes they boil pans of water to keep things working."

Carrollee nodded her head.

"When do we break out the oxygen masks?" she asked.

"They fall down from the ceiling in an emergency. Seriously, are you feeling all right? It's getting pretty thin. We're two miles above sea level."

"I'm okay. I was just thinking about one time we went skiing in Colorado. It took some time to get used to the altitude. I would get sick if I exercised too much."

"Yeah, altitude sickness. We shouldn't have a problem though, I don't plan on skiing, or even walking much. Just watching them take the pictures and then getting off this frigid rock."

"With Bree-geet up here I bet it's not frigid."

Emmett felt the prick.

"Some of those who work up here have trouble adjusting. The air is dry and oxygen poor. Thinking can be affected. A problem you might solve in fifteen minutes at the university can take an hour up here. But if you are going to build an observatory this is one of the best places in the world to do it."

Emmett leaned toward the windshield and looked up at the sky. Carrollee did likewise, and they both found themselves lost in the speckled black ink. After a few minutes she turned to Emmett.

"We'll be there soon. Don't you think it's time to tell me what's going on? You didn't seem all that surprised by what we found on the beach. I know I'm not security cleared or anything, but neither are you. After all, I'm a coconspirator in whatever it is we're doing."

Emmett had no real reason not to tell her everything he knew. The reports on the news were filling in enough pieces of the puzzle to make it obvious to anyone. He worried briefly about the legal implications but suspected there were enough problems in the world now to keep even the most officious bureaucrat busy and away from Carrollee. So, he told her. She knew of the various floods, fires, avalanches, tidal waves, and blackouts, and she had her own experience with the plesiosaur, but like most of the public, she had no idea how widespread these events were. When he finished explaining, Emmett found Carrollee wasn't frightened by the idea of dinosaurs. Instead she seemed tickled.

"Imagine," Carrollee said, "*Tyrannosaurus rex* roaming the earth again. How would you contain something like that? Electric wire three stories tall? Trenches? Fire? Oh, man-oh-man wait until my brother, Richard, hears about this. He's going to want a hunting license. Of course he'd need a trophy room the size of a barn to put the head on the wall."

After fifteen minutes she came to the fundamental questions.

"Why did this happen? Is it over? Will it happen again? Where did the people go who were where the dinosaurs are now?"

Puglisi explained as best he could about the effect of dense matter, the time waves and the displacement. He told her about the various theories and the extension he made in the Gomez model and how it might affect the moon. When he reported his contact with Dr. Paulson, Carrollee looked at him skeptically but seemed to realize that was no more impossible than dinosaurs showing up in the modern age.

"So what are you looking for up here?" she asked.

"Support for the theory. Evidence that the effect on the moon is reversed. Any data that can help fill in the picture. Dr. Paulson seemed particularly interested in the data. He didn't say getting it was urgent, but he put some time into arranging it, time he could have used for any number of tasks. So if it's important to him, it's important enough for me to climb this ugly Popsicle to get it."

Carrollee, silent, slipped into one of her rare pensive moods. After a few minutes Emmett missed her conversation.

"What are you thinking, Carrollee?"

Carrollee shook herself out of her mood and sat straight up in her seat.

"I'm thinking about my family on the mainland—my

mother and my sister. I haven't been able to reach them, but I know there have been telephone problems. I figured they were probably safe. Now I'm thinking they may not be there at all. Not dead, just gone. Gone somewhere in time. Is that what you're saying? It makes me wonder if it could happen again? If it did, I wouldn't want to be sent off to the future by myself. So, I guess I should stick pretty close to someone I would want to disappear with."

"I don't think it will happen again, not if we don't start nuclear testing again."

But Emmett began thinking of people *he* would want to be near if he were displaced. He didn't have any immediate family, only an uncle in Iowa. After considering and discarding several names, he realized he was sitting with the only person who had a certain spot on the list.

The switchbacks became sharper and more irregular, telling them they were near the summit. The landscape was a monotony of frosted, cracked, black lava. The winds continued to pick up, blowing white granular material across the road.

"Is that snow?" Carrollee asked. "Incredible. Snow in the tropics. I knew it was up here of course, but I guess I never really believed it."

The summit appeared suddenly. The flat of the barren lava dome was sprinkled with the high technology toys of civilization. Half a dozen observatory domes were spaced across the peak, most perched on square bases that housed support facilities. Other support buildings were situated nearby. It gave an altogether eerie effect, as if time displacement had shifted the trappings of a high-tech civilization to the cooling lava of the ancient earth. Each of the domes they could see had a four-wheel-drive vehicle or two parked at it, but Emmett was unsure of where Bridgette might be. Four cars were parked in a level area at the end of the road by the administrative building, and Emmett decided to start there.

They parked in the lot and then dressed more warmly. Carrollee's red checked sweater would only be adequate for a short walk in this kind of weather. When they opened the doors the cold dry air immediately sucked out moisture and warmth. Carrollee led the way, trotting to the building and bursting through the door. Inside they found chairs and tables making up a rudimentary lounge. It was empty, but music drifted down the hall, then a man came toward them, tall and slender, balding, with glasses pushed up on his forehead. He paused when he saw the visitors, staring at Carrollee, amused.

"We're here to see Dr. LaSalle."

"I'll tell her you're here." The man continued to survey Carrollee, but with another amused glance he turned and walked back down the hall. While they waited, Carrollee wandered around, picking up astronomy journals and leafing through them. Suddenly the door opened.

Bridgette was as beautiful and sexy as Emmett remembered her. She was wearing what must have been designer overalls, baby blue and trimmed in white. Her matching jacket was trimmed in what looked to be needlepoint. She was as color coordinated as Carrollee, but more understated. Bridgette would draw attention, Carrollee screamed for it. Bridgette's figure pushed and pulled at the fabric in ways that made Emmett's body long for their old days together.

When the look on her face said she had none of those old feelings left for Emmett, his lustful reminiscence evaporated. Then Bridgette turned to look at Carrollee, eyeing her from the big bow on her head to her matching red socks.

"*Qui est-ce que cela pourrait-être, Emmett? Elle reassemble à Minnie Mouse.*"

Emmett wanted to laugh, but bit his lip. He had to admit that Carrollee did look like Minnie Mouse, with the short brown hair, and the red checked outfit topped with a big checked bow. You wouldn't have to know any French to pick out the reference to Minnie Mouse. Carrollee's face was red, but with anger, not embarrassment. You couldn't dress like Carrollee and be easily embarrassed. Emmett held his breath when Carrollee's mouth opened.

"It's so nice to meet you, Dr. LaSalle, I've heard a lot about you from Emmett. He said you were so . . . well . . . easy . . ."

Emmett waited for Carrollee to add "to get to know" but she just let her unfinished sentence hang in the air. Bridgette bristled, but rushed on, as if she had not understood.

"How did you get Dr. Paulson to go along with this? If he hadn't called I never would have consented to . . . this . . . abominable waste."

"It was Dr. Paulson's idea to confirm—"

"It doesn't matter whose idea it was, it is a waste of resources. Come here, I want to show you something."

Bridgette turned and walked outside. Emmett turned to follow, catching Carrollee's eyes.

"Minnie Mouse! Everyone knows Minnie wears only polka dots and never checks!" Carrollee snorted. "Warm, isn't she?" she continued. "She must have been awfully good in bed for you to put up with that kind of crap."

Emmett didn't answer. He just followed Carrollee out the door.

"Look over there," Bridgette was saying, pointing to a dome set apart from the others, a road curving up to its rectangular base. "That's NASA's IRTF. Infrared telescope," she translated, looking directly at Carrollee. "The only single-mirror infrared telescope bigger than NASA's is right there," she said, pointing to another dome that blended smoothly into its base. "And over there," she continued, "is the seventh largest optical telescope in the world. And do you know what this telescope is doing right now?"

"Taking pictures of the moon?" Carrollee offered.

"That's *right*," Bridgette said patronizingly, turning to face Carrollee.

"It's not my idea," Carrollee said defensively. "I just came along to keep Emmett company. If I had my way I'd be taking pictures of Pluto."

Clearly Carrollee was referring to Bridgette's comments about Minnie Mouse. But Bridgette continued coolly.

"There are many things in the sky more worthy of an instrument of this power. I would have refused Paulson's request outright if we hadn't had some cancellations."

"Cancellations?" Emmett prompted.

"Well, no-shows actually. We have some gaps in our observation rotation, and we've had trouble contacting those on the waiting list."

Use of the facilities was highly competitive, and not showing up was unheard of. Emmett understood why there were gaps in Bridgette's schedule, but obviously Bridgette was uninformed about what had happened to the world below her. He decided not to tell her. He wanted his photographs.

"You said the photographic survey has already begun? Do you need any help?"

"We don't need help. If you want the plates developed and printed it will take another hour and a half."

Emmett decided it was worth the wait. He wasn't sure he could get the developing done at the university, given the situation.

Two hours later they were traveling down off the volcano with a sheaf of photos. Carrollee drove while Emmett shuffled through them futilely, looking for some obvious change.

"I just don't know enough about moon topography to do a good job on this," he said finally. "Besides, I'm getting car sick."

"Emmy not take his Dramamine?" Carrollee said in a babyish voice and clucked her tongue. "Just what are you looking for, anyway?"

"Something different. Some kind of change. Something that would support my model. Dr. Paulson wasn't very specific."

"Maybe you could ask someone to help you?" Carrollee suggested.

"I suppose you will be busy with your babies."

"Nothing to do now but wait. I don't enjoy staring at sand."

Emmett knew Carrollee was as hooked as he was on the project. But she wanted to know he wanted her help.

"Carrollee, would you help me examine the photos?" Emmett asked it politely and seriously, although it came out sounding a little forced.

Carrollee stifled a smile and then said, "*Oui*."

53. Modern Death

It wasn't the wheel that gave man dominance over other species, nor any other implement, save one; the weapon.

—Sir John Hammond, *A Philosophy of History*, 1872

Warm Springs Indian Reservation, Oregon
PostQuilt: Tuesday, 10:30 p.m. PST

Colter's survival instinct barely saved him from drowning. Already physically exhausted, he dove repeatedly, searching for any sign of Petra, but when he found none, he finally splashed to shore and collapsed. He meant to rest briefly and then search again for Petra, but his good intentions faded with his consciousness. While his body struggled to renew itself, he was near comatose. Badly chilled and without food to replenish his resources, he woke to find himself still near exhaustion.

It was nearly too much for him. The loss of Ernie and Mrs. Wayne scarcely crossed his mind because he hadn't witnessed it. The losses of Dr. Coombs and Dr. Piltcher were painful, but manageable. He had liked the people in the group. Sure they were kooks, but they were nice kooks. Kind of interesting, if you didn't take them too seriously. He was sad to know how they died. But the death of Petra caused personal pain, something Colter had never experienced. He'd never been as close to anyone as to Petra. He'd never told her, but he loved her. Now she was gone.

They were all gone. And it was because of the monsters, the dinosaurs, whatever Dr. Piltcher called them. These animals came, they terrorized, they maimed, they killed.

Well, I can kill too, Colter thought. I'm a human, and humans kill better than any animal ever could.

He got to his feet and ran recklessly through the brush toward the RV, feeling invulnerable, even though he was nearly naked, exhausted, and unarmed. He defied any dinosaur to cross his path. He'd be an easy target, of course, but now he didn't care. He was going to kill, or be killed.

When he burst in the door Moose scrambled to the cabinet, and Sarah waddled to the back and buried herself under a pile of clothes. Colter flared when he saw them. But he only cursed at them and then began digging in the piles looking for a pair of jeans. Still angry and reckless, Colter threw things violently to the side, working his way toward the back. When he spotted his jeans in the bottom of a mound he jerked at them, eliciting a squeal of pain from Sarah.

The painful cry melted some of the ice from Colter's heart. Gently, he pulled the clothes off the pile one by one to uncover Sarah. She had one back foot stuck in his jean's pocket, and when he pulled on it, it twisted her leg up and back. Sarah flinched when he reached down, but didn't snap. Slowly, Colter untangled her back leg, and she limped away to another pile and tried burying herself again.

Feeling guilty, Colter dug around in the cabinets until he found a package of raisins. He tore it open and dumped about half of it in front of Sarah's clothes pile, and after only half a minute her head and neck collar emerged from under the clothes to sniff at the raisins. Something pink and lacy was dangling from her collar. Colter smiled at the sight, but then frowned when he realized it was a pair of Petra's panties. When he reached down to retrieve them Sarah cringed, but didn't run away. He threw the underwear out the shattered window. Sarah looked up briefly, then started nibbling on her raisins.

He was surprised at how much pain a piece of Petra's clothing could bring. The look and the touch triggered memories of what had been and would never be again. Now Colter sorted through the pile, pulling out whatever pieces of Petra's clothes he could find, and threw them out the window. It was crazy, he knew, but it was also therapeutic.

When he was done, he thought about starting on the belongings of the others, but he had something else to do. Something to do with killing. He pulled on a sweatshirt to finish covering himself, and then put on his old Nikes. When he was done he looked up to see Moose staring longingly at the raisin pile Sarah was devouring. While Moose cringed against the wall, Colter pulled another handful of raisins from the package and dropped them on top of the cabinet. The animal was on the food as soon as Colter stepped away.

It took over an hour to hammer the crushed metal of the wheel wells away from the tires. Colter worked by flashlight, bending, prying, and hammering. When he was sure he had enough clearance to turn without cutting the tires, he climbed into the driver's seat to start the engine. The egg they had found in the clearing was still wrapped in a towel on the dash. Colter placed it into a lower cabinet and then tried starting up the RV, which roared to life on the second crank. Pulling forward, he turned away from the prehistoric world toward what he hoped was still civilization. When he adjusted the rearview mirror he spotted Moose on top of the cabinet.

"All ashore who's going ashore. Let's go, guys! Last stop! End of the line!"

Moose stared at him from the top of the cabinet, but didn't move. Colter swore, set the brake, and walked back to grab Moose and throw him out. Moose skittered away to the back of the RV and disappeared behind a pile of debris on the bed. Instead of chasing Moose, Colter reached for Sarah, but when she ran to avoid his reach he noticed her slight limp. He felt a sharp pang of guilt.

"Okay, guys," he said resignedly. "You had your chance. Let's go to town."

He put a handful of raisins on top of the counter and then dumped the rest into a pile on the floor of the RV. The two little dinosaurs were eating again by the time he reached the driver's seat. As Colter rumbled down the road toward town, he shouted back to his little passengers.

"If either of you has to take a crap, you hold it until we get to town, or no more raisins."

The dinosaurs looked up but then returned to their snack. A few minutes later Moose lifted his tail and left a little pile on the top of the cabinet.

Colter found the town with only a thin veneer of civilization left. Refugees and trapped tourists were everywhere, trying to buy everything. Panic was setting in. Colter was only interested in getting a gun, but he nonetheless picked up pieces of information. The town's people didn't want to believe the information that was trickling in, but Colter knew the terrible truth. Whatever put those dinosaurs in Oregon had done things all over the country. The people in town weren't just terrified of what was now roaming just outside their town, they were terrified of the unknown. Colter had little sympathy for them. Why couldn't they take what was and live with it? To him, this endless search for understanding was a mystery. But not death. Death could be understood, and death of a friend—a lover—demanded response.

Colter tried two sporting goods stores looking for a rifle. It was late, but every store had a light on. The owners weren't taking any chances on losing their stock. The first store he tried still had some rifles, but the owner wasn't selling them for paper money. Colter begged, pleaded, and threatened, but came away without a rifle. At the second store, he got the same reaction. Then he drove to a garage and managed to rent some time with a torch, telling the owner he wanted to work on his vehicle. Colter blamed the hole on an accident, but the owner was suspicious. Still, Colter could weld the hole in the side at least roughly, then took the torch into the RV. In one of the lower cabinets Dr. Coombs and Dr. Piltcher had bolted a small cheap safe to the floor. It wouldn't stop a professional thief, but it would stop the ordinary jockey-boxer looking for tape players and loose change. Colter cut the combination lock out, careful not to set the contents on fire. As he expected the safe was full of money—several thousand dollars in currency, and six thousand in traveler's checks. Behind the paper money Colter found two heavy wooden boxes. Colter opened one to find a long row of gold coins lined up like mints—twenty coins. Colter took six of them and put the rest back in place and welded the door closed.

He tried the first sporting goods store again. The owner was belligerent until Colter held out his hand with two gold coins. The owner looked over the coins and even bit one to make sure they were real. Then the negotiation started. While interested, the dealer wouldn't sell Colter the rifle he wanted for only two of the coins. Colter mournfully told the man he had only four coins and a family back in Ashland and wasn't sure he could go back without protection.

"Boy," he said, "you could kill an elephant with a rifle like that. Now if you want personal protection I've got an assault rifle here that will give you the rapid-fire capability you need. I might even be able to get you a banana clip to go with it, if you don't say where you got it. They're not legal, you know."

Colter held his ground and the negotiation continued. Colter didn't want to give him four gold pieces—but there was no way to make change. Colter now understood why pirate treasure was often pieces of eight—breaking his gold coins into eighths would make the negotiation simpler. Finally, Colter thanked the man and said he'd try the shop down the street. That's where he got the deal he wanted—the rifle, three spare eight-round clips, and three boxes of ammunition for three gold coins. Then Colter went looking for supplies.

The only open grocery was guarded by six police officers, and the people going in were coming out with only small quantities of food. Colter drove to one of the closed stores and banged on the glass door until a thin middle-aged man came from the back waving a pistol and hollering to Colter. Colter put the gold coin against the window and held it there with his finger. The man stared at it, then walked forward and put his nose right up against the glass. Then he put on a pair of glasses and Colter watched the guy's eyes light up. The man motioned Colter around back, through the delivery entrance, where he traded his coin for groceries, propane, bottled juice and water, and raisins and other fruit for Sarah and Moose.

54. The Den

We were recovering our net by reeling in on our drum, when one of the hands yells 'lookit there.' Well, I looked and sure enough there was a head . . . sitting on a neck as thick as a good-sized cargo boom. But it was the eyes that held me; they were large, but sort of deadlike. . . . In all my years of working drift nets . . . I ain't never come across the likes of that . . . But that animal was big indeed.

—Captain Mario Lapana, in *Sea Monsters and Other Dangerous Marine Life*

Warm Springs Indian Reservation, Oregon
PostQuilt: Wednesday, 1:10 a.m. PST

Petra woke in darkness, her body aching from head to toe. When she tried to lift her head, the agony threatened to drive her back into unconsciousness, so she lowered her head gingerly until it met the wet surface. When the pain subsided a little, she was able to localize her injuries. Her head was the worst, but her left foot and ankle throbbed and pain kept her from bending her ankle more than a fraction of an inch. Petra lay still again, and when the pain in her ankle subsided she became aware of her other senses. It was almost pitch black, so her eyes were nearly useless, but there was a terrible stench in the air. Some of the smell was familiar—and Petra realized she was lying in her own vomit. Still, when she tried to scoot away, the pain was worse than the smell, so instead she lay still and tried to remember what happened.

The first memory to return was Colter's face. She could see it through a murky gloom. He was moving away, pawing at the air. No, not pawing. He was swimming, and it wasn't Colter who was moving away, it was Petra.

Then it all came back. That strange fish. The one that came out of the water, walking on its flippers and then grabbing her ankle. It had pulled her under the water, and she had drowned. But she hadn't drowned, not unless this was hell. It sure wasn't heaven. But where was she, and why wasn't she dead?

Petra kept her head as still as possible and reached out slowly with her right hand, sliding it across the wet surface. The bottom was clearly rock. Then her hand touched something slimy and scaly. She jerked her hand back and froze. It was the fish.

Her heart pounded so loudly, she feared the fish would hear. But nothing happened. It didn't move and made no sounds. When Petra's panic subsided, she began to think more clearly. The fish she'd touched couldn't have been the one that grabbed her; that one was covered with hard scales. This fish was slimy. Petra forced her hand back out to the fish and touched it again, poking it with a fingernail. It didn't move. She ran her hand along its length. It was four feet long with a long fin on one end. She couldn't bring herself to explore its head, after she discovered that the fish was well decayed. She went to wipe her hands on her pants but found she wasn't wearing any. In fact she wasn't wearing much at all.

She reached out above her head and found something covered with smooth skin, not scaly, with a long thin neck and at least two well-muscled back legs. Petra realized she was in a den. She was part of the food supply of that walking fish that snatched her. Somewhere on the trip to the den she had passed out, but she hadn't drowned. At least not quite. Her head told her she had been without oxygen for a while. She worried briefly about brain damage but realized there was a more immediate problem. She was part of some prehistoric fish's larder, and she didn't want to be its main course at the next meal.

Petra lay still, listening as hard as she could, but heard nothing. She was pretty sure the fish wasn't in the den with her. There were no sounds that weren't her own. She reasoned that if the fish could walk out of water, and snatch her and other land animals, that it must be an air breather. The only sounds of breathing were her own. No, this den was filled with death and rot, not life. Except her life.

Petra lifted her head slowly, pausing frequently to let the stars clear from her eyes. The pain kept her at the edge of tears, but she was almost to a sitting position when her head, with a dizzying pain, hit the ceiling. It seemed to be made of sticks and mud. There *was* air in here, she realized, stale putrid air, but air. She must be near the surface of the lake. She thought about digging through the roof but didn't know what was above. Could this part be under the lake? Surely not, if it was made of mud.

She sat semireclined, holding her body up with her hands, and looked around. It seemed brighter now. But where was the light coming from? Petra looked above and behind, seeing nothing but the gloom. Then she spread her knees apart and looked between. There was a soft glow on the floor of the den. It took her a minute to realize she was looking at a pool of water, and the pool was glowing softly. That was the way out. But even if she could stay conscious, could she swim far, weakened as she was and with a crushed ankle? She was debating whether to try it when the light suddenly disappeared and the water began to ripple. Something was swimming up the tunnel.

She flopped back down and froze, trying to remember the position she had been in. The water of the pool sloshed violently enough to splash her ankles. She began to tremble with fear and bit her lip, trying to stop the shaking. Suddenly there was a loud splash and the wet sound of blowing air—she could feel the walking fish behind her. It puffed and blew a couple of more breaths, tasting the air of its den as if to make sure it had not been disturbed. Petra knew her only chance was to play dead, but reflexively she wanted to run or fight.

Still, she suppressed her instincts as the fish pulled its body from the water. She heard its flipper-feet pad across the wet surface, its body or tail dragging across the floor of the den.

Then something pushed her in the back. Petra tried to remain limp, but she panicked again. Rigor mortis. She should be stiff, shouldn't she? Too late. She couldn't change her act now. It pushed her again, this time higher in the back. Petra rocked gently again, acting limp. She'd play stiff later. Then the fish walked forward and began rummaging around in the back of the den. Soon Petra heard the sounds of chomping and eating. Relief swept her body. She was too big for an after-dinner snack, so unless it planned to taste her, she didn't think she was on tonight's menu. From the smell of the cave this prehistoric fish liked its food well decomposed.

When the fish finished its meal it rummaged around a bit longer, then padded back toward Petra. She held perfectly still when it approached, but then to her horror, it plopped down behind her, its back pressed against hers. She waited for it to move, but it didn't. After a few minutes she heard rhythmic breathing. It was asleep, its back against Petra. Now she couldn't move. She was trapped.

---

55. PAT AND PATTY

The killer whale has no peer; it fears nothing in its domain and has no qualms about attacking any other beast it makes contact with, even the true whale. Would it kill a man? Probably yes.

—James B. Sweney, *Sea Monsters and Other Dangerous Marine Life*

West of Naples, Florida
POSTQUILT: WEDNESDAY, 7:12 A.M. EST

Hey look, a fin!" Chris yelled.

Ron woke to see a black fin break the surface, and then disappear again. Another fin appeared farther out and then another.

"Are they sharks?" Carmen asked.

"No," Rosa answered. "They're too big."

"They're over here too," Chris said excitedly.

Ron looked right to see two more fins. Then one of the animals leapt out of the water. It was black on the top but white on the bottom, the clear markings of orca. It was a pack of killer whales—there were at least ten.

The whales circled Patty and Pat, coming closer with each pass. Then Chris shouted and pointed straight down. Ron looked to see a black shape shoot between Patty and her baby. Another orca followed, but this one rammed Pat, driving him away from his mother. More whales swam between Pat and Patty, driving the baby farther away from its mother.

"They're after the baby," Rosa said sadly. "We've got to help it."

Suddenly the baby let out an ear-piercing squeal. The

mother immediately whipped her head around, wrenching her body into a partial turn. Ron and the others dropped spread-eagled, to keep from being thrown off.

When the mother was satisfied the baby was still following she resumed her course. Ron looked down at the baby and heard rapid, deep breathing, punctuated by a slight whine. Rosa pointed silently to the baby's wake; everyone saw that Pat was leaving a pink trail in the water.

Suddenly Pat dipped deep into the water, nearly submerging his head, and screamed again. Chris put his hands to his ears to block the horrible sound, but Patty wrenched around again and Chris had to spread his arms wide to keep from rolling off. Ron looked back to see two more fins rushing toward Pat. Now the fins dipped below the surface and a few seconds later Pat shuddered twice in quick succession.

Pat screamed continuously now, and his wake was a crimson stream far into the distance. The orcas were in a blood frenzy and the pack circled closer. The flashing orcas were designed for this kind of attack. Sleek and powerful, they darted in and out, biting into the struggling Pat, who squealed with every blow. Patty's huge tail might have been formidable on land, but in the water it was nearly useless in the defense of Pat. Occasionally Patty's tail would break the surface and slam down into the sea with a deafening slap. The orcas seemed bothered by the sound at first, but then ignored it, dodging it every time.

The kids were horrified. But Ron realized that to the orcas it was just feeding time, and Pat was the target. Even in the civilized world justice is fleeting; in the animal world it is meaningless.

The attack on Pat was going on at a leisurely pace. The orcas were enjoying the hunt, streaking up from below—their attacks drenching Patty's passengers with bloody spume.

"I want to get out of here," Chris moaned.

"Me too," Rosa said. "Let's swim away."

Ron had never heard of orcas eating people, but he wasn't sure anyone had ever swum through a feeding frenzy, covered in the blood from the kill. Apparently Carmen agreed.

"We're still safer here, kids," she said. "If we get in that water they might come after us. Let's stay up here as long as we can."

Ron nodded. He decided now was the time to use the last of the water and passed the bottle to the kids. They each drank about a quarter and passed the bottle to Carmen—who started to refuse, but Ron frowned at her. There was no point in saving the little that was left. After Carmen drank her share she passed the bottle back to Ron. As he drank the last of the water, he noticed dozens of seabirds gathered overhead. They must have been following the killer pack, scavenging the remains of their victims. The birds circled and screeched, waiting like vultures.

Pat was barely moving now, although he still seemed to have little trouble floating. Patty was getting frantic, and began bleating defiantly at the circling orcas. Then as Pat slowed to a near stop, Patty turned in a wide circle, around him. Carmen yelled for everyone to lie flat, to get as much traction as possible. Patty, even with the long dragging tail, couldn't come close to encircling her baby.

The orcas paused, apparently considering Patty's new strategy. As Patty circled, Pat floated in the reddening water, squealing for his mother's help. Ron began to think it was time to get off.

"Here they come again!" Carmen shouted.

Ron turned to see an orca darting toward Pat, skimming along just below the surface, timing its attack to just clear Patty's massive tail. They could feel the muscles along her spine bunch as she suddenly lifted her tail and stopped swimming. The whale continued forward, confident it would clear Patty's tail, but Ron realized the orca had miscalculated. The refugees felt the collision when several tons of tail slammed into the attacking orca, and then her whole body wrenched to the side.

The whole family cheered.

"You show them you're the mama!" Carmen shouted.

"Way to go, Patty!" Rosa yelled.

"Yeah, way to go," Chris echoed, and then added, "one down, nine to go."

Chris's mention of the odds sobered the group. There were many more orcas, and they had no idea how badly their member was hurt. Then it surfaced outside Patty's protective circle. When it blew its lungs clear the spray was pinkish. It dove again and then quickly surfaced, again blowing pink spray.

The family watched the injured whale swim off to the west,

tilted at an angle, zigzagging through the water. Ron realized it was being followed by the flock of scavenging birds.

The orcas continued to circle, now deadly efficient, businesslike. Then an orca split off and angled in at Patty broadside, disappearing beneath the waves a hundred yards from them. Suddenly something slammed into her, shaking Ron and his family. Patty screamed, swinging her tail up and down violently, and the family reached out, grabbing onto one another's hands and holding one another up. Another hit came from the opposite side, and Patty wrenched again, twisting toward the new attack. Another hit came from the front and Patty's screams became deafening. The attacks stopped for a moment, and Ron looked for the rest of the orcas—now busy with Pat.

The baby was twisting in the water, whipping his neck back and forth as the orcas took turns hitting him. Pat began to list to the right and fought to keep himself upright. As he rolled, Ron could see his left front leg come up toward the surface. It looked like the leg of an elephant, thick with baggy skin, but with three distinct clawed toes. Now an orca buried itself in the flesh of the leg and whipped its body back and forth, tearing free meat and skin.

Pat had no more screams left in him. Another hit to his belly finished pushing Pat to his side, and his head disappeared into the water. Pat would die soon, either of blood loss or drowning. As he rolled over, Ron could see the left rear leg was nothing more than a thick white bone with a few chunks of bloody meat still dangling.

The attacks on Patty continued, even though the orcas were at the same time making a meal of Pat. It was getting harder for the family to stay on her shuddering back.

Orca after orca slammed into Pat's body, tearing away bloody chunks that now floated in the crimson water, making a gory soup. The seabirds were beginning to risk dropping briefly into the water to feed on the scraps.

In her pain, Patty forgot about Pat and began swimming away from the attack, out of the red soup, but leaving a pink trail of her own. For a moment the attacks on her stopped. She resumed her eastward swim, returning hope to Ron and the rest of the family. A sense of relief spread through the little group, but they kept glancing back, fearful the orcas would follow.

56. Mariel from the Window

They do not know the hidden meaning of what is taking place now, nor have they even understood the lessons of the past. Consequently, they have no knowledge of what is coming upon them.

—The Coming Doom, The Dead Sea Scrolls

New York City
PostQuilt: Wednesday, 7:50 a.m. EST

Luis woke to the beat of a drum pounding in his head, the rhythm of his pulse, but with each beat came a stabbing pain. It was another blinding headache, but he managed to push himself up, using the arms of the rocking chair, and then stepped close to the window.

His vision was coming back, but his eyes were blurry, making it difficult to see into the distance. In the bathroom he washed his eyes with a little water from the toilet tank, now three-quarters gone.

Back in the living room, he saw a large still form in the meadow. Still groggy, Luis left the apartment and went down the stairs one step at a time, his hand firmly gripping the rail. The trail was easy to find. It was marked with blood.

Following the flattened sticky grasses, Luis moved slowly, keeping his eyes on the ground and placing each foot with care. When he looked up, he spotted a dinosaur in the path ahead. It was small compared to Mrs. Weatherby's dinosaur, and only half as tall as Luis, but it stared, unmoving. Finally, he shouted at the beast.

"Shoo. Shoo! I said get the hell out of my way!"

The dinosaur stared back at him blankly. Suddenly Luis took three running steps forward, screaming at the top of his lungs. The dinosaur bolted to Luis's left and disappeared into the shoulder-high grass, but two more appeared and darted across

Luis's path, following their sister. Luis stood still, shocked, then laughed at himself despite his throbbing headache. If he had known there were three of them would he have charged? Certainly not. Sometimes, he reflected, the victory goes to the lucky, not the wise.

Walking faster now, Luis plunged ahead. The path began to curve left as if the wounded dinosaur had lost its way. Luis paused and stood on the tips of his toes. He could see the form of the dinosaur over the tops of the grass. Luis turned, cutting through the grass, and then he froze. Something was moving ahead. He could see the tips of the grass waving. He squatted, waiting and listening.

He should be with Melinda and his kids, he thought. He longed to see them all, but especially little Cinda. Luis had to get out of this conjured meadow and out of the war zone that surrounded it. Thinking about all of this, Luis still moved ahead. He would leave, he told himself, but with Mrs. Weatherby.

Moving slowly, he found himself behind the iguanodon, who was lying on its side, his massive hind legs just in front of Luis. At more movement in the grass, Luis dove behind the animal's legs for cover.

Something slammed into the ground where Luis had been—the iguanodon's tail. That meant the animal was alive. It also meant Luis was sheltering himself between the legs of a wounded dinosaur.

Afraid to stand, he crawled along the creature's belly. Now Luis saw the dinosaur's head rise a foot off the ground, staring with a massive brown eye. As Luis froze, transfixed, he heard a soothing voice pleading with the dinosaur.

"No, don't move. Please lie still. You'll only hurt yourself."

The voice was weak and hoarse, but it was Mrs. Weatherby's. When the dinosaur's head settled, Luis walked slowly forward. Mrs. Weatherby was lying in the grass, nestled against the shoulder of her dinosaur. The grass under the dinosaur's head and neck was soaked in blood. Mrs. Weatherby's eyes were closed and she was talking to the dinosaur in a hoarse whisper.

"Go to sleep. Please go to sleep. It won't hurt as much if you can sleep."

"Mrs. Weatherby? Mrs. Weatherby? Can you hear me?" Luis asked.

Mrs. Weatherby stopped talking when Luis called to her.

"Is that you, Luis? Oh, dear boy, what are you doing here? Why aren't you with your family?"

When she spoke she opened her eyes and looked at Luis, but her eyes couldn't seem to focus on him. Luis realized she wasn't wearing her glasses.

"I've come to take you home, Mrs. Weatherby."

"I can't leave him. He's hurt . . . he's dying."

"I'm so sorry, Mrs. Weatherby. I didn't mean to get him shot. I only meant to scare the Zombies away so I could get to my family. I didn't mean to hurt him . . . to hurt you."

"I know, Luis. To you he was a big scary monster, but to me he was a friend. And friends don't leave friends when they're hurt."

"Mrs. Weatherby, I won't leave without you. This time I mean it."

Mrs. Weatherby was still protesting when Luis reached her, and he looked at her, shocked. She was pale and sweaty, and when he bent to pick her up she had no strength to push him away. He lifted her, one arm under her knees and one across her shoulders. She wasn't heavy, but the effort started the pain in Luis's head again.

"No, Luis. I don't want him to die alone. No one should die alone, not even an animal."

"Maybe he won't die, Mrs. Weatherby," Luis lied, trying to calm her. Something was seriously wrong with her. She hadn't been this pale or weak when she faced off with the Zombies.

"He's dying, Luis, I know it. Don't lie to me."

"All right, Mrs. Weatherby."

"He shouldn't die alone."

"No, he shouldn't. But maybe his animal friends will come if we leave."

Mrs. Weatherby was silent for a minute after that. As he carried her off, Luis swung his head back and forth to keep an eye on both the thumb spikes and the dinosaur's head. Now the mouth opened slowly, not sudden or threatening, and Luis heard a familiar sound.

"Aaaaaahhhhhh—"

Mrs. Weatherby's head came up. Luis stopped and turned so Mrs. Weatherby could see her friend. The two of them looked at each other. The sadness in Mrs. Weatherby's eyes was clear. Maybe Luis was imagining it, but he thought he saw the same emotion and intelligence in the dinosaur's eyes. The animal's mouth opened again and another soft "aaaahhhh" came gurgling from its throat. Then the head sank to the bloody grass, the eyes closed, and a long slow breath blew from its nostrils. It didn't move after that.

Mrs. Weatherby began to cry, tears streaming down her face. Luis quickly turned away and carried her into the grass. She never tried to look back. The old lady hung limply in Luis's arms, still pale and sweaty. Since the day was cool but not cold, the perspiration worried Luis. He stopped frequently, resting his aching head more than his arms. Twice things moved through the grass around him, but he ignored them.

When Luis paused near the apartment to rest again he heard a new sound: gunfire. The battle for the streets was raging again. Luis waited with Mrs. Weatherby, trying to locate the sounds, muffled but not distant. Perhaps on the other side of their apartment building?

Luis looked down. Mrs. Weatherby seemed to be asleep. He didn't know if that was a good or bad sign. He felt he could reach the safety of the apartment without getting shot, so he carried Mrs. Weatherby across the open space, past her garden, and into their building, pausing twice on the stairs before he reached her apartment. He lay her on the couch.

"It smells like home, Luis."

Luis was surprised when she spoke, thinking she was asleep.

"It is home, Mrs. Weatherby. Lie still. Get some rest."

"Are they shooting again?"

"Yes, in the streets. Not too near, probably."

Mrs. Weatherby, silent, was breathing shallowly. Luis wasn't sure if she was asleep but used the quiet time to get a washcloth from the bathroom and soak it in the water from the toilet tank, and used it to wipe the perspiration from her face.

He didn't know what else to do. Until the shooting stopped he had little hope of getting her any help.

The wet cloth seemed to revive her and she opened her eyes and looked up at Luis.

"There's blood in your hair again," she told him.

"I know. I'm okay."

"I'll wash it out for you."

"When you're feeling better."

Mrs. Weatherby lifted her head but didn't have the strength to sit up. Then she sank back down and looked at Luis.

"Help me to my window chair."

"You're better off here. Maybe in bed?"

"My window chair. That's where I always sit, well or sick."

Mrs. Weatherby seemed agitated. Making her unhappy wouldn't help her heal, Luis realized, so he set her down gently in the rocker by the window.

Mrs. Weatherby turned her head and looked into the distance. Luis had forgotten about the iguanodon's body, and to his dismay, he saw animals around it. Mrs. Weatherby's friend was being recycled.

"Luis?" Mrs. Weatherby spoke in little more than a whisper. "I lost my glasses in the meadow. Can you see him? Did his friends come to be with him?"

"Yes, I can see him, and he's got lots of friends with him."

"I'm so glad. I wanted to be with him too."

"I took you away. Don't blame yourself."

Mrs. Weatherby was silent for a few minutes and then whispered again to Luis.

"Please, dear, can you fix me a cup of tea?"

In the kitchen, Luis lit the stove and then put the pot on to boil. Then he sat with Mrs. Weatherby to wait. Her skin was ashen, now, and she perspired profusely. As he watched her she involuntarily shifted from sweating to shivering. Taking the crocheted blanket from the couch, Luis covered her. She managed to sit, clutching it in her hands and staring out the window.

The teakettle whistled and Luis returned to the kitchen. Then he took the tea back to Mrs. Weatherby—she didn't move when he set it down. Her eyes were open and staring out through the window.

Luis watched her chest and lips. She wasn't breathing, and she didn't blink when he passed his hand in front of her eyes. Luis rejected the idea of trying to revive her. She wouldn't want to be brought back to the loneliness and the pain of grief. Besides, she had died as she wanted, with a friend.

Luis left her in her chair by the window, her head turned to the meadow, her lifeless eyes forever open to take in the view. A cup of tea lay at her right and her crocheting on the floor next to her.

She would never finish the girls' bedspreads. Luis knew someday she would need to be buried, but he believed she should be entombed just this way, like a pharaoh sent to the next world with everything he needed. Luis wished he could seal this room in concrete with Mrs. Weatherby just as she was. A thousand years later some archeologist could open it and see how one woman's life had ended.

It bothered Luis when he speculated that the archeologists of the future might think she had died alone and friendless. It hadn't been that way. She had had two good friends in her final hours. One a dinosaur, who had come out of time and befriended her, and the other a human, no relation, who now grieved over her death.

Luis left, closing and locking the door and went to his own ransacked apartment. On his couch he listened to the sounds of the gunfire in the street. It was more sporadic now. Someone was winning the battle. Luis dozed for a few minutes and when he woke there was silence in the streets. He waited another hour before he ventured out.

When he peeked through the front door of the building he saw two soldiers walking up the street. They wore helmets but carried their guns casually, as if they felt safe from fire.

When Luis stepped from the doorway and called to them, their guns pointed at him and he instinctively put his hands in the air. When the guardsmen demanded identification, Luis started a long explanation about being mugged and losing his wallet and pointed at his injured head to prove it. Though they listened skeptically, they only searched him for weapons and then escorted him down the street to a looted furniture store used as a holding area. He joined a room full of old men and women who were waiting for transportation.

An hour later Luis was called to a desk and a woman soldier asked him a long list of questions and filled out two forms with the answers. Luis gave her Steve's phone number and address, but she reminded him the phones were not working, then sent him back to sit with the old men and women.

Luis sat against the wall with his head on his arms, finally dozing off. Someone shook him awake. It was the woman soldier. She was moving all the sleeping people out. He followed the crowd to find two canvas-covered army trucks and crawled in the back of one.

Luis watched out the back of the truck as he left his neighborhood behind. Bodies lay here and there in the streets, some wearing the colors of the Zombies, then in the colors of the Diablos. Finally the truck left the bodies and the burned-out buildings behind.

When the truck stopped, soldiers began helping the passengers out. Luis looked for a familiar face but found none, so he pushed through the crowd, trying to find a street sign to orient himself. He was nearly to the edge of the crowd when someone slammed into him from behind, wrapping her arms around his waist—his daughter Charlotte, hugging him.

His other kids—the older ones—ran up behind. After he had hugged each one he looked up to see Melinda with tears in her eyes, and he opened his arms for her. They both cried.

After a minute they separated and kissed and then looked into each other's eyes. Melinda immediately noticed the blood in his hair.

"Luis, you're hurt—" she began.

Luis shushed her with a finger to her lips, nodding to the kids. He didn't want to scare them. Melinda, comprehending, quickly changed the subject.

"We were so worried. Steve and I both tried to look for you, but we couldn't get through. It's almost like a war."

"It is a war. Where's Cinda?"

"With Steve and Tanya. She's fine. What about Mrs. Weatherby?"

Luis shook his head furtively, knowing Melinda and Charlotte would understand.

"She's with a friend now. A friend who'll never leave her," he explained. Later he'd report the details.

Then Luis picked little Katrina up in his arms, and he and his family walked off into what was left of the city.

57. Moonscape

Major Cox called today with a most bizarre report. He claimed that the pond at his Sussex home had disappeared. I investigated, as was my duty, to find it indeed was gone, boat, dock, water, fish and all, leaving nothing but a muddy hole.

—Constable Clarke, October 6, 1921

Honolulu, Hawaii
PostQuilt: Wednesday, 3:25 a.m. AHT

The moon photos were spread all over Dr. Wang's office. Carrollee and Emmett had divided them up for analysis. Few university classes were going on, and they might have recruited a couple of graduate students to help them. But they were scientists, and if there was a discovery to make here, Carrollee and Emmett wanted to be the first to make it.

Each of them compared the new pictures with file photos taken long before the disaster. Each also used a schematic of the moon's surface that pointed out features and labeled major craters. Every new photo was scanned quickly, first for obvious changes, and then painstakingly viewed through a magnifying glass, comparing it with those from the file.

They flipped a coin to decide who got to examine the Sea of Tranquility. Emmett won, but Carrollee looked over his shoulder anyway, trying to spot something before he did. But they found nothing that varied from the plates they had pulled from the files. Frustrated, they divided up the rest of the lunar landing sites and examined each of those areas carefully. After that they began systematically searching the surface of the moon. Emmett sat up and stretched his arms high over his head. His photos were on Dr. Wang's desk and he'd been bending over them most of the night, and his back ached.

"My back is killing me," he complained.

"At least you got the desk," Carrollee pointed out, rubbing her own back, and then her eyes.

Carrollee was on the floor on her hands and knees, wearing a white knit shirt with white Bermuda shorts. White would be fine on most people, but Carrollee was not most people. She'd added a shiny white belt, white socks, white shoes, white globular earrings the size of Ping-Pong balls, and a large white barrette. A white fanny pack had been deposited in a chair. In a blizzard she would be invisible, better camouflaged than Russian snow troops. Emmett regarded her briefly, rubbed his back again, and then leaned over the desk.

He had gotten the focal point of his magnifying glass just right when he felt Carrollee behind him. Then she put her hands on his hips and pressed hers against his bottom. As soon as her hands touched him, his breathing stopped, and his heart started to pound. He felt her hands massaging his shoulders, but Emmett knew he would never relax with her body pushed up against him. Her hands worked their way down his spine, and he began to breathe again, not deeply, in relaxation, but in short ragged bursts. He remained bent over the desk, enjoying the sensations and changes taking place in his body. It's only a friendly back rub, he told himself, over and over. This may not be the signal to cross the line from professional friends to something more personal.

Emmett had nearly convinced himself it was an innocent gesture when Carrollee stopped her massage and folded herself over Emmett's back, slipping her hands around his waist, and then sliding them up to rub his chest. Her breasts against his back and her hands on his chest told him her true intentions. Then she gave a ragged sigh, and put her head down on his back.

"I want a back rub next," she said, and then added, "or something to relax me. Too bad we didn't find something in the obvious spots, like the Apollo sites. I thought you had a good idea there for a while."

The hands were still rubbing Emmett's chest, sending warm rushes through his body, and he was afraid if he spoke she would stop.

"You know, I just thought of something," Carrollee said.

Carrollee's hands stopped moving and her head came up, although she remained folded over his back.

"How did they map those landing sites? Weren't there some missions before the Apollo landings? . . . I mean, unmanned missions?"

With that Carrollee stood up, her mind and mood now clearly back on the problem at hand. Emmett wanted to shout at her not to think so much, but he answered her.

"Sure, they had to pick a good landing site, so they crashed some unmanned photographic craft into the moon. Landed a couple too, I think." Emmett stood up, shaking his head to disperse the fog of lust. "They had a terrible time with them—they were called Rangers. Yeah, now I remember. It took six or seven tries to get one out of Earth orbit, and then they missed the moon entirely. There were some other failures too." Emmett searched while he talked, looking for the *Space Almanac* he used to locate the Apollo landing sites. When he found it he looked up Ranger. "Three Rangers crashed into the moon."

"Give me the sites."

"Ranger seven impacted in the Sea of Moons; Ranger eight in the Sea of Tranquility, and Ranger nine in the highlands near the Sea of Clouds."

"You take the Sea of Clouds and I'll take the Sea of Moons."

Carrollee rushed back to her photos on the floor and shuffled through them, matching the photos to her *Lunar Atlas*. Emmett, suddenly feeling competitive, leafed hastily through his own photographs.

Twenty minutes later they were still frustrated.

"Carrollee, we're expecting too much. This is only a theory. Even if it's accurate it doesn't mean there would be any evidence of it on the moon."

Carrollee listened, but her face showed she was unconvinced. She was in her research mode, a hunter after a prey. Without a kill, a discovery, she would be terribly frustrated.

"You said they landed a couple of craft too? Rangers?"

"No, they were called . . . Searcher . . . no, Surveyor." Emmett turned to his *Almanac* again and found the surveyor project. He read through the section quickly. "Okay, we have landings in the Ocean of Storms . . . two there, Sea of Tranquility, Central Bay . . . there's a crash site there too, and the highland region near Tycho Brahe. You start with the Ocean of Storms, and I'll start with Central Bay. Whoever's done first gets Tycho Brahe," Emmett added to heat up the competition.

They both examined their photos, trying to match them as quickly as possible. The early competitive rush, however, soon faded as the monotony of correlating details returned. Emmett began blanking out and found he had to review sections. Convinced he had covered all of Central Bay, he searched Tycho Brahe, mildly happy that he had beaten Carrollee.

Taking a break, he decided to stretch, and needle her a little, but when he looked at her the back rub feelings came back. She was bent over on the floor, her bottom up and head down, staring through the magnifying glass. Suppressing an urge to fold himself over her, as she had him, he stared for a full minute, savoring her body and his feeling. Then he realized she hadn't moved her magnifying glass in all that time.

"You've found something?"

"I don't know. This is peculiar though. It might just be a shadow."

Emmett grabbed his magnifying glass and got down next to Carrollee.

"Right here," she said, pointing. "Right there in that crater. I think it's called Flamsteed Crater."

Since there wasn't room for both of their heads, Carrollee leaned back so Emmett could get a good look. He looked first at the *Lunar Atlas* and then at Bridgette's photo. This was no shadow, and what he saw hit him like a slap in the face.

"This is it. This is what Dr. Paulson is looking for. We've got to get this to him, but how? We need a high-definition fax machine."

"My brother Richard's in the military, remember."

"Great! This could be important—What am I saying? This is incredible. I'll type a message while you call him."

When everything was arranged they turned to leave and Carrollee rubbed Emmett's back with her hand. Emmett warmed at her touch and slipped his arm around Carrollee's shoulders, pulling her close and crossing the border from friendly to personal.

"When we get back," he suggested, "maybe I can give you a back rub."

Carrollee smiled and then said, "*Très bien.*"

---

58. The Guys

I will hand you over to brutal men, men skilled in destruction.

—Ezekiel 21:31

Forest, former site of Portland, Oregon
PostQuilt: Wednesday, 6:44 a.m. PST

Ripman did come back in the morning, but with a take-it-or-leave-it offer.

"I'll take you to the edge of dinosaur country, then you're on your own."

"What about John and Cubby? They're your friends, Ripman, your good friends," Ellen said.

"Friends will get you killed in here. Hey, I hope they make it, but it's not my problem. You want me to get you out of here or not?"

Ellen had no choice. There was little chance she could find John on her own. With Carl and the guys on the loose and dinosaurs to worry about, she needed help. Besides, Angie deserved to get out of this alive. They had known each other for only a few days, yet they were friends for life.

Ripman agreed to get them out on the Carlton side and led off through the trees. His pace was brisk, and keeping up was difficult but manageable. A fall chill greeted them when they climbed out from beneath the roots of the fallen giant. It had been snug in the hole, but goose bumps brought Ellen thoughts of her coat left behind in the clearing. Still, Carl and the guys could have it, she told herself, but they were never going to have her.

Ripman kept up the fast pace of the previous day, and Ellen's chill quickly turned into a light sweat. The trail he blazed led them up and down hills, which he never tried to go around. Fortunately, the dense canopy of the giant trees prevented significant underbrush and walking was relatively easy. The occasional fallen trees were problematic, since they seemed to explode into new growth, but the detours were few. Ellen was disoriented, but it appeared that their path was the closest thing to a straight line. Tired, she began watching her feet, letting herself be absorbed by the right-left rhythm, which replaced her thoughts, and her fears for herself and for her son. Suddenly she ran into Ripman, knocking him into a stumble.

"Listen."

Ellen and Angie looked at each other and shook their heads. Ripman turned his head toward the southern sky. Ellen and Angie followed his gaze. A few seconds later they heard a distant roar, the sound of a jet. It grew louder, and they looked through the towering canopy to glimpse the plane, but it was futile. The sound reached a peak and then faded.

"This is just too weird, Ellen."

"What is, Angie?"

"Standing here in this . . . this impossible forest, with dinosaurs running around, following some teenage Jungle Jim, and having jets fly overhead."

Ellen was going to respond but then noticed Ripman's head was still cocked. She listened too and picked up a low rumble, a sound that was not the jet. He motioned them to stand still and be quiet and then padded softly up the hill. As he approached the crest he slowed, bending into a crawl. He lay still for a minute and then signaled Angie and Ellen forward. They mimicked his movements, crawling the last few feet to his side, hearing a crunching and thumping as they approached the crest. Ellen peered fearfully through the ferns at the crest and over the top but saw only trees. She was about to ask Ripman what he was looking at when Angie's finger shot out, pointing to movement in the distance. The trees were dense, but here and there through the gaps they could see dinosaurs. As she watched, she realized there were more than just a few. There was a herd.

These dinosaurs were not like the trophy Carl and the guys had killed. These were bigger, and deep green. They were angling up the side of the hill but away from them. Ellen could see the animals were traveling on all fours, measuring ten to fifteen feet at the shoulders. Three horns protruded from each forehead and an armored collar was around each neck. Their long tails were tipped with three spikes. Ellen leaned into Ripman and whispered in his ear.

"Shouldn't we get out of here?"

"Relax, they're just big cows. They don't eat people. Probably never seen a person before. There's a meadow over that way. That's where they used to be. For some reason they seem to be on the move. Let 'em pass."

They lay in the grass as the dinosaurs came closer, their noise now a cacophony. Despite Ripman's reassurance Ellen's apprehension remained until the last one disappeared into the trees. Ellen started to rise, but Ripman held her arm pulling her back down.

"We've got a problem. If we move straight ahead we cut across the path of those dinosaurs."

Ellen and Angie looked at each other, neither seeing the problem.

"Those dinosaurs are on the move for some reason. They were happily stuffing themselves with grass and ferns yesterday."

"You know what they say about greener pastures," Angie offered.

"Maybe. Maybe they're moving because they don't want to be somebody's lunch."

Ellen blanched at the thought of whatever might eat one of those dinosaurs for lunch.

"Well then, let's head back the other way and find another way around." Angie looked to Ellen for support.

"If we go that way we head back toward Carl and the guys," Ellen reasoned. "If we go in the direction the dinosaurs came from we could be heading right toward whatever was hunting them. But if we cut across . . ."

"I see," Angie said, her mind weighing the risks. "If we cut across we better move fast, since we don't know if something is following the herd, and how far back it might be."

Ripman seemed impressed and sat quietly, letting them analyze the options. Angie decided first.

"I'd rather be eaten by a dinosaur than raped by a bunch of assholes. I say our best bet is to cut straight across as fast as we can and get the hell out of this place. Remember Coop!" Angie spoke the name sadly. Ellen realized Angie was depressed over more than a senseless death. She had cared for Coop. Seeing how Angie used her sexuality to manipulate men, it had never occurred to Ellen that Angie might have feelings for those men. Because Ellen had loved only one man, she assumed Angie was the same.

"Let's go for it," Ellen said to Ripman.

Ripman was nodding his head in appreciation for their clear thinking. "El-ah-mental," he cheered.

He led off through the trees at his usual pace, but this time with occasional pauses to listen. Ellen and Angie listened too, but depended more on their eyesight. The trees were far enough apart to see quite a distance. But Ripman was right, you'd hear a dinosaur before you'd see one in this forest.

They were nearly across the track of the herd when Ripman slowed to a walk, then stopped, dropping to his knees, his eyes riveted on the ground. Ellen and Angie approached slowly, still watching for dinosaurs. Even before they reached him they could see a large pool of blood. Ellen immediately thought of John, but realized it was too much blood for him. It formed part of a trail that angled off through the trees, one corresponding to the dinosaurs' path. Suddenly Ripman's head snapped up and his face went pale.

"Come on. *Run.*"

Ellen and Angie followed Ripman, running and struggling to keep him in sight. They trusted his instincts. As they ran, they heard something coming—something big.

Cubby and John were awakened by the roar of a motorcycle engine. John felt his insecurity come back. He immediately assumed he cut the wrong wire or tube, and Cubby obviously agreed. Ripman would have blamed John too. When Cubby shot John an accusing look, he protested, "Hey, it could have been you, Cubby."

The engine was being revved, and every time it slowed it sputtered. Finally it sputtered once more and died. Cubby and John left their hiding place to get closer to the clearing, John crossing his fingers and hoping it wasn't one of the bikes he had disabled. The engine roared to life again but died almost instantly.

When the boys got closer they saw the bikes had been moved; they were now parked around the still-smoldering fire. To John's relief he couldn't tell which bikes he had worked on. He could recognize only the deputy's gaudy blue one; the rest were mostly chrome and engine.

All four of the men were crowded around one bike. After a few minutes one of them climbed on and jumped down on the starter. After three kicks the engine roared. The rider revved it to keep it going while another one did something on the engine. It died again. The rider climbed off angrily and began yelling at the one working on the engine. They traded places and tried it again. It took eight kicks to start and died almost immediately. It didn't start again after that.

Carl, his leg bandaged with a folded shirt, shouted the guys down and then took control. After they argued for a while, Carl and two others picked up their rifles and headed into the forest. The third man picked up his rifle and watched the others go, then he went back to the bike and kicked it three times till it rocked over onto its side.

Cubby pulled on John's sleeve, and they slipped deeper into the forest.

"Do you want to take him?" Cubby asked.

"How? He's watching now, and he's got a rifle. We couldn't get far enough across that meadow to hit him with that pistol before he'd plug us both. Besides, I've never shot a pistol before, have you?"

"Once, except it wasn't like this one exactly." Cubby doubtfully looked over the gun. "I think this is the safety," he said weakly. "Okay. Let's follow the others then. Once we're sure Ripman got your mom and her friend away safe, we'll head for my house."

They detoured wide around the end of the clearing and

headed in the direction they had seen Carl lead the other men. With Cubby in the lead, they moved quickly, nearly jogging so they could catch up. Soon they spotted one man in the distance, carrying his rifle behind his neck with his arms looped over the stock on one side and the barrel on the other. He looked lackadaisical, as if he didn't give a damn.

Cubby and John could not see the others, but when they heard a voice to their right they dropped back, easily keeping out of sight. Occasionally they caught glimpses of the other men. Carl was limping along, the wound in his leg apparently hurting but not enough to suit John. He hoped Ripman had dipped that arrow in dinosaur shit before he stuck him with it. It might give him some incurable prehistoric infection.

The sound of a jet engine stopped the men as they looked up, but the plane passed quickly and the men resumed their search. The boys soon realized the men weren't following tracks, and they became confident that John's mom and Ripman would get away.

When they heard a distant animal roar, the men froze and checked their rifles. Another roar sounded closer and they marked the direction and moved toward it. Knotting together in a small group, they followed Carl, who limped in the lead.

The next roar was much closer—the dinosaur was coming toward them. John spurted ahead to catch Cubby and pulled his arm to stop him.

"Let 'em go. I hope the dino eats them."

Cubby looked thoughtful for a minute, then nodded. "Yeah. Ripman's long gone by now."

Then they heard the scream—a woman's scream.

Ripman pounded uphill and down, running full speed. Angie and Ellen soon lost him in the forest ahead. But they kept on the same path, following blindly. Ellen, ahead, quickly saw Angie was falling behind. Pounding up to the top of a rise, Ellen intended to wait for her friend. A downhill start would get her to top speed as quickly as possible. At the top Ripman's voice came out of the tall grass.

"Get down!"

Ellen dropped down next to Ripman, disappearing into the grass. Angie was having trouble with the hill, barely trotting by the time she reached the top. Ellen pulled her down. Angie wheezed and Ellen gasped nearly as hard. Ripman lay quietly, trying to listen, shushing them over and over. When they caught their breaths, Ripman turned his head to listen to the forest.

"Won't it follow the blood?" Ellen asked. "Why would it come after us when there's all those dinosaurs to eat? We're too small, aren't we?"

Ripman, irritated by the noise of the questions, ignored Ellen for a full minute. Finally he answered, "If it's a carnivore it's probably following the herd because that's its food supply, but if it just ate one of those suckers it's not going to be hungry."

"So it's not dangerous?" Angie suggested.

"It's more dangerous to us. If it smells us it might get curious. It can always pick up the trail of that herd. A full belly means it can afford to explore, look for new food. Easier food."

"Us," Ellen concluded.

"Just a little cheesecake for dessert," Angie added with a false laugh.

"Quiet," Ripman said suddenly.

Ellen listened hard and picked out the distant sounds almost as soon as Ripman, who lay still waiting.

The density of the forest and the dinosaur's deep brownish green coloring made the carnivore difficult to see. It walked on two powerful back legs, leaning forward so far it looked as if it would fall. Somewhere behind it was a massive counterbalancing tail. It had long forelegs, nine or ten feet in length, and a huge head that was mostly jaws. Deep breathing sounds rumbled past bloodied teeth, and it swung its head back and forth as it walked.

Ellen started to get up to run, but Ripman grabbed her arm and kept her down. Then he leaned into her and whispered, "Slowly and quietly. If you can't keep up this time, I'll leave you. Tell your friend."

Ellen relayed that to Angie in a whisper, and Angie's face fell. Ripman inched his way down the hill away from the dinosaur, moving as little grass as possible. His bow was still slung over his shoulder, but Ellen realized it would be of little use. She and Angie followed, keeping their heads below the top of the grasses. Halfway down the hill Ripman turned and padded softly through the forest, his speed and noise increasing as he put distance between himself and the dinosaur.

Again, Ellen and Angie followed, but their best speed would not keep Ripman in sight for long. Angie pressed her hand against her waist, wheezing again and slowing. Ellen trotted beside her. They settled into a low running rhythm, a pace Angie seemed able to sustain.

After a mile they heard the roar.

Ellen looked back to see the dinosaur's head staring at them from around a tree. As they gaped in horror, the dinosaur's mouth opened wide, and another deafening roar rattled their nerves. Angie poured the rest of her energy into her feet and picked up the pace, as Ellen, risking another look behind, saw the dinosaur in pursuit, gaining fast.

Suddenly they broke free of the forest into a small clearing. On the other side was a section of tumbled-down forest—smoke drifted up from the far side of the clearing. Ripman's head appeared above the grass and his arms began waving. His voice drifted over the clearing. "Here, this way!"

Angie and Ellen raced across the clearing, too afraid to risk a look behind them. Ripman was waving frantically, signaling them to pass him and keep on going. As they passed, Ripman dragged a flaming bundle behind them, setting fire to the grass. When Ripman passed her at a dead run, she looked back to see the dinosaur pound through the fire, extinguishing the small flame with its massive feet. Now Ellen knew they weren't going to make it.

Ripman made it to the fallen trees first, dodging around the massive foliage of one and climbing over the trunk of the next, using broken limbs like a ladder. Ellen followed his lead, throwing herself over the log, panicked by the crashing sounds of the dinosaur behind her. She reached back to pull Angie down with her, only to see her friend silhouetted on the top of the tree trunk behind her, leaning forward to roll down the other side. But she never made it. Towering over Angie was the dinosaur. A nine-foot foreleg with razor sharp claws swept the length of the tree, shearing off limbs six inches thick. Angie screamed when she saw the arm coming toward her, and with a whipping motion it caught her full in the side. Her left arm, across her body, was severed above the elbow as the claws buried themselves into her torso, and it tumbled down Ellen's side of the trunk disappearing into the grass six feet from Ellen's face. When the dinosaur swiped Angie off the tree and threw her back in the clearing, it followed the body with a triumphant roar.

Ellen lay in the foliage under the trunk paralyzed with horror, seeing only the blood stains in the grass. Then she felt someone pulling on her, jerking her out of the foliage.

"We've got to go while it's busy. It won't take long."

Ellen became an automaton. She followed Ripman over and under trees carelessly, her footing and grip mattered little. She tripped, fell, and fell again. Her pants and blouse tore and shredded. Her skin underneath was scratched and cut by broken limbs. She felt nothing and saw nothing except Angie's blood in the grass.

Every time she fell she got up more slowly. Soon Ripman was helping her to her feet every time and supporting her with an arm around her waist. They worked their way across the fallen trees and to a small stand of upright trees, then back into fallen trees. Sometime after that Ripman pushed her up onto another tree with his hands on her bottom. When she reached the top she collapsed spread-eagled, her eyes in a glassy stare, her mind filled with bloody grass. This time Ripman didn't help her off the top.

Shouts and laughter filled her ears. Slowly the bloody grass was replaced by another image. It was Carl's laughing face. She forced her eyes to focus and realized the face was real. It was Carl and behind him were the guys. Carl smiled, showing all his teeth.

"Now, where were we?"

59. The Toolmaker

According to the rabbinical authority Rashi, ancient tradition knows of periodic collapses of the firmament, one of which occurred in the days of the Deluge, and which repeated themselves at intervals of 1,656 years.

—Immanuel Velikovsky, *Worlds in Collision*

Warm Springs Indian Reservation, Oregon
PostQuilt: Wednesday, 7:10 a.m. PST

Moose was riding on the dashboard, stretched out and soaking up the rays of the morning sun while Sarah was curled up on the passenger seat with a blanket. The two of them had gorged on raisins and apples. Behind them, tucked safely in a cabinet, was a rifle with a bore big enough to bring down an elephant, and three boxes of ammunition. Colter was retracing the route Dr. Coombs had taken, except Colter had a different purpose in mind. Dr. Coombs, Dr. Piltcher, and Petra had come to explore, to understand what had happened. Colter was going back for only one reason: to kill the monsters that had taken Petra from him, and especially one. He didn't know how he was going to get it, but he wasn't leaving without its head.

Colter knew he was close now. The road was nothing but two ruts. He cleared the top of the hill, and then rolled to a stop, surprised. He expected to see the dinosaurs, but not one fifty feet away, walking down the road ahead of him. When it heard Colter's engine the animal turned and looked at the RV.

It was like the one that had killed Dr. Coombs. Colter's anger flared. He set the brake and dug the rifle out of the cabinet, checking the clip to make sure he had a full load, and then jacked a round into the chamber. When he aimed the rifle through the front window at the rear of the walking dinosaur, he looked down the sights to see Moose's head staring from the end of the barrel.

Colter put the weapon down and shooed Moose out of the window, and then carried Sarah, blanket and all, to the back of the RV. To keep them busy and out of the way he put a few raisins on top of Moose's cabinet and a bigger pile on the floor for Sarah. Moose immediately attacked Sarah's pile, knowing his would still be there when he was done. Colter snickered. He liked Moose. He was a thinker.

Now the dinosaur was well down the road, so Colter released the brake and pulled up on its left. The creature kept walking but looked nervously at the RV rumbling along beside it. Something was wrong, Colter thought. Why wasn't it scared? Colter pulled ahead of the dinosaur and parked, getting out with his rifle. He checked the load. There was one round in the chamber and eight in the clip. He had three more clips tucked into a fanny pack.

Colter scanned the area, making sure none of the big carnivores were around. When he did, he noticed other dinosaurs like the one on the road were milling around in the prairie grass bordering their meadow. Everything looked the same as when he left, except the grass. It was wilting. Not enough water? Colter wondered. Maybe it was the cool air. The dinosaur land *looked* almost tropical, but if it was too cold for the grass and brush, maybe it was too cold for the dinosaurs. Maybe they were dying. Colter smiled at the thought. Then something blew across the road—one of Petra's T-shirts he'd thrown out the RV window. Colter flushed at the thought of Petra, and he turned, bringing the rifle to his shoulder. The dinosaur was lumbering toward him at a slow pace. Colter waited with his finger on the trigger, letting the dinosaur come closer. He didn't want to miss. He knew the head and neck were heavily armored with bone, and he needed to hit it dead on to kill it instantly. If he just wounded it, it would be as dangerous as the mother whose egg they had stolen.

Wait till you see the whites of their eyes, he said to himself.

The dinosaur came on straight toward Colter. Slowly he began to pull back on the trigger, the sights lined up between the dinosaur's widely spaced eyes. Just before he pulled the trigger it turned, angling to Colter's left to go around him. Colter kept his aim, but the head began to swing, occasionally blocking his shot with the bony collar. Colter's frustration grew, and he lowered the rifle. He wanted a head shot, but he didn't want to get too far from the safety of the RV. Frustrated, he raised the gun to his shoulder, aimed at the neck of the passing dinosaur, and pulled the trigger.

The slug entered just in front of the dinosaur's shoulder. But the dinosaur only jumped from fright at the gun's loud report—then it jogged down the road. Colter jacked another cartridge into the chamber and chased the animal. He didn't have to go far. Suddenly it collapsed to its knees, breathing deeply through its nose, and then fell to its side, its chest heaving. Colter watched it dying, a feeling of deep satisfaction filling his soul. After a few minutes the breathing became irregular and Colter worried it might die by itself. So he put another slug into its throat and then another into its exposed chest. It didn't breathe after that.

"Man, that felt good!" Colter screamed. Then he put two more rounds into the dinosaur's belly and one into an eye. "Yes!" he screamed. "How does it feel to be the hunted? Huh? See what a toolmaker can do? Huh? That's why you guys are extinct, you dead piece of crap!"

Colter enjoyed the kill for another few minutes and then walked back to the RV. It was going to be a good day. These evolutionary rejects would learn who the real top predator was, and Colter would be the teacher.

He looked around for another target; the other monoclonius, scared by the sound of the gunfire, were positioning themselves defensively in the prehistoric clearing. Colter jeered, then screamed down the hill at them: "It ain't gonna do you any good. I got the magic!" Then he held the rifle above his head, whooped and danced, and ran back to the RV.

He parked the RV near its earlier spot. Debris from the dinosaur attack, as well as Petra's clothes, littered the clearing. Leaving Moose and Sarah in the RV, Colter approached the dinosaurs. Six of them stood lined up in two rows. Their heads were down, the horns pointed at Colter. He walked parallel to the dinosaur wall, watching the horns track him every step of the way. When he reached the end of the line he lifted his rifle, lined the sights up between the eyes of the last dinosaur, and pulled the trigger. The rifle kicked into his shoulder, and the loud report startled the lines of dinosaurs, but they didn't bolt. The one on the end took the slug just above the snout. Colter was disappointed, he thought for sure at this distance he could put it right between the dinosaur's eyes. But it didn't matter. The dinosaur's front legs buckled, and it dropped to its knees. Its back legs seemed locked and held its rear haunches high. Then its eyes closed, and with the back legs still locked, it tipped left and fell onto its side, dead.

The back row of dinosaurs moved nervously back and forth, swinging their heads. They looked like they wanted to bolt for the taller brush, but their instinct told them staying in the line was the best defense. Colter smiled. These poor dumb bastards were too stupid even to save themselves. He walked down the line to the next dinosaur. When he was directly in front, it pawed the ground. Colter raised his rifle and was about to shoot when a dinosaur in the back moved out of line and ran behind the one he was about to kill. Colter froze but held the moving dinosaur in his scope. The newcomer trotted up to the dead one, pushed it in the back with its horns, then raised its head and bellowed, prodding the carcass again and again. It then turned toward Colter, put its head down, and charged.

This time Colter's life was on the line. The huge monster was picking up speed and closing fast, so he kept the rifle aimed between its eyes, fired, and then dove to the side. When he hit the grass he rolled to get well clear of the monster, and swung his rifle up to fire another shot if needed. It wasn't. The bullet had hit the dinosaur in the head, killing it instantly, but the momentum carried it into a skid, then a tumble.

Colter crawled forward and then stood, using the dinosaur's body to steady his gun. He sighted on another dinosaur and fired. This time the shot was wide and buried itself somewhere in the dinosaur's neck, but it roared in pain and began swinging its head, then turned and staggered away. Now the rest of the herd bolted for the tall brush and were soon at a full gallop. Colter fired another round at the wounded dinosaur, hitting it in the rump; it roared again but kept walking even as blood streamed down its left rump and leg. When Colter put another round into it, the retreating dinosaur only whimpered and Colter was disappointed, but at least it bled more. Another shot got no further response, and as Colter watched, the bleeding dinosaur walked across the clearing and disappeared into the tall brush.

Colter was satisfied. It was heading into the heart of the dinosaur land and bleeding bad enough to attract a pack of scavengers. He smiled. This was one dinner party he planned on crashing.

He returned to the RV and packed some water, a little food, and a box of ammunition. Then he stretched out on a mattress on the floor to take a nap, his hands behind his head. He wanted to give the scavengers time to gather before he went after them. Besides, he was days behind in his sleep. Sarah came out from under a pile and sniffed all around Colter, looking for food. When she was sure there wasn't any, she flopped down next to him, pushing her head into the warmth of his armpit. Her closeness bothered Colter, bringing back memories of Petra, but he soon fell asleep.

When he woke, Moose was stretched out on his chest, but as soon as he stirred the animal was up the wall to the top of the cabinet. Sarah stirred but didn't wake. Colter realized she was shivering and he covered her with a blanket. It was just too cold for them, he realized. Colter remembered Dr. Coombs or Dr. Piltcher talking about the extinction of the dinosaurs. He remembered one of the theories was that a comet slammed into the earth, kicking up enough debris to block out the sun and bring winter to the entire planet. The dinosaurs just plain froze to death. Colter hadn't paid much attention to the theory then, but he could see that Moose and Sarah weren't equipped for an eastern Oregon fall, let alone winter. They were both lethargic and slept much of the time.

Of course there's another thing that might have happened to the dinosaurs, Colter told himself, something Dr. Piltcher or Dr. Coombs never would have thought of. Maybe the dinosaurs died off because they all came to the future and were blown away . . . by me! Colter frowned as a memory of Petra drifted through his mind. Then he put out a bowl of water and more fruit for Moose and Sarah and left.

Outside the RV, the position of the sun told him he had been asleep for hours. The carcasses nearby were still intact. Probably the gunfire had scared the scavengers deeper into the forest. But there was still the one that got away, leaving a blood trail, and it should have drawn a crowd by now. Checking that all his clips were fully loaded, Colter slid a hunting knife in a sheath onto his belt, picked up his pack, and left the RV. The trail was easy to follow. It led him straight into the tall brush, and toward the clearing where the big carnivore had eaten Dr. Piltcher. It also led toward the lake where that walking fish had killed Petra. That suited Colter fine. First he would kill the dinner guests, and then he would camp by the lake and wait. If he had to, he'd wade out into the lake making himself bait. But he wasn't leaving until that walking fish paid for what it did to Petra.

There was so much blood, Colter guessed the animal must have a severed artery, but the track went on and on. He was approaching the clearing when he heard growling. Making sure the rifle had a bullet in the chamber, he crept forward. The monoclonius had made it through to the clearing and its carcass—picked nearly clean from neck collar to tail—was fifty feet from the brush line. All of its ribs were bare. Three of the fifteen-foot carnivores were in the clearing chewing on rib bones, and half a dozen of the three-footers were reaching around looking for tidbits. It was just what Colter wanted, a shooting gallery.

Colter crept right to the edge of the clearing, crawling under a bush until he had a clear shot. Then he lined up his first one, aiming at the head of one of the fifteen-footers. As its head came up with something red from the body cavity it turned to look around. When the head was parallel to Colter he fired and it screamed in pain. The other dinosaurs froze at the sound of the rifle, trying to spot the danger, their heads pointed up. Colter realized that in this food chain, none of them would think to look under a bush for an enemy.

The wounded dinosaur was using its small front legs to paw at his jaw. Colter, skilled from his first killing spree, turned and shot another of the fifteen-footers in the side, leaving the first wounded dinosaur for later. The second dinosaur screamed like the first and spun, looking for its attacker. Blinded by its pain and rage it sunk its teeth into its wounded brother's neck. The first dinosaur crumped and bellowed and the fight was on. The dinosaurs fell, rolling to the ground. The first one still had its teeth in the neck of its friend, but the one on the bottom was using its three toes to rip at the belly of its attacker. The noise was deafening, but Colter couldn't have been happier. He loved it. They were killing each other.

Colter decided to add the last dinosaur to the fight, the one who had backed off a few feet and was watching the fight from a safe distance. He put a slug into its chest. But this dinosaur simply shuddered and stood dumbly, watching. Colter shot it in the leg, trying to get a reaction. This time it spun around and Colter shot it in the tail. When it spun again, Colter excitedly repeated the tail shot—again and again as the beast whirled and shrieked, ten times in all. It took two shots at the head before he dropped the spinner.

By now, the dinosaur fight was over. The one on the bottom had died in the grasp of its brother. Colter took aim to kill the winner but never fired the shot.

Something was coming up behind him, and from the sound of the crashing brush, something big. He realized it was almost on top of him, its progress covered by the noise of the gun and the dinosaur fight. He rolled onto his back and looked up through the brush. There, towering three stories above him, was the dinosaur that had chased Colter and killed Dr. Piltcher. He was about to shoot when he realized the dinosaur wasn't looking at him. It didn't seem to know he was there. Instead it was looking into the clearing at the remaining carnivore.

Colter began to worry about the dino's feet. If it kept coming it might step on him. He quietly got to his knees. He couldn't get all the way up without noisily pushing branches out of his way. Colter watched the huge legs for movement, but nothing happened. Then he heard the loud sounds of a dinosaur sniffing and saw the giant's head dropping toward his bush, where it paused and inhaled loudly and deeply. With its head low over the brush it bellowed, blasting Colter with its warm putrid breath. It remembered him.

Colter pushed the rifle up into the bush above him until the barrel pointed up. Then he steadied the gun and pulled the trigger. The dinosaur took the slug in its snout and blood gushed from its left nostril. The dinosaur reared, blinded by its agony, and Colter slithered out from under the bush, then turned just in time to see three huge, clawed toes, swinging toward his head. He rolled out of the way and came up firing wildly, hitting the dinosaur in the side. It didn't flinch. Instead, it turned toward Colter, a murderous gleam in its eyes.

Colter bolted into the clearing, running past the cringing fifteen-footer, hoping the big monster would pick on something closer to its size. It didn't work. As the monster followed him, Colter had a terrifying feeling of déjà vu—running from the monster again, toward the trees where Dr. Piltcher had been eaten, and the lake where Petra had been taken.

Hours had passed, and with each one Petra had become more miserable. She was terrified of the fish, she was in throbbing pain, and she had a new fear: She was afraid of falling asleep, of moving and alerting the fish to the life still in her. So Petra spent the hours lying motionless, enduring the pain, and fighting to keep herself conscious. She spent most of the hours grieving for Dr. Coombs and Dr. Piltcher, and fearing for herself. Strangely, she never worried for Colter. The last time she'd seen him he was swimming after her, but somehow she knew he was safe. But was he looking for her? No, he was probably back at the RV with Moose and Sarah. She hoped he was grieving for her. An image of Colter sitting in the RV, knees pulled up to his chest, head down and crying, flashed through her mind. It was too much for her. She began to cry over Colter's grief, over her own death. In her exhaustion and pain she lost control and one sob wracked her body. It was enough. The fish stirred.

Petra felt the fish rock back and forth against her back as it struggled to its rudimentary feet. Petra lay there too exhausted to be terrified, too exhausted for anything but resignation. She lay there motionless waiting to see what came next. She would fight. But there was little life left in her. Too little to fight long.

The fish's scales scraped skin off her bare back and tore at her panties, shredding them and the flesh underneath. Then it was up and moving. Petra listened and waited, sure it knew *she* had moved. But it walked deep into the den and began to feed. Petra's body ached from lying motionless for hours, and her ankle was still throbbing, but her head was clearer. It still ached, but now the blinding pain was reduced to a bad headache.

The walking fish finished its meal and then waddled back

toward Petra. It paused by her back and sniffed up and down her body, pausing at her bottom. Petra realized it was smelling the fresh blood. The fish was confused. Probably few of its meals bled. It sniffed higher up onto her back and then pushed her again. This time she resisted slightly, trying to mimic rigor mortis. After one more push, the fish snorted, the warm wet spray from its nostrils coating Petra's back. As Petra lay there, eyes wide open, the fish padded to the pool and splashed into the water.

Petra counted to five hundred and then moved slowly. Her head throbbed when she rolled over and sat up, but she hung on to consciousness. The pool was glowing much brighter now, making Petra wonder how long she had been in the den. She scooted her bottom across the stone until her feet were dangling in the water, so cold it brought out the ache in her ankle. It also revived her, however. She sat there breathing deeply, trying to oxygenate her blood for what might be a long swim. Her own feeble efforts might not be enough to reach the surface. Finally she sucked in air, filling her lungs, and let her body slip down into the pool.

As soon as she was below the surface, she pushed off hard from the edge of the pool. Only one leg was working, so she had little speed. She kept her eyes open, focused on the brightest glow ahead of her. Mostly she pulled herself along by grasping on the rocks that lined the entry tunnel. She made slow progress, however, and her air was running out. The glow was brighter, she was sure of that, but a ceiling still hung over her. She kicked and pulled again, desperate to clear the overhang. She had only seconds of air left when she turned, swam out, and kicked upward. Her lungs demanded air and she felt faint—then she broke the surface.

He made the treeline a few steps ahead of the monster and darted around the trunks. Still the beast came on, shearing off limbs and bulldozing smaller trees. This time it wasn't going to let the forest keep him from his prey. Colter knew he was little more than snack-size for this beast, but this wasn't about hunger; his tormentor had a personal mission. That was fine with Colter; his was personal too.

At the lake shore, the enraged monster was still forcing itself through the trees. It was perfect. The beast had little maneuvering room and Colter could hide behind a tree and take his time pumping out lead, one well-placed shot at a time. A large limb lay at the edge of the little wood, and Colter turned toward it. The monster was still coming, still angry; the snapping of big and small limbs filled the air.

Petra gasped and sucked in fresh, oxygen-rich air. Her starved brain cleared itself and her headache faded slightly. Now she found herself too weak to tread water and kicking with only one leg was nearly useless. Petra turned in the water, scanning for the fish, and saw the shore was close. She stretched out in the water and began swimming, one weak stroke at a time.

The shore, with its grove of trees, inched closer. Petra thought it might be the grove where Dr. Piltcher had died. She knew there was a tree there she could climb. It wouldn't save her from that big monster; Dr. Piltcher had proved that, but it would keep her safe long enough to rest and get some strength back. Suddenly something moved in the woods ahead. A figure jumped over a large fallen branch and then turned its back to the lake. She recognized it: Colter.

Colter was exhilarated as he planned the perfect shot. He decided to aim about where a lung should be. That should slow it down in case he had to run again. A lungful of blood should cut you down to size, he silently told his enemy.

Colter smiled and began to squeeze the trigger, but then he heard something new. It was coming from behind him, the sound of splashing and dripping water. Something was coming out of the lake.

He turned at the sounds behind him to see a ghostly stick figure emerging from the water. It was a human figure, pale, white, and deathly, and looked zombielike as it walked through the shallows. Most horrifying of all, though, was its resemblance to Petra. Colter knew he was losing his mind. Petra was dead. She had been at the bottom of the lake since yesterday. She couldn't be alive. Yet here was her body returning from its watery grave. Unnerved, he slumped to the ground with his back to the fallen limb and stared at the phantom, forgetting about the dinosaur behind him.

* * *

Petra staggered along the bottom toward Colter, wading through the water and pushing herself along with her hands. She'd just about made it to shore when Colter suddenly turned and pointed a rifle at her. Petra froze when she saw the look on Colter's face; he meant to kill her. Then she saw the monster behind him, and it was coming.

Now the dead body limped through knee-high water, favoring its left leg. Colter remembered the fish chomping down on that leg. It must still hurt Petra, Colter thought. But why would a corpse limp? No, death was a painless state. That's the only way it made sense. That realization snapped him up short and he stood and stepped toward Petra.

"Petra? Petra? Is that you?" Colter shouted.

It was. And she was alive. As he watched, Petra pointed a finger at something behind him, but before she could speak there was movement in the water behind her, the walking fish was racing toward Petra.

"Run, Petra!" Colter shouted. "It's behind you!"

Petra's eyes were still fixed beyond Colter, but at his warning she glanced behind. She broke into a run—but the pitiful run of an exhausted, lame person. The walking fish was in the shallows now, and using its flipper legs to splash after Petra, its powerful tail helped to propel it forward. Colter took two steps to the right to make sure his shot would be well clear of Petra and raised his rifle and fired, the shot sailing over the fish's body and into the water. He jacked another round into the chamber and raised the rifle again, but the fish had come close to Petra. Colter hesitated, but fired a slug into the fish's back, near the tail. The fish flinched, slowed for a second, and then lunged for Petra's flailing legs, tripping her, and she belly flopped into the shallow water. When the fish lunged again, Petra's left foot disappeared between its powerful jaws.

Her head vanished in the water but she came up screaming. Now she was again too close to the fish but Colter once more raised the rifle, aimed at Petra, moved the sight slightly to the right, and fired. This time the slug hit the fish's body dead center, and it began to thrash, still holding on to Petra's leg. Colter fired again, hitting the fish just behind its jaw. The violent thrashing continued, whipping Petra's legs back and forth. She kicked at the fish, trying to dislodge her foot, and suddenly she was free, and pushing herself away with her good leg. Colter opened fire again, putting three more slugs into the fish, and finally it lay still.

"Yes! I got you, you sonovabitch!" Colter rejoiced. He was still celebrating when he heard Petra yelling, and he remembered the other dinosaur.

He spun to see a huge three-toed clawed foot swinging toward his head and started to raise his rifle, but there wasn't nearly enough time. Instead, he dropped the rifle and dove forward. He hit the ground and rolled toward the limb he'd been hiding behind, clear of the foot but not the huge tail, which swung to the left as the dinosaur turned. Colter crouched low beneath the limb, hoping it would protect him, but the tail knocked it sideways. He covered his head with his hands while the branches tore at his shirt and skin. Colter felt the limb break and its weight and the beast's tail pounding him.

Petra watched in horror. She couldn't see Colter, but the frantic turn of the dinosaur told her he was still alive. She ran to the side, then, above the din, she heard Colter's shout.

"Get the rifle, Petra! Get the rifle!"

Petra could just make out Colter's body beneath a huge fallen tree limb. Then he threw something at Petra. It landed just clear of the dinosaur and Petra approached warily. But the dinosaur was single-minded in its attack, so Petra retrieved the object—a loaded clip for the rifle—and then retreated.

She spotted the rifle under the dinosaur. There was no way to get to it except by running in the shadow of the towering behemoth.

When Colter hollered for help again, Petra trembled in indecision.

Now the dinosaur decided to get at Colter with its feet, stepping up close. With its huge three-toed foot, it clawed away turf. Its digging grew frenzied, throwing huge hunks of dirt toward Petra.

Petra was trying to time a run for the gun when the dinosaur clawed up the gun in a clod of dirt. Dodging the flying earth, she retrieved the gun—scratched and filthy. She hoped it would still work.

Suddenly Colter screamed as if he were being killed. Petra raised the gun, aimed it dead center at the dinosaur's back, and pulled the trigger. As it fired it knocked her to the ground, and she saw the dinosaur's head turning toward her.

Petra pulled on the bolt but it wouldn't move. She looked at the mechanism, then lifting it, she pulled and to her relief she saw one bullet pop out of the clip, but there wasn't another one behind it.

Petra closed the chamber. The dinosaur was turning toward her, and she knew she'd be easy prey, with no strength and little fight left. She lifted the rifle, her weak arms swaying under the weight, and aimed at the dinosaur's left leg, waiting for it to turn and expose its chest. She had to get the heart, but where was the heart? In the center? The left side? Would a single bullet do enough damage to such a huge animal? As the dinosaur turned, Petra saw its head hung low. Suddenly she changed her mind, pointed between the beast's eyes, and pulled the trigger.

The slug hit the dinosaur above the left eye, smashing through the thick skull. As bullet and bone fragments shredded the brain tissue, the dinosaur lost consciousness, closed its eyes, and then collapsed to the ground. A wave of hope and relief swept Petra until she saw the dinosaur was falling on Colter's hiding place. The few branches still on the trees snapped off as the limp monster crashed to the floor of the little wood, and then lay still.

Petra stood stunned. She had killed the dinosaur, but she had crushed Colter beneath its mass. She ran around the dinosaur shouting Colter's name, looking for some way to get under him, for some depression or crawl space. The ground was uneven because of the dinosaur's digging, but there was no space big enough for a body. Finally she sat down. She had no tears left, and no energy to mourn. Instead, she just let creeping blackness fill her.

There was no point in staying. They were all gone now. First Mrs. Wayne and Ernie Powell, and then Dr. Piltcher and Dr. Coombs. And now Colter. She couldn't bring them back. Maybe she could find Phat, or perhaps she should go back to Ashland and see if any of her friends were still alive. She knew she should go see if the RV was still there. If it was, she could get out of here, away from this nightmare. She didn't know what kind of world it would be now, with dinosaurs running around, but whatever was out there wouldn't carry these kinds of memories.

Still, she sat motionless. Depression weighed her to the ground. She sat and fiddled with the gun listlessly. One part of her mind was working on how to reload it while the rest of her mind flowed from one unhappy pool of memories to the next. Finally, she found the clip release and replaced the expended clip with the one Colter had thrown her. She was about to leave when she heard a muffled sound.

Suddenly alert for danger, her head snapped up. She worked the bolt again, still awkward, hoping she wouldn't have to fire off several rounds in quick succession. Petra held perfectly still, facing the jungle and waiting for the sound again. It came from behind her. She turned, holding her breath to hear better; the noise came from under the dead dinosaur. She ran along the dinosaur's back to where she estimated she had last seen Colter, and the sound was louder near the dinosaur's shoulder.

"Colter, is that you?"

When Colter yelled back it was with a touch of irritation.

"Of course it is, you—"

Petra couldn't make out the last word but smiled anyway. She didn't care what he said as long as he was alive.

"Can-you-dig-me-out-of-here?" he screamed one word at a time.

It came out muffled, but Petra understood and shouted back she would. With her hands she made slow progress. She tried Colter's dog paddle technique, but this wasn't the soft pile of humus where they found the egg. One by one Petra's fingernails broke off, two of them leaving bloody tips. When the last one broke Petra paused and found a stick, then alternated with the stick and her hands. Still the progress was slow. Her arms ached and she'd dug only a small depression. Still she avowed she would dig all night if she had to.

She was digging out cupped handfuls of dirt when something ran by in her peripheral vision. Dropping the dirt, she picked up the rifle, standing slowly. The dead dinosaur was too big to see over, so she began walking along the dinosaur toward the tail, the rifle pointed in front of her.

Suddenly she heard a growling and tearing sound. She froze, trying to locate it, but it came from somewhere near her. Another growl sounded followed by more tearing and chomping sounds. Petra moved forward one step at a time. She heard Colter's muffled yell behind her, but whatever was making the sounds ahead either couldn't hear Colter, or didn't care. Petra took a few more steps and then knelt and crawled along the tail until she was sure she could stand and look over it. Two carnivores were on the other side of the carcass, burying their teeth into the flesh of the monster's belly. As she watched, a bigger carnivore came out of the forest and snarled at the others. The smaller ones snarled back but moved toward Petra a few steps. Once the big one had the space it demanded, the new dinosaur tore into the belly of the carcass.

Petra squatted back down and continued crawling along the spine. Halfway back to Colter, a three-foot dinosaur with a huge head ran between the trees toward her. Petra pointed the rifle at it, but it ignored her and ran along the length of the tail and to the other side. Petra sighed and continued her crawl, her bare knees scraped and jabbed by rocks buried in the grass and her body scratched by small branches. As soon as she could stand she got up and tiptoed along the dinosaur's back. When she heard Colter's muffled call, she wanted to yell for him to be quiet but couldn't risk it. The sounds on the other side of the dinosaur suggested a gathering horde. Another small dinosaur ran through the woods and to the other side. Petra sighed again, then began to dig. But another movement caught her attention and she turned to see a fifteen-foot dinosaur coming at her through the trees.

Petra lifted the rifle and pointed it at the dinosaur's chest. Shooting it would only attract the other dinosaurs' attention. She hated to leave Colter, but didn't see any options. Keeping the rifle on the carnosaur, she inched along the body toward the head. The creature watched her, but it wasn't going to trade an appetizer for a meal. Finally, she limped into the trees.

Something moved to her left, so she dodged right. A tree with a low overhanging branch loomed ahead and she pulled herself up on it, balancing the gun on the limb. She kept climbing until she was sure she was out of the reach of most of the predators, then wedged herself between a limb and the trunk with the gun across her lap, and relaxed for the first time in days.

---

60. Guard Duty

Before long everything will be organized, but not in the evil century of the great year.

—Nostradamus

Medford, Oregon
PostQuilt: Wednesday, 9:37 a.m. PST

The dispatcher's call pulled Deputy Kyle away from his post in front of the grocery store. Guard duty was usually easy, but the world had gone mad, and nothing was easy duty now. Food purchases were limited to prevent hoarding, leaving customers frightened and frustrated. Kyle knew it was only a matter of time before a riot broke out.

Karon was vague about his recall, referring to some sort of "special duty." Kyle didn't want any more special duty, especially after the cave incident. Kyle's worst fears were confirmed when he saw Shirley in the parking lot wearing climbing clothes. Kyle tried to slip into the station, but she intercepted him.

"How's your nose, Deputy?"

"Fine," Kyle said, his face reddening. "I can't talk now, I'm needed inside."

"I'm why you're here. We need your climbing skills again."

Shirley smiled when she said it, and Kyle fought to keep from smiling back. Whatever she wanted was going to be hard work and dangerous.

"Shirley, I'm needed here. You're pulling me out of a potentially volatile situation."

"Anyone can stand in front of a grocery store and look tough."

Kyle was embarrassed. Shirley had a way of making him look ridiculous.

"There's more to it than that," he said defensively.

"Maybe," she conceded with a smile, "but I've got a job only you can do."

"It involves climbing, doesn't it."

"There's a little girl trapped up on a ledge. We need to go up and get her."

Shirley's smile faded when she mentioned the little girl.

"Is the girl hurt?"

"Maybe, but we won't know until we get there."

Kyle felt Shirley was holding something back.

"A little girl, huh? All right, I'll get my climbing gear out of the station."

"It's already in my car," Shirley said.

"Okay, then. Let me get something to eat—"

"Got something already," Shirley said, reaching into the car and holding up a McDonald's bag.

"I thought they were closed."

"I've got connections." She looked proud and mischievous.

"Get me something to drink?"

Shirley smiled and reached in the window and came out with a large soft drink. She seemed a little too efficient for Kyle, but he liked the way she thought of his needs. He lowered his eyes, taking in Shirley's figure. Yes, there *was* a lot to like about her.

"I hope that's a Big Mac in there."

"Large fries too."

Kyle was into the fries before they were out of the parking lot. Compared to what was going on in town, rescuing an injured little girl didn't sound too bad. In fact, Kyle thought as he stuffed another fry into his mouth, this might be the closest thing to easy duty left in the world. Kyle was just starting on the Big Mac when they turned onto I-5 and headed north.

61. HELICOPTER

The railroad workmen were cutting the way with dynamite and a steam shovel when they discovered the cavern. It was filled with a strange assemblage of animal remains. Animals from cool northern climates, wolverine, lemming, long-tailed shrew, mink, red squirrel, muskrat, porcupine, hare and elk, were mingled with animals from warmer climates, peccary, crocodilid, and tapir. How species of such diverse climates all came to be in the enclosed cavern is a mystery.

—J. W. Gridley, Cumberland, Maryland, 1912

Forest, former site of Portland, Oregon
PostQuilt: Wednesday, 10:00 a.m. PST

The demarcation between the time-quilted area and Portland was not as sharp as in New York. Portland was a small town busting out of its britches, but from the air the city looked like an octopus sending tentacles of development up over the hills and down into valleys. Because the urban area intermixed with rural and forested land, the contrast between city and the time-quilted area was harder to spot. At first the quilted forest looked like any to Terry, but then he began to get a sense of scale. The smallest of the trees was easily the match of the largest PreQuilt Douglas fir. Terry and Bill hadn't seen any dinosaurs, but Terry was already a believer. He had seen the I-5 mountain, and if a city could disappear, couldn't dinosaurs appear?

Bill's connections seemed as important as his rank, and he'd gotten them a military jet out to Nevada. Then one "buddy" shuttled them to Hillsboro, where another buddy arranged a helicopter. On the way, Bill exchanged unclassified information with them on what was happening in the civilian sector. Power outages were keeping about a third of the country in the dark, literally, but the rest of the country was getting news, unbelievable news, and was near panic. Food hoarding had begun, and frenzied shoppers had caused riots in Los Angeles, Chicago, and Seattle. A third of the state governors had declared martial law and were begging for federal help. Massive flooding, tidal waves, and landslides had devastated the country. Hospitals near the disasters were jammed, and rescue workers and relief agencies found themselves overwhelmed by requests and stymied by missing bridges and roads.

Yet while chaos reigned in and near affected areas, major portions of the country stayed at home, watched reports on the television, went to work, and sent their kids to school. The disasters were tremendous but highly specific in nature. Los Angeles, for example, was largely intact, but just south of the city there had been a massive flood. After the water found its way out to sea, rescue workers found precious little to search. San Juan Capistrano and San Clemente were gone. Not demolished, but completely gone, leaving no wrecked homes, cars, or bodies.

Terry and Bill tried to contact Ellen and Angie by phone, to tell them they were off to look for John, but long-distance phone calling was impossible. AT&T had been hurt by losses in Atlanta and New York. MCI and Sprint, devastated by satellite ground station losses, had good service only between the Midwest and Southeast. Coast-to-coast calls could not be made. And concerned parents and children overwhelmed the remaining phone capacity.

During the stopover in Nevada, Terry worked the civilian phone circuits while Bill tried the military. He returned with bad news.

"Angie and Ellen checked out. They left a message saying they were going to find your son."

"What? But he may not be there to find." Terry had never admitted that, and saying it now the words gave it a grim finality. "He may be somewhere else," he added, convincing neither Bill nor himself.

"Ellen and Angie don't know what's happened. They could be in dinosaur country already. But that's not all. Something's going on. A friend of mine says they've ordered the Portland area target mapped—bit mapped for a terrain guidance system."

"They use those to guide bombers, right?"

"Mmmm—yes, bombers and cruise missiles. The system allows them to fly at treetop level. That kind of guidance system is very reliable, and very accurate."

"You don't think they're going to bomb those dinosaurs, do you?"

"I can't believe you would need a bomb to keep them at bay. Remember what caused this in the first place?"

Terry tried to recall Dr. Paulson's explanation of the computer models and their relation to patterns of explosions. Large nuclear detonations had caused this; detonations in the megaton, not kiloton range. Then Terry made the connection.

"You don't think they're going to—" Terry stammered.

"Hair of the dog—"

That realization sent a shiver through Terry. He was going to be flying into the land of dinosaurs, not knowing whether his wife made it to Portland, or what had happened to his son, and wondering whether a Stealth bomber would suddenly unleash nuclear hell on them. He wanted to say it couldn't get any worse than this, but every time he thought that, he was wrong.

The helicopter was there as promised. Although Bill kept saying he'd "get the hang of it again soon," he proved himself a reasonably competent pilot. They circled to identify the quilted segment, and then entered from the southeast. The skyscrapers in city center were gone, and most of the urban sprawl that covered the valley and hills had vanished. The shape of the land, however, was the same. Terry picked out the Columbia River glistening in the distance, and the Tualitan River, where it should be. The Willamette River was gone, but something reflected silvery light through the trees on the east side of the valley. If that was the Willamette it had been drastically rechanneled. The new forest itself was not uniform. Sections of it looked like they were being clear-cut, with the trees dropped on top of one another in a confusing jumble. Other sections seemed collapsed in, the trees holding one another up, as if they had been badly crowded. Other sections appeared to be normal forest. Then Bill spotted something.

"There! In that clearing!" he shouted.

He banked the helicopter to the right, bringing it full circle and dropping altitude at the same time.

The clearing looked more like a river bottom to Terry, a long earthy gouge that disappeared in the distance. The strip was speckled with large sheets of water that reflected the sun and clouds.

Bill pointed again and brought the helicopter around so Terry could see a herd of animals. Terry first thought of buffalo, but dismissed the thought. These were much bigger, four-legged animals with long necks and tails.

They were dinosaurs. They seemed to be slowly walking along the bank of what had been a river. Bill and Terry watched the herd in silence, considering the implications. Then Bill made a wide circle and began searching again. West of the dinosaur herd they spotted a clearing. In it were three horses with riders, one horse carrying two. As Bill banked the helicopter, and circled, the riders stopped and watched it land. Bill kept the blades rotating while Terry jumped out.

Even from the air Bill and Terry could tell Ellen and Angie weren't there, but the riders might have information. They looked to be a family. The man was riding double with a boy of about twelve, and the other two looked to be his wife and teenage daughter. They all looked comfortable on horseback and wore denim and flannel. But they seemed watchful. Everyone but the boy had a rifle. Terry approached carefully.

"Hi there. Can you help me? We're looking for some people, two women."

"I'd get back up in the air if I were you. There's killer lizards in here, big ones."

"I know, that's why I need to find these people. One's my wife."

"She better not be in here. We just lost a horse to one—nearly got my boy." The man nodded to the boy riding behind him.

"It killed Copper," the boy sniffed. He had been crying.

"Came out of nowhere," the man continued. "It was about half the size of my boy's horse but had jaws you wouldn't believe. Sank its teeth into the horse's neck and brought old Copper to the ground. If my boy hadn't jumped free he'd be dead."

"Have you seen anyone else in here?"

"Saw some people this morning, but they were heading out, two men and a woman. You should do the same. Now we gotta go."

The man nudged his horse with his heels and headed off.

"Hey, how far does this go, anyway?"

The woman turned before she followed the others.

"Don't know for sure. I heard Vancouver's still there, but the bridges are down. Someone said it goes all the way to Wilsonville."

John thanked her as she rode to catch up with the others. Wilsonville, he said to himself. They had already seen how far south the affected area was, and the woman had mentioned Vancouver. That meant not only was his house gone, but 90 percent of the metropolitan area was now dinosaur-infested forest.

Bill took them up again and deeper into the quilt. Two clearings later Terry spotted something orange—fluorescent orange and certainly not natural. Bill couldn't land so he hovered at treetop level, giving Terry a better look. There were four three-wheeled ATVs in the trees. Two of them lay on their sides. Each one carried an orange flag on a seven foot whip pole—that was the orange Terry had spotted. They circled slowly but saw no signs of any people. Even when they widened their search circle they never found the owners of the bikes.

Terry directed Bill into the valley, using the few landmarks he could recognize, but mostly relying on his best judgment. Terry was directing Bill toward his house, or at least where his house had been. That would be the logical place for Ellen to look for John. Terry let Bill fly past the location before he directed him to circle. There was nothing there but forest. Bill's circles grew wider and wider, and still they saw nothing but trees, no houses, roads or buildings. Surely, Terry told himself, Ellen and Angie would have realized the futility of their search by the time they got this far.

Bill's air force eyes were used to seeing things from overhead, and again he spotted something new. Motorcycles were parked around a black spot in a clearing. He circled the clearing but again saw no people, only movement in the grass, small animals scurrying for hiding places. Bill landed near the bikes and left the rotors turning, then climbed out, offering an M-16 to Terry. Terry refused. He didn't know how to shoot it and felt he'd be a danger to Bill if he tried.

The motorcycles were parked around a fire, still smoldering, littered with empty liquor bottles. In the grass on one side was the head of a dinosaur, about twice the size of a human head. Its eyes were gone and insects crawled over it. Terry was mesmerized. Even though it was as much a product of evolution as Terry, it seemed unearthly.

Bill climbed on one of the bikes, turned the key, then tried kick starting it. The loud whirring startled Terry and also something in the grass. Walking slowly toward the movement, Terry saw the grass had been trampled or run down in the makeshift path. More grass rustled to his right, and he froze. Then he stepped into the grass toward the movement. He took two steps down a slight hill before he saw it. It was a body, a human body, in worse shape than the dinosaur head. Large and small animals had been feeding on it, and it was nothing more than blackened meat. Terry turned away, struggling to control his nausea.

Bill was looking at the engine on the motorcycle when he returned.

"There's a body down there," Terry said slowly.

Bill stood up and merely looked in the direction Terry pointed.

"Well that might fit. These bikes have been sabotaged. Someone got mad and cut up their wiring, and maybe killed a guy."

Before Terry could respond something big ran behind him. Bill shouldered his rifle and stared into the grass.

Suddenly a head popped up. It was larger than a human head, with an elongated snout and two rows of needle teeth. Hissing at them, it ducked its head and continued walking. Bill fired blindly after it.

"What are you doing, Bill? That's an extinct species—*was* an extinct species."

Another movement to Terry's left brought Bill's gun around again. Another head popped up and then disappeared, similar to the first. At the sound of more movement in the grass, Terry realized they were surrounded.

"They're hunting us in a pack," Bill said. "Stay close to me and when I say run, you run."

Following Bill's gesture, they stepped toward the helicopter. Terry wished he'd not turned down Bill's other rifle. A pounding behind them caught their attention, and Bill and Terry turned to see a dinosaur about the size of a Shetland pony charge through the grass. Its body was gray-green, with a short thin neck and a tail held up almost to head height. It was running on two back legs and had short clawed arms folded against its chest. Its mouth was open, revealing its double row of teeth, but it made no sound. Bill fired three shots into the chest in quick succession and the dinosaur collapsed into the grass, tumbling toward Terry and Bill, yelping and screaming, drowning out the thump of the helicopter. Bill fired three more shots at movement to their left and was rewarded with another yelp.

"Run!"

Terry bolted toward the helicopter, gritting his teeth and pushing his legs to move him faster than he had in years. Bill pulled ahead of him, but Terry had nothing more to give. Terry's eyes darted back and forth as he ran, watching for any signs of attack. As he pounded and puffed through the grass, he realized the sounds of the helicopter's engines would drown out the noise of dinosaurs in pursuit. They could be surprised at any moment. Bill scrambled in as Terry ran to the far side, swung the door open, and climbed onto the seat. Just as he was closing the door he heard Bill yell a warning. Instinctively Terry leaned into the cockpit and pulled his exposed leg high. Teeth buried themselves into the seat beneath Terry, and the dinosaur struggled to pull the seat out from under him. Then Bill's M-16 slapped down on Terry's other leg. Terry froze, but Bill hesitated. Suddenly the dinosaur lunged for a better mouthful. Quickly Terry shoved himself up off the seat, his back arched. The jaws snapped closed just below his crotch.

"Kill it, Bill! Kill it!" he screamed, and Bill fired a shot into the dinosaur's head. Blood spattered Terry's face and crotch. The dinosaur stopped moving and slumped, but its jaws were still set in the seat.

"Get it out of here. We've got to take off before another one gets us!"

Terry leaned on Bill and kicked the head. With each kick he heard the seat tear, but the dinosaur's blood made the head slippery and Terry's blows began to slide off. A dozen kicks later, the head flopped out the door with a piece of seat still in its mouth.

Bill increased rotor speed and pulled up immediately. As they lifted off, Terry could see two more dinosaurs running off through the grass. When they were safely away, Bill turned to Terry with a grin and shouted over the rotors.

"Now what was that about those things being extinct species?"

Terry, shaking, tried to maneuver his body onto what was left of the seat. As he put his headphones on, he heard Bill chuckling.

"That was the quickest conversion I've ever seen. 'Save the endangered species' to 'kill it quick,' in less than a minute. Say, Terry, you know what kind of dinosaur that was, don't you? Ballosaurus. It eats only one thing and it nearly had yours."

Bill kept laughing, but Terry wasn't amused and quietly fumed, watching below. But for a long time all he could see were razor sharp teeth snapping an inch from his crotch.

"What's this? I don't believe it."

Terry looked but saw only foliage.

"No, up here. Over there."

Terry looked to see skyscrapers shimmering in the distance—translucent skyscrapers. Portland was there now, but it hadn't been just minutes ago. But was it really there? Did Terry and Bill need to see Portland so badly that their minds were creating it? Terry looked for landmarks, picking out the Bank of California, and the KOIN tower. Terry tried scanning vertically to the base of the skyscrapers, but they blurred into indistinguishable light and shadow at their base, making it impossible to distinguish cars and people.

"Think Ellen and Angie made it into the city? Maybe my son is there now. Let's fly into it, Bill. See if we can find them."

Bill hesitated, holding the helicopter in a hover. Terry had never seen him indecisive before.

"What's the problem? Let's go find our people."

"Something's not right . . . mmmm . . . It doesn't look real . . . doesn't look stable."

"If it's not real it will disappear as we approach it." Terry said it with more confidence than he felt. Why was the city flickering like a mirage?

The helicopter tilted nose down and started forward. Bill stiffened noticeably, shaking Terry's confidence as they moved forward. Terry found it difficult to stay focused on the city. His eyes seemed to fix on the hills shining beyond the city. Then the buildings began to fade. Terry blinked to bring the image back, but it continued to fade until it was gone. Bill slowed the helicopter, hovering again, staring at the forest where the city had been.

"Hallucination?" Bill asked.

"Two people sharing a hallucination is extremely rare. Maybe a mirage."

"We're low on fuel. A couple more passes, then we need to head back."

Bill turned back to resume his spiral search pattern and Terry returned to his watch, surprised at how easily he could put the vanishing city out of his mind. It was, he realized, just one facet of a mystery that had consumed his son, and perhaps his wife.

---

62. CAPTURED

It happened mid morning when everyone was about their daily tasks. Suddenly burning planks began to fall from the sky. The fiery planks were of similar width, but varied in length, and all were aflame. The planks were quickly extinguished. The villagers turned to the priest, fearing witchcraft and seeking explanation, but he had none to offer.

—François DeLaine, Province of Tournaine, France, August 15, 1670

Forest, former site of Portland, Oregon
POSTQUILT: WEDNESDAY, 10:05 A.M. PST

"Ellen, you look like shit. You gotta take better care of yourself."

Kishton was holding Ellen's hands behind her back and Carl was looking her over like she was a piece of meat. Which she felt like now—bloodied from a hundred tiny wounds, with dirt covering her arms and legs and tattered blouse and pants. But as his eyes smoldered, Ellen knew the dirt didn't matter to Carl.

Ripman stirred and sat up, drawing Carl's attention. He had been lying on the ground unconscious, but the bow was still slung over his shoulder. Carl jerked it off angrily.

"So you're the sonofabitch that shot me. You fucked up our bikes too, didn't you?"

Ellen saw that Ripman's eyes showed no surprise at the mention of the bikes. Had he slipped into their camp while Angie and she slept?

"He killed Bobby," Miller added, and then kicked Ripman in the side, knocking him over again. "You shot him in the back. That ain't the way it's done."

Ripman pushed himself into a sitting position again and looked up at Miller. The right side of his face was swelling.

"Sorry. What's the right way to kill a rapist?"

"Sonofabitch!" Miller shouted, and kicked Ripman again.

Carl pushed Miller back and took center stage.

"Rapist? Hell, they were asking for it!" Carl shouted in Ripman's face. "They sure as hell weren't no virgins. Did you see the size of Angie's tits?" Carl said. "And the way she was wigglin' around? She wanted it, and we have it. A match made in heaven. By the way," Carl asked, lowering his rifle so it pointed at Ripman's head, "where is Big Tits?"

Ripman gave Ellen a look she couldn't interpret and then jumped up and shouted in the direction they had come.

"Run, Angie, hide! Run!"

A blow from Carl's fist sent him back to the ground.

"I'll get her, Carl," Miller volunteered. "Sounds like fun to me."

Miller headed off recklessly, climbing over and under trees. Ellen looked in the direction of Ripman's shout, trying to spot the dinosaur, but an isolated patch of standing trees was blocking the view. How far had they come while she was semiconscious? Was the dinosaur gone? Was it following like before?

Carl grabbed a fistful of Ellen's blouse, pulling her close. She could feel his hot breath and could smell liquor.

"Let's you and me go someplace more comfortable." He shoved Ellen ahead of him. "Kishton, bring Robin Hood, and watch him close. You can kill him if you want to."

Kishton looked scathingly at Ripman, but there was no murder in his eyes. Talking of killing someone was easy. Actually killing was hard. Only Carl was sociopath enough to do it in cold blood. Pulling Ripman to his feet, Kishton shoved him in the direction of Carl and Ellen.

They were nearly out of the fallen trees when they heard three quick shots, followed by a roar. As they all turned and looked back, a loud thumping and crunching sound nearly frightened them off the log they were standing on. Then Miller appeared around the corner of the tree stand, his rifle in one hand, climbing one fallen log, and then jumping from tree to tree. Another roar trumpeted and a dinosaur came around the tree stand, the one that killed Angie. It had trouble negotiating the fallen trees and picked its way slowly. Miller tripped over a trunk and disappeared, then popped back up, steadied his rifle across the trunk, and fired another three quick shots. When the dinosaur bellowed in pain, Carl and Kishton brought their guns to their shoulders and fired, missing it.

Miller raced to another fallen tree looking for a way over, then began climbing limbs recklessly. The dinosaur swiped at him, but too late, and Miller jumped down between trunks. Before Miller reappeared the animal stepped up on one trunk, and then another, and another. Then, poised precariously on two logs, it looked down. As the tail slammed down, acting as a stabilizer, the dinosaur bent its head between its feet, using the forelegs to swipe. Two quick shots came from beneath the trunk.

"Reload, Miller, reload!" Kishton shouted.

Miller's first scream was shorter than Angie's, but he got two more out before the digging claws silenced him.

"Move it!" Carl yelled, shoving Ellen again. "And you, you sonofabitch!" Carl screamed, kicking Ripman in the groin and knocking him to the ground. "You did that on purpose. You knew that thing was there!" Ripman groaned, then whimpered as Carl kicked him in the back.

"He wanted to be with Angie, didn't he?" Ellen said, hoping to distract Carl. "Now they'll always be together."

Carl whipped around at the sound of her voice, his face red with fury, the lust in his eyes replaced by murder. Ellen's mind raced as she searched for a way out.

"I think it's coming this way," she lied.

Carl's head snapped back to the dinosaur, which still had its head poked under a log.

"You'll pay for this! You'll both pay," Carl hissed.

Carl shoved Ellen and once again they were climbing toward the forest. Everyone except Ripman kept looking back. Occasionally the animal glanced in their direction, but it was preoccupied with eating.

Again Ellen was facing what her psychologist husband would call an avoidance-avoidance conflict. If she tried to escape she would probably be killed by Carl or Kishton, and if she did escape, this dinosaur, or some other, would probably eat her just like Angie. But if she didn't escape she would end up being gang raped first and then killed. Then there was Ripman. He could have left her and Angie to the dinosaur. Instead he tried to help them. Now it looked like Carl and Kishton would beat him to death. If she escaped, she resolved, it would be with Ripman.

The standing forest was only a few logs away when a bullet slammed into a fallen tree next to Ellen, followed by the report of a pistol. Confused, Carl and Kishton looked in all directions. Two more bullets whined over their heads, and all four people ducked behind the nearest log. Then a voice rang out of the forest, a deep menacing voice, a voice that was vaguely familiar to Ellen.

"Let the woman and boy go!"

"Who are you?" Carl shouted back. The voice repeated its demand. Carl gave Kishton a quizzical look, but Kishton merely shrugged. Carl then turned, his rifle on Ripman.

"Who's out there, kid?"

The right side of Ripman's face was swollen and purplish. He could scarcely move his lips, but he whispered, "Someone with a gun."

Carl slapped Ripman across his discolored cheek. As Ripman grimaced with pain he gasped and moaned. Satisfied momentarily, Carl turned to Ellen, who flippantly offered, "Someone with a gun and an attitude?"

Carl slapped her down, then jerked her up by her hair.

"They ain't gonna get you. You're mine."

Two more shots echoed out of the forest, and the bullets

whined overhead. From the log, Carl fired three quick shots in response.

"Come and get them, if you want them!" he shouted. "We got plenty of ammunition, and we ain't movin'."

"Look behind you!" the deep disembodied voice called.

They all turned to see the dinosaur looking in their direction. When it stepped toward them Kishton kicked Ripman twice more.

Carl looked around wildly for another escape route, but Ellen could see they were trapped and hoped Carl was smart enough to see it too. They could move parallel to the forest until they were out of range of the gun, but there was no way to know that the man in the forest wouldn't follow them. And it would be slow, and the dinosaur was getting better at walking through the fallen trees.

"What we gonna do, Carl? Maybe we better let them go?" Kishton offered hopefully.

"Let me think. Just shut up and let me think!"

Ellen was watching the dinosaur, afraid it was moving faster than Carl could think.

Carl finally shouted into the forest defiantly, "If we let them go, how do we know you'll let us out of here before the dinosaur gets us?"

"Let the woman and the kid go. We have no interest in you."

At the word *we* Ellen felt hope. Whoever they were, they couldn't be any worse than Carl and the guys. Ripman, his head down, showed no reaction. Carl and Kishton were taking too much time. If they didn't act soon they wouldn't be able to release her and Ripman and make it to the forest themselves before the dinosaur caught up.

"All right, all right!" Carl shouted to the forest.

Then to Ellen and Ripman he said, "This isn't over. Now you go, and you go fast, or I'll shoot you in the back just like you did Bobby."

As soon as they climbed on top of the log, the dinosaur spotted them and picked up its pace. Its enthusiasm spoke of an acquired taste for people, Ellen realized.

"Hurry it up!" Carl shouted behind them. "Hurry it up or I'll shoot you!"

Ripman was slowing them down. His swollen face impaired his vision, and Ellen had to help him climb and guide him toward the forest. But if she held his arm too firmly or too long, Ripman pushed it away. When they went around the foliage of the last fallen tree, they ran into the forest.

Now a familiar voice whispered to them, and a hand motioned from a tree. Ellen guided Ripman there and around the other side.

At the sight of her son her knees went weak and she collapsed into his arms. After a long relieved squeeze Ellen opened her eyes to see Cubby holding a pistol.

"Hello, Mrs. Roberts."

The voice wasn't as deep as the one shouting from the forest, but she realized both were Cubby's. He smiled at her, then turned to Ripman.

"Ripman, you look like crap."

Ripman turned his head to look at Cubby with his good eye. "We'll all be crap tomorrow if that dino eats us today."

In her relief Ellen had forgotten about the dinosaur. She leaned out around the tree to see Carl and Kishton climbing over a log, moving fast. But so was the dinosaur.

"It's coming . . . they're coming."

Cubby leaned around the tree and fired three times at Carl and Kishton, who were running the length of a trunk to reach another tree and dove between the two logs. Cubby fired another shot before the gun clicked on an empty chamber.

"Time to go," he said and ran off through the trees.

As they followed Cubby, semiautomatic rifle fire echoed through the trees, quickly drowned by roaring and bellowing. Carl and Kishton were putting up a fight.

Ripman's breathing was heavy and ragged and he stumbled frequently. Ellen and John bracketed him, taking turns supporting him, but he didn't tolerate their touch for long and pushed their hands away.

The rifle fire continued behind them, the sharp cracks and pops competing with the screaming roars of the enraged dinosaur. Then a tremendous crash and splintering drowned out the gunshots. When the new noise faded, the rifle fire and the screams were gone.

Cubby pulled up behind a tree and plopped down, pretending to catch his breath but keeping his eye on Ripman. He remained standing, leaning against the tree, but slowly sank onto his bottom like the rest of them, looking down to avoid eye contact. Ellen knew he was in pain, some of it physical, but most of it emotional. He hated needing their help.

After a few minutes, Cubby took charge again.

"Let's get going. Maybe we can still make it to my house."

"Your house?" Ellen asked. She was puzzled. Could Cubby's house be in this primeval forest somewhere? "Your house is still here?"

"It's over that way a few miles. We saw my dad's church yesterday, isn't that right, John?"

John responded with a reluctant nod, and Ellen realized there was something her son was holding back. Ellen looked around the woods. It was like nothing she'd ever known. Some of the trees were the size of the biggest redwoods in the nation, and there were thousands of them. The plants were strangely unfamiliar, and the insect and small animal life seemed alien from an ancient world, one ruled by dinosaurs and gone for sixty-five million years. Yet Cubby talked of going home, home to a parsonage. The impossibility of what had happened hit her hard.

"Well, if you're sure it's there, and it's not too far, I guess we should head for it."

She said it without conviction. Her own inclination was to make directly for the nearest piece of confirmed civilization. At last Ripman lifted his eyes and used the good one to stare at Cubby.

"I wouldn't say it's there, and I wouldn't say it's not there," he muttered thickly through his swollen lips.

Cubby turned on him angrily.

"I'm not buying that rapture crapola of yours, Cubby," Ripman continued, "I'm just telling you what I've seen. I've seen Portland too, I've seen it come and go."

"What's that supposed to mean?" Cubby snarled in his deepest voice.

"It means what it means. Sometimes it's there and sometimes it's not. Even if it is there it doesn't look right."

"I saw it. John saw it."

"That right, John?" Ripman turned his good eye to John,

defying him to support Cubby. "Did it look all right to you?"

"It was there . . . but it was . . . hazy."

"See, John saw it. Now give it a rest, Ripman, we're going to my place."

Ripman turned his head back and forth, reading facial expressions with his good eye.

"If it's there why haven't we run into any of the people from Portland?"

"It's too far away, that's why." Cubby spoke with conviction, but no one shared his certainty.

"It's not that far away. You're sitting on Mount Tabor."

Cubby's eyes went wide and he mouthed "Mount Tabor" silently. Ellen had been to Cubby's church on several occasions, and she knew it was on the hill just south of Mount Tabor. Now, Ripman stood and threw a rock into the forest.

"That means your house is about that far away. You see your house? Your church? It's gone, Cubby, gone. Get used to it. Better yet, get out of here. You don't belong here, none of you do. Get out of here before you get me killed."

Ripman collapsed back onto the ground, pulled his knees to his chest, burying his head between his knees. Ellen impulsively reached out to put her arm around him but held back. Her gesture would only add to his pain. Ellen didn't know how to comfort Cubby either. She only knew that it was time to get out of the forest.

She turned to John to ask for his support, but a new noise pulled their attention to the sky—the distinctive thump, thump, thump of a helicopter, flying low. She, John, and Cubby spread out looking for a thin spot in the canopy to attract the attention of the pilot. Ripman remained under the tree with his head between his knees. The thumping got louder when the helicopter was nearly overhead. Then leaves began fluttering out of the trees, hundreds of them, blocking her view. As they drifted toward her she realized these were long elongated leaves, and that evergreens have needles, not leaves.

The whirling blades were directly above them when the first of the leaves drifted down to head height. Suddenly the leaf changed course and swooped to Ellen's shoulder. She turned to find an eight-inch lizard staring her in the face, its tongue slithering in and out. It was a mottled green with a brown bone collar around its neck. Spines, extending from its neck on either side, were folded flat along its body. Screaming, Ellen knocked it from her shoulder, but its claws snagged her blouse and it hung upside down by its back legs. Then it extended the spines from its side, stretching the attached webbing wide. Its claws released and it rolled and glided to the ground, reared on its back legs and ran into the underbrush. Other lizards landed nearby and ran off, some scrambling up trees and disappearing into the foliage. Another scored a direct hit on Ellen's head, its claws enmeshed in her hair. Ellen, in panic, tried to pull it free, and when it came loose with a hunk of hair in each fist, Ellen flung it to the ground, where it ran off with the others. The lizard flights diminished, and when the air raid ended the helicopter was gone.

Tears filled Ellen's eyes. She resolved then and there to take no steps that didn't lead out of this hell. She saw the same desire in her son. Cubby looked mostly confused, and Ripman was still hiding his emotions. Ellen regarded the boys in a new light. They were still young in many ways, struggling for an identity, not sure of their direction. She had depended on them, and they had saved her. Ripman had tried to save Angie too; he'd been remarkable, and so had her son. But now they needed her. She was going to lead them out of there.

Before she could act, she heard a new sound, growing louder. Cubby and John looked at each other accusingly.

"It was your bike," Cubby said.

"Uh-uh! It was yours," John replied defensively.

Ellen didn't have time to ask what they were talking about. Cubby pulled Ripman to his feet and into the forest while John grabbed her arm and dragged her along behind. The sound grew loud enough for her to recognize. It was a motorcycle.

63. Oscillations

Einstein's failure to explain time's arrow . . . is closely linked to the concept of causality . . . the notion that effects never precede their causes. Consider a world in which causality is violated. It might mean that a pebble could levitate off the ground so that you could grasp it; worse than that, you might be struck down by a stone before it fell, or kill your own grandmother before you were born.

—Peter Coveney and Roger Highfield, *The Arrow of Time*

Washington, D.C.
PostQuilt: Wednesday, 1:15 p.m. EST

The PresNet was rich with data now. Scientists who had been absent from their labs studying local phenomena were back on-line providing reports. They were still mostly descriptive but some included analysis and theorizing. Unidentified plant life, unusual microscopic sea life, dinosaur sightings—the reports went on and on. They were fascinating and seductive but Nick needed to concentrate on cause, not effects, so he programmed his computer to screen for messages on Gomez's theory.

That theory was receiving both support and criticism. A physicist at the University of Virginia had organized commentary into confirming responses and invalidating arguments. Nick skimmed the listings, but there was none for E. Puglisi. A few minutes later a messenger delivered an envelope.

It was from E. Puglisi. Nick tore it open and extracted a thick stack of photos and a two-page typed report. Puglisi wrote in an efficient style and, like a good science writer, began with a summary of the entire report. Nick read the summary, excitement building with each word. When he finished, he dropped the report and thumbed through the pictures, finding the photo the summary referred to but unable to see the details. His hands shaking nervously, he brought a magnifying glass down over the crater named Flamsteed until it came into focus. There it was.

Nick leaned back in his chair and stared at the ceiling, trying to take in the implications. He had been somewhat vague when he asked Puglisi to make the survey, but Puglisi had immediately taken the initiative. Puglisi's report noted that he and his colleague Chen-Slater had reasoned that only three types of changes to an airless body like the moon could be passed from the future to the present. Changes from internal events, like moonquakes. Changes from celestial events, like meteorite impact. Or man-made change. Puglisi and Chen-Slater found only the third kind.

Nick leaned back over the photo to make sure he hadn't imagined it. It was there, in the crater. A rectangular structure, so symmetrical and sharp-edged there was no confusing it with natural phenomena. Something from the future was now on the moon. What could it be? Nick wondered, his mind racing through endless possibilities. Most likely, he thought, it's part of a permanent moon base. But in the future we would know the time displacement was going to occur. Knowing that, wouldn't we take steps to make sure a base would not be constructed in a location to be displaced? Or at least built under the surface, where the effect doesn't seem to carry? Of course it could be from such a far future that civilization had lost its collective memory for this time. Perhaps civilization collapses, only to rise again. Or perhaps the structure was placed there deliberately to travel to the past—to Nick's present? Would future scientists be able to predict the time displacement that accurately?

A knock interrupted his thoughts, irritating him. "Come in!"

Elizabeth came through again, this time accompanied by Samuel Cannon. Nick had exchanged pleasantries with the CIA director on occasion, but never had closer contact. He and Elizabeth pulled chairs up close to Nick's desk and leaned forward, talking in low voices. As usual Elizabeth's face was impassive, but Cannon's look told Nick this meeting would be all business. With her usual bluntness, Elizabeth jumped right to the problem.

"Nick, the President is going ahead with Gogh's plan. The cruise missiles have been armed and the terrain mapped. They are going to launch as soon as the timing is right."

"What about the site selection? Aren't they going back to the Security Council to consider sites?"

Elizabeth and Samuel Cannon exchanged glances, and then Cannon answered in a subdued voice. "There is nothing to be considered. The site has been selected. It's the Portland site. They can't confirm the dinosaur report in Alaska, and the glacier site is too near the Canadian border. Besides, the glacier might be from the Ice Age. We have no way of knowing."

Nick knew what he meant. Everything suggested the time displacements were all from the Cretaceous period, but if the glacier was from the Ice Age there might be people somewhere there. It was unlikely that killing them would alter the present, and if it did who would know? Nick understood the danger, however. Severing a lifeline in the ancient past would kill all succeeding generations. Who might be eliminated from history by such an act? While you might want to eliminate Hitler or Stalin, you would also risk Jesus, Gandhi, and Einstein. But if you killed Einstein, would we have nuclear weapons at all? Perhaps Hitler would have developed them first and won World War II. And if we didn't have the bomb, how could we drop it to kill Einstein in the first place? Nick's mind reeled for the second time in a few minutes. He understood why they were avoiding the Alaskan site—still, risking the population of Portland for an untested theory was immoral.

"But Portland is a city. Can't you convince the President to wait for confirmation on the glacier site?" Nick argued.

"Nick, the President is only listening to Gogh. Gogh is telling him what he wants to hear, and what he wants to hear is that he can get his wife back. Nick, do you think this will work—this bomb theory?"

"I've been monitoring the debate over Gomez's—Gogh's theory, and only one in ten physicists support it. The rest are suggesting modifications or outright doubt about its validity. No one is supporting Gogh's idea that simultaneous nuclear detonations will return things to normal. It's also not clear that the explosions will actually take place in the past. Those bombs could be delivered to our present."

Elizabeth exchanged glances with Cannon again, and when she gave him an encouraging look, he nodded reluctantly.

"There's something else you should know," Cannon continued. "This is classified, you understand? We sent a team into Atlanta to try to locate and recover the first lady. They never came back."

"What? How did you do it?"

"The first attempt was an air drop. We sent up an aircraft that orbited the Atlanta site until they got a good solid image of the city below them. Then they parachuted in. We monitored the descent from the ground and from the aircraft. Everything went normal, their chutes opened and they descended into the city. Then the city was gone again and we never heard from them. We've been trying to contact them ever since."

Nick's concern made his voice quaver. "Sorry about your men, but that could partially support Gogh's theory. If we deliver the warheads when the past is . . . present . . . then the warheads may go off in the past . . . but of course that would be in this present . . . or would it?" He berated himself. He had only confused them and embarrassed himself. Changing the subject, he asked about the other incident.

"The ground team monitoring the drop had a good vantage point and reported that as the parachutists dropped into the city they saw that kind of fuzzy transparent look the city has. The crazy thing is the ground team reported that from their vantage point the city appeared off in the distance, but the aerial shots showed the ground team's position as in the city. Since we had radio contact with the ground team, we sent them toward the heart of the effect—Atlanta—and told them to maintain radio contact. We had positive contact until, suddenly, they were gone."

"We get nothing now," Elizabeth added, her voice uncharacteristically tremulous.

Nick was puzzled. Dinosaurs, like the ankylosaur in Montreal, were coming out of the displaced segments into Nick's present, but apparently the people from the present made only a one-way trip. Nick wondered whether the dinosaurs could go back. Could movement be only from past to the future? That would be consistent with time's arrow. If so, then was Atlanta displaced to the future, and was that why Cannon's people could not come back? But what of inanimate objects? Would they have the same restrictions? Probably, Nick realized. He was thinking in terms of the human disruption that could occur if one traveled to his or her own past.

Like most people, Nick was psychologically unwilling to meet himself in the past. But in one sense people were nothing more than organized chemicals. Would chemicals from the future meeting themselves in the past cause disruption? Not likely; but if the disruption occurred in a forward direction, then Gogh's bombs could be carried into the future. That is, if the effect was not disrupted by the blast. He resisted speculating out loud again. Elizabeth and Cannon came to him for his expertise. It's disquieting to people when experts act human.

"I'll put this information on PresNet. Maybe someone can make sense of it."

When Elizabeth and Cannon looked as if they wanted more, Nick wasn't sure what to give them.

"This means the timing is crucial," he added. "If the bombs are delivered when the present is—present, then the bombs will go off over Portland. If the past is present, then everything in the present will be intact. Of course the past will be incinerated."

Nick meant it to be reassuring. There was nothing more he could do. And apparently Cannon and Elizabeth had lost their influence. What Nick needed was sweet lemon rationalization. No matter how sour things turned out he was going to make the best of it.

"Tell him the rest, Sam."

"The timing is the problem. Gogh thinks the effect will be disrupted, but he isn't sure of the outcome. He thinks each segment will return to its own time, but he admits there is a chance the explosions will freeze the displaced sections in whatever time they are in. The problem is the oscillations for various locations are different."

Nick saw where Cannon was going, and a horrible thought formed in his mind. Cannon had been looking Nick in the eye—but now Nick's expression made the CIA director drop his head to study his shoes.

"Mr. Cannon, have they timed the oscillations in Portland?"

"They're working on it, but the data from out west is coming in slow. It won't matter though. They're going to use the Atlanta oscillations for the timing."

"They can't do that."

"The President can, and he's ordered it."

"They could kill everyone in Portland."

"Elizabeth and I argued that. The President sees it as a lesser of two evils. Lose everyone in all the affected locations, or risk the residents of Portland."

"He could minimize the risk by waiting for the oscillation analysis."

Cannon had no heart for arguing the President's position and slumped back in his chair, just as Elizabeth leaned forward.

"This isn't about saving anyone but the President's wife," she said urgently. "He's going to time the blast to freeze Atlanta in the present. We think it's a mistake."

"It is, it's a deadly mistake."

"We want you to come with us. We're going to talk to the President one more time. We need you to handle Gogh."

The President was in the Oval office, his back to his desk, staring out the window, his fingers involuntarily twirling a paper clip. Gogh and Natalie Matsuda were there too. As usual, Elizabeth ignored them and took charge of the meeting.

"Mr. President, I think you need to reconsider this plan to bomb Portland."

The President whirled around in his chair and threw the paper clip onto the desktop; it bounced onto the floor at Elizabeth's feet.

"Elizabeth, I told you before, we're not going to bomb Portland! We're going to detonate nuclear explosions in the distant past to return things to normal. If it works, and I'm confident that it will, Portland, and every other city in this country . . . and everywhere in the world, will return to normal."

The President spoke with venom.

"A decision had to be made," he added, "and I made it. The longer we wait the less chance there will be of it working. Isn't that right, Arnie?"

"The effect is stabilizing," Gogh said. "If we don't act soon, we may lose our only opportunity."

"What about the timing?" Nick cut in. "How will you time the blast?" The question reduced some of the President's self-righteousness, and he deferred to Gogh.

"We are timing the explosions with the most accurate data available," Gogh said crisply.

"Portland data," Nick offered.

"That is not available. The best available data is from the Southeast."

"From . . . ?" Nick prodded.

"From Atlanta!" the President roared. "Is that what you want to hear? I ordered it, I'll live with it."

"People may die with it, sir. I've been monitoring the debate over Gogh's plan on the PresNet. There is no support for it."

The President sank back in his chair and picked up another paper clip.

"There is debate, I know. But what else—"

"We're only asking you to wait a little longer. Data are coming in rapidly now. We might get the timing information you need."

The President didn't answer and wouldn't look Nick in the eye. Nick glanced at Gogh, but he too turned away. Reluctantly, he handed the Puglisi photo to the President.

"There's been a new development, sir. The time displacement has been from the past to the future on earth, but on the moon the future comes to the past." The President's eyes remained on the paper clip in his hands. "I have evidence something from the future is now on our moon. You can see it in this photo."

The President looked up at Nick, confusion in his eyes.

"Here, sir. In this crater."

"We should investigate, sir, before we do anything else. It may be something that helps us."

Finally the President spoke.

"Investigate with what? The Florida launch facilities are gone. Only two shuttles remain, and they're strictly close orbit vehicles."

"This is nothing but a shadow," Gogh cut in. "This is nonsense, Mr. President. You've made the right decision."

"A rectangular shadow?" Nick protested.

"Not impossible. There is a face shadow on Mars, you know."

"It should be investigated—"

"Too late," the President said, and then turned his chair back to the window. He twisted the new paper clip into a crank and began to twirl it furiously. "The decision has been made, and the order has been given."

Endless PresNet messages scrolled before Nick's eyes. He had no interest. Gogh's bombs were on their way—everything else paled in comparison. Images of children playing in Portland streets and people strolling in parks occupied Nick.

The moon photo was tacked on Nick's bulletin board. The ultimate mystery out of his reach—maybe forever. If Gogh's plan worked, whatever was in that crater would disappear. If it failed, in a decade maybe, they might be able to explore Flamsteed crater. Guiltily, Nick realized a part of him wanted Gogh to fail.

The computer beeped for his attention, as something he'd requested came across the screen. It was another variation of the Gomez model. Nick looked it over for the differences, but found himself thinking about the beep the computer made. He wondered if he could program it to jangle instead.

---

64. Landfall

We were out on the ice trying to free the *Terra Nova*. Suddenly the pack of killer whales attacked. They smashed their backs against the ice trying to knock us into the water. Such was their power that the ice exploded, showering us with fragments. We were lucky to scramble to more solid ice.

—Captain Robert Falcon Scott, January 5, 1911

West of Naples, Florida
PostQuilt: Wednesday, 1:20 p.m. EST

Patty's crimson trail steamed into the distance as far as Ron could see. She was losing massive amounts of blood, yet she kept swimming. Her breathing was labored and she was wheezing, and Ron regretted the burden he and his family were to her. Still, they had no choice but to stay.

No one had slept since Pat had been killed, but weak from

thirst and hunger, they sat quietly on Patty's back, with no energy for talking. Ron had no desire to sleep, fearful of the nightmares Pat's grisly death might generate.

Ron sat up and looked behind him again for signs the orcas were following. Pat was surely enough to fill the killer whale pack, Ron assured himself, but looked anyway. There was no sign of the pack. Ron looked ahead and got a shock—he could see land.

"Look! We made it! We made it!"

The others roused themselves and looked past Patty's head to the thin line of brown along the shore. Hidden reservoirs of energy were released and the Tubmans cheered and hugged one another.

"Good old Patty," Rosa said, leaning down to rub her sides. "I'm so sorry about Pat."

The family watched the shore creep closer, Ron estimating the spot where they could make it to shore in case something happened to Patty. Carmen turned to Ron, her mouth open to speak, but said nothing. She was staring past him to the sea. Ron turned to see a flock of birds in the distance. It took him a moment to understand the importance. The orca pack was following.

Looking back to shore Ron realized it would be close. The kids picked up on their parents' looks and were soon as worried as Ron and Carmen.

"They're coming, Dad."

"I know, Chris. But we're close to shore." Ron didn't add they weren't close enough. "We can swim if we have to." Chris didn't look reassured.

Soon the flock was close enough to make out individual birds, but the shore remained despairingly far. Suddenly the sleek form of a killer whale leapt from the water and splashed the Tubmans. There were no other whales in sight, but Ron knew the others would be there soon. The whale breached again, by Patty's head, and she bleated from fear. Then the whale leapt across her path and Patty heeled over, nearly throwing her passengers into the sea.

Ron feared she would be driven off course, but quickly she came around again. The orca leapt again, but this time Patty wouldn't be driven off. Two more tries, and two more failures, then the orca gave up and simply swam alongside, waiting.

Now the flock was nearly overhead, and they could see the fins of the pursuing whales. They split into two groups, one coming up on each side.

"Hang on, everybody."

The family flattened, ready for the attack. Just as before the orcas went for the legs.

Patty's shudder announced the first blow, and her scream the second. The orcas angled in, diving deep and then jetting up, attacking Patty's dangling legs. The blows continued, and soon Patty was streaming blood from all four limbs. Still she struggled toward the nearing shore.

Three blows in quick succession rocked Patty, and she rolled to the right, nearly tossing the family, before she righted. Patty lost all sense of direction and swam aimlessly for a few minutes, and then turned toward shore again.

It was close now; Ron could make out buildings behind the beach. "Come on, Patty!" Ron whispered. "You can make it."

The whales picked up the attack, sensing the nearing shore. Quivering silently now with the blows, Patty continued her struggle. The water was red now, not pink, but still she swam. Then an orca hit her undulating neck, severing an artery. When the neck cleared the surface between waves blood spurted from the wound. In a few minutes her head began to sag, and her body listed to the right.

"Time to get off?"

Ron asked, rather than ordered. Carmen hesitated briefly, looking at the crimson water and then the attacking orcas.

"All right, kids," Carmen announced. "Down the side."

The kids didn't hesitate. Rosa checked the catches on her life jacket, folded her left arm across her chest, and then slid down Patty's side into the water. She pushed herself a few feet away and waited for Chris. Patty was still swimming, and Rosa was falling behind. Carmen checked Chris's life jacket and then pushed him down the side. Rosa immediately swam to Chris and began towing him away from Patty's bloody wake.

Carmen turned to Ron and held out her hand. Ron took it and smiled.

"For better or worse, isn't that what we said?" Ron asked.

"You should have been more specific," Carmen responded,

then slid down, pulling Ron down after her. They were still swimming when Patty's screams started again, and kept on until they were outside what they considered the orca's circle. They finally stopped, exhausted. They were completely spent, and the adults hung on to the kids' life jackets to keep their heads above water.

Patty swam slowly in circles, suffering the constant attacks of the orcas. They could see her shudder with every piece of flesh torn from her body. Shortly she fell silent and rolled over in the sea, her head disappearing into the waves. Her blood slowly diffused through the water, and soon the Tubmans were swimming away, fearing the orcas, but also sharks and other predators.

The family swam for shore, under a canopy of screeching seabirds. They were coated with Patty's blood and left a pink trail of their own, and Ron worried something might follow it. Slowly the waves washed them clean and Ron switched to worrying about making it to the beach. It was there, tantalizingly close, but they had little strength.

They lost speed with each stroke, and soon were doing only a slow crawl. Without life jackets, Ron and Carmen struggled through the waves. Ron found he didn't have the strength to ride the waves, and they began breaking over him. Each time he went under it took longer to come up.

Ron popped to the surface to see Chris well ahead of him, Rosa right behind. Carmen was to his right. As he watched, a wave caught the kids and washed them toward shore, pushing them well ahead. They would make it, he knew—he didn't know about himself and Carmen. Ron relaxed between waves, then stroked furiously, trying to catch a wave and bodysurf in. Without enough speed, the waves kept washing over him.

Ron was semiconscious when he felt hands pulling him. Rosa and Chris dragged him through the surf, then dropped him in the shallows. Ron crawled the rest of the way to shore and turned to see the kids helping Carmen out of the surf. Soon they were lying side by side on the warm sand, thankful to be alive.

The joy of survival renewed Ron's strength, and he pushed himself into a sitting position. The remains of a shattered dock littered the beach and a parking lot. Behind that was what was left of a small town—it had been hit by a tidal wave.

"Come on, everyone," Ron urged. "Let's find something to drink."

"And eat," Rosa added.

"Do they have a McDonald's?" Chris asked.

Then a bloody wave washed over them and they hunkered down to keep from being sucked back to sea. Turning, Ron saw Patty thrashing in the surf. She struggled to get what was left of her legs under her and stand. Weak from blood loss, she couldn't lift her long neck, and only her head was held above the waves.

"You can make it, Patty!" Rosa yelled.

"Yeah, you can make it!" came Chris's echo.

But she couldn't. The orcas hit her again from the oceanside and Patty staggered through the waves and then fell onto her side, washing the family with another bloody wave. Her head came up out of the water briefly, then slipped below the surface for the last time.

Hoping she would recover, they stood silently and watched for a long time. Then Carmen took charge and turned them toward the remains of the town. Ron looked back at the mound resting in the sea and felt sadness, as if he'd lost a family member. She'd saved his family, but he could do nothing for her or poor Pat. He regretted that, but it also made him cherish his own family more. Stepping closer to Rosa he said, "Well, Rosa, how do you like sailing?"

Rosa turned and smiled, then reached out and took his hand.

65. Magic Mountain

Early one morning, a young woman looked through the mist to see a herd of buffalo approach. Then an opening appeared in the mountain and inside she could see the world as fresh and green as it once had been. The buffalo walked into the opening, and the mountain closed behind them.

—Kiowa legend

The I-5 Mountain, Oregon
PostQuilt: Wednesday, 11:32 a.m. PST

Kyle needed a bath and a night's sleep. Instead, he found himself staring up the sheer face of a mountain, preparing to climb into the unknown. Kyle had listened to the stories of the I-5 mountain with mild interest. He liked a mystery as well as the next person . . . until it involved him. And it involved him when the little girl had been carried up the mountain by the bird-thing.

The state police had taken charge at the mountain and were trying to send trapped motorists back down I-5. Many of the motorists were resisting, however, preferring to stay and watch the drama with the little girl unfolding. The congested traffic had dissolved a little, but it still meant driving up the median. To Kyle, the mountain looked like a scene from Disneyland. Right where the freeway should continue was a tall rock mountain, surrounded by boulders and a small meadow. Hundreds of people milled around the clearing, radiating fear and excitement in the air. Kyle half-expected to see hot dog vendors.

"It looks like a carnival," Shirley whispered.

"It looks like the 'Twilight Zone,' " Kyle responded.

A state police officer named Murphy was giving orders and greeted Kyle and the other climbers. He talked directly to Kyle, ignoring Shirley and the others.

"Thanks for coming. You can see the situation," Murphy said. "We got no idea where this sucker came from," he said, jerking his thumb toward the mountain, "and no way of getting up the damn thing. The little girl makes noises once in a while, so we're pretty sure she's still alive. We've tried climbing up, but we can get only about a third of the way. Can't get good footholds."

"What about this bird that picked up the little girl?" Kyle asked. "Not many birds could do that."

"You got that right," Murphy assured him. "It was a big sucker for sure. Had wings fifteen or twenty feet across. Funny thing though, it seemed to have trouble picking up that little girl. Like it didn't have much strength. Witnesses said it kind of floated her up."

"What kind of bird was it?" Shirley asked.

"They said it was a diseased condor. Didn't have any feathers, but it was too big to be anything but a condor."

Shirley shook her head in disbelief. How could a diseased, featherless condor fly?

"Where's the bird now?" Kyle asked.

"Shot. Probably dead. Fell down behind those rocks up there with the little girl. Christy, her name is—no, Chrissy." Murphy pointed to an outcropping a few hundred feet up the mountain.

"Probably dead, or dead?" Kyle asked.

"Haven't heard the bird for a while. Not since the other one left."

"Other one?" Kyle probed.

"Where's the mother?" Shirley cut in. Murphy pointed to a woman sitting on a blanket in the clearing, surrounded by people. Two men with guns were standing nearby. Shirley walked off toward the mother.

Kyle waited until she was out of earshot. "Other one?" he repeated.

"Yeah. There's another one. Every once in a while it floats out over the peak of the mountain. It came down low at first, but we scared it off with shots. It doesn't come down anymore. We figure it's the mate. Probably gave up when the other one died. I don't think you have anything to worry about. If it comes back while you're climbing, we'll give you cover fire."

Kyle found no comfort in the thought of Murphy and his men blasting away over his head.

"Murphy, when we're up there I don't want any cover fire.

I don't want any fire at all. I don't want to risk a ricochet or bringing some of that mountain down in an avalanche."

Murphy didn't exactly disagree, so Kyle began hauling the climbing gear over to the mountain. As he walked a man separated from the crowd and joined him, a tall thin pale man with black-rimmed glasses. He obviously had something to say.

"It's not a condor."

"What?"

"I said, it's not a condor. I got here just before those fools over there shot the first one." The pale man jerked his head toward the two civilians with rifles, who began following within earshot. "Those two brainless wonders blew the wing off a living, breathing pterosaur."

Kyle stopped in his tracks and stared at the man.

"What are you talking about? Are you trying to tell me it was a dinosaur? A pterodactyl?"

"Certainly not. It was too big to be a pterodactyl. Surely it was part of the pterosaur family, but it most assuredly wasn't a pterodactyl. More likely it was a pteranodon. They were much bigger. Cretaceous period, I believe."

Kyle stared incredulously as the pale man continued talking.

"It was magnificent. So graceful in the air, and so huge. Nature's finest flying creation, perfectly designed to conserve every ounce of energy. The aerodynamics involved stagger the imagination. You see as the wingspan increases, the weight increases exponentially. Theoretically anything this big shouldn't fly at all. Even with the hollow bone structure. But it uses the surface area of its wings to maximize use of the thermal—"

"What about the little girl?" Kyle cut in.

"Well, they were most likely scavengers. Carrion eaters. I imagine that little girl was too tempting a target to ignore, just small enough to lift off the ground. The way it swept down and grabbed her . . . nature's perfect flying machine. And those two men shot it. They should be shot, not that beautiful pterodon."

Kyle couldn't stand it. He turned and walked back to the two men with guns.

"You the two that shot that thing?" The two nodded nervously. "Well, I'm going up there to see if that little girl's all right and when I get back I want to punch that man," he said, pointing at the pale one behind him. "Just in case I don't come back, will you see that it gets done?"

The two men looked at each other and then smiled. The pale man turned even paler and then walked hurriedly toward the crowd, the two following.

What had the jerk called it? Kyle wondered. A pterodon? Kyle had heard strange reports of disasters coming through the station house, but they were explainable. But what could explain dinosaurs flying around?

When Jay and Kimberly carried the rest of the equipment to the base of the mountain, Kyle tried to examine the rock face. It would be an easy climb over the boulders and loose rock at the bottom, but above that the rock face quickly became vertical. Shirley returned from talking to the mother while he was still mapping his climbing route.

"She's terrified. We'd better get up there quick and settle this one way or another." Shirley looked up to the overhang where the girl had disappeared. "We can do this free climb."

"No we can't," Kyle responded quickly.

Shirley looked at him and raised her eyebrows.

"There's two of them, remember? We want to be anchored if the other one comes after us."

Sure that Shirley saw right through him, Kyle quickly changed the subject.

"Not only that, but that guy back there," he said nodding to the pale man, "well, he said the bird up there was a dinosaur. Really! He called it a pterodon."

"No such thing, Officer Kyle."

"You think a condor could lift a little girl?"

"Depends on how much she weighs," Shirley said thoughtfully. "But I doubt it in this case. Chrissy is three years old. I'll bet she weighs thirty pounds."

"Then what lifted her up this mountain?"

Shirley frowned, then turned to Kyle with an infectious smile.

"I give up. Let's go see."

"Another thing, Shirley. I want you to take a gun."

"No thanks. I don't know how to use one anyway. I'd probably end up shooting you. I'll take the first aid pack," she said holding out her hand.

Kyle had no intention of getting shot, so he quickly agreed with Shirley. The first part would be a free climb through the loose rock and boulders. Then they would take separate routes up the face, setting pitons. Once the first piton was set Jay and Kimberly could belay their fall. Because of the size difference it was decided Jay would act as belayer for Kyle and Kimberly for Shirley.

Kyle stood at the base of the mountain, running over his training in his mind. His climbing skills were a tool, not a hobby, and seldom used. Shirley and the others, however, spent weekends scaling mountains for fun.

When Kimberly and Jay were ready, Kyle followed Shirley, who was scrambling up the boulders to the beginning of the rock face. Kyle followed easily enough but found himself breathing hard when he caught up with her. Shirley was examining the rock above her and mapping her route. Kyle picked a spot thirty feet from Shirley and checked the rock face. It would be easier for Shirley. The cracks weren't made for a size eleven climbing boot.

"Climbing!"

Kyle turned to see Shirley with her toe fitted into a crack about knee high.

"Hey, Shirley!" Kyle called, stopping her before she could get started. "You like movies?" Shirley nodded her head and smiled like she'd just been asked out on a date.

"Me too. I saw one once with a dinosaur like that one up there in it," Kyle said, jerking his thumb upward.

Shirley looked at him quizzically. "What happened?"

"It swooped down and swallowed a person whole."

Shirley shook her head, then smiled and patted her own bottom.

"Race you to the top, Officer Kyle."

Kyle yelled, "Climbing!" and Jay's "climb" followed immediately. Kyle jammed his right toes into a good-size crack and then felt for others wide enough to grip with his fingers. When he found a satisfactory one he pulled himself up, ready to set his other foot.

Kyle made good progress. He was fifteen feet up when he noticed that Shirley was ahead of him. He managed a couple more steps before he heard Shirley yell "slack," and set her first anchor. Kyle picked up his pace and climbed to a spot a few feet above Shirley's anchor to set his own. He clipped a D carabiner to it and passed his rope through the spring catch. A wave of relief came as he realized his fall would now be limited by the anchor.

Only after his third anchor was Kyle climbing ahead of Shirley, which gave him great satisfaction. They continued seesawing up the rock face, setting pitons, clipping carabiners, and looping kermantle. As they approached the outcropping they angled in toward it with one of them on either side. Twenty feet below the ledge Kyle motioned for Shirley to stop and be quiet. He listened intently but heard nothing—no little girl, no prehistoric bird.

They proceeded up on either side of the outcrop, neither willing to hammer in a piton this close to the pteranodon. Now Kyle and Shirley had to climb out and up, and they lost sight of each other. As Kyle neared the top he debated whether to pop up suddenly, jump onto the ledge, and then pull his gun, or peek over the top slowly. He decided on slow and cautious. Caution was natural for Kyle.

He found toeholds and fingerholds and then slowly pulled his head above the rim of the outcrop. The first thing he saw was the massive head of the pteranodon—six feet of it lying against Kyle's rock. Two enormous eyes were set in the middle of the spear-shaped face. Kyle sighed with relief when he saw the eyes were closed.

The pteranodon's wings filled nearly the entire ledge, concealing the little girl. Across the other side of the ledge he saw Shirley. First her eyes appeared searching for the child. Then she stared at the pteranodon, caught Kyle's eye, shook her head in disbelief, and mouthed, "Is it dead?" Kyle mouthed back, "I think so." Shirley nodded, and then pushed herself up a little higher and took hold of the collapsed wing of the pteranodon. As she lifted it, stretching it out so that she could look under it for the little girl, the creature blew air through the nostrils in its beak.

Kyle dropped his head down and froze. It was alive. He thought about shooting it, but he couldn't and still hang on.

Kyle pulled his head up again to find himself staring at the back of the pteranodon's head. It had moved; its head was up now and its beak pointed at Shirley. The crest that protruded out the back was inches from Kyle's face. Kyle followed the creature's stare to Shirley, who had lifted the wing and was looking under the membrane for the little girl. As she started to lift another piece of wing, she looked up to find the pteranodon staring at her, and she froze. Kyle decided to grab the crest and hold the bird. He made sure his feet were secure, detached his rope and secured it in the rock, and pushed up slowly with his legs.

When Shirley started to lower the bird's wing, the pteranodon's mouth opened in a high-pitched screech. Then it lunged at Shirley, using its beak like a spear. Shirley flinched, bringing her hands up to deflect the thrust, but the bird was too fast—as her hands grasped the beak, the momentum of the thrust carried the beak into her chest, knocking her over the edge. Controlling his panic, Kyle reacted by pushing himself up and flopping onto the ledge. As soon as Kyle's chest hit the rock, the pteranodon twisted to look at him. The crest was suddenly out of Kyle's reach and he found himself staring down the three-foot beak into a pair of black, angry eyes.

The bird screeched again and began hopping, its unfolded left wing partially obscuring Kyle's view. Kyle pulled both legs up onto the ledge as the pteranodon hopped trying to get at him. It was handicapped by its huge wingspan and its crippled wing. Now it began beating at Kyle with its good wing. Then the bird lunged again.

Kyle, stumbling backward, tripped over loose rock, falling against the cliff wall. The bird danced around and Kyle saw the beak coming at his stomach. He leapt sideways and grabbed the beak with both hands, holding it closed. The huge wings slapped at his body and face, but he kept his head down and let his shoulders absorb the blows. He was gaining confidence when something tore through his shirt and sliced the skin on his right shoulder.

In sudden pain, Kyle realized the creature had small clawed feet attached to its wing. Wincing, Kyle maneuvered himself to his left and away from the good wing, in a frantic dance with the pteranodon, keeping it at arm's length. Around and around they went until the partners collapsed in exhaustion.

Still, Kyle held on, feeling the deep, rapid breaths coming out of its nostrils.

He was still considering the options when he heard a voice.

"I want my mommy."

Kyle looked around but couldn't see where the voice was coming from.

"Chrissy? Where are you, honey?"

"I'm here. I hurt."

Kyle could hear the voice, but the wing was blocking his view. Desperately, he searched vainly for an option. Then Shirley's head appeared.

She pulled herself up over the ledge, flopped onto her stomach and then rolled to her back, smiling.

"I saw you dancing with that thing, Officer Kyle. And while on duty too. You two made such a lovely couple," she drawled sarcastically.

Kyle felt foolish but spoke authoritatively. "The little girl's here somewhere, I heard her voice. See if you can find her."

Shirley nodded and crawled to look under the massive wings, then poked her head up and looked at Kyle mischievously. "Hey, Kyle, give me a hand, will you?"

When she picked up the wing, the pteranodon began twisting sideways.

"Mommy?"

At the sound, Shirley abruptly turned around and crawled to the cliff wall, reaching for the broken wing.

Kyle tightened his grip. When Shirley lifted the bird's injured wing, Kyle could feel the bird's whole body shudder. Now Shirley lay on her stomach looking down into a crack between the ledge and the cliff wall.

"Hello, Chrissy," she said. "Your mommy sent us to get you."

"I hurt."

"Where, Chrissy? Where do you hurt?"

"Here. And here."

In the dim light, Shirley could see the child's gestures.

"I'll be right back, Chrissy," Shirley said soothingly. "She's in pretty good shape," she announced. She rolled to face Kyle. "Some cuts and abrasions. Her shoulder looks the worst, but her arm's hurt too." Looking at Kyle and the pteranodon, she frowned.

"Since you've got your hands full, I guess I'll take care of her."

"Shirley, get my gun and shoot it. Then I can help."

Shirley thought it over for a second, and then shook her head.

"I don't know how to use it. Besides, you've got it under control. Why kill it?"

Shirley grinned. Then she rolled over, reached down into the hole and began checking Chrissy's injuries while Kyle watched helplessly. After a few minutes she slowly pulled the child out of the crack, pausing to reassure Chrissy when she began to cry.

Chrissy started to sit up, but Shirley restrained the child, talking soothingly as she splinted the right arm, put it in a sling, and tied it across Chrissy's chest. Next she bandaged a wound on Chrissy's head, then cut away at her shirt, exposing the injured shoulder. It was caked in dried blood and Shirley shook her head. She was still looking at the injury when a shadow passed over the ledge.

Kyle looked up to see another pteranodon. The newcomer looked like a 727 orbiting above them.

"We've got company, Shirley."

Shirley didn't pause. Instead she quickly bandaged the shoulder and then got Chrissy to the edge and propped her up.

"Kyle, we don't need a backboard, so I'm going to take her down myself." Then Shirley looked up at the circling pteranodon. "Maybe you could hold one in each hand."

A shot rang out, followed by a ricochet. The captive pteranodon began twisting and turning and Kyle tightened his grip until it settled down. Waving her hands, Shirley stood up slowly, leaning out over the ledge to shout. "No firing! We're coming down! We've got the little girl."

Kyle knew the last sentence would mean new hope to a mother down in the clearing. Shirley pulled Chrissy to her chest and began crisscrossing kermantle to secure her. Kyle watched helplessly, his frustration growing with each second. Another shadow passed over them. Kyle looked up to see the pteranodon closer than before. The shadow passed twice more, growing bigger each time.

"It's coming," Kyle warned.

Shirley ignored him and finished strapping the little girl firmly to her chest, the injured arm safely tucked between her own and Chrissy's body.

"Gotta go now. Hang in there, I'll be back."

Kyle was about to answer when the second pteranodon swooped low over the edge, knocking Shirley backward onto a loose pile of rocks. Shirley gasped with pain. The fall set off spasms of pain in Chrissy, who began sobbing wildly. Desperate, Kyle got to his feet and began dragging the pteranodon toward the edge. If he couldn't shoot it, and if he couldn't let go of it, he was going to throw it over the ledge. Sensing the danger, the pteranodon renewed its struggle. For Kyle, this wasn't a dance, it was a tug of war. The pteranodon used its good wing to push back and beat at Kyle, but it was losing the fight, and Kyle pulled it closer to the ledge. As he struggled, Shirley slid over the side and disappeared. Kyle took another step and stumbled over a rock, falling to his knees but holding on to the bird. He was ready to stand when a rush of wind behind him announced the other pteranodon. Then he felt a jab of pain.

The second one had stabbed him in the butt with its beak. Kyle flinched and screamed, letting go of the first to protect himself from the attacker. When he released its bill the dinosaur tumbled backward, finally winning the tug of war. Kyle turned in time to dodge another jab, stumbling backward and falling onto his wounded behind. Both birds now screamed simultaneously, deafeningly, but he picked up a rock and hit the pteranodon who had stabbed him. Spreading its mammoth wings, it launched itself off the edge, only to float back up and hover, looking down. Kyle remembered his pistol and fired, punching an insignificant hole in the webbing. The sound drove the pteranodon off, and it floated out of sight.

Kyle turned to face the injured pteranodon, his pistol still in his hand. But when he swung around, the pteranodon was thrusting at him with its beak. As Kyle brought his arms up to deflect the jab, the dinosaur's mouth opened revealing rows of needlelike teeth, and then closed them over his gun arm just above the wrist. Then the dinosaur jerked its head back. When it did Kyle pulled his arm out, the rows of teeth shredding three inches of skin. Overwhelmed by pain, Kyle dropped his gun—

just as the pteranodon jabbed into Kyle's sternum, knocking the wind out of him. The beak stabbed once more, jamming between two ribs. Kyle grabbed the beak and pushed it back. His bottom, chest, and wrist were throbbing, and he was in a fight for his life. The adrenalin poured into his system. Then he stood and dragged the pteranodon toward the edge again.

Twisting savagely, Kyle pulled the beak close to his chest, flexing his arms, and threw the dinosaur away from him. Only the good wing held it to the ledge, its body suspended in air. Kyle walked to the edge, ready to break the wing with his boot and send it over, but he paused. It was truly helpless now and no threat to him, except that it was hanging over his rope. He was considering a different way down when he heard Chrissy scream.

Kyle raised his boot and broke the wing with a quick stomp. Shrieking, the dinosaur dropped over the edge, fluttering and twisting in the air until it hit the rocks; then it lay silent and motionless.

Kyle leaned out looking for Shirley and Chrissy but couldn't see them. The ledge must still be obscuring his view, he hoped fervently. But now the other pteranodon floated by below him, circled, and headed back toward the cliff. He heard another scream when it disappeared, but then it floated below him again. Kyle looked back for his gun. When he started away from the edge to find it, another scream spun him in his tracks.

Picking up the rope, he wrapped it around his good wrist and arm, and when the pteranodon appeared below him a second later, he jumped, pushing out with his legs, to avoid the rocks. Kyle yelled, "Falling," and prayed Jay was awake on the belay. Kyle fell toward the pteranodon, angling head down, his rope trailing out behind him like a bungee cord—but kermantle rope has very little give. His stomach elevatored as he dropped and the cliff flashed by. The pteranodon was rushing up toward him, but laterally away from him. He hoped it was far enough.

As he fell below the ledge, he could see Shirley and Chrissy dangling on the other side, being lowered down by Kimberly on the ground. The pteranodon continued to rush toward him. Stretching out his arms, he angled down, trying to close the distance with a glide, though he realized he wouldn't get enough glide to close the gap. Then the pteranodon pivoted on its right wing, slowing its forward motion. As Kyle reached out to hit the wing he reached the end of the rope.

The kermantle snapped his wrist up, the rope burning and removing skin. He snatched it with the other hand and managed to stop his slide down the rope. As his arms pulled his shoulders and head up, his legs snapped low beneath him and he kicked out with them, bringing his feet under the pteranodon's wing, and up into the membrane. Kyle could see the impression of his climbing boots in the tautly stretched skin, and he pushed up with his entire body. The pteranodon rolled left away from the kick, emitting a shocked screech, and continued toward the cliff. Kyle lost sight of it then, because his rope finished snapping him away from the fleeing dinosaur. Now he was swinging by his arms, toward the mountainside.

He took the crushing collision full on his right knee and leg, then hung semiconscious. Slowly he realized the rock in front of him was moving. Panicky, he looked to his wrist—the rope was blood soaked but secure. Then Kyle realized he was being lowered by Jay.

He blanked out briefly. When he opened his eyes, people were laying him flat, stretching out his injured leg and sending more spasms of pain through his body. Discovering the wound on his backside, they rolled him over and cut away the seat of his trousers. Kyle was just aware enough to be embarrassed as they worked on his bottom for a while and then applied a compress. Then they lifted him and laid him on a stretcher facedown, his bare buttocks sticking up for the crowd to see. Mortified, Kyle closed his eyes, but he felt a touch on his face. He looked to see Shirley's brown eyes staring into his own.

"Chrissy's going to be okay. They've already transported her."

Kyle flashed a smile to acknowledge he'd heard. Then Shirley looked over at his exposed bottom, and shook her head in disbelief.

"My hero," she said, and then kissed him on the cheek.

66. Noah's Raven

Civilization comes in long waves. Whether Babylon, Ur, or ancient Guatemala, the mystics of those civilizations understood this, and used mathematics to try to understand why theirs and other civilizations come and go. Ours may be the only wave of civilization that has not made such an effort.

—Dr. Carrie Simpkins, *Mathematics and Prophecy*

Forest, former site of Portland, Oregon
PostQuilt: Wednesday, 12:30 p.m. PST

The sound of the motorcycle put them on the move again. Cubby led the way with Ellen and John taking turns jogging with Ripman, who let slip occasional groans. The motorcycle sounds continued in the distance, but did not approach. Then three gunshots echoed from the distance—followed by more motorcycle sounds and two more gunshots.

"Think a dino got him, Cubby?" John asked.

"I don't know," Cubby responded softly, and then with a touch of anger added, "How should I know?" To Ellen, Cubby seemed uncomfortable with the role of leader. His irritability was one symptom. The other more serious one was his unwillingness to consider any plan of action except heading to his house. For now they were moving away from the sounds of the motorcycle, but they'd need to settle the question of direction soon. As if in response to Ellen's thoughts, Cubby slowed to a walk, and the rest dropped abreast.

"Did you guys sabotage their bikes?" Ripman asked without looking up.

"Yeah, we did," Cubby said with pride. "We saw them go after John's mom and that other lady, and you take Mrs. Roberts off into the woods, so me and John waited until dark and then snuck into their camp and cut up their wiring so they couldn't follow you."

"All of the bikes except one."

"That was one John was supposed to do," Cubby snapped.

"Up yours, Cubby. You don't know which bike that was."

"Yeah, maybe. Hey, where is that other lady?"

Ripman finally looked up and caught Ellen's eye. When he didn't say anything, Ellen just shook her head. She couldn't bear discussing the details. Cubby and John sensed her pain so Cubby quickly changed the subject.

"We also got this gun off a dead guy," Cubby said, holding it up.

Other visions immediately filled Ellen's head—terrible visions. Ellen wondered if they'd found the gun on Coop, or Bobby, but didn't bother to ask. Someday she would have to cleanse herself of these memories by talking them out, but this day called for repression and denial.

"Elemental, guys," Ripman said. Ellen noticed that Cubby and her son glowed in the light of Ripman's praise. "Except for one thing," Ripman continued. "You used up all the ammo shooting at those assholes back there."

"Wrong again, Sherlock," John said, pulling two clips of ammunition out of his jacket pockets. "Now if we can only figure out how to change the clips."

Cubby kept walking but began fumbling with the gun, turning it at different angles and pushing and pulling on anything that looked like a release. Ellen and John flinched every time the barrel of the gun turned toward them.

Finally, Ripman snorted derisively and said, "Let me do it before you shoot someone." Cubby gave up the gun reluctantly. Ripman turned partially away, so Cubby and John could not see what he did, and when he turned around the empty clip was out of the gun. John handed over another clip and Ripman slipped it in the handle, then slapped it home with the palm of his hand. He didn't volunteer to show anyone how to change the clip, and it was then Ellen realized how insecure he was.

Ripman, she saw, needed an edge over John and Cubby to stay their friend. They were willing to give their friendship to Ripman, but he needed to earn it, or perhaps, Ellen thought, buy it. Ripman wouldn't take anything for free or do anything the easy way. He didn't want anything from anyone that he didn't pay for. Cubby's and John's friendship was paid for in myriad ways, but mostly by the way Ripman doled out esoteric knowledge, bits and pieces of skill, and expertise he had been husbanding for just that purpose. Her son and Cubby's resourcefulness at disabling the motorcycles and obtaining a gun had disturbed Ripman's balance with his friends. Their independence had devalued the only commodity he felt he had, skill. So Ripman ridiculed them for missing one motorcycle, and then reestablished his value by changing the clip in the gun. He needed that edge and Ellen was willing to let him keep it for now.

Cubby held out his hand. Ripman hesitated, then slapped the gun into Cubby's palm.

"Wish I still had my bow, guns are a crutch, but a bow—"

"I know, Ripman," Cubby cut in, "a bow is el-ah-mental." When John harmonized the word with Cubby, all three of them laughed, diffusing the tension and reaffirming their friendship. They walked in silence for a way, not wanting to disturb the good feeling.

Ellen grew impatient. They needed a plan, a goal, and in her mind the only goal could be to get out of dinosaur land as soon as possible. She was about to speak when Ripman saved her the trouble.

"Cubby . . . it's really gone, Portland's gone. You can't go home."

Ripman's tone was conciliatory, his comments an act of compassion.

"It is there! We saw it!"

"I've seen it too, Cubby. But something's not right. It comes and goes, and when it's there, I'm not sure it's really there."

Cubby walked in silence, sorting his thoughts, while Ellen hung back. She had already decided on her course of action. She and John were getting out as fast as possible. If Portland was there, it wasn't all there, and her part of it, her home, her friends and neighbors, were gone. She had her son, a husband somewhere, and a daughter. So far she had lost only things, and of the things lost only the mementos mattered, those markers of personal passage through time. And they mattered little compared to her family. She cared about Cubby and Ripman for their family's sake, but she would not risk her son and herself for them. She and John were leaving.

"I know the city doesn't look right, Ripman, but it's something," Cubby said. "My family is in there, my mom and dad. This isn't the rapture, I'll admit that. But it's something, something only God could do. There's a purpose behind this, a plan. My dad will understand it, he's probably explaining it right now. You guys don't have to come with me," Cubby finished. "I'm going into Portland."

Cubby's decision sounded as firm as Ellen's, but she wanted to give him options.

"Cubby, you can come with us, live with us as long as you want. I know your mom has relatives in Georgia or someplace, we can get in touch with them. You too, Ripman. We'll move down to the beach until someone figures out what is going on."

Ellen could tell by their faces they were looking for a kind way to say no.

The return of the helicopter spared them for a moment.

When Ellen heard the distant sound she sprinted ahead looking for thin canopy and began waving her arms. The helicopter never passed within sight of their group, but when the sounds faded they heard the brief distant roar of an engine, which soon died, replaced by the silence of the forest. The machine roar returned, and then faded, only to come back again. The rhythm continued, the sounds coming closer and closer.

"They're tracking us," Ripman said. "We better find a place we can defend."

Ripman lead off, but his injuries kept his pace down. As tired and hungry as he was, even Ellen could keep up with him. She was more than just physically tired, she was tired of being afraid, and tired of being a victim.

Something moved in the trees up ahead. Ripman spotted it with his good eye and veered to the right. The others followed his lead. Ellen spotted a long green tail protruding from behind a tree, but no head was visible. Whatever it was, it was content, and they ran on ignoring it. Ripman led them into a tiny clearing and to an ancient fallen tree on the far side, which had sprouted new trees along its entire length. Ripman paused looking around rapidly.

"This is as good as—" He stopped in midsentence, distracted by the noise behind him.

They all followed Ripman's gaze to see a dinosaur coming

through the trees. It was half the size of the one that had gotten Angie, but its jaws were still big enough to bite a person in half. Cubby was pointing his gun at it, waiting for a clear shot.

"Don't shoot it with that, Cubby, you'll only make it mad. Everyone spread out, back away slowly," Ripman ordered.

Ellen fought down the urge to run and obeyed him, looking to see where John was. She was next to Ripman, then Cubby, and John was on the far side. She punished herself mentally for letting John get so far away. The dinosaur stepped into the clearing, walking on two huge hind legs, dragging a long muscular tail behind. Its forelegs were small but powerful looking. Its triangular head had massive gaping jaws showing rows of pointed teeth; its breath came in liquid heaves. Most noticeable were its eyes—its *eye*. The left was a brown orb barely distinguishable from the olive skin, but the right eye was a large crusted scab. Blackened blood stained the right side of its face down to its shoulder. John gasped, and Ellen heard Cubby say, "It's One Eye."

The animal was swinging its head from side to side, keeping its good left eye on them all. As they backed away it became more difficult for it to keep them in sight and the arc of its swings increased. Seeming confused, it paused at the edge of the clearing, its head continuing to swing, watching them inch backward.

The four continued backing slowly while the dinosaur watched. They were only a few yards from the trees when the dinosaur started forward again. Ellen watched its head swing wide, tracking each of them, and it gave her an idea. If they waited until the head started its swing away, and they peeled off in sequence, it would give them a precious few seconds head start. She was about to yell instructions to the others when Cubby tripped and fell backward, the gun in his hand firing wildly into the air.

Now the dinosaur screamed and charged directly toward Cubby, who was struggling to his feet. Ripman began hollering and waving his arms, and Ellen followed his lead, but the dinosaur's dead eye was blind to Ellen and Ripman, and its own screams drowned out their voices. Cubby started firing at the creature's chest. Either the impact of the lead slugs or the report of the pistol froze the dinosaur in its charge, stopping just in front of Cubby, its head thrown back into a scream.

John yelled something to Cubby but no one could hear him. Cubby emptied the last bullet into the dinosaur and then fumbled with the gun, trying to eject the clip, forgetting John had the spare one.

All Ellen could do was yell and wave her arms. Blood, from the bullet holes, speckled the dinosaur's chest. The creature took the last step toward Cubby, its gaze fixed on the boy's head, its jaws opening. Cubby threw the useless gun into the gaping mouth and turned, stumbled to his feet, and ran.

The dinosaur shook its head throwing the gun out toward Ellen and Ripman. Ellen jumped for it, forgetting that it wasn't loaded. But as she moved she saw John charging at the dinosaur from the other side, a stick in his hand. Blind to Ellen, the dinosaur swung to take John's charge, but as it turned the tail swept toward Ellen, catching her as she bent looking for the gun, tumbling her over her right shoulder into the fallen tree. Her ribs flexed, absorbing enough of the impact to keep them from breaking, but the blow knocked the wind from her. When she collided with the log, she put out her right arm to absorb the shock. But her arm slipped, breaking as it slammed against the wood.

In agony, flat on her back, she saw the tail fly over her head splintering tree limbs above. When the tail fell toward Ellen, she screamed, then rolled up on her broken arm, flattening her body against the log. The tail slammed behind her and then was gone. She slipped back toward the ground, but arms encircled her chest and began pulling her through the grass. They were Ripman's arms. Through her tears she saw Cubby and John dancing in front of the dinosaur, poking sticks at it, wide apart, with Cubby keeping on the blind side, so the dinosaur had to keep swinging its head to keep track of him.

With a roar the motorcycle entered the clearing, carrying two riders, and Ellen's dread became hope. The animal did a quick, powerful pivot to face the new threat, its tail sweeping through the clearing. Diving into the grass to avoid it, Cubby and John disappeared.

With Ripman's help Ellen was up and running. The boy stopped inside the forest and leaned Ellen against a tree, then turned to check behind them. A rifle fired rapidly three times and Ellen saw the dinosaur charging the motorcycle as Butler revved the engine and Carl stood behind the bike firing his semiautomatic until the dinosaur collapsed to the ground screaming in pain.

Carl yelled in triumph. Butler said something to Carl that Ellen couldn't hear and then reached down to pull his rifle from the sheath. As he did the engine died. In the silence Ellen could hear the wet gurgling breathing of the dying dinosaur and the triumphant "all rights" of Carl and Butler as they walked forward to deliver the coups de grace.

Ripman pulled on her arm to go, but Ellen hesitated, her eyes searching for her son. John and Cubby were nowhere to be seen. Ripman pulled harder, and as she started to turn she noticed the dinosaur's back legs were pulled up under its body, its tail still moving slightly. With a paralyzing roar its head jerked up, its one good eye targeting Carl and Butler, and then its muscular hind legs launched at its executioners. Butler shouldered his rifle and fired two quick shots. At the same time Carl threw himself out of the dinosaur's path. Butler dropped his rifle at the last second and brought his arms up in a futile attempt to protect himself before he disappeared under the dinosaur's falling body.

Ellen tried running but the movement bounced her arm, blurring her vision with pain. Finally, Ripman circled her waist with his arm to support her. Her ribs, bone bruised, ached nearly as badly as her arm, and Ripman's support was almost too much to bear. They had just managed to develop a walking rhythm that minimized Ellen's pain and maximized their speed when the sharp crack of a rifle buried a bullet into the tree ahead of them.

Ripman helped Ellen turn to face Carl, whose leg bandage was black with old blood while new blood stained his arms, legs, and chest. The biker's smile was finally gone and his swagger lost to a bad limp. The rifle was leveled at them from Carl's hip, and Ellen recognized the murderous rage in his eyes. She pushed Ripman's arm off and tried to step away from him; the semiautomatic rifle could kill them both in a second unless they moved apart.

"You take another step, Ellen, and I'll kill you both."

Ellen and Ripman froze. They had no doubt Carl would do

it. Carl switched his hate-filled gaze from Ellen to Ripman. He leveled the gun at Ripman's stomach.

"Kid, I owe you big-time. Now Ellen here still has somethin' I want, but you . . . I mean you backshoot my friend Bobby, you send Miller off to get eaten by that dinosaur, and then you double-cross us. You and those friends of yours were supposed to give us enough time to get out of there before that dinosaur got to us. That was the deal. We kept our part of the bargain, we let you and her go, but you tried to kill us—kill me!"

Ellen once again tried to distract Carl.

"What happened to Kishton, he get away too?"

"I'll tell you what the fuck happened! It bit his head off, that's what happened. But when it did I pumped five bullets into its brain. I killed that mother—twice as big as that other one—the one that got—"

Carl's eyes glazed over as he realized the last of his friends was dead. He was alone now, but in an instant his eyes refocused in a cold stare.

"Carl, I'll give you what you want. Just don't hurt him," Ellen pleaded.

"Give? I'll take what I want, and do what I want, when the hell I want to."

Carl swung his gun back to Ripman just as Cubby's deep menacing voice came out of the trees to Ellen's right.

"Freeze, maggot, or I'll blow you away."

Carl spun and fired twice toward the voice. As the second report sounded, another gun fired three times, the slugs ripping through the flesh of Carl's back, pitching him forward. Ellen, stunned, tried to understand what had happened. Carl had fired at Cubby but Carl ended up shot dead from behind.

Now Cubby emerged from the forest on Ellen's right, and then John emerged from the left, holding the pistol. Waves of relief swept over Ellen followed by concern for John: Her child had killed.

Ripman sent Cubby and John back to the clearing to retrieve Butler's rifle and ammunition. While they were gone he used his hunting knife to cut three limbs the length of Ellen's arm. Then he cut strips of cloth from Carl's clothing. Ellen's broken bone wasn't protruding, so to Ellen's relief, Ripman didn't try to set it. The splint did nothing to relieve the pain, but the sling made it easier for her to immobilize it. Ripman finished the first aid just as they heard the motorcycle again.

Ripman ran for Carl's rifle and aimed it in the direction of the sound, but something was not right. The sound was approaching very slowly. Finally, Ripman shouted and pointed through the trees. Ellen had to stand to see above the ferns and grasses. Cubby was driving the bike, with John behind him, his arms around Cubby's waist. It was clear Cubby was a novice on a motorcycle. The bike was in one of the high gears, and Cubby kept revving it, releasing the clutch, and lurching forward, almost losing John each time. Ripman shook his head, and then laughed.

"Those bozos can't even ride a motorcycle."

When they finally lurched up to Ripman he shook his head in appreciation.

"You bozos finally did something right. Does it have much gas?"

It turned out to have about a quarter of a tank. Not even Ripman had any idea how far that would take them. Since they couldn't all ride the bike, Ellen insisted that Ripman take John and Cubby out first. John insisted Ellen go first, and Cubby protested going at all. He wanted to ride into Portland if they could find it.

Cubby did agree that Ellen needed to get to a doctor and should go first. They then argued over who should have which weapons. Ellen wanted to take only the pistol. John insisted she take a rifle. Cubby agreed, pointing out that he and John had survived without a gun. Ripman muttered something about dumb luck under his breath, then sided with Ellen. With the bike they could outrun the dinos, so they would take just the pistol. Cubby and John didn't want to stay with Carl's body, it would attract scavengers. So the three boys scratched in the dirt working out a plan to rendezvous. Ripman started the bike as if he knew what he was doing, then Cubby and John helped Ellen on the back, John giving her shoulder a squeeze. It was too painful for Ellen to turn around, so she didn't see her son waving good-bye.

67. Out of the Pit

. . . the mountains shall be molten . . . and the valleys shall be cleft, as wax before the fire, like water rushing down a slope.

—Micah 1:4

Warm Springs Indian Reservation, Oregon
PostQuilt: Wednesday, 4:52 p.m. PST

Petra, still wedged against the tree trunk, shivered uncontrollably. A bra and torn panties were inappropriate for an autumn day in Oregon. The sounds of splashing came from the lake. She wondered if more of those walking fish lived in the lake, and wished Dr. Coombs and Dr. Piltcher could have seen that fish. It walked, it breathed air, it swam under the water. Half-fish and half-mammal, it was some in-between species, like millions of other variant forms. As such it must have been ancient, much older than the dinosaurs onshore. Dr. Piltcher would have given his life to see it, but unfortunately he gave his life a little too soon.

Determined not to spend another night with the dinosaurs, Petra climbed down, stiff from the cold, and worked her joints. When they were loose enough to let her run if she had to, she crept back toward the carcass.

Petra approached from the back side again. It had been the least popular side.

She was shocked when she saw the carcass. It had been hollowed out and stripped of most skin and flesh, leaving bare bones. A huge bloody pool lay around the bone pile and a dozen dinosaurs of different sizes surrounded the remains, gnawing on bones and digging pieces of bloody flesh from inside the carcass. One small dinosaur was peeling skin away from the head.

Petra worried she had waited too long. They were digging deep into the carcass, and from the look of it they had emptied the chest cavity of every bit of soft tissue. Had they eaten clean through to Colter? Was he still alive under that bloody mess somewhere?

Petra approached slowly, gun ready, walking out between the trees until the dinosaurs spotted her and froze. None of them was bigger than about ten feet. Apparently the giant dinosaurs had eaten their fill and moved off; still the ten-footers were terrifying. Sucking up her courage, she ran forward screaming at the top of her lungs. The sound was pitiful compared to those of the giant lizards, but it got their attention. She charged and just before she reached the nearest one fired a round into the air, the noise scattering the feeders. After Petra fired another round, they moved off a safe distance. Now to find Colter.

"Colter? Colter?" she called. "Colter, are you still here somewhere?"

Petra listened for a reply but heard none. She walked to the carcass, her feet squishing in the blood-soaked grass, and then reached out gingerly with one hand and pushed on one of the still standing ribs. It didn't budge. Petra put her bare shoulder against it and pushed with all her strength. It still didn't budge. The ribs were still attached to the backbone and weighed tons. She had no hope of moving it off Colter. There were only two choices now. Go back to digging, or climb inside and try to get through past the backbone. Petra peered into the carcass. Something was moving.

She backed up, raising the rifle. The carcass began to rock ever so slightly, the still-hanging skin flapped with the movement. Then something rose out of the carcass, covered with blood and reddish mud. The figure rose, then slipped back only to rise again, grabbing on to the hanging skin and flopping over the side and out. Like some bizarre cesarean-born baby, Colter had emerged from the dinosaur.

Hysterical, overwhelmed with joy, Petra ran to him and cradled his head in her lap. She wiped the blood from his face to see he was crying, then rocked him in her lap and cried with him. She continued to clean his face and head, but had nowhere to wipe the blood because it had soaked the ground too. Petra opened Colter's torn shirt gently and realized some of the blood was his. There was a gash from above his left nipple running all the way to the right side. She looked closer to find perforations in his shirt along his left arm. A splinter was sticking out of one of the holes. Petra reached down and yanked the splinter out. That sharp jab of pain made Colter stop sobbing and he complained instead. "Ouch. That hurts, Petra!"

Petra laughed at him sadly. "Colter, you've got a gash across your chest. You've been buried alive under a dinosaur, and you're complaining about a little splinter?"

"Lots of splinters," he replied. "I pulled out as many as I could reach."

"How did you survive down there?"

"I nearly didn't." Colter paused, but he fought back his tears. "I got down flat when it started to fall. It had dug out enough of a space for me, I guess. It jammed that limb down on me though. I think it broke a rib or two. That's when I got the splinters."

Petra was going to ask about the slash across his chest, but Colter looked like he was trying not to remember some things, so she let him tell it his way.

"I heard you outside and I tried digging out, but it was no use. I could hardly move. Then I heard the feeding start. You can't believe how horrible it sounds from underneath. It was coming toward me."

Colter was getting louder and losing control over his emotions.

Petra tried to calm him. "It's okay now, Colter. You're out."

"Then the blood started. It was just a wetness at first. I didn't know what it was. It had a salty smell to it. It just kept coming, filling the hole I was in. Other body fluids too."

"Don't think about it, Colter."

"I nearly drowned in it."

"Time to go, Colter."

"Oh God, it was horrible."

"The dinosaurs might come back, Colter."

"I want to go. I want to go out of here."

"Yes, Colter. Me too."

They stood, helping each other to their feet and then with Petra holding the rifle, they stumbled through the trees and back toward the RV. They leaned on each other, more for emotional support than physical.

Monoclonius stood in the clearing, but they ignored the humans, allowing them to cross the clearing without incident, and then they were into the tall brush on the other side. Petra hated the brush. There was no visibility and they had too little energy to walk stealthily, so they crashed through it. Petra slowed when she saw the RV. Near it were two piles of bones. Then Petra urged Colter to go faster. As they walked, Petra scanned the clearing nervously for predators.

The RV was close now. So close she began to feel its safety. It could take them away, and she wanted that badly, and the more she wanted it the more she feared something would snatch it away again. At the door of the RV Petra pushed Colter up and inside. Then with a last nervous look around she climbed in, vowing not to leave the vehicle until she was safe with other people.

Colter handed her a quart of orange juice and raised a second quart to his lips, drinking down huge gulps. Petra drank half of her juice without pause. After a couple more swallows, Colter walked into the back of the RV and collapsed on the bed. Petra started back to join him but jumped back in fear as something came out from under a pile of blankets—Sarah. Petra had forgotten about the little dinosaur. It stared at her, but unlike earlier, she didn't seem panicked by Petra's presence. Then to Petra's surprise Sarah waddled over and banged into Colter's dangling legs.

"Petra," Colter moaned. "Feed them will ya?"

Opening the fridge, Petra pulled out an apple and rolled it to Sarah. Then Moose launched himself from the top of the cabinet, landed next to Colter, and then jumped down to the floor. Petra sliced up another apple, and he quickly carried a piece to his place on top of the cabinets. Petra was amazed by the little dinosaur's new confidence. They had lost all fear of people.

She flopped down next to Colter, lying on her back with one arm over her face, and both were soon asleep. When Petra awoke she found Moose sleeping next to Colter on the other side, but when she stirred the little animal scrambled up the wall and to his hiding place.

Petra propped herself up with one elbow and looked down at Colter. His face was caked with blood and red mud, so she got up, soaked a towel with water and began to clean his face. He woke and stared at her blankly.

"Colter, you're coated with . . . well, why don't you take your clothes off? You're a mess."

Colter nodded and sat up, unbuttoning his shirt. Now Petra could see the wound on his chest more clearly. It was deep, crusted with dried blood, and should have been stitched. But at least it didn't seem to be oozing, so Petra decided it would heal. Colter slipped out of his bloody pants and shorts and put on a clean pair of pants and a T-shirt that he dug out of a cupboard.

Petra looked at her own body. She wasn't as severely injured as Colter, but blood and dirt were all over her. Petra used the wet towel to wipe off as much of the grime as she could, and then took off her bra and bloody panties to wipe the rest of herself. Petra felt scabs on her bottom.

"Here, let me," Colter said, holding out his hand for the towel.

Petra was momentarily embarrassed. He was fully clothed and she was naked, and she felt helpless. Still, she turned and let him help her.

"It's not too bad," he assured her.

"Good. Give me some of my clothes to put on."

Petra turned, covering her small breasts with her arms as Colter stared at her with a strange look on his face.

"Well . . . I . . ."

Colter never got to finish. Something rattled behind him. He turned and looked for what was making the noise in the front of the RV. Petra cringed behind Colter as they walked forward, looking for the sound.

Colter stooped, reaching down to a cabinet door near the floor, hesitated and then yanked it open. A baby dinosaur rolled out, its lower half still in the eggshell. About a foot long, its skin was the bright green of spring leaves. The wet little baby had a small flexible neck collar and a short stubby tail, its snout tipped with a small hooked horn. It was clearly a baby monoclonius.

Colter reached down and pulled the rest of the eggshell away and then wiped it with the towel he had been using on Petra's bottom.

"It's cute, isn't it, Colter?"

"Cute now, sure. It won't be so cute when it weighs a few tons."

Colter picked it up and handed it to Petra. It was heavier than it looked and wriggled in her grasp.

"What do we feed it?"

"I dunno. Probably some mashed fruit. Maybe some milk. Moose and Sarah seem to eat everything."

"We'll figure that out in a minute." Petra put the baby down on Sarah's blanket, and she sniffed at the baby, but wasn't hostile. Then turning to Colter Petra said, "First, where are my clothes?"

"Well . . . you see I was kind of upset when I thought you were dead. I mean, I didn't know you were alive. How did you get away from that fish anyway?"

"Don't change the subject. Where are my clothes?"

"I kind of threw them away."

"Colter! Why would you do that?"

Finally he got the courage to look Petra in the eyes and tell her.

"Your things kept reminding me of you, and how you were dead and stuff. It was too hard for me. It hurt pretty bad."

Tears welled up in Petra's eyes. It was only a couple of sentences but Petra knew the rest of what he could never say. She wrapped her arms around him and hugged him, and then pretended to be mad at him.

"Oh great. Someone dies and you immediately hold a garage sale. What am I supposed to do for clothes?"

"I like you the way you are."

"I don't like being the only one naked."

"I can fix that," Colter offered.

"Don't bother. Neither of us is in any shape for that."

Petra turned and opened several cabinets until she found one of Colter's sweatshirts and pulled it over her head. Though it hung down covering her bottom, she still felt exposed and she never wanted to feel that way again. Colter's pants were way too big, but she put on a pair of his boxer shorts. The flap gaped open when she tried sitting in them, so she found a safety pin and pinned it closed. It would have to do until she could get to a town.

Then Petra opened a can of peaches and mashed them up, pushing spoonfuls into the baby dinosaur's mouth. It chewed reflexively. When Petra was sure it had swallowed enough, she poured in some of the juice from the can. Most ran down its neck and pooled in the collar. Colter watched the feeding with amusement.

"Moose and Sarah aren't this sloppy," Colter said.

"It's just a widdle thing," Petra said in baby talk.

"Just what are you gonna call the little orphan?"

Petra set the can of peaches to the side and put the little dinosaur on the floor. The baby got to its feet and wobbled a few steps. Then it stopped and licked at the peach juice on its chin.

"Well, what if we call her Peaches?"

"Her?"

"Her until we know better. We should get a bottle somewhere for this poor thing."

He rolled his eyes, nodded, and moved to the driver's seat and started the engine. Petra sat down in the passenger seat gingerly, holding the sleeping baby dinosaur in her lap. Now that she was rested, she was beginning to feel every bruise, cut, and aching muscle. Colter, she knew, was feeling his pain as well.

They were about to leave when they heard the sound of padding feet. Petra flinched when Moose scrambled up the dash and stretched out in the window. Sarah waddled forward and looked perturbed that Petra had taken her place, so instead she curled up on the floor between the seats. Petra and Colter looked at each other and smiled.

"Well, honey," Colter said. "It's been quite a vacation."

"Yes, dear," Petra replied. "But the kids are exhausted. Let's go home."

Then they drove away from the clearing and back up the road.

68. CHOICES

In the age of no time, what came before will come again, and what is yet to come, will come before. I do not understand it myself, but I know it will be heralded by a great fire.
—Zorastrus, Prophet of Babylon

Forest, former site of Portland, Oregon
POSTQUILT: WEDNESDAY, 5:05 P.M. PST

They walked with a new confidence. Someone watching would say it was the rifles that gave them confidence; a store-bought, machine-made and polished confidence. But this was homemade confidence. Everything and nothing in their experience had prepared them for what they had gone through over the last few days, but what they found inside had been enough, even more than enough.

They'd had a happy victory celebration after Ripman left with Ellen. Exchanging insults, they argued over who should get credit for bungling the sabotage on the motorcycle, since that had saved them from One Eye and now was saving John's Mom. But as they moved toward the rendezvous point, Cubby fell silent.

Cubby and John could hear the helicopter come back, circling, its thumping sounds reverberating down the valley. But the rendezvous point was in a different direction, so the noise grew fainter as they moved away. An occasional lizard skittered across a log or glided from tree to tree above them. Once a crashing and thumping in the distance sent them running for cover, but the sounds finally moved off.

Finally they reached the dry riverbed Ripman had described. It disappeared around a bend to the southwest and then into the forest. The boys surveyed silently from the bank, scouting the forest on either side for animal signs. Then Cubby tugged on John's arm and pointed.

A movement caught John's eye. In the shadow on the far bank were several animals, four-legged with long tails, and long necks, resembling brontosauri, but only a fraction of the size. Occasionally a head would appear towering over the bank, look around, and then dip back down. The animals appeared to be grazing. Cubby and John finally stepped out of the shadow onto the bank, fully exposing themselves. A minute later a head came up, spotting them and grunting. Then three more heads popped up. The dinosaurs and the people stared at one another, then one by one the dinosaurs went back to eating.

Ripman was nowhere to be seen, so Cubby and John found a pile of rocks to settle on. They had no food, but large puddles in the riverbed would provide enough water for now. At least, if Ripman came back.

After a long wait the engine of the motorcycle announced Ripman's return. First the heads of the dinosaurs all popped up again, and they moved up the riverbed out of sight. Finally, John saw Ripman riding around the bed of the riverbed. Cubby and John cheered, then Cubby put his fingers in his mouth and blew several shrill whistles.

Ripman pulled up in front of them revving the engine loudly. His face was still swollen, he was cut and bruised and covered with dirt, yet he was also proud, even arrogant, and Cubby and John loved it. He finally let the engine die and untied a grocery bag from the back of the bike.

"How's my mom, Ripman?"

"She's fine. There's a bunch of houses over that way," he said, pointing. "The forest goes right up to their front doors. Some of the houses have been smashed up pretty good. It looks like some of the dinosaurs came to visit. The people who live there have blocked the streets with cars. There's cops there too, keeping people out, and keeping the dinosaurs in. The police took your mom to the hospital."

Ripman opened the pack and tossed cans of Coke Classic to Cubby and John. John drank a third of his in three gulps. When the carbonation burned his throat and nose he belched, but Cubby soon belched a belch that put John's to shame. Ripman kept digging, passing out another can of Coke to each, and then threw his friends a package of Twinkies and a Three Musketeers bar. They tore into the junk food till finally their ravenous gobbling turned to slow savoring.

"Where'd you get the goodies, Ripman?" Cubby asked.

"Hey, there's civilization out there. After I got John's mom to the cops, they wouldn't let me come back. They were going to round up some volunteers—mount a rescue mission. Jeez, you'd think it was some big deal. So I had to find a way around. I ran into a 7-Eleven down the road. It was semiopen, so I picked up some supplies."

"You pay for these?" Cubby asked suspiciously.

"They gave me a bag, didn't they?"

"You stole the bag too, didn't you?" John suggested.

"Hey, you don't want the stuff, give it back." Ripman said it good-naturedly.

John and Cubby knew he craved to be thought bad, and they were willing to support him. The sugar quickly replenished their strength and they joked and kidded for a few more minutes. Then Cubby began praying in whispers. When done he turned to the others.

"I'm not leaving. I'm going into Portland. My family is in there somewhere . . . my church."

John, uncertain how to respond, sat silent, watching a two-foot lizard slither down the bank and into a puddle. Ripman finally spoke, but gently, looking at Cubby with his good eye.

"Cubby, Portland's not right. I watched it. It seems to come and go . . . sometimes it's there, sometimes it isn't, and it's going away. Even if we headed to it, we'd probably go right through it. I think it's just some sort of mirage."

"Maybe, Ripman, but I've got to know. I've got to know!"

"It's not the second coming, Cubby."

"I know, but God's hand is in this."

"Maybe."

That "maybe," John realized, was the only concession to the possibility of God's existence Ripman had ever made. Ripman, the militant atheist, wouldn't have made this concession a few days ago.

"Let me run John out on the bike, then we'll go looking for Portland."

"You don't need to come, Ripman. Take John out, come back for me, I'll take you out, then I'll take the bike in toward Portland."

As Cubby and Ripman continued to argue, the helicopter sounded in the distance, somewhere out of sight. John, looking for it, ignored the argument. He didn't like what his friends were saying anyway. Cubby and Ripman were assuming he needed taking care of, and only after that would they see to their own needs. No one realized that he, John, had outwitted the dinosaur that chased them. He had given One Eye its name. He had helped disable the motorcycles, and he even shot—killed—Carl. His heart sank at that thought. After all that, his friends could not think of him as an equal. If the last three days hadn't changed their thinking, nothing would.

"Hey," he cut in, "nobody has to take me anywhere. You two take the bike and go find Portland. I'm walking out."

John swigged down the rest of his Coke, picked up his rifle, and started walking down the riverbed, following the bike's tire marks.

"Where are you going, man?" Ripman called. "Hey, wait up."

"Come on back, John, what are you so mad about?" Cubby added.

John stopped and turned back.

"I'm not mad. I'm just trying to save you the trouble of looking out for me. You two head on into Portland, have a good time. If I don't see you sooner, I'll see you later . . . maybe at the beach house." John turned to walk off and then stopped.

"I hope you find your folks, Cubby. Hey, Ripman, thanks for the food. See ya guys."

John walked off, deliberately splashing noisily in the puddles to keep him from hearing what they were saying. As soon as he was out of sight around a bend, he gripped the gun tighter, as feelings of loneliness replaced his bravado. The motorcycle came to life behind him, then he heard the put-put of someone riding it. He thought about hiding, making it easy for them to leave him, but that would be cowardly.

To John's surprise, Cubby was driving, and Ripman was hanging on behind. They rode up next to him, and Ripman climbed off to face John.

"We decided, John. We're all going home."

"It was great wasn't it, Johnny my boy? Let's do it again sometime," Cubby said, then released the clutch and rode the bike in a slow circle and disappeared around the bend.

"He's crazy. Ripman, couldn't you talk him out of it?"

"He's a fanatic. I never could talk sense to him."

They started walking again, this time side by side.

Terry stood by the helicopter rubbing his eyes. His head ached from the refueling vapors and from staring through the tops of trees trying to spot his wife. He realized finding her that way was unlikely, but he wasn't ready to give it up—he had no other choice.

Bill returned. Even Bill's size and official manner had failed to get free fuel from the crusty operator of the airfield. But he'd taken a Visa card—obviously, he didn't understand what had happened.

When Bill climbed back in and lifted off, Terry tried to find a way to sit comfortably on what was left of his seat. It was late afternoon and there was little daylight left to search with. This would be their last trip. After this, he didn't know what to do or where to go.

The house was a two-story Colonial, with a bay window and a dinosaur forest for a front yard. The windows were broken, but otherwise the house was intact.

"Through there," Ripman said pointing, "is another house and on the other side of that a cul-de-sac. Go up the cul-de-sac and over the fence of the blue house at the end. There's a highway on the other side. Follow it north and you'll find that roadblock. The cops will take you to your mom."

"Aren't you coming too?"

"Like I said, we're all going home. Your home is with your parents. Me, I don't have anyone. My dad's gone wherever Cubby's folks are, and he never gave a damn anyway," Ripman said with both sadness and bitterness in his voice. "Besides, I like it here. It's the best home I had."

"You can't stay here! Sooner or later those dinos will have you for lunch. Come with me. My mom asked you. We'd have a great time."

"Naw, I'm too elemental for you Yuppie types, but I'll trade you the pistol for the rifle. A bow won't cut it in here."

John traded, then handed back the pistol. "You're gonna need both, Ripman. If you change your mind, man, we'll be at the beach house."

"I know."

John walked through the trees a short distance, then turned and looked back. Ripman was still there watching him. John wanted to tell Ripman he'd miss him, that he would think about him, that he loved him. But none of that was elemental, at least not in Ripman's way of thinking. So instead John simply nodded his head. Ripman nodded back.

"See ya, Ripman."

"Later, John."

Cubby followed the riverbed, the noise of the bike chasing dinosaurs from his path. When the river angled off away from Portland, Cubby cut into the trees. Occasionally he came to clearings, some small, some larger, but as he looked into the distance no skyscrapers appeared.

He rode on, the sun setting on his left. It would be behind the hills soon, leaving the valley in shadow, and still the city could not be seen. He passed a section of collapsed forest, ran into an impassable rock slide, and headed uphill to skirt it. At the crest, he skidded to a stop. The view was unobstructed, and to his dismay he saw Mount Saint Helens in the distance. There was no city. Tears blurred his vision, and he wiped his eyes. Then he realized Mount Saint Helens had disappeared into a haze, and shimmering before him the city appeared. Skyscrapers towered above the trees as he looked around. He was in a city that wasn't there.

From this close Portland wasn't transparent. It was back, but Cubby didn't know for how long. If God had opened this door for him, he wasn't going to let it close. You don't need certainty when you have your faith, his father always said. Cubby sucked down his doubts, revved up the engine, and released the clutch. "Time to go home," he said to himself, and angled the bike down the hill toward the city.

* * *

Now Terry rubbed his aching eyes with both fists. He admitted defeat to himself and was ready to convince Bill.

"Bill, this is useless. We don't even know if Angie and Ellen are in there."

"Yeah, I know. I just don't know what else to do. Where do we start looking if we don't look here?"

"Will this thing make it to the beach . . . say about ninety miles? We can check our summer house."

When Bill didn't answer right away, Terry rubbed his eyes again, and opened them to see the return of the phantom city.

"Bill, it's back."

Bill straightened the helicopter, and hovered facing the city.

"We can try flying into it again. What do you think?" Terry suggested.

"Mmmm—I don't think—"

Something zoomed past the helicopter on the left, banked to the right on stubby wings, and flew directly toward the city, taking Terry by surprise. Bill spun the helicopter around and throttled up the engine until the rotors screamed.

"What's going on, Bill?"

"It's a cruise missile. We're in big trouble."

Terry looked around, trying to follow the flight of the cruise missile, and when he did he spotted another missile in the distance, then suddenly he realized the sky was full of them. Terry was trying to make sense of what was happening when the sky went white, as if a giant strobe light had just flashed. At the same time there was a burst of static over the earphones, followed by the acrid smell of ozone. The helicopter's engine sputtered and then died. Terry's stomach made him think they were suddenly in an elevator going down. The rotors continued to spin but without any power, making more of a whistle than a thump. The churning of his stomach increased and the helicopter's nose dipped, giving Terry a good view of the onrushing forest.

When John stepped out from beyond the last tree and onto the front lawn of the Colonial house, he felt tension being swept out of his body. His legs went weak with relief and began to shake. He hadn't realized how much fear and adrenalin had powered him, and he now felt every ache and pain, and he was exhausted.

He thought of his mom in a hospital, his dad in Washington, D.C., or somewhere, maybe with his sister. That meant John should be with his mom.

He found the cul-de-sac and the blue house Ripman had described. Two other houses at the end of the cul-de-sac were surrounded by fences six feet high, making the end of the street look like Fort Apache. The owners of the blue house had settled for a four-foot fence. John jumped up and straddled it. Balanced on the top he looked back down the cul-de-sac toward the forest. Ripman and Cubby were in there somewhere, and that meant he was leaving a part of himself there too. He knew the closeness they had shared was too good to last a lifetime, but he never expected it to end so abruptly. It wasn't the way childhood friendships should end. They should end slowly, day by day, month by month; each of them taking different paths that would lead them farther and farther apart. The forest had replaced the slow march to separate lives with a race to adulthood, and to loneliness.

John stared at the forest one last time, knowing there was no going back. As he turned to look for a soft landing spot beneath him, a blinding flash of light knocked him off the fence into the azalea bushes on the other side.

The New World

69. Beach House

The New World
North Oregon Coast

Cable TV was out, since the Portland feed was gone. At their beach house, Ellen and John could still pick up the Eugene and Salem stations, although the reception without the cable boost was terrible. It didn't matter though. The stations weren't carrying anything but disaster coverage, and John was sick of it. He wanted escapism, some mindless sex or violence to distract him.

The network news people were dominating the coverage, sitting in anchor booths and telling the camera what other people were telling them. John could only pick up two of the networks, but neither had its regular anchor. Apparently the New York problem had taken some of the network people; the second string was now anchoring from Chicago.

The news might have been fresh at one time but was now a series of recycled reports, including oft-repeated interviews with the President's chief of staff, Elizabeth Hawthorne. "The President is devoting himself to dealing with the crisis, but will meet with the press when the time is right," Ms. Hawthorne was shown saying over and over again. John watched Ms. Hawthorne deny rumors that the President was ill, take questions about relief efforts, and defer questions requiring an explanation of what had happened to the President's science advisor.

Dr. Paulson was interviewed repeatedly by the networks. He labeled what happened as time quilting, and described it as a natural result of the interaction of strings of dense matter created by nuclear detonations. When asked if it was true that only the former U.S.S.R. had detonated devices of sufficient size to create the effect, he deferred to Natalie Matsuda, the secretary of defense, who proceeded to blame it on the U.S.S.R. and single out the Russian Republic in particular to inherit the blame. She also claimed credit for preventing a worse disaster with the action taken in the Portland area. John noticed they never referred to it as a nuclear attack, calling it instead an "action."

There was quite a bit of debate over what had happened at Portland. Some experts claimed the explosions destroyed Portland, others claimed the blast more likely took place somewhere between the two space/times involved. John thought of Cubby during these discussions. Had he been incinerated in a nuclear holocaust, or was he where he so badly wanted to be, with his family and church?

The networks interviewed a Dr. Gomez of the Fermi Institute about the effect itself, but her explanation made little sense to John. She talked of explosions in the sixties and the time quilting, as if they were concurrent events. She referred vaguely to possible future events. Apparently the first computer models had correctly predicted the focal point and the time quilting but had not projected the events into the future. More sophisticated models were being tested and some of these projected additional events. She also said something about effects on the moon, but being unable to confirm them until the space program could be reestablished. That point was then lost in questions about identifying where the displaced people had gone. John realized there was cold comfort in knowing that friends and relatives could be alive in some other time period.

Dinosaur horror stories filled the rest of the news. Of course the media concentrated on made-in-America stories. Attacks by tyrannosaurs were the most popular. Occasionally a story sympathetic to dinosaurs would surface. The story of an old woman in New York with a pet dinosaur got a lot of play, and John was particularly touched by the story of the mother apatosaurus and her baby that saved a shipwrecked family, despite a killer whale attack. There were also stories of organized protests of animal rights activists who were fighting for dinosaur rights. There were many stories of food shortages, fuel shortages, and medical supply shortages. These were invariably followed by predictions of more shortages, and how the poor were disproportionately affected. The only silver lining in these reports was that the human losses were out of proportion to the crop losses. In other words, they lost more people than crops to feed them.

John's mother came out of the bedroom to make a cup of tea. Her right arm was in a cast, which she carried in a sling. He watched her until he was sure she could handle fixing the tea one-handed. The hotshot's noise drowned out the sound of the TV.

Ellen was more animated now than when she had learned of her husband's death, but her grief was still compounded by the fact she had been angry the last time she saw him. She couldn't make peace with him now and would live the rest of her life with that knowledge.

They couldn't get through to John's sister, Carolyn, until after her father had been buried. It wouldn't have mattered though. Civilian air travel was restricted. Ellen offered to bury Colonel Conrad next to John's father and include Angie's name on the marker, but the military took charge of Colonel Conrad's body. John remembered vividly his mother sobbing as she explained what had happened to Colonel Conrad's wife, and after that Ellen had been more depressed than ever.

With her tea, his mother sat on the other end of the couch watching the TV. The constant repetition couldn't hold her attention any better than it held John's, and her eyes wandered to the window and the distant ocean. But that only reminded her of more death. Animal carcasses mixed with debris had begun washing ashore. The carcasses were victims of nature's recycling process and hard to identify. Some of them were dinosaurs, of course, but with live ones loose in the countryside, the carcasses received scant attention. At their beach house, John's parents used to walk the shore endlessly, occasionally collecting glass floats or unusual pieces of driftwood. To walk the Oregon beaches now, though, was to risk an encounter with the bloated remains of a prehistoric animal, victim of something they could never conceive of. Most sickening of all was the realization that somewhere in time there were undoubtedly human bodies washing ashore in the same condition.

The sound of a car outside distracted them. They had few friends at the coast, since they were weekenders, and no one had come by to see them since they moved in.

John opened the door and stepped back with the shock. Cubby's van was parked behind Angie's Jeep. The glare on the tinted windows prevented John from seeing inside. Behind him he heard his mother's gasp of recognition. The driver's door opened, and Ripman stepped out, grinning sheepishly. They smiled at Ripman and then turned and watched the other door. Ripman lost his grin.

"He's not with me. I looked for Cubby after the . . . light, bombs, whatever. I never found him. Never found Portland either. It's really gone now."

Ripman stayed by the car, making no move toward them, seeming uncertain. John felt his mother's hand on his shoulder and stepped aside to let her pass. She walked around the car toward Ripman. He stepped back, but she kept coming, wrapping her good arm around him in a big hug. Ripman's hands went up, but he couldn't bring himself to hug her back. His face went red, but the smile returned.

"What's the matter, Ripman?" John teased. "A hug is as elemental as things get."

"Screw you," Ripman mouthed over Ellen's shoulder.

"Up yours," John replied silently.

Ripman looked at John and mouthed the word "El-ah-ment-al," then let his hands fall and hugged Ellen back.

70. The New Country

South Oregon Coast
The New World

Petra was driving while Colter dozed in the seat next to her. Peaches was cuddled in his arms and Moose was settled on his shoulder. Sarah was on her blanket beneath his feet. Petra guided the battered camper down a forest service access road not marked on many maps. The dirt road was poorly maintained and filled with deep ruts and huge mud puddles, and Petra could do no more than twenty-five miles per hour. Colter found the road, remembering it from deer hunting. The main roads were filled with confused people or blocked by state police who were restricting travel.

Petra found herself driving along a hill so steep it was indistinguishable from a cliff. Some tractor driver had carved a road across the middle. Tons of debris littered the lower side of the hill, which dropped sharply to a creek. Rockslides covered parts of the road. Petra snaked around rock piles, fearful of triggering another rock fall. Once across she cornered left around a huge boulder, following the road as it dropped off sharply. Suddenly she was out of the forest into a clear-cut, those great ugly scars that peppered Oregon's great forests. Clear-cut is a funny name, thought Petra. Sure, the towering firs were gone giving a clear view of the sky, but nothing resembling a clearing was left behind. The "clear-cut" was filled with massive stumps, limbs shaved from the fallen ancients, and junk timber felled to reduce the competition for sunlight for the newly planted fir seedlings.

The road led down to the creek, which flowed over and around boulders creating a swirling frothing stream. Petra found herself hypnotized by the creek and slowed to enjoy it. Something moved in the trees on the far side and Petra stopped to watch. Peaches lifted her head briefly, looked around, and then snuggled into a new position. Colter and Moose never moved. Petra understood. She slept like the dead now too. Her body was still replenishing and renewing itself, and the poor little dinosaurs had little energy in the cool weather.

Then a doe walked out of the forest and down to the stream for a drink. The deer stared at the RV long and hard before it finally dropped its head and drank. Petra watched with an odd feeling. Something as normal as a deer now seemed strange to her. Petra had been in the company of dinosaurs for too long; she longed for mammals.

Suddenly the deer's head snapped up, its oversized ears erect and cocked sideways. Out of the shadows of the forest came something ancient—something no deer had ever contended with. It was five feet high, lizard green, and ran on two large back legs. The body of the animal was small compared to the massive head. The deer jumped but wasn't up to running speed before the jaws of the dinosaur tore into the flesh of its neck. The deer went down in a tumble with the dinosaur, rolling once and ending their struggle in the stream.

There had never been any doubt about the outcome. When the deer stopped thrashing the dinosaur dragged its kill from the stream to the shore and only then released the death grip of its jaws. The dinosaur examined its kill, licking its lips, perhaps tasting the blood of a mammal for the first time. Then the dinosaur began its meal. Petra had no desire to watch another bloody feast, so she put the RV in gear and gave it some gas. When the engine revved the dinosaur looked up and watched the RV drive away.

Petra continued down the road, now aware the forests of Oregon were a different place. The radio reports told of patches of prehistoric land here and there all over the state. The dinosaurs must be exploring the turf of the mammals. There were no fences to prevent it, and no fence would stop some of those dinosaurs. The question now was could they live in this new climate? Oregon winters were mild along the coast, not like east of the Cascade Mountains. Certainly dinosaurs in Florida or closer to the equator could live, but Oregon's dinosaurs would struggle. Petra wondered if the government would try to kill them or save them. All levels of government were working on survival—restoring transportation for food and fuel, restoring communication, and restoring order. But soon it would have to deal with the marauding dinosaurs.

The dirt road intersected a gravel road. A forest service sign directed Petra to the left, and soon she had the RV up to forty miles per hour. Even at that speed the gravel pounded away at the underside of the RV. Still her little family slept, oblivious to the rock rhythm being pounded out on the floorboard. After they drove through a couple of miles of forest, the road intersected blacktop, which led through a small valley dotted with dairy farms. Dairy cows watched with disinterested eyes from behind barbed wire fences as the RV passed. Petra left the valley and entered another stretch of woodland, winding up a hill and then back down. As she started down she could see the ocean ahead. They were almost there.

Petra lost sight of the ocean as she wound down the hill and through the woods again, but then suddenly there was the coast highway, and there on the other side was the Pacific Ocean. Petra felt a sudden sense of freedom cleanse her soul. She could almost forget what had happened to her, and to the others. She always felt this way by the ocean—renewed, or at least recharged. Petra turned left, heading south. There were few cars on the road. Gas was rationed and only necessary trips were taken. The RV was an obscene use of fuel, but it served as both home and transportation. Petra had asked Colter how he managed to get its three fuel tanks filled, but he had only smiled and mumbled something about the golden rule.

Petra gave the RV more gas and soon was doing fifty miles per hour. Colter stirred, disturbing Moose, who scrambled from Colter's shoulder to his place on the dash. Soon Colter's eyes flickered open. He remained slumped in the seat for a minute and then pushed himself up. Peaches still cuddled in his arms. When he was upright he discovered the ocean.

"All right, we made it. How far is it?"

"We're almost there."

Colter watched the ocean in silence for a few minutes, stroking Peaches's head. The baby dinosaur kept its eyes closed but make a little squeaking sound with each stroke. Colter scratched behind its little collar eliciting more squeaking, then he leaned over and put Peaches on the blanket next to Sarah and went into the back of the RV. Petra heard the refrigerator open.

"Petra, want a Pepsi?"

"I'll split one with you," Petra offered.

Colter came back with two cans of Pepsi, opened one and put it on the dash.

"Drink as much as you can; I'll finish the rest."

Petra shook her head. "Colter, we better start taking it easy on some of this stuff. You've heard all the reports on the shortages and all the rationing."

"They aren't rationing pop."

"That's because it's not a necessity."

"That's what you think."

Colter opened his can and swigged down half of it. When he was done, he saw her watching him, and frowned. "All right, from now on you're in charge of supplies," he said.

"I don't want to be in charge, I just want you to take it easy."

"I want you to be in charge. You know, and I know, I don't have any self-control."

Petra could see he was serious—he was asking for her help. This was a new Colter. She knew she would never be the same person, but she had wondered about Colter. She appreciated his new self-awareness but hoped some of the reckless courage and other traits remained. She had fallen in love with the old Colter. Then he opened his mouth and loosed a long, loud belch. Yes, some of the old Colter remained.

The sun was nearing the horizon when they came to the turnoff and followed the road around a hill to the parking area. The lot sat on a little bluff overlooking the ocean. A narrow gray sand beach separated the ocean from the massive piles of driftwood directly below. There was one other car in the parking lot but looked abandoned. Colter opened the door, and the cool sea air rushed in, cleansing the RV of animal smells. When the door opened Moose quickly retreated deeper into the RV out of the cool air. Sarah roused herself from her blanket and waddled down the aisle to the back. Petra picked up Peaches and found a snug corner for her next to Sarah. Sarah wriggled around until she was comfortable with Peaches next to her.

Petra could hear Colter outside getting the shovel. She pulled the blue and white plastic cooler out of the cabinet and checked the contents again. It was all there. Petra closed the cooler and headed for the door. When she reached it she turned and went back for the rifle, then joined Colter outside. The air was cool and the sky overcast. When was the sky not overcast at the Oregon coast Petra reminded herself.

"What's the rifle for?" Colter asked.

"In case there's any deer hunting going on. Never mind, I'll explain later."

Colter shrugged his shoulders and said impatiently, "Let's get this over with."

Two paths led from the parking lot. One well-traveled path led to the beach, but the other path wound up the hill into the trees. Colter followed the path uphill. It was a gentle climb, marked frequently with signs identifying the vegetation. A quarter mile up the trail they left the path, turning into the trees. Soon they could see the ocean again on their right and a rocky cliff to their left. Colter stopped by a small fir tree, looking out to sea, and then turned and looked at the cliff. Then he walked to another young fir, looking again in all four directions.

"This is the spot, right."

Petra stepped behind the fir and looked out to sea, lining the fir up with a large rock formation just offshore. Then she stepped to the other side and lined the fir up with a large crack in the rocks of the cliff behind them. Finally she stood to one side and made sure the fir lined up with a notch in the distant hills.

"Yeah, this is the spot."

Colter stood with his back to the tree and then took two steps toward the sea.

"About six feet?"

"Close enough."

Colter began digging with the shovel. The ground was moist and soft but there were many rocks, and the digging wasn't easy. When Colter looked disgusted and ready to call it deep enough, Petra took the shovel and dug. That shamed Colter into digging again. Finally, he buried the tip of the shovel in the ground next to the hole and turned to Petra.

"I say that's three feet deep."

Petra agreed but held back the cooler when Colter reached for it. Opening it she checked the contents one last time. Inside was a record of what had happened. There were newspaper clippings about the disasters and the sudden appearance of dinosaurs and the sudden disappearance of people. There were also articles about the bombing of Portland and the debate over whether Portland had been destroyed or not. There were many articles about the dinosaurs and the problems they were creating. Of all the items in the cooler, however, the most important was a history Colter and Petra had written of all that had happened to them and the group. They wrote of the group's meeting with Kenny Randall and his strange story of corn falling from the sky. They wrote of the group's research, and their discovery of Zorastrus. They described the model Kenny and Phat had programmed and their search for confirming evidence. They told the story of a boy who nearly drowned in saltwater in the middle of a prairie and of Yellowstone and the ice falling from the sky. Then after recapping the before events they told in even more detail what happened next. How they had divided into groups to be as widely dispersed as possible when it happened. They told of losing contact with Mrs. Wayne and Ernie Powell. They told of their search for their friends and the discovery of the dinosaurs. They told of their discoveries, especially Sid, Moose, Sarah, and Peaches. Then in painful detail they talked of the death of Dr. Coombs and Dr. Piltcher. Colter wrote of his adventures and Petra of her time in the walking fish's den. When every painful detail was down they had taken the record, made three copies of it, and sealed them in plastic. The first copy had been buried in Dr. Piltcher's backyard. The second was in a small cave east of Medford, and the third copy would be buried here, by the sea. Like the other two copies it would be buried in a plastic cooler. Dr. Piltcher had assured everyone the plastic would last for centuries.

When Petra was sure the record was complete she put it in the cooler, latched the top securely, and placed it in the hole.

Colter filled the hole in a little at a time, compressing the earth as he filled by stomping on it. Soon the hole was firmly packed with earth. Colter took the shovel and scattered the leftover dirt into the trees. Then he spread pine needles and dried leaves over the hole. Finally he pried a nearby rock out of the ground and placed the rock on top of the buried cooler. When he was done he looked to Petra for affirmation.

"Good enough," she said.

Colter picked up his shovel and Petra the rifle and the two of them started back down the path. The clouds had broken up, letting the setting sun peek through, but the air was cool and evaporated the sweat from Petra's body, making her shiver gently. Colter put his arm around her shoulder and they walked together, their arms around each other. There was no hurry, they had nowhere to go.

"Petra," Colter said softly, not wanting to break the feeling they were sharing. "Do you really think anyone will ever dig that up?"

"If Dr. Piltcher was right, then the others may be digging it up right now."

"Right now? They disappeared, remember?"

"I mean right now in the future."

"Now in the future. That makes no sense."

"I know. What I mean is if the dinosaurs came here then the people and things that were here had to go somewhere. Maybe they went to the future. If so, Ernie and Mrs. Powell would know where to go to find our message. Maybe Phat and Kenny too. We don't know what happened to them."

Colter walked on in silence, a puzzled look on his face. Petra knew what he was feeling. It didn't all make sense to her either—maybe it never would. But she and Colter had to learn to live with what had happened. They had lost all their close friends—the friends that made up their support network. Colter still had a family in northern California. That's where they would head next. Petra still had her father, but there was little support to be found there. Still they were lucky, they had each other. So many had lost so much.

"Look," Colter shouted.

Petra followed his point to see something moving along the ocean shore. Colter broke into a run and Petra followed down the path to the wire fence along the edge of the bluff. To the north was a point of land that blocked the view farther up the coast. Coming around that point was the biggest dinosaur they had seen yet. It walked on all four legs and had a long snaking head and dragged a long tail. It was a brontosaurus, except they remembered it was technically an apatosaurus. Everyone was quickly becoming a dinosaur expert.

The apatosaurus walked purposefully along the beach, its head held high, its gait slow but steady. When it cleared the point coming fully into view, another appeared behind the first. The second was only a little smaller and walked with the same steady pace. Petra and Colter watched in awe as the majestic monsters moved down the beach toward them, the sun setting into the sea behind, creating an orange backdrop. A third apatosaurus appeared behind the second, and then more, each descending in size, all following the mighty beast in the lead.

"It looks like a bizarre circus parade," Petra said.

"Where do you think they're going?" Colter asked.

"South, I guess. Instinctively heading for the warm weather."

"Should we go too?"

"No, Colter. Let's watch for a while."

Colter put his arm around her shoulder and pulled her close. They stood like that until dark, watching the new world go by.

A special preview of

Fragments

by James F. David

Available in hardcover in July 1997
from Forge Books

October 19, 1953

The flashing red lights of the police cars lit the crowd that had gathered to see something they could later tell their friends they wished they'd never seen. He joined them, acting curious, planning to stay just long enough to deflect suspicion.

The crowd was thick, and those in the back whispered questions to those in front. What, who, how, and why? the new arrivals asked, and in reply came fact, rumor, and surmise. He joined the crowd and whispered his own questions to a short man with a brown hat. The man turned, anxious to stare with a newcomer.

"It's another dead body."

"College age?"

"Probably. Someone said he has a university decal on his car window."

"Was he killed with a knife?"

"Yeah, just like the others. Cut up too—you know—especially his private parts. It's the same em-oh. That's what the police call it. Modus operandi, or something like that. My brother-in-law's a cop. He says you can always tell when it's the same killer from the MO."

"Do they know the boy's name?"

"Naw, but they found his body in a '49 Chevy. Know anyone driving a green one?"

He shook his head—a silent lie—then let the man turn to answer the questions of a young woman.

Now he moved on, quickening his pace to a brisk walk. He tried to look casual, like someone out for a walk on a warm October evening—someone going to the twenty-four flavors for a double dip, or down to Hickman's for a cold pop. He strode up the tree-lined street, a feeling of dread growing with every step until it was almost too much to bear.

He rounded the corner at Elm and turned down Lincoln. His house was there on the left, halfway up the block. It was a big house, much bigger than he needed now. Filled once with a family overflowing its six bedrooms, now the house—and his family—was little more than an empty shell.

Every light was on, giving the empty rooms the glow of the living. He liked the house bright. If he couldn't have the people in the house, he at least could drive out the shadowy memories they left behind. He looked up at her second-floor room but saw nothing but her white lace curtains fluttering out the open window. He went up the walk and then the flight of stairs to the porch. The front door was closed and locked, just as he had left it. Entering, he quickly climbed the stairs to the second floor, pulling himself along with the handrail. Checking her room first, he hoped to find her in bed reading, or playing her forty-fives. It was empty, as were his and the other bedrooms. Downstairs he found the living room, library, and den just as empty, so he cut through the dining room to the kitchen. There was an empty glass on the table, lined with a film of dried milk, and a plate with cookie crumbs next to it. He was about to search the side porch when he noticed the back door slightly ajar. The yard was dimly lit by the light coming from the kitchen windows, but there were too many shadows and shrubs for hiding laces for him to be sure the yard was empty. Closing the door his hand came away sticky with blood.

Blood drops on the floor led him through the kitchen to the basement door. There was more blood on its handle, and the lights in the basement were on. Softly, he walked down the stairs, trying to avoid the creakiest steps. The basement was filled with bits and pieces of his old life. There were mattresses and bed frames from the now empty bedrooms upstairs, and bicycles that would never be ridden again. Nearly new children's clothes and toys were packed away in boxes—he couldn't bring himself to give them away. His wife's things were there somewhere too, long since removed from the room they had shared.

When he reached the bottom he could hear the sound of running water. The laundry room was to the right, but the sound was coming from the left—his shop was there, a small room in one corner. He passed through the piles of rummage, careful not to make a sound, and past the shelves for canned goods until he could see. She was there.

Bent over the stainless-steel sink she was washing her hands and arms. She wore a pair of white shorts but no top, only her bra—her blouse on the floor. Her washing was methodical and thorough. Over and over she soaped up her hands and then washed up and down her arms, clear to the elbow. First her right hand and arm and then her left. When done, she started over with her right again. He watched her wash, trying to imagine another explanation for why she might be in the basement doing this, but when she pulled a knife from the bottom of the sink to scrub, he felt all hope drain from him. He recognized the knife—it was from the set in his kitchen. He had used it many times since the murders began. Then he was filled with a terrible resolve.

Slipping back past the shelves, he picked through the rummage until he found an old set of golf clubs. He pulled a driver from the bag, freezing when the other clubs rattled into the empty space. When he was sure the water was still running he crept back along the shelves. Intent on cleaning the knife, she didn't see him coming.

Raising the club above his head, he ran the last few steps, then swung down. She looked up at the last minute, understanding flashing across her face, but there was no fear in her eyes, only surprise that her father could do this to her. But in that she was wrong. He couldn't kill her. At the last second he lost his resolve and tried to soften the blow. The club head came down as her arm came up to deflect the blow. The force left in his swing was too much and her arm was knocked down by the shaft, the club continuing down and contacting her head with a sharp crack.

She crumpled to the floor in a limp pile. He raised the club for a second blow, determined to finish what he had begun; then he saw her face. Her eyes were closed and her blond hair lay loose across her cheek. He'd seen the look many times before, at night when he would check on her and her sisters. His sleeping children always brought out the tenderness in him, and sometimes he would sit watching them until his wife came to drag him off to bed. He knelt now and brushed the hair away from her face. She had that look of a sleeping angel, and he was suddenly transported back to their common past, a time when they both were innocents. There was no murder in him now, no matter what she had done. A small streak of crimson spread through her hair, but it was a small wound and she was breathing strongly. He hoped she would live.

He carried her from the shop, setting her gently on an old mattress, then tied her hands and feet. She was crazy, of course, but not so crazy that she couldn't act normal. That was how she had fooled him and fooled the boys. She would never be his little girl again, or the woman she could have been. He didn't blame her, she didn't ask to be what they made her, but he couldn't let it go on, and he couldn't let the State finish the killing he couldn't do himself.

He went to work in his shop, dismantling the lathe, table saw, and jigsaw and moving them out. He had boxes of tools, a wall full of hooks with more tools, and two vises to move. After he had worked for an hour, she began moaning. A few minutes later she began to talk to him.

"I didn't do anything—" she began.

He hushed her with an angry look. Her pleading expression instantly turned to flashing anger.

"What did you expect? You know what they did to me."

He hushed her again, but she wouldn't be still. She kept after him.

"You didn't do anything. I had to. Someone had to."

He couldn't take it, and he pulled a dishcloth from the laundry basket and wrapped it around her mouth. She screamed and cussed him as he did, using words girls shouldn't know. Then he went back to work dismantling the workbench. He worked through the night until he had the room emptied out. There was no window in the room and it had a sturdy door. He dug through the piles of tools and supplies he had dumped in the basement until he found a hasp and latch and attached them to the door and frame. She was asleep when he finished but she woke when he tried to pick her up. Her struggle made it impossible to carry her, so he dragged her into the room and laid her in the corner. She rolled over, venom in her eyes. He dragged the mattress into the room and then retrieved a blanket from the linen closet upstairs. He tried to move her to the mattress but she wriggled out of his grasp. Instead, he threw the blanket over her and then left, closing the hasp and securing it with a padlock. It was a temporary solution at best. Then he went upstairs and fell onto the bed and slept the sleep of the grieving. He'd just lost another daughter.

He woke to the sound of a distant thumping. He was groggy and his head pounded a painful rhythm in synchrony with the thumping. His mouth was pasty; thick with mucus. He felt like he had a hangover, but he didn't remember drinking anything the night before. He sat on the edge of the bed letting his body adjust his blood pressure to keep himself from blacking out; then he walked to the open window and looked into the street. It was another hot afternoon, and the street near his house was empty except for Mrs. Clayton, who was watering her shrubs with a hose. Mrs. Clayton watered incessantly. It was her way of keeping an eye on what was happening on the street. He turned back to his bedroom, trying to clear his thoughts. Why was he so confused? Then he noticed the thumping again. *What was that pounding?* When he heard splintering wood, he remembered.

Down the stairs he ran at breakneck speed, into the kitchen and down into the basement. He jumped the last four steps and hit the floor running, turning in time to see the shop door kicked open, the frame splintering. She came out screaming in fury. He crashed into her with full momentum. His bulk gave him the advantage and he bowled her over, but he wasn't prepared for her fury. She clawed and bit like a wild animal and he quickly found himself bleeding from a dozen places. He tried wrapping his arms around her to control her, but her violent motions made it impossible to hang on. When he feared she might get away and break to the stairs he hit her. Over and over he pounded at her head. Soon her arms came up, protecting her face. He stopped hitting when he heard the sobs.

She would be manageable for a while and he worked fast. He carried her into the shop and put her back on the mattress. She turned away from him, curling into a fetal position, her body racked by sobs. He could see bloody circles on her wrists where she had worked at the ropes until her wrists bled, lubricating the ropes. He retrieved the bloody ropes and then left her and checked the door. The frame was split where the hasp had been pulled free. He found a hammer and nails and put the frame back together and then reattached the hasp. It wouldn't be as strong as it was before, so he found a two-by-four and nailed it across the door to keep her in until he got back.

He found what he needed at the hardware store and was back in thirty minutes. He'd dismantled his shop, so he worked on the basement floor. When ready, he pried off the two-by-four and opened the door. She was huddled against the wall, hugging her knees to her chest. The venom was back in her eyes.

"Why are you doing this to me?" Her voice came out in a coarse whisper.

He didn't answer. How do you tell someone they're not sane? Especially when you're not sure you're sane yourself? He ignored her and came in brandishing the two-by-four.

"Turn around or I'll let you have it!"

She hesitated but then turned.

"Put your hands behind you."

"You can't keep me tied up forever."

"Give me your hands or I'll hit you with this!"

Her hands came around and he quickly tied them with rope. Then he tied her feet again. He left the gag off but ordered her not to speak. He went to work with a masonry drill and attached a steel plate to the concrete of the exterior wall. He ran a length of heavy chain through a ring attached to the wall plate and then snapped a keyed lock onto the chain to secure it to the ring. The heavier chain connected to another ring, which had a lighter chain looped through it. He then wrapped one end of the light chain around one of her wrists and secured it with another lock. When he had the other wrist secured the same way he cut the ropes off her wrists and ankles. As soon as the ropes were gone she came after him. He retreated out the door, grabbing his toolbox as he ran. She came screaming, but the length of chain pulled her up short at the door. She stood there pulling on the chains, bloodying her wrists again and screaming at him with foul language. There was none of his little girl left in her now.

He closed the door, shutting out her epithets, and the sight of what she had become. He didn't want to see her this way ever again. He chose to remember her as his little girl, even though somewhere just past childhood that little girl had died, leaving the monster now kicking at the door.

He brought her food but she kicked the tray out of his hands as soon as the door opened. Later he brought her another blanket. She was still only wearing her bra but there was no way to dress her without removing the chains.

The next day he rented a truck and bought a supply of bricks and mortar. Then he went to work in the backyard building a barbecue. When he had a good start he began surreptitiously moving bricks into his basement. He started along the wall of the shop, bricking it from floor to ceiling. It took him three days to do the walls, leaving only the door. She began eating on the third day, accepting the food tray from him. Her attitude had changed, too—she was contrite and apologetic, begging him to forgive her and understand. He couldn't do either.

When he was ready, he entered her room holding the golf club as a weapon and shortened her chain so that she was held back from the door. Then he carried furniture into the room: a bed frame and box springs, a table, and a chest of drawers. Then, as she watched with mounting horror, he took the door from its hinges, busted out the frame, slapped down mortar, and fit the first brick into the opening. Screaming, she lunged at him, but was pulled up short by the chain. Quickly the screaming became soft pleading.

"Please, Daddy. Please don't."

His heart softened but didn't melt and he kept spreading mortar and slapping bricks into place. He paused in his work to build a small wooden frame, which he set in the center of the doorway, and then he bricked up and over the frame. Then he worked nonstop from a stockpile of bricks, quickly filling in the doorway until only the small opening at the bottom remained. When he finished, he heard her voice from the opening at the bottom of the door. Her voice echoed as if from a tomb.

"Why didn't you just kill me quick?"

"Because I love you."

He never spoke to her again.

He waited three days before he slid the keys to the lock through the opening, making sure the mortar was well set. She immediately began pounding on the wall with the chains. He kept her food for two days until she slid the chains and locks out to him. He brought her food three times a day, after that, coming home at lunch to make sure her needs were taken care of. There was waste to be dealt with, too, and he kept her supplied with toiletries. He pushed clothes through the opening regularly and she would push out her dirty clothes. He kept her supplied with books, and when she asked for pencils and a sketch pad he slid those underneath, although no pictures ever came back through the opening.

Her friends called at first, but she had only a few. Most had been driven away after it happened. He told them she had run away to Seattle and they believed him. It helped that she had been morose for some time, and distant. Running away was something unhappy teenagers did. Besides, she was old enough to be on her own anyway. Her friends married and were soon immersed in their own lives and eventually even persistent best friend Jean stopped calling.

Sometimes she would refuse food for days at a time, or send out books and other offerings shredded, but she always came around. It disappointed him in a way. If she had been stronger she could have starved herself to death. But if she had been stronger maybe it wouldn't have happened to her in the first place, and maybe she wouldn't have turned into a monster.

He regretted not putting a radio in the room for her. They were too big to get through the opening, so he took to sitting downstairs and listening to the radio loud enough so she could hear it. She never asked to hear anything in particular, so he mostly listened to the news and band music. When TV finally seduced him away from the radio, he would turn the radio on in the evenings, putting it on a rock-and-roll station. He didn't know if she liked the music; she never said. But one day when